IDA MAY

broadview editions
series editor: Martin R. Boyne

Mary Hayden Green Pike, date unknown. Image courtesy of
Special Collections, Fogler Library, University of Maine.

IDA MAY:
STORY OF THINGS ACTUAL AND POSSIBLE

Mary Hayden Green Pike

edited by Jessie Morgan-Owens

broadview editions

BROADVIEW PRESS – www.broadviewpress.com
Peterborough, Ontario, Canada

Founded in 1985, Broadview Press remains a wholly independent publishing house. Broadview's focus is on academic publishing; our titles are accessible to university and college students as well as scholars and general readers. With over 600 titles in print, Broadview has become a leading international publisher in the humanities, with world-wide distribution. Broadview is committed to environmentally responsible publishing and fair business practices.

The interior of this book is printed on 100% recycled paper.

PERMANENT   100%   BIO GAS ENERGY   Ancient Forest Friendly™

Library and Archives Canada Cataloguing in Publication

Langdon, Mary, 1824-1908, author
        Ida May : story of things actual and possible / Mary Hayden Green Pike ; edited by Jessie Morgan-Owens.

(Broadview editions)
Includes bibliographical references.
ISBN 978-1-55481-225-7 (softcover)

        I. Morgan-Owens, Jessie, editor II. Title.
III. Series: Broadview editions

PS2587.P5I33 2017   813'.3   C2017-902619-4

Broadview Editions

The Broadview Editions series is an effort to represent the ever-evolving canon of texts in the disciplines of literary studies, history, philosophy, and political theory. A distinguishing feature of the series is the inclusion of primary source documents contemporaneous with the work.

Advisory editor for this volume: Denis Johnston

Broadview Press handles its own distribution in North America
PO Box 1243, Peterborough, Ontario K9J 7H5, Canada
555 Riverwalk Parkway, Tonawanda, NY 14150, USA
Tel: (705) 743-8990; Fax: (705) 743-8353
email: customerservice@broadviewpress.com

Distribution is handled by Eurospan Group in the UK, Europe, Central Asia, Middle East, Africa, India, Southeast Asia, Central America, South America, and the Caribbean. Distribution is handled by Footprint Books in Australia and New Zealand.

Broadview Press acknowledges the financial support of the Government of Canada through the Canada Book Fund for our publishing activities.

Canada

Typesetting by Aldo Fierro
Cover design by Aldo Fierro

PRINTED IN CANADA

For Nathaniel

Contents

Acknowledgements

By the twentieth century, Mary Hayden Green Pike's novels were largely forgotten, and they would have remained so if not for the scholarship of Rachel Griffin in the 1940s, Don Liedel in the 1960s, Nina Baym in the 1970s, and Cindy Weinstein in the early 2000s. Their foundational scholarship on *Ida May* brought this book back to scholarly attention. The digitized version made available at the Antislavery Literature Project by Joe Lockhard brought *Ida May* within reach of a new audience, including myself, and for that I am grateful.

The American Antiquarian Society's newspaper and print holdings made it possible to locate items reprinted here in the Appendices. I would also like to thank the Massachusetts Historical Society, the Boston Athenaeum, the Boston Public Library, and the University of Maine at Orono. I am grateful to the Susan and Donald Newhouse Center for the Humanities at Wellesley College for its year of support while I researched this project, and to the American Antiquarian Society for its long-term fellowship and congenial support.

I wish to thank Kathy and Rick Morgan for their timely assistance in preparing this manuscript.

Introduction

"Nothing is denied to patient and well-directed effort."
—*Ida May*, p. 342

Who Wrote *Ida May*?

The sentimental antislavery novel *Ida May: Story of Things Actual and Possible* appeared so like its predecessor in the genre, *Uncle Tom's Cabin*, that for the month of November 1854, newspaper reviewers looked for Harriet Beecher Stowe's hand in the new book. Some even considered *Ida May* superior, for its improvements in style and in the accuracy of depiction of Southern life and language. Once the book's publisher, Phillips, Sampson and Company, publicly denied in late November 1854 that Stowe was the author of *Ida May*, the guesswork as to "who is to wear the honors of this very clever book"[1] continued in the press through January 1855.

With glowing reviews and stirring extracts in all the premier antislavery papers—*The National Era*, *Frederick Douglass' Paper*, *The Liberator*, the *Boston Telegraph*, and New York's *The Independent* and *The Evening Post*—the new novel *Ida May*, brought out during Thanksgiving week in late 1854 under the pseudonym Mary Langdon, became an immediate success, selling 60,000 copies in American, British, French, and German editions. *Ida May*'s author, Mary Hayden Green Pike (1824–1908) of Calais, Maine, had chosen with her debut to participate in a growing interest in sentimental approaches to the antislavery question. In doing so, she joined a cohort of women writing fiction to affect politics, both before and after the 1852 publication of the enormously influential *Uncle Tom's Cabin*, widely held to be the best-selling novel of the nineteenth century. *The Evening Post* article entitled "Who Wrote *Ida May*?" (see Appendix A1d) notes that among contemporary writers, women novelists rule the scene: "that the most popular living novelists, in the strictest sense of that term, [are] women; that the fictions of American females [have] attained a wider circulation than those of either sex of any other nation"; and that the author of *Ida May*, whom

---

1 *The Evening Post*, 6 December 1854; see Appendix A1d, p. 348.

the reviewer never doubts to be a woman, "strengthens that supremacy ... as a new recruit to the already strong array" of women writing controversial novels.

While on an antislavery lecture circuit in 1859—after the secret of *Ida May*'s authorship had been revealed—Caroline F. Putnam and Sally Holley of the American Anti-Slavery Society paid a visit to Mary Pike at the home of mutual friends in Calais. Reporting for *The Liberator*, Putnam writes that Pike and two other "Maine ladies" had spent a winter in Aiken, South Carolina, for their health. While there, "Mrs. P learned much which suggested to her the narratives of *Ida May.*... She has given us this afternoon many reminiscences of that Southern winter— some shocking atrocities which she could not shut her eyes to" (Appendix E1, p. 383).

On the title page, the American editions of *Ida May* quote a New Testament passage: "We speak that we do know, and testify that we have seen." The conclusion of the verse is implied: "and ye receive not our witness."[1] Pike's contemporary audience considered her depiction of South Carolinian plantation society both accurate and sympathetic, and the reviews collected here in Appendices A and B unhesitatingly map Ida May's story, taken as "Story of Things Actual and Possible," onto a contemporary political landscape. As we can see in Appendix A, part of the impulse to identify the author of *Ida May* was not only to determine its genre but also to map the author's political geography. Abolitionist literature, as reflective of a splintered movement and widely criticized genre, made the most of geographic placement. Proximity to slavery made a difference, as did party affiliations. Contemporary reviews demonstrate a growing anxiety around the issue of where in American letters to place the political novel, and in particular of how to assess an emergent popular genre of sentimental antislavery novels written by women.

Claiming the status of an eyewitness, Pike asserts in her Preface that Ida May's fictional story should be "recognized and accepted" by the public as truth: a fair, "true picture" of Southern life (p. 43). Her reviewers responded accordingly. The *Boston Daily Atlas* asserted that *Ida May* makes an influential "home thrust" for antislavery, "the more telling in its influence, because it will be found to contain no exaggerated pictures, and nothing that can be pointed to as a caricature of everyday realities" (Appendix A2a, p. 348).

---

1 John 3:11.

As Don Liedel argues in his study of the promotional tactics that led to the success of *Ida May*, Phillips, Sampson and Company precisely timed the book's publication to capitalize on renewed antislavery fervor in the months following the Kansas-Nebraska Act of May 1854, which opened the Nebraska territory west of Missouri to slavery. The status—slave or free—of these territories would be decided by popular sovereignty, a term meaning local or regional democratic process. This repeal of the Missouri Compromise of 1820, which had held the boundary at latitude 36°30 for more than 30 years, actualized fears that slavery would one day extend into the vast territory to the West once promised to non-slaveholding farmers and settlers. Pike's Preface refers to encroachment directly when she calls for "a more firm protest against the extension of that system" (p. 43). In 1854, the struggle shifted from an ideological debate over the basic human rights of the enslaved to a struggle between "systems" for control of the federal government.

Then, in the summer of 1854, the slave system demonstrated its national reach when Anthony Burns (1834–62), a fugitive who had been living in Boston, was marched back into slavery under military escort after failed attempts by abolitionists to intervene on his behalf. This rendition was made possible by the Fugitive Slave Law, which required the federal government to bring fugitives living in the North back into slavery in the South.[1] This bill, one of five that made up the Compromise of 1850, reinforced the Fugitive Laws of 1793, which by this time were customarily violated, by revoking judicial process and shifting the jurisdiction over fugitives into the hands, and scrutiny, of federal commissioners. The Fugitive Slave Law legalized the practice of "slave-catching" and deputized federal commissioners across the Northern states to find and return fugitives from slavery. Under the new legislation, only an affidavit was required of the "claimant," or master, to prove ownership of a fugitive. If the commissioner decided that a person was not a slave, the federal marshal was paid five dollars, but if the commissioner decided that the person was a fugitive, the marshal got ten. Clearly, this provided an incentive to rule against the runaway in doubtful cases. A person suspected of being a fugitive slave could be arrested without warrant and turned over to a claimant on nothing more than the claimant's sworn testimony of ownership.

---

1   For a detailed account of the rendition of Anthony Burns, see Von Frank.

A suspected slave could neither ask for a jury trial nor testify on his or her own behalf.

The Fugitive Slave Law of 1850 also stated that any person aiding a fugitive by providing shelter, food, or any other form of assistance was liable to six months' imprisonment and a $1,000 fine. Thus the Law in effect deputized the entire Northern public as slave-catchers, regardless of their politics, which in turn radicalized abolitionism in those who resisted the law. Anthony Burns's rendition proved that local activists could do little to protect their neighbors from enslavement; even moderate Northerners found their liberties infringed upon by this provision in the law that would fine or jail a citizen for aiding a fugitive from slavery.[1]

Stowe (1811–96) cites this law as the impetus for her writing; Pike makes the possibility that slave-catchers could steal and sell children living in the North into slavery, under the provisions of the Fugitive Slave Law, to be the central motif of her novel. Pike's villains kidnap a child who looks like Stowe's heroine "Little Eva"[2] and thrust her into a plot not unlike that of the free-born Solomon Northup's story of abduction and enslavement in *Twelve Years a Slave* (1854).[3] Not three chapters into *Ida May*, the precocious, beautiful heroine is kidnapped on her fifth birthday from her white middle-class family in Pennsylvania, stained brown, and sold into slavery in the South. *Ida May* upends the concept of the fugitive by reminding readers that slave status hinges on the *viewer's* perception of race. Under the Fugitive Slave Law, persons assumed to be slaves because of the color of their skin could be sold into slavery without recourse. The novel *Ida May* contends that the Fugitive Slave Law shifted the border of slavery far enough north as to threaten the freedom of all Americans, not only those with dark skin. The new law exposed how easily the slave system could wrongfully trap, or allow to escape, persons of every race. *Ida May* is not a "passing"

---

1 The full text of the Fugitive Slave Law is available at Yale Law School's Avalon Project, http://avalon.law.yale.edu/19th_century/fugitive.asp. Eric Foner explores the implications of the Fugitive Slave Law in the lives of the enslaved in *Gateway to Freedom*.

2 Cordelia Howard (1848–1942), the child actress who made Eva's role her own in theatrical versions of *Uncle Tom's Cabin*, performed as "Ida May" in a stage adaptation of Pike's novel, sometimes playing both roles on the same day. Cordelia's father, George Howard (1818–87), produced the first stage version of Stowe's novel in 1852.

3 Northup's memoir was made into a critically acclaimed film in 2013.

novel,[1] or a story about the enslavement of mixed-race children, for the plot of *Ida May* discards these tropes to incite white indignation more directly. *The Liberator* called Pike "ingenious" (see Appendix B3) for making her heroine Ida entirely white, yet mistaken for a slave for five years.

As Cindy Weinstein argues in her groundbreaking study of the generic innovations of Pike's novel, "*Ida May* is fundamentally about a sentimental heroine kidnapped into the genre of the slave narrative" (95). In the novel, traumatic amnesia brought about by a severe beating prevents the title character from knowing who she really is until, after five years in slavery, Ida recovers her identity in a dramatic flash of recognition. Her former master Charles Maynard adopts her as his ward, at his nephew Walter Varian's insistence, and they provide for her education as she grows into a woman with her adopted family at Wynn Hall plantation in South Carolina and at boarding school in the North. At the midpoint of *Ida May*, Pike's novel hybridizes into a sentimental romance, once redeemed from its slave narrative beginnings, but with a twist: in Ida's marriage plot, her future husband Walter must first purchase, emancipate, and then educate Ida into middle-class femininity. The master narratives of sentimental romance allow Pike to challenge slavery from the safety of "women's fiction." In *Women's Fiction* (1978), Nina Baym introduced Pike's novel to a new generation of readers as "ideologically appalling," due to its conflation of the story of slavery with the popular stories of "feminine trials-and-triumph" then in vogue (268). Baym neatly summarizes how much *Ida May* keeps in common with the popular novels of its day: "This 'anti-slavery' novel has all the trappings of a woman's fiction— an apparent orphan, uncongenial surroundings, a decision that requires defiance of one's guardians, moral influence exerted on a weak male (her husband-to-be), a malicious female rival, a cruel patriarch, and finally the formation of a utopian family centering on the heroine" (269). However, what distinguishes *Ida May* from other sentimental novels with a similar romance plot is how Ida's story is *wholly* tied to the slavery question. Pike does not simply exploit enslavement as an uncongenial setting; instead, she presents antislavery as a world view born out of the

---

1　The genre of "passing" narratives features characters that cross the color line and present themselves as white. These novels dramatize the social and emotional risks inherent in hiding or abandoning one's black heritage in order to experience the benefits of white privilege.

experience of enslavement. As Weinstein noted in 2000, "Ida's *bildungsroman* [i.e., coming-of-age story] is inextricably linked to her position *vis à vis* the peculiar institution, whether as a slave, as a freed slave, or as an anti-slavery advocate" (105).

The problem of education, which she is legally denied until her whiteness is discovered, brings Walter to recognize and enunciate Pike's message of racial equality at the novel's midpoint:

> ... what reason and justice is there in the difference we make between her condition, now we know she is the child of white parents, and the treatment she would have been considered entitled to if we had not made that discovery? Why wouldn't she have needed knowledge as much then as now, and been as capable of receiving it? Who knows how many children sold in the slave market, as she was, have minds equally susceptible of cultivation? What sense is there in making the color of the skin, or the difference of lineage, outweigh every other indication? (p. 175)

Ida May needs only to prove her whiteness to escape the tragic plot that is perpetrated on all the black characters in the novel. In her 1834 short story for children, "Mary French and Susan Easton" (see Appendix D3), Lydia Maria Child (1802–91) makes Walter's point more directly. In Child's story, two free little girls are kidnapped—one white and one black—but only the white child is redeemed. Child concludes her tale: "the only difference between Mary French and Susan Easton is that the black color could be rubbed off from Mary's skin, while from Susan's it could not" (p. 378). When Ida (known as "Lizzy White" in slavery) recognizes her name, and with it that of her father, she rejoins the white world of privilege and reward: a private education, recognition in society and by her suitor Walter, and even the inheritance of a small plantation of her own. The subtitle of *Ida May* for the 1879 German edition announced Ida's transformation from the first page: *Ida May, oder, Durch Nacht zum Licht : Eine auf Tatsachen beruhende Erzählung*, or "Through Night to Light: A Factual Narrative."

Antislavery activists, both black and white, took aim at the very foundations of race-based enslavement and prejudice. In response to their political climate, the recent abolition campaign of the 1850s made an unsettling strategic move: it sought to undermine racial classification with images and stories of enslaved persons who appear white. Looking at the canon of antislavery fiction as a whole, Don Liedel points out that "*Uncle Tom's Cabin* provided the inspiration, but not the model, for novelists. The antislavery novelists of the 1850s turned their attention to delineating the effects of slavery on white society. They generally discarded the Negro male hero of *Uncle Tom's Cabin* and substituted a heroine of mixed blood. By making her heroine in *Ida May* entirely white, Pike had fashioned the ultimate appeal to Northern readers" (294). For Northern white audiences to sympathize with the enslaved before and after *Uncle Tom*, it was assumed that antislavery writers must build resemblances where none existed before, across what appeared to be an impassable racial divide. We can recognize today that Pike's strategy of resemblance generated sympathy at a high cost: it elicited sympathy along white lines while continuing to deny sympathetic experience to persons of color. However, by throwing into question white and black "fitness" for enslavement, characters such as Ida May confirmed the message and vision of a shared humanity propagated by leaders in the black abolitionist movement, including the prominent former slave Frederick Douglass (1818–95). To the abolitionists of the period, white enslaved children such as Ida offered a crucial possibility: to unsettle the legitimacy of a race-based system of enslavement.

The Making of an Abolitionist

Incorporated in 1809, nineteenth-century Calais was a small forestry town on the Maine frontier. Its proximity to the mouth of the St. Croix River encouraged the free circulation of capital and ideas for eight or nine months a year. In the summer of 1838, when Mary Hayden Green was 14 years old, radical abolitionism arrived in Calais in the form of the antislavery lecturer Ichabod Codding (1810–66). At that time, Codding was in his second year with the Anti-Slavery Society, just two years out of Middlebury College, but he would make a life's work of the lecture circuit for reform. Upon arriving in Calais, he lectured for three evenings to increasing audiences on "the sin and wrong of negro slavery," and on Sunday evening he sermonized in the Baptist church, where Mary's family were prominent members.[1]

---

1 Rev. I.C. Knowlton, *The Annals of Calais, Maine, and St. Stephen, New Brunswick; including the village of Milltown, Me., and the present town of Milltown, N.B.* (J.A. Sears, printer, 1875), 138; http://archive.org.

The following day, local politicians and lawyers, fearing the influence of Codding's agitation for the Liberty Party, convened a public meeting to expel him from the town. The Reverend Mr. James Huckins (1807–63), whose church Codding had filled on Sunday, spoke of "the farce and buffoonery of the evening before, and that Mr. Codding owed him an apology for desecrating his house." Codding attended the meeting and demanded the right to speak; but once he had the floor, he used his hour to deliver another impassioned speech on the subject of slavery. The debates continued for a week, until a vote was taken. Codding lost his right to speak to the citizens of Calais: yeas 68, nays 85. A mob led by "a set of desperadoes called 'the Indians,' from the fact that, dressed as Indians, they committed acts they dared not commit in their real characters" beset Codding before he could leave town, pelting him with rotten eggs and "shouting, yelling, howling, like so many demons from the infernal regions."[1] (Mary Pike would later re-enact this mob scene in the final chapters of *Ida May,* when Ida and her father are run out of South Carolina.) Deacon Samuel Kelley, who "felt a deep interest in the down trodden colored race," garnered support to keep Codding in the safety of the Baptist church, and to give a final lecture, against Minister Huckins's wishes (Knowlton 138). Codding's early lectures argued that slavery was a sin because the slaveholder overruled the slave's right to follow God. "If God has no right to rule over any, he is no God: this would be *No-godism*—ATHEISM." Codding warned, "every man who apologizes for slavery is warring against God's throne."[2] According to the *Annals of Calais,* Huckins left his post as minister, to serve a more amenable congregation in Texas (Knowlton 139).

A consequence of Codding's visit was the total conversion of the Green family, inextricably bound to their devout Baptist faith, to abolition. Mary's father, Elijah Green, was a founding deacon at the Baptist church in Calais, and he sided with the abolitionists during the Codding affair. Two years earlier, Mary Hayden Green had been called to baptism in the dead of winter; a hole had to

---

1 Austin Willey, *The History of the Antislavery Cause in State and Nation* (Portland, ME: Brown Thurston, 1886), 115; http://archive.org.

2 D.W. Bartlett, *Modern Agitators, or Pen Portraits of Living American Reformers* (Auburn, NY: Miller, Orton, and Mulligan, 1855), 216; *Making of America,* http://name.umdl.umich.edu/ABT6622.0001.001.

be cut into the ice at the river's edge for twelve-year-old Mary's immersion.[1] As a devout member of her church, Mary felt that her faith demanded her antislavery position, a perspective she would later make clear in *Ida May*. Like others of the genre, *Ida May* is a religious text rooted in the author's Baptist faith. The heart-wrenching subplots of enslaved motherhood, performed by Maum Abby and Maum Venus, are deeply informed by a Protestant view of God's will. This religiosity distinguishes the strong black characters from their weaker, slaveholding counterparts. Religious faith in *Ida May* is a sustaining, moralizing force, and this novel unfailingly has a double conversion in mind—toward both antislavery and Protestantism.

In her teens, Mary became an ardent reader of social-reform texts, including those from the temperance and antislavery movements. It was through the circulation of these texts that she met her husband, the young lawyer Frederick Augustus Pike (1816–86), who shared her political views. Frederick and his brother James (1811–82) took the nascent Calais library as their philanthropic mission in the 1840s, furnishing it with books and funds and curating their town's literary taste and politics though subscriptions. The town's first permanent newspaper, *The Calais Advertiser*, was established in 1841, and the editorial leaning of the paper was first Whig, then Republican. Frederick edited and wrote for this local newspaper.

Frederick did not know his father, William Pike, who had helped establish Calais in the early years of the nineteenth century, much as their Puritan ancestor, Robert Pike, had founded Salisbury, Massachusetts, in the seventeenth century. William Pike drowned in 1818, when he fell overboard en route to Eastport, Maine, to celebrate the end of four years of British occupation due to a boundary dispute. All four of his sons would carry on his legacy of public service (Griffin 24–30). Mary and Frederick married in 1846. In 1850, Calais became a city, and soon afterward, Frederick became its mayor. They would maintain a home in Calais all their lives. On 29 May 1852, Mary's cousin, steamboat captain William Henry Clark Stearns, was killed by a boiler explosion on board the *Eastern City*. With no children of their own, Mary and Frederick adopted Stearns's ten-year-old orphaned daughter, Mary Sophia Green Stearns, known as "May" (Griffin, chs. 2 and 3).

---

1 *Dictionary of American Biography* (New York, 1934), XIV, 597; cited in Griffin 22.

With the rest of the country, Mary Pike read *Uncle Tom's Cabin*, and she decided to take up her pen in support of causes she held dear: Protestantism, antislavery, and racial justice. She would publish three novels in the 1850s, each with plots that pivot on prejudice and racial identities in the United States. In *Ida May* (1854), the enslaved heroine is a white child; in *Caste: A Story of Republican Equality* (1856), the romance centers on a white woman who discovers she is legally black; and *Agnes* (1858), set in the Revolutionary era, concerns the place of Native Americans in the new republic. Mary Hayden Green Pike did not step forward to claim authorship of *Ida May* or *Caste* until 1858 with the publication of *Agnes*, her third and final novel. According to a letter written by her husband Frederick, who managed her literary affairs, Mary had difficulty convincing her publishers to print *Agnes*. Her first book had been a signal success, but her second—a romance that results in a controversial interracial marriage—decidedly not. *Caste* was her "passing" novel, repeatedly depicting the pervasive racism of the Northern states; it sold only 13,000 copies. Frederick Pike accused her publishers of a "mercantile blunder" when they published *Caste* under a new pseudonym, Sydney A. Story, with no indication that this was the second novel by the author of *Ida May*.[1] It seems likely that for *Agnes*, Pike put the text in her own name in an attempt to win back her once large audience.

That year, 1858, was also when her husband began his career as a congressman and as a Republican. In 1858, Frederick was elected to the state Senate, and from 1861 to 1869 he served Maine's 5th and 6th districts in the federal House of Representatives. His older brothers were also in the prime of public careers: Charles E. Pike served as representative of Newtown in Boston to the Massachusetts state Senate in 1856, and as solicitor for the Washington Internal Revenue Bureau during the Civil War. James Shepherd Pike was invited by Horace Greeley (1811–72) to write increasingly radical, "racy, epigrammatic articles" (Barnes 273) from Washington as an associate editor for the *New York Tribune*. James Shepherd Pike was appointed Minister Resident for the United States to the Netherlands during the war. Frederick's constituents may have seen Mary's books as evidence of the political and social leanings of the Pike household.

---

1 Letter from Frederick A. Pike to Moses Dresser Phillips, 21 June 1857. Manuscript Collection, Boston Public Library.

The family was not always in agreement. While we can see in Pike's novels a dramatization of her husband and brother-in-law's Republicanism, we can also find humanizing challenges to the party platform: caught between slave and free, black and white, her heroines cross the very borders that first Free Soil and then Disunion politics sought to maintain.[1] James Shepherd Pike, though vehemently against slavery, was openly hostile to blacks. In 1853, while Mary was beginning her manuscript for *Ida May*, James was writing racist screeds for the *Tribune*, such as "we want no more ebony additions to the Republic."[2] James consistently argued for containment, believing that the best solution to "the African problem" was emigration of blacks to the West Indies, thereby ridding North America of slavery and "the burden and hindrance of the black population" in one move. In his article "What shall we do with the Negro," Pike shows himself as viscerally anti-black as he was antislavery: "We say the Free States should say, confine the negro to the smallest possible area. Hem him in. Coop him up. Slough him off. Preserve just so much of North America as is possible to the white man, and to free institutions" (qtd. in Durden 31). It bears mentioning that Greeley censored Pike when these columns first appeared; however, given free rein in his post-war diatribe *The Prostrate State: South Carolina under Negro Government* (1874), James Pike is openly, shockingly racist.

While the more moderate and politically savvy Frederick Pike spoke only once on slavery during his time in Congress, he would be remembered as the first to call in Congress for immediate emancipation. His speech of 5 February 1862 on the Legal-Tender Bill concludes: "these three—tax, fight, emancipate—shall be the trinity of our salvation. In this sign we shall conquer" (see Appendix E3, p. 384). When the Amendment to end slavery reached Congress three years later, in January of 1865, he argued for its ratification: "Let the amendment be adopted, and slavery be destroyed, and hereafter the only contest upon the subject will be, Who did the most to bring about this consummation so devoutly wished for by all good men" (qtd. in Barnes 277).

---

1 The Free Soil movement sought only to protect new territories in the West from the slave system. Disunionists fought to dissolve the federal union between North and South. For a more nuanced view of the many political forms that abolitionism took, see Sinha.

2 "Mr. Everett's Dispatch on Cuba," *New York Tribune* 10 Jan. 1853.

Mary Pike's poem in honor of the martyred abolitionist John Brown (1800–59), included in Appendix E4, makes clear that like many of her contemporaries, and with her husband Frederick, she recognized that it would take a war to end slavery. Mary lived in Washington during the Civil War. Her only brother, Captain Thomas Hayden Green, was stationed there too, awaiting orders as staff in General Henry Prince's Western Army. Thomas died in the battle of Cedar Mountain, on 9 August 1862, in an attempted rescue of his general, who had been taken prisoner. Mary's memorial for her brother poignantly depicts how committed she was to God and country during the war years:

> when asked with irrepressible bitterness what did he for the proud beautiful flag ... there comes the whisper of Christian faith, saying that no deadly missile speeds its way in the midst of battle unguided by the will of Him with whom are the hours of life and death, and that a man has learned life's lesson well when he can dare to die in obedience to duty.[1]

Her husband's biographer called Mary in her forties "a lady of rare endowments of heart and mind. After the experience of a winter in the South, she wrote *Ida May*, and some other novels, which were received by the public with great favor. Her mental activity and acquirements have been chiefly displayed, however, in a rare conversational talent, which makes her the charm of the social circle" (Barnes 277–78). Following Frederick's final term in Congress, the couple went on a European tour. In an unverified family story recorded by Rachel Griffin (44), Mary aided General Lew Wallace in collecting material for his popular novel *Ben Hur: A Tale of Christ* (1880) when they were both in Constantinople. Upon the Pikes' return to Calais and Frederick's return to business, they purchased a spacious new home at 293 Main Street, which they called "Thorncroft," with five acres of gardens and groves. For the next ten years, they lived primarily in Calais and wintered in Florida or in Baltimore.

Frederick lost his seat in Congress by becoming a Democrat in 1872; in 1877, the Democrats and Republicans nominated and elected him to his old post in the Maine legislature. He did

---

1   Letter dated 22 May 1865, from Mary Hayden Green Pike to Charles B. Hayden, containing a memorial of her brother for Bowdoin College; qtd. in Griffin 43.

not retire from public life until after his brother James's death in 1882. Frederick died four years later, after which time Mary chose to live with her daughter May and her growing family in New Jersey, and with her sister Emma in Baltimore. Mary and Emma, both in their seventies, dedicated their retirement years to mission and educational work through the Baptist Church, working primarily with the Chinese community in Baltimore. A Calais friend remembers Mary in her retirement as "an unusual woman, unusual to look at, fine in strength of features, and lively in expression."[1] Though she was gone from Maine nine months of the year, she continued to spend the summers at Thorncroft for the rest of her life.

Writing the White Slave

The paragraph that describes five-year-old Ida the moment before she is kidnapped is one of the longest in the novel. Ida is seen in three ways: from the perspective of her nanny Bessy's care, from a narrator's "painterly" vantage, and from the villainous slaver's point of view:

> Bessy was accustomed to having strangers compliment the beauty of her little charge, and never had she looked so beautiful as now. She had taken off her hat, and her long dark curls were hanging carelessly down her cheeks, and over her neck, twined with a long spray of delicate pink flowers, with which she had ornamented herself. The mourning-dress showed her clear, dark complexion to great advantage; her cheeks and lips were like blushing rosebuds, and her brilliant eyes were lighted with merriment. Seen in the softened light of her leafy resting-place, with the deep shade of the forest for a background, she formed a picture on which a painter's eye would have rested with untold delight. But other thoughts were in the mind of the dark-browed man who now approached them. (p. 55)

The narrator focalizes the "painterly" portrait of Ida through her maid Bessy, before the passage concludes with a deliberate misreading of the scene by the slave trader. This scene fore-

---

1   Letter from Mrs. Albion H. Eaton, Portland, Maine, 12 Aug. 1934; qtd. in Griffin 45.

grounds the work of representation, which in turn inscribes Ida with blackness: her black curls, her mourning clothes, and her "clear, dark complexion" find but little contrast in the pinkness of her cheeks and the pink flowers in her hair. Pike contends with a representational crisis over how to present Ida's race as both ambiguous and white. Why else would the "dark-browed man" choose to kidnap Ida, unless he thought he could pass her off as a slave? Ida's racial ambiguity in these moments creates, for the abolitionist and the modern audience, an ideological jam: to dismiss *Ida May* as unrealistic or inaccurate because of how clumsily Pike handles race denies the injustice and prejudice of the era that the novel records.

Each time Ida's physical appearance is described, the word "dark" is used for her eyes and hair. In the racialized societies of antebellum America, these were significant details, for one looked to the hair and the eyes to categorize a stranger as black, white, or of mixed race. Ida's ability to "pass" as a slave in her narrative was made possible by prior narratives featuring near-white enslaved women. The pioneering antislavery novel *Archy Moore* by Richard Hildreth (1807–65), republished in 1852 as *The White Slave*, was reprinted in 1854 and 1855 to take advantage of *Ida May*'s celebrity. George and Eliza Harris, central characters of *Uncle Tom's Cabin*, pass for white on their path to freedom. Francis Colburn Adams (fl. 1853–80) published two books on slavery in South Carolina in the 1850s—where the redemption scenes of *Ida May* take place—one a non-fiction response to *Uncle Tom's Cabin*, the other a novel about near-white slave children caught up in their father-master's debt (see Appendix D4). Both novels re-imagine the non-fictional narratives of near white fugitives. The white slave child—and white slave girl in particular—was a phenomenon by 1855.

Scenes featuring white children at auction or the whipping post, and living under the threat of sexual violation, populate these books and their illustrations. In her subtitle for *Ida May: Story of Things Actual and Possible*, Pike insists that the depictions, not only of Ida May but also of the conditions of slavery in which she finds herself, are real. Such unimaginable, improbable "things" like enslaved white children, as Pike implores in her Preface, are both "actual and possible." Political and social theory of the eighteenth and nineteenth centuries claimed that sympathy hinges on an imagined resemblance between ourselves and the person whose suffering we witness. To sympathize is to put oneself in the place of another, to imagine, as philosopher

Adam Smith (1723–90) does, that our bodies can experience the suffering we witness in another.[1] *Ida May* maintains a racial bias in order to court a white audience's sympathy through a strategy of resemblance; the narrator laments in its pages the capture of the one white child in a carriage filled with nameless, kidnapped children of color. In contrast, *The Liberator* reminded reformers in its first number: "There were kidnapped during the past year, and reduced to remediless bondage, MORE THAN FIFTY THOUSAND INFANTS, the offspring of slave parents!!!"[2] This narrative, and others like it, make the troubling assertion that white children are unintended victims of the slave regime. Even so, *Ida May*'s predicament and redemption ultimately call into question the justice of the slave code that claims her as property. Eliza Lee Cabot Follen (1787–1860), in her tract "To Mothers in the Free States," makes the connection for white audiences: "There is even a more painful picture than this for American mothers to see, and one that God and man call upon them to look at and remember. You have a daughter; you are a proud, tender, virtuous mother," Follen writes, and dares her audience to now "[i]magine her exposed to ill usage.... Is the picture overdrawn?" She concludes, "Every honest and intelligent man and woman in the land must know that *Uncle Tom* and *Ida May* owe much of their power to the ghastly truths they reveal."[3]

William Craft's 1860 memoir *Running a Thousand Miles for Freedom* (see Appendix D2) opens with the problem of kidnapped white children to appeal to the basic similarity between kidnapping and enslavement. His wife Ellen Craft (1826–91) "passed" for a male white invalid in their escape narrative. Although she was the daughter of a slave and her master, William Craft (1824–1900) reminds us that other slaves in the historical record were born free to white parents. He expounds on a simple truth that "slavery in America is not at all confined to persons of any particular complexion," and he fears "it is almost impossible for a white child, after having been kidnapped and sold into or reduced to slavery, in a part of the country where it is not known (as often

---

1 *The Theory of Moral Sentiments* (1759), Part I, Chapter 1: "Of Sympathy."

2 William Lloyd Garrison, "Today," *Liberator* 1 Jan. 1831.

3 Anti-slavery tracts, No. 8 (New York, 1855), 1–2; Slavery and Anti-Slavery Digital Archive (http://gale.cengage.co.uk/product-highlights/history/slavery-and-antislavery-a-transnational-archive.aspx).

is the case), ever to recover its freedom" (p. 372). He refers to a case heard before the Louisiana Supreme Court sixteen years earlier. Salomé Müller (b. c. 1814) was an orphaned German immigrant who was held in slavery in New Orleans from 1818 until she was recognized in 1843. When she successfully sued for her freedom the following year, it was seen by the abolitionist press as making a fissure in the racial foundation of slavery, even as Southerners saw the same case as a confirmation of the primary construct of race. Historians have since concluded that Salomé was in fact Sally Miller who, like Ellen Craft, was born into slavery (see Wilson). The case of Salomé (Sally) Müller is pointed to in reviews of *Ida May* as substantive evidence for the veracity of Pike's fictional narrative. A review in the *Boston Daily Atlas* begins, "It is a criticism not infrequently made upon *Ida May* that the ground-work of the plot—the kidnapping of a white girl into slavery—is too improbable, too outrageously improbable, to come within the legitimate scope of slavery. Those who urge this objection are of course ignorant of the commonest facts of slavery" (Appendix D1, p. 367). The phrase "the commonest facts of slavery" refers the reader not only to kidnapping but also to sexual slavery and the resulting children; the word "legitimate" is carefully chosen. When Craft or *Ida May*'s reviewers remind readers about Salomé Müller or Solomon Northup, they expose a trend of misplaced attention: the conversation remains focused on the details of these sensational kidnappings, when what should be analyzed are the mutable and mistaken foundations of chattel slavery. Sally Miller and Ellen Craft both made the most of their mistaken racial identities, while Solomon Northup was made vulnerable to kidnapping by his. If the peculiar institution could not certify, in the Louisiana Courts, the "legitimacy" of one man or one woman's enslavement, then all property in humans ought to have been brought under suspicion.

In February 1855, at the height of *Ida May*'s popularity, the Senator from Massachusetts, Charles Sumner (1811–74), sent a daguerreotype of a little girl to his supporter Dr. Stone in Boston, with this message:

> Dear Doctor—I send you by mail the daguerreotype of a child about 7 years old, who only a few months ago was a slave in Virginia, but who is now free by means sent on from Boston, which I had the happiness of being trusted with for this purpose. She is bright and intelligent—another *Ida May*. I think her presence among

us (in Boston) will be a great deal more effective than any speech I could make. (Appendix D5, p. 381)

The child, Mary Mildred Botts, was in appearance and age similar to Ida during her enslavement. Mary Botts did not "look" like a slave, and it is precisely for this reason she was daguerreotyped: to confound her contemporaries' confidence in their ability to see race, and to threaten the racial architecture of the slave system. "Meanwhile I send this picture," Sumner wrote, "thinking that you will be glad to exhibit among the members of the Legislature, as an illustration of Slavery. Let a hard-hearted Hunker look at it and be softened" (p. 381). Stone forwarded Sumner's letter to the editor of the *Boston Telegraph*, Richard Hildreth, who published it in full the following Tuesday. Mary's image passed hand-to-hand through the Capitol, her story was reprinted in newspapers up and down the East coast, and, by the middle of 1855, Mary joined Senator Sumner on the lecture circuit "as an illustration of Slavery." During her first three months of freedom, Mary stood as "Little Ida May," as she shared platforms with Anthony Burns, the famous fugitive captured in Boston and escorted by federal troops back into enslavement, and freeborn Solomon Northup of New York, whose narrative of wrongful enslavement in Louisiana had just been published. The "Boston Correspondent" for *Frederick Douglass' Paper*, William Cooper Nell (1816–74), covered her first appearance:

> Honorable Charles Sumner, the pride of Massachusetts, has arrived home, and brings with him "Little Ida May." She is perfectly white, and on that account produces intense excitement. We see daily white fugitives, and the cupidity of a slaveholder would suffer him to keep anyone, even his mother, in slavery. When white men learn this, and that their own liberties are in danger, then they will see the reasonableness of an unconditional emancipation.[1]

A black abolitionist, Nell succinctly summarizes what Mary Botts, as "Little Ida May," meant as an icon for white abolitionist audiences. As a "perfectly white" slave, she draws astonished attention and "intense excitement"; as "Ida May," Mary reminds white audiences that all liberty is endangered by a slave system.

---

1 *Frederick Douglass' Paper* 16 Mar. 1855.

And Nell confirms that the trumpeted spectacle of white slavery was, in fact, an everyday affair.

Sumner's speech, "The Anti-Slavery Enterprise; Its Necessity, Practicability and Dignity," solidified his position as a leader in the antislavery movement. As he would argue in his speech, with Mary Botts by his side at the podium, the message Sumner borrows from the plot of *Ida May* is this: if race cannot be identified, as it could not be in this child Mary or in the fictional Ida, then how can race serve as the basis for the legal status of slave or free? Sumner's line of reasoning begins from a position of racial indeterminacy, whereas pro-slavery arguments depended on an untenable distinction between the races. "First, of the alleged distinction of race," as Sumner opened his argument, "it is apparent in the obvious fact, that, unless such distinction be clearly and unmistakably established, every argument by which our own freedom is vindicated ... must plead trumpet-tongued against the deep damnation of Slavery, whether white or black."[1] While he leaves open the possibility of racialism, hinting at the social assignment of attributes and stereotypes according to race, he concludes that, to be comfortable with the institution of slavery, the American public must also be prepared to countenance white slavery.[2]

Mary Botts's precipitous conversion from a slave child into an illustration of white slavery writes the open secret of sexual slavery into the political discourse: in Sumner's letter or beside him at the podium, given Mary's personal ancestry, she embodies living evidence of rape, and her skin color foretells an anxious future of sexual slavery. As Karen Sánchez-Eppler writes in *Touching Liberty*, "As the child of lawless sexuality she has inherited the role of being exploited. Her body displays not only a history of past miscegenation but also a promise of future mixings" (34). Historian Walter Johnson explains that "according to the ideology of slaveholders' racial economy, which associated blackness and physical bulk with vitality," slave women that were "light-skinned and slender" like Mary Botts embodied the opposite: "their whiteness unfitted them for labor." Thus she represented a different economy, narrowly escaped: "for slave-buyers, near-white enslaved women symbolized the luxury of being able to pay for service, often sexual, that had no material utility—they were

---

1 Charles Sumner, *Recent Speeches and Addresses, 1851–1855* (Boston: Higgins and Bradley, 1856), 486.
2 For more of Mary Mildred Botts's story, see articles by Morgan-Owens and Mary Niall Mitchell, and Morgan-Owens, *Poster Child* (W.W. Norton, forthcoming).

'fancies,' projections of the slaveholders' own imagined identities as white men and slave masters" (18). Though the history of sexual enslavement nominally legible on the white enslaved child lurks outside Pike's plot, this future troubles our heroine every time she is sold. Her kidnappers offer Ida to James Bell at a bargain due to her emaciated, feverish, and mentally broken condition, with this hard sell: "I tell you, it goes to my heart to have to part with her this way, for she'll sell for a thousand dollars, as a fancy girl, in ten years" (p. 84). Five years later, when Ida's health and beauty are recovered, Mrs. James Bell insists that Ida be sold off to save herself the ignominy of a tempted husband. At the moment of her purchase by Charles Maynard, her future guardian, the narrator comments that Mr. Maynard, who "was acquainted with the market value of such articles," hurried the proceedings to avoid conversation with the slave-driver, "whose coarse jokes and allusions to what Ida would soon be worth as a 'fancy girl,' aroused disgust and anger" (p. 144). Insinuated only in a few discreet passages, sexual enslavement is notably not a part of *Ida May*; if the white child Ida were to become a "fancy girl" or a slaveholder's concubine, Northern audiences would be outraged and her romantic future would be unredeemable.

Walter Varian, Ida's future husband, scrutinizes Ida's race shortly after he has insisted upon her purchase: "I have no doubt she is of white parentage," he claims. "You notice that though she is not very fair, her skin has the clear darkness of a brunette, and not the yellowish tinge which marks the lighter shades of the negro race. Her features, her whole form and mien, show that she is wholly of the Anglo-Saxon lineage" (p. 164). Walter establishes Ida's "indisputable" lineage through an examination of her skin color, which reclassifies the "clear darkness" that singled her out for kidnapping, as white. Everywhere Mary Botts went in the spring of 1855, audiences similarly examined her for traces of the African race in her skin, the shape of her features and head, her hair, and her eyes. Walter's facility in negotiating the markers of race in his dark-haired brunette slave underscores how practiced, and falsely confident, nineteenth-century audiences were in this kind of looking. But Ida May reclaims her identity as a free white woman, not with a legal document or a public examination, but with a private domestic token—a scrap from her lace-trimmed undershirt—that has passed through the hands of Ida May's three mothers in the novel: her deceased white mother, her surrogate black mother, and her plantation mistress. Her protector and guardian during her five years enslaved, Maum Venus, recounts a different kind of phenotypic examination scene, one that occurred when she was first given the broken and bruised Ida to care for:

> "Well, den, I has my 'flections on de subject, all the time I'se undressin' yer, and when I come to take off *dis* thing last, and see how nice 't was through all de dirt, and de stain dat was on it where de rapscal done painted yer neck, to make it like you was black baby; 'specially after I see de lace 't was round it, den I say, 'Sure 'nuff, dis a'n't no nigger, nor no poor buckra child neither. Dis yer poor baby must b'long to somebody dat'll cry powerful a'ter her.' O, honey, den I cry myself, to think o' your poor mammy dat had her baby stole, and toted 'way from her." (p. 123)

This token of a stained lace collar inscribed with the name "Ida May" signifies for Venus the privilege that Ida, had she not been kidnapped, would have experienced. Hers was not a black or poor white "buckra" mother, but a mother who will cry after her. The distinctions Venus draws between sentiment and race seem to ring false in this passage. At this point in the narrative, readers know that Venus's children were "stole, and toted 'way from her," to her great grief, and she fears at this moment that the same will happen to her adopted favorite. When her master gave her a beaten, unconscious white slave to raise, Venus did not hesitate to love the mysterious child she calls "Lizzy" as one of her own. As told to the mistress of Wynn Hall, Venus's words are intended to reach beyond her simple narrative to touch the hearts of a reading audience made up of "Mrs. Wynns" and "Mrs. Mays," the middle-class women who find themselves and their mothering practices reflected in this garment.

Pike makes free use of the racial stereotypes common to her genre, and her protagonists are invariably white women. Even so, Pike does not fail to create individualized black characters with plot-lines motivated toward the same selfhood, security, and belonging that her white protagonist desires. Though appearing over one hundred times in the novel, the word "nigger" as an epithet is relegated mainly to the speech of morally corrupt and uncouth whites. When black characters use the word to describe themselves, it is not in reference to race, but to slave status. The following exchange occurs when Ida wakes in Venus's cabin, after coming out of unconsciousness:

"Who are you?"

"Laws bless the child!" said the delighted woman,—"she'll get peart now, mighty soon; she's begun to ask questions. Who I be?" she continued, shaking all over with a convulsive giggle. "I's an old nigger-woman—don't ye see?"

Again there was a pause, and the child looked from the dark face of her nurse to her own emaciated hands, that were now returned to their original whiteness. After some moments of mental comparison, she said, "Am I a nigger, too?"

"Dono', honey," replied Venus. "Dey say you was, and mighty sick one, too. What be ye? Where was you raised?"

"What is *raised?*" asked the child.

"What, where'd ye *grow*—where ye *come from?*"

"I don't know—I can't remember," replied Ida; and her face grew anxious and troubled. (p. 89)

The next day she wakes up and continues the conversation:

"Did I always live here?" she asked, at length.

"Laws, no, honey!" replied Venus, giggling at this question. "Don't ye see I'se an old black thing, and you's white?"

"A'n't I a nigger, then?" persisted Ida.

"Dono' 'bout dat," replied her nurse. "'Pears like you wasn't; but Mass' James say you was, and some niggers *is* white. It's my suspinion," she continued, after a pause "dat you'se kidnap."

"What is kidnap?" asked Ida.

"Laws, bless de child, she dono' nothin'!" said Venus. "Why, dey kidnaps 'em away off from dere mammys and daddys, and sells 'em to white folks. I reckon somebody done kidnap you, and dat de way Mass' James come to find you."

"Who is Mass' James?" asked the child.

"Mass' James—why he our massa, your massa and mine. He bought us, so I s'pose we b'long to him." (p. 91)

From this moment forward, whenever the narrative is presented through Ida's eyes, we see that she is race blind. For example, when Pike introduces Alfred and Elsie through Ida's eavesdropping, she carefully has her character Ida make no mention of their race or their enslavement. The characters are presented as clandestine lovers everywhere.

As readers will no doubt recognize, Ida May experiences small measures of heartbreak in this novel compared to the ancillary characters Maum Abby, Maum Venus, and Aunt Chloe. The narrative does not flinch from describing the devastating losses experienced by these enslaved women. They see their children taken from them, time and time again, and in their stories the agony and searching experienced by Ida's parents is retold. In Chapter 5, Venus narrates how each of her children has been lost through slavery, and how the slow road out of grief now grants her the vulnerability to love another child in Ida. Venus's strength serves as a foil to the first black character we meet in the novel, the kidnapper's accessory Chloe, who appeases the pain of losing her own children by beating others. The middle third of the novel turns its focus to the story of Abby and her son Alfred, the pride of her heart. Their master, Mr. Wynn, enforces his will upon Alfred through torment and confinement, which drives Alfred to suicide. Readers experience Abby's devastating grief, while Ida becomes a secondary character who administers hope to a broken woman. The success of Abby's recovery is attributed to her strength of character, her faith in God, and Ida's tireless ministrations. The spiritual repercussions for Maum Abby following her son's failed fight for liberty meaningfully illustrate the psychological burden and torment faced by enslaved mothers.

The kidnapper's accessory Chloe has a great deal to say in her chapter, and her backstory interrupts the narrative at its highest pitch. While readers wait to hear what will happen to terrified little Ida, we learn the life history of her torturer instead. With this redirection, Pike accounts for how a woman could become capable of committing cruel torture, by providing a motive for the crime of beating Ida senseless. Chloe was once a mother with a loving home, but she suffered a series of cruel masters who beat and sold her children from her, to be forever lost in slavery. This commonplace in antislavery literature is refigured to be a warning that mothers pushed to such limits are justified in their rage, madness, and desire for revenge. Chloe issues an impassioned lecture on how little color matters to the body that is being whipped. Kelly admonishes Chloe, "it don't do to whip white children like they were niggers," and Bill joins in: "Yes, ... white folks is white folks, and niggers is niggers." Chloe doesn't hold back when faced with this absurd tautology: "'Niggers is niggers, is dey?' rejoined Chloe. 'I neber could see, fur my part, but de nigger flesh feels jest de same tings as white flesh does. Dem two little niggers you toted in here last month, dey was mighty sight like dat white young 'un ater I broke 'em in; didn't know but dey was dead sure 'nuff, dey swine 'way so long'" (p. 76). "Breaking in" hurts black and white children equally, black and white children miss their parents equally, and black and white children fall unconscious under her whip, equally. Chloe is a monster, but her story offers a clear moral. "'Dey's all like me,' interrupted Chloe, 'ony dey keeps it in, 'cause dey's scare ob de white folks, and dey *purtends—dey purtends*—it's de ony way to get along easy, is purtendin' '" (p. 74).

Ida moves between races and social classes and thus offers a unique vantage point on plantation life as experienced by the women in the novel. While Pike's contemporaries made free rhetorical use of the metaphors of slavery to describe women's lives, Ida's story, time and again, reminds us that despite limitations placed on her by her gender, in her womanhood Ida is *free*: free to act on her conscience when enslaved property comes her way, free to marry whom she loves, free to learn and study, free to create and maintain a family of her choosing. As Weinstein points out, when Ida becomes self-pitying, "she is reminded of the obvious by an elderly female slave that 'you'se *rich*, and you'se *white*, and you'se *free*'" (125). Pike's recognition that her heroine has limited access to the experience of slavery and prejudice haunts the narrative from Chloe's scene forward. According to Chloe's logic, the enslaved characters in the novel, even those closest to Ida, may be pretending their affection. Chloe's admonishment— "Dey's all like me, ... ony dey keeps it in"—serves as a reminder that Ida's view is limited by Pike's benighted perception of Southern plantation life *and* the active barriers maintained by the enslaved characters for self-preservation.

Even Venus, whose love appears genuine, is described as inscrutable. She sits secretively behind a facade of prejudice:

No one who looked on Aunt Venus's inexpressive face, as she sat there steadily sewing, would have imagined her capable of the mingled train of wise and bitter reflection that was passing through her brain. She kept her thoughts to herself, and few were aware of the delicate feelings, the womanly refinement, and germs of keen intellect, that lay hid beneath that dark and unpolished exterior. (p. 92)

Pike has created interiorities that she holds out of reach, restricting emotional access to the experience of the enslaved, whose sufferings cannot be fathomed, and whose demonstrative feelings could be pretended. Though she engineers plot coincidences and innumerable reunions to retrieve her characters from the black box of slavery, these twists and turns undermine her claim that *Ida May* is a realistic and noteworthy portrayal of life in bondage. In other words, reading *Ida May: Story of Things Actual and Possible* in the twenty-first century as an encounter with slavery and sentiment in the nineteenth century brings us up short against that which we can never know.

Mary Hayden Green Pike:
A Brief Chronology

1824   30 November: Mary Hayden Green born in Eastport, Maine, to Elijah Dix Green, a bank director and militia officer, and Hannah Caflin Hayden.

c. 1826   The family moves to the lumbering village of Calais, Maine, where Elijah Green prospers. They set up house at 267 Main Street.

1836   Baptized a Baptist at the age of twelve in the icy St. Croix River.

1838   Abolitionism comes to the Calais Baptists: abolitionist speaker Ichabod Codding delivers a contested course of lectures at the First Baptist Church that divides the town of 2000 and splits the church. The minister and a number of the Calais congregation leave. The Green family remain staunch abolitionists.

1841   Elijah Green becomes a deacon of the newly inaugurated Second Baptist Church of Calais.

1840–43   Attends and graduates the Charleston Female Seminary of Calais, Maine.

1844   Makes the tour of the South that would serve as the basis for *Ida May*. The mayor of Aiken, South Carolina, threatens to kick her out of town for her abolitionism.

1845   Marries Frederick Augustus Pike, a lawyer and Bowdoin graduate.

1850   Frederick's brother, James Shepherd Pike, begins writing radical Republican columns as correspondent for the *New York Tribune*.

1852   Cousin Mary Sophia Green Stearns (b. 1844) comes to live with Frederick and Mary after her father's death.

1854   24 November: Publication of *Ida May: Story of Things Actual and Possible* under the pseudonym Mary Langdon. Sixty thousand copies are sold. Sales from the novel are used to build a house at 278 Main Street in Calais, which they name "Ida May." Frederick and Mary formally adopt Mary Stearns.

1855	Publication of initial German and French translations of *Ida May*.
1856	*Caste: A Story of Republican Equity* published under pseudonym Sydney A. Story, dealing with the racial prejudice faced by mixed-race families in the North.
1858	Publication of *Agnes*, a novel that explores female independence against a backdrop of the American Revolution. Mary also claims authorship of *Ida May* and *Caste*. Frederick elected to Maine State Legislature.
c. 1859	Pike publishes her final piece, a memorial poem "John Brown in Prison."
1860	Frederick is Speaker of the Maine House and begins to campaign for Congress.
1861–69	Frederick serves the Republican Party for four successive terms as US Congressman, with six years as chairman of the Committee for Naval Affairs. The Pikes live in Washington, DC, where Mary becomes an accomplished landscape painter.
1862	5 February: in Congress, Frederick makes historic call for emancipation. 9 August: Mary's brother Captain Thomas Hayden Green dies in the battle of Cedar Mountain.
1870	Adopted daughter Mary "May" Stearns Pike marries Morgan Smith Taylor of New Jersey. They will have three children: Mary, Edith, and Frederick Taylor.
1871	May–January: Following the end of Frederick's fourth term in Congress, he and Mary travel abroad.
1872	Frederick leaves the Republican Party to run for Congress as a "Greeley Democrat." After his defeat, he turns his attention to managing his extensive holdings in timber, railroads, granite, gas, and plaster. They move to "Thorncroft," a small estate in Calais.
1877	Supported by both Democrats and Republicans, Frederick is nominated and elected to his former seat in the Maine legislature.
1882	Death of James Shepherd Pike. Frederick retires from politics, law, and business in the ensuing months.
1886	Frederick dies in Calais, leaving Mary with a comfortable estate. Their daughter May, now in Plainfield, New Jersey, invites Mary to live with her family. Mary spends nine months each year with her daughter's family, and the summer months at Thorncroft.

1895   Mary, May, and Edith spend the summer at Davos in Switzerland. Upon her return in 1896, Mary joins her sister, Emma Sophia Smith, in Baltimore. The sisters, in their seventies, are actively engaged in mission and educational work in the Chinese community, through the Baptist Church.

1904   Emma dies. Her daughter, Kate Oudesluys, cares for her aunt Mary in subsequent years of declining health.

1908   15 January: Mary Pike dies at the home of her niece in Baltimore and is buried next to her husband in Calais.

A Note on the Text

This text is from the twentieth-thousand printing of the first edition of *Ida May*, published by Phillips, Sampson, and Company in Boston, released at the end of December 1854. No manuscript is extant, and the plates for all three of Pike's novels were destroyed by fire in 1870. Her popularity so sharply waned after the Civil War that *Ida May* has not been reprinted until now. An electronic edition of *Ida May* produced by the Antislavery Literature Project, which appeared in 2006, also relies on the first edition of the novel.

For passages that do not appear in dialect, I have silently modernized and regularized punctuation and spelling.

IDA MAY:

Story of Things Actual and Possible

BY

MARY LANGDON.

"We speak that we do know, and testify that we have seen."

TWENTIETH THOUSAND.

BOSTON:
PHILLIPS, SAMPSON AND COMPANY.
NEW YORK: J. C. DERBY.
1854.

PREFACE.

This story, which embodies ideas and impressions received by the writer during a residence in the South, is given to the public, in the belief that it will be recognized and accepted as a true picture of that phase of social life which it represents.

In the various combinations of society existing in the slave States, there may be brighter, and there certainly are darker scenes, than any here depicted; but I have preferred to take the medium tones most commonly met with, and have earnestly endeavored to

> "nothing *exaggerate*,
> Nor set down aught in malice."[1]

I have not written in vain, if the thoughts suggested by the perusal of this book shall arouse in any heart a more intense love of freedom, or bring from any lip a more firm protest against the extension of that system which, alike for master and servant, poisons the springs of life, subverts the noblest instincts of humanity, and, even in the most favorable circumstances, entails an amount of moral and physical injury to which no language can do justice.

M.L.[2]

---

1 From Shakespeare's *Othello*, 5.2.341–42. In his final speech, Othello asks Lodovico to "Speak of me as I am. Nothing extenuate, / Nor set down aught in malice." Pike has changed the word "extenuate" to "exaggerate" to better suit her claim to truth.

2 Mary Langdon is the pseudonym that Mary Hayden Green Pike used for *Ida May*, to protect her husband's nascent political career from the potentially negative publicity that could arise from a woman writing a political novel. She did not claim authorship until 1858; see Introduction, p. 20.

CHAPTER I

"A child is always a charming novelty, although Cain was the only really venerable and truly original baby."[1]

DR. O.W. HOLMES

Everybody thought that Ida May was a wonderful child, and everybody said that she would be completely spoiled; and it was a matter of congratulation to all who desired her preservation from ultimate destruction, when one day it was announced that Mrs. May had given birth to a son.

Great, indeed, was the rejoicing; not only among the "dear five hundred friends,"[2] but in the quiet home of the Mays. Every face wore a peculiarly happy and relieved expression—from the old doctor, who met the three years old Ida on the stairs, as he descended from the sick-room, and, patting her dark curls, said, "So, miss, your nose is out of joint, now," to the little nurse-maid Bessy, who made an idiotic face and imitated the wailing of the new infant, by way of illustrating to the child the inestimable treasure of which her mother had become possessed.

But when Miss Ida was ushered into the darkened room, and saw the formidable array of phials and caudle-cups[3] on the mantelpiece, and the stern face of the nurse, who hushed her first rapturous greeting of her little brother by pointing to the bed where her mother lay, the young lady began to doubt the extreme benefit she had been told was to be derived from this addition to the family. She stood a moment, gazing around, with her large, dark eyes wide open, and her rosy lips set in a queer expression.

"Come here, my darling," said her mother's feeble voice. "A'n't you very glad you have a little brother, and won't you love him very much?"

---

1   Quoted in *Merry's Museum and Parley's Magazine*, Volumes 27–28 (S.T. Allen & Company, 1854). Oliver Wendell Holmes Sr. (1809–94) was a doctor, celebrated poet, essayist, and Cambridge wit. The quotation begins, "We like new forms of the poetic element, even if they resemble the old; as the birth of a child is always a charming novelty...."

2   William Cowper (1731–1800), *The Task* (1785), Book Two: "She that asks / Her dear five hundred friends, contemns them all, / And hates their coming."

3   Two-handled silver cup used for "caudle"—a drink of warm ale or wine with gruel and spices—administered to convalescents and to women after childbirth.

But the child was not in the mood for sentiment. Climbing up into a chair, in order to reach her mother, she pointed with one chubby hand to the fireplace, where the nurse was rocking the baby, and said:

"Mother, did *God* send that baby here?"

"Yes, my love," replied Mrs. May.

"Well, then," said little miss—dropping her hand and curling her lip in great scorn—"I should think *God might know better* than to send him now, when you are so sick you have to hire that great ugly woman to take care of him."

But the little stranger, about whose coming the child thus irreverently expressed her opinion, was not destined long to endure the joys and sorrows of humanity. Not many weeks had elapsed before the immortal flower was transported to bloom in the gardens of Paradise, and then this bright beautiful girl was watched over with even a tenderer devotion, and clasped more closely than ever to the parent hearts which death had so cruelly wounded.

The baby died and was buried; and, as Ida sat in her father's arms that evening, vainly trying to comprehend what was *death*, that had thrown such an unwonted gloom over the household, she suddenly broke the silence by saying:

"Where is the baby, now?"

"The baby is an angel in heaven," replied the father, sadly.

"And my little chicken, you know, father, that I killed hugging it, the other day, and you buried for me—I suppose by this time that is an angel in heaven, too. I wish God knew it was mine, and then, maybe, he'd let our baby have it to play with."

The chicken thus referred to was one of a number of its race that had been the victims of Ida's fond but overzealous care; for, about this time, and during the summer that followed, she gave her almost undivided attention to that branch of ornithology that concerns the habits of domestic fowls. Her great delight was to watch the chickens in the henery, and many hours each day were spent in following them about, and imitating their motions, until the feathered bipeds came to regard her as one of themselves, and ceased to feel alarm at her presence. Sometimes she was found with her rosy mouth covered with dust, after attempting to peck from the ground, as she had seen her favorites do; and she came near having her eyes picked out by an indignant hen, under whose wings she tried to introduce herself, along with the chickens that were brooding there. Often she would climb the hen-roost, and there, supporting herself in some angle, would sit patiently for a long time, balancing herself on her hands and feet; and the only drawback to her pleasure in this position was the melancholy fact that, notwithstanding all her efforts, she could not *put her head under her wing.*

One evening she was missing when bedtime came, and, when her mother went to the door to seek her, a childish voice, that seemed to come from the clouds, answered her call. Looking up into a tree that stood near, she discovered Ida safely perched among the branches.

"Mercy!" exclaimed the terrified mother, "how came you up there, my child?"

"I a'n't a child now," was the reply; "I'm a *hen*, and I'm gone to roost, and I've got up high so the cats shan't catch me."

Fortunately her father was near, and his firm arm soon withdrew the little girl from her perilous position.

One afternoon her mother was telling her of God's care over us all, and that he sent his angels to guard us from evil and incite us to good.

"Are they round us always; in the night, too?" asked Ida, her eyes dilating with wonder.

"Yes, they are always with us," replied Mrs. May. "They guard us while we sleep, and give us happy dreams. My darling, you need never feel as if you were alone, for the blessed angels are always near to protect you."

Ida was not at all timid in regard to physical danger; but the idea of the supernatural, thus suddenly presented to her excited imagination, impressed her powerfully. She said nothing more, however, and, unconscious of her feelings, Mrs. May pursued the subject some moments longer.

That evening, after she had been undressed and left alone in her little bed, her parents were startled by hearing her call them in a loud, distressed voice; and, going to her room, found her sitting up in the moonlight, her face agitated with vexation and fear. To their inquiries, she answered with a burst of tears, which could no longer be restrained,

"I wish the old angels would stay in heaven where they belong. They'd better be playing on their harps than standing here watching me."

It was a great pleasure to Ida to attend church. Her quick sensibilities were impressed by the solemn hush of the place. The softened light, the pale face of the minister in the sacred desk, and the music of the organ, thrilled her with a mysterious awe. She was always wide awake then, and her childish soul overflowed with ecstasy; and, as she was allowed to sleep quietly during the sermon, she was inclined to consider the Sabbath worship, upon the whole, a very pleasant institution. Great, then, was her disappointment when, one day, she was detained at home by a slight illness. She begged and cried to be permitted to go, and, as a final argument, she said, looking up into her mother's face, with the greatest earnestness,

"Do let me go, mother. If you will, *I'll indulge a hope*—I will, mother—and be a *little mite of a candidate*."[1]

"My dear," was the reply, "I cannot allow you to go to church, and if you really want to be good, you won't tease me any more." The child turned away with a deep sigh, and stood by the window, listening to the ringing of the church-bells, that came musically over the fields on the pleasant summer air. When they had ceased, she turned again to her mother.

"Mother," said she—a curious expression of triumph breaking over her face, and sparkling through the tears which had been slowly gathering in her downcast eyes—"I don't care if I can't go to church today. One of these days I'm going to heaven, and it is Sunday there always, and I will go to church whenever I've a mind to."

Think not, reader, that, in giving these few anecdotes of her childhood, I can convey to you any proportion of the quaint expressions with which my heroine was continually electrifying this admiring household. Even if circumstances had not made her so peculiarly dear, it would have been impossible to withstand the winning ways and childish graces, the sprightliness and intelligence that sparkled in her dark eyes, and moved her restless limbs, and filled her busy brain with the oddest ideas and the most amusing fancies.

Thus brightly and calmly, tinged with warm roseate hues, and musical with song, dawned the day of life that was to be so changeful ere its close. Thus tenderly, in a down-lined nest, was the birdling brooded, whose wings should wander so far over strange lands, and beneath such darkening skies.

---

1 Ida childishly misquotes language about the path to conversion.

CHAPTER II

"What, *all!* did you say *all?*
What, all my pretty chickens and their dam
In one fell swoop?"
MACBETH.[1]

"World! world! O, world!
But that thy strange mutations make us hate thee,
Life would not yield to age."
KING LEAR.[2]

"Good-evening, doctor."

"Ah, Mr. May, good-evening. Chilly weather this. By the way, I saw Mrs. May out today. It won't do for her to breathe this air; you must keep her indoors."

"Do you think her disease progressing?" said Mr. May, anxiously.

"No, no. Don't be alarmed; I am not; but we must be careful;" and the worthy doctor hurried away.

A shadow fell over Mr. May's face, and he sighed heavily as he proceeded homeward. His way lay over the brow of the hill, on which stood the church where he worshipped, and, to shorten the distance, he usually went across the churchyard. As he entered it, a cloud passed from before the moon, and her light fell brightly on the cross that crowned the church tower; and the sight of that blessed emblem of our faith raised in his mind associations and feelings that stilled the deep throbbing of his heart.

Leaning thoughtfully against the low paling that enclosed one of the graves, he gazed around him.

The village lay beneath him on the slope of the hill, and in the valley with its houses gleaming white in the moonlight, and the same radiance glittered on the surface of the river, where a vessel was slowly sailing, with her snowy wings spread to the soft breeze. Light gleamed in many windows, but the quiet of evening had fallen on the streets, and the low rustling of the night wind among the trees was almost the only sound that fell upon his ear.

---

1 Shakespeare, *Macbeth*, 4.3.217–19: Macduff's reaction to the news that his wife and children have been murdered.
2 Shakespeare, *King Lear*, 4.1.10–12.

"Yes," said he aloud, "the scene suggests only ideas of peace and comfort; and yet in every home are fears and cares as great as those which disturb mine. Happiness, love, and the domestic ties that make life beautiful—all must end *here!*"

He paused, for with startling vividness there came over him the thought, "What if this were really *the end?*"—and his memory ran back to the ancient time when the grave was indeed the parting place; when the eye of Faith was dim, and Hope questioned fearfully of an afterlife. Alas for the bereaved one then! From the wide expanse of nature there came no answer to the soul's great question. From the shadowy bourn, whither it had fled, never might the spirit return. Never might the cold lips of the dead murmur a reply to the anguish of that thrilling question, "If a man die, shall he live again?"

Hardly can we imagine the agony of the last hours of those blind heathen, when their grappling hold on life was loosened.

> "Dark must have been the gushing of their tears,
> Heavy the unsleeping silence of the tomb
> On the impassioned soul in elder years,
> When, burdened with the mystery of its doom,
> Mortality's thick gloom
> Hung o'er the sunny world!"[1]

With what a gush of exultation should gratitude ascend to Him whose death, rending in twain the mysterious veil that for ages had hung darkly over the portals of the tomb, brought life and immortality to light! Still doth Love weep over the unconscious bier, but her tears fall not despairingly as of yore. Christ hath risen. O, words of triumph! The cherished form is not given up to darkness and the worm, without the assurance that even from corruption shall come forth incorruption, and the glorified body be reunited to the soul that made it sentient.

Christ hath risen! And we, too, in whose frail nature is enclosed a type of his infinite being, we shall rise from the sleep of the tomb, and ascend to those bright regions where there is no more night.

A smile came over his face, and his heart grew less sad, as these thoughts passed through his mind; for he was a man of strong religious feelings, and now, more than ever, he seemed to find therein the consolation which he sought.

---

1 From "Easter-Day in a Mountain Churchyard" by English poet Felicia Hemans (1793–1835).

Eight years had passed since Ernest May brought to his father's home a gentle and beautiful bride, whom time had only served to make more dear to him. A pleasant home it was; nestled cozily in a grove of trees on the hillside, a little out of the town of M——,[1] in the interior of Pennsylvania. He had inherited from his father this house, in which he was born, and a sufficient fortune to satisfy his unambitious desires; and here, occupied with his favorite pursuits, and in the society of his wife and child, he had enjoyed a happiness that, until within a few months, seemed wholly without alloy.

But now dim shadows were stealing over the brightness of his days. A vague fear haunted him, and would not be driven away. The husband and wife gazed on each other, and felt that there was in the heart of each a thought of terror, which they dared not speak. As she leaned more and more heavily on his arm, and her light step grew slow and faltering in their daily walks—as he marked the quick panting of her breath and the fixed flush on her cheek—as he saw how, day by day, her voice grew weaker, and her fair flesh wasted—his heart sank within him; for he feared that consumption[2] had marked her for its victim.

She knew it also. Well she recognized the footsteps of the silent destroyer, who had borne to the grave all the rest of her family; and, as she felt those icy fingers sealing up the fountain of life, she turned shuddering from the tomb, and clung with trembling hope to the home where love had surrounded her with so many blessings. For a while the weak human nature prevailed over the divine, and she seemed to struggle vainly for the attainment of that strong faith that triumphs over death.

The moon was again hidden behind thick clouds, and the rain was falling, when Mr. May left the churchyard, and, after a few minutes' walk, reached his own door.

Mrs. May sat in a large armchair by the fire, in a quiet room, adorned with pictures and books, with a stand of flowers in one window; and the soft light of an astral lamp[3] filled it with brightness that shone like a welcome into the night-darkness without. She had been musing silently for some time, but, when her ear caught the sound of her husband's step, her pale face lighted with a smile, and she half rose to meet him as he entered.

---

1 Possibly Middletown, Pennsylvania.
2 Pulmonary tuberculosis.
3 Star-shaped, star-like lamp, with its oil contained in a flattened ring, so as to give uninterrupted light.

"You look tired, tonight, and sad, or thoughtful. Which is it?" said he, when he had returned her greeting.

"Perhaps both," she answered; "for I took a walk this afternoon, and I have been sitting here thinking, since I came in; and that is sad work now, is it not?" she added, looking up with a faint smile.

Her husband shook his head playfully. "Ah! Imprudent woman, where did you go? I shall have to stay at home and watch you, if you are not more careful."

"I did not think it would grow so damp, or I should not have ventured," she replied. "I went to see Mrs. Allin, and sat a long time talking with her. How wonderful it is that she should be so resigned to the death of that favorite child! He was her only comfort in life; but yet I believe she is willing, in her inmost heart, that the will of God should be done. She prefers it; she is really satisfied that her plans for earthly enjoyment should be thus suddenly crushed. When she was talking about it today, I was forcibly reminded of the words of David, 'Thou shalt keep him in perfect peace whose mind is stayed on thee.'"[1]

"There is something sublime in such exalted piety," she added, after a pause. "This conquering of all self-will, so that the soul can welcome all things in a holy silence—O, is not this a state of mind worth suffering much to attain?"

"There are many qualities of mind, and many conditions of life, that go to make up such a character," said Mr. May, "and few attain it. Few have strength to continue the self-discipline alike amid the smooth and the rough passages of existence. We are too apt to sink under affliction, with a kind of dumb despair, which, if it does not murmur at the hand that chastens, says, sadly, 'Never was sorrow like unto my sorrow.'"[2]

"And in our happy days," said his wife, "we find it easy to content ourselves with a cold and careless gratitude, that lessens self-control more than even the pressure of grief. We grow cold-hearted and careless, and then, when the hour of trial comes, we find ourselves weak and helpless. O, if it were not so hard to feel right, and to do right!"

Poor Mrs. May closed her eyes, to keep back the tears, and sank down into her armchair with a deep sigh. Her husband gazed upon her with a throbbing heart, for he knew whither her

---

1 Isaiah 26:3: "Thou wilt keep him in perfect peace, whose mind is stayed on thee: because he trusteth in thee."

2 Lamentations 1:12.

thoughts tended; and like a shadow falling darkly down to shut her from his sight, there glided into his mind the image of *death*.

A shudder passed over him, and, for a moment, his eyes were dim; but he would not yield to his emotions, and, taking in his own the hands that had clasped themselves involuntarily, as if in prayer, he said, cheerfully,

"Courage! courage! dear one. These tremblings and fears are not for those whom the strong arm of God upholds. This darkness is not for those who walk in the light of his love."

"O, Ernest!" she answered, mournfully, "I am weak. Never till now did I feel how weak, how incapable of self-abnegation. I admire the perfection of Christian character, but I shrink, weakly, wickedly, from the conflict by which alone it is to be obtained. I am as one who struggles faintly, in a dream, with shadows. Life passes over me, and her warm breath encircles me, but there is no answering life and energy within. Day after day glides from me; hour after hour more surely my destiny reveals itself. Ernest," she cried, suddenly, raising herself and gazing intently into his eyes, "Ernest, can you read it?"

With an irrepressible cry of anguish, her husband caught her in his arms and clasped her to his breast.

"O God!" he said, "it must not be! It shall not be! What can I do without you, Mary; and you—could you be happy, even in heaven, without me?"

"Oh, hush!" said his wife, placing her thin hand over his quivering lips. "This is wrong. We are both wrong. We have lived too much for each other. Ernest, for thy sake, even the eternal life, on which thou canst not now enter with me, seems less dear, less glorious to me! And O, who will guard our child with a mother's care? Who will love her with a mother's untiring sympathy and patience, if I am taken away? How can it be best that she shall sustain such an irreparable loss? O, it is hard! it is hard to die! O, my husband! O, my child! my little child!"

She paused suddenly, and a change came over her face as she pressed her handkerchief to her lips. When she removed it, it was colored with a bright-red stain. She had ruptured a blood vessel.

In a moment all was alarm and confusion in that once happy home. The doctor was called, and the usual remedies applied to stanch the bleeding, and, gently as one would bear an infant, Mr. May bore the wasted form of his wife upstairs to her bed, in that room she was never to leave again till shrouded in the garments of the grave. From the moment of that fatal hemorrhage the cruel disease, whose approaches had hitherto been so silent and slow, threw off all disguise, and with sure and rapid progress consummated its work.

But in that chamber of suffering, where human love wrestled vainly with death, there was felt the presence of an unseen Power, making strong the weak-hearted, and upholding the footsteps that trod the dark valley. The prayers that were offered, the ceaseless, imploring cries for help and comfort, were not in vain. In that fierce furnace of affliction, beside those chastened ones, there walked "One having the likeness of the Son of God," and in that divine companionship the anguish and the terror passed away. He touched their eyes, and the barriers that hide the invisible were removed. All that had seemed dark was lightened, all that was obscure was revealed. Calmly they took the bitter cup, and drank it slowly to its dregs; and lo! it became a holy sacrament, whereon the soul feeds as on heavenly manna.

When the last word was said, and the last token given, he who was left alone at midnight with his dead, bowed his head in a holy and tearless silence; for he seemed to himself to have seen the portals of heaven opened, and heard the unutterable words wherewith a beautified spirit was welcomed to eternal bliss.

But the child, the little one over whom that mother's heart had yearned with inexpressible tenderness, the child who had been borne sleeping to the silent room, and laid on the bed beside the dying, that her hands might, till the last moment, retain their hold of her dearest treasures; how sad was her waking from that sleep beside the dead! how pitiful the wailing cry of childhood, "O, my mother! Give me back my mother!" Sadder still, and more touching, if possible, was her endeavor at self-control, when she became sensible that her paroxysms of grief added to her father's distress, and her efforts to amuse him, wiping with her small, soft hand the tears from his eyes, and striving to amuse him with the playthings of which she took no notice at any other time. How often, in the deep and terrible trouble which afterwards befell him, did that desolate father recall these winsome acts, and the musical tones of her voice, and wonder that he should have esteemed himself so forlorn while he held that treasure to his heart!

For, one day—it was her fifth birthday—three or four months after her mother's death, little Ida and her nurse walked out to gather flowers that grew along the side of a lonely road, which led through a piece of woodland, not far from the house. It was one of those glorious days in June, that make poets overflow with inspiration, and awaken the dormant organ of ideality in the most prosaic; and the clear air, the sunshine shimmering through green branches, and the melody of birds that rang through the woods, tempted them to prolong their walk till they reached the top of a hill, up which, after the fashion of our ancestors, the road had been made to ascend. This had once been the mail route from Philadelphia, westward, but a more direct and less hilly one having been constructed, the old road was left to solitude, except for the occasional passing of the farmers' carts, and the loitering carriages of the few pleasure-seeking travelers, who preferred it on account of the picturesque scenery through which it wound. Having ascended the hill, Ida seated herself to rest on a fallen tree that lay along a bank by the roadside, and Bessy, the maid, who had gathered her apron full of flowers, sat down beside her to weave them into a wreath with which to ornament her straw hat. As they were thus occupied, a closed carriage, drawn by two horses, came slowly up the hill, followed by two men, who sauntered along as if enjoying the beauty of the hour and the scene. When nearly opposite the fallen tree, the horses stopped of themselves, as if waiting for their driver, who, with his companion, soon came up with them. When they saw the two children—for Bessy, a maiden of fifteen, was small of her age, and looked much younger—they paused, and, after looking at them a moment, said a few words to each other, and then one of them got into the carriage and took the reins, while the other approached the place where they were sitting. Bessy was accustomed to having strangers compliment the beauty of her little charge, and never had she looked so beautiful as now. She had taken off her hat, and her long dark curls were hanging carelessly down her cheeks, and over her neck, twined with a long spray of delicate pink flowers, with which she had ornamented herself. The mourning-dress showed her clear, dark complexion to great advantage; her cheeks and lips were like blushing rosebuds, and her brilliant eyes were lighted with merriment. Seen in the softened light of her leafy resting-place, with the deep shade of the forest for a background, she formed a picture on which a painter's eye would have rested with untold delight. But other thoughts were in the mind of the dark-browed man who now approached them. Standing beside Ida, he twined her curls around his fingers, and asked her a few questions, such as are usually addressed to a pretty child, seen for the first time, to which she replied fearlessly. At length turning partly away, as if to regain his carriage, the stranger stopped suddenly, and said to Bessy, "I find I've dropped my whip, walking up—there 't is, lying in the road," he added, pointing to something on the ground, about halfway down the hill—"come now, you're younger 'n I am; s'pose you run down and get it, that's a good girl, and I'll stay with the little girl until you come back."

Bessy hesitated a moment, not that she thought of danger, but she feared the child might not like to be left alone with a stranger. "Will you stay here while I go get the man's whip?" she asked Ida.

The child turned her eyes earnestly upon him for an instant, and then, unwilling to own any fear, but yet detecting, with a child's instinct, something sinister in the gaze that was fixed upon her, she rose from her seat, and said simply, "I will go with you."

"O, no!" replied Bessy; "you can't run quick enough, without getting tired, and there's no good place there to sit and rest, as there is here. I won't be gone but a minute."

"Well," said the child, reseating herself with a dignified air which she sometimes assumed, and which was amusing in one so young—"the man may go get into his carriage, and I'll stay here alone and see you go."

The stranger laughed, and took a few steps forward, and Bessy ran down the hill; but when she arrived at the object pointed out, she found it only a dry stick, and was turning to go back, when a shriek struck her ear, and she saw the child struggling in the arms of the stranger, who put her into the carriage, jumped in after her, and immediately the horses dashed away out of sight. Fear lent her wings; but when she reached the spot whence they had started, they were in the valley below, and galloping at a pace that made pursuit hopeless. Still she ran after them, filled with terror and anguish for the loss of the child, and yet hoping it might be that the men were playing some rude joke to frighten them both, and expecting every minute to see the carriage stop, and allow her to take her little charge. But no; it kept on and on, never slackening its speed, and the poor girl followed, calling wildly, and entreating the pity of those pitiless ones who were far beyond the reach of her voice. So long as the carriage remained in sight, although far distant, she had still a little hope; and when now and then she paused for an instant, to take breath, she heard, or fancied she heard, the piercing cries of the poor child, and the sound stimulated her to almost superhuman exertions; so that, when at length a turn of the road hid it from her eyes, and she fell down on the ground, almost dead with exhaustion, she was more than two miles from home.

How long she lay there, faint and insensible, she never knew, but she was roused by someone shaking her arm a little roughly as he raised her, and a voice that said, "Bless my soul, if this a'n't the little gal that lives to Squire May's! What on airth be you doin' here?"

"O, Miss Ida!—dear, little Ida!" moaned the girl—"they've carried her off; did you meet them—have you got her?" she added, the sudden hope awakening her to life and energy.

"Got who? Who's carried off? What you talking about, gal, and how come you here?" asked the astonished farmer, who, having nearly driven over her, as he rode lazily along to town, now stood half supporting her. "Why, ye poor cretur," he added, "one o' your shoes is off, and your foot's a bleeding, and you're all over dust. Who's been a hurting of ye?"

"O, Mr. Brady!" said Bessy, who, having by this time collected her scattered senses, now recognized her companion, "did you meet a carriage, with two horses, driving like mad? I was with little Ida, on the top of the hill, just out on the Bridge-road, and that carriage came along, and two men were after it, and one of them stopped and spoke to us, and asked me to go get his whip that he had dropped, and while I was going, they took the child. I heard her scream, and turned round just in time to see them drive off with her, and so I ran after them till I dropped down here."

"Bless my soul!" said Mr. Brady—"who ever hear'n tell! So they carried away the poor little girl, did they? I thought they was driving awful fast."

"Did you meet them?—O, did you see her?" said Bessy.

"Well, I s'pose 't was them. There was a carriage and two horses, jest down by widder Wilby's farm, in the hollow there, and they was driving like mad. I saw them coming down the hill, and so I hauled up, till they was by."

"O, then they do mean to carry her off!—O, dear! O, dear! what shall I do? I shall never dare to go home and tell her father!"—and the girl wrung her hands in despair, and sank down again in the road.

"Well now," said farmer Brady, in his slow, calm manner, "I guess the best thing ye can do is to go home as fast as ye can—I'll give ye a lift in my wagon—and tell her father, and he can go after 'em, with horses that'll stand a better chance o' ketchin' up with 'em, than you will."

This advice was followed, but the Brady "colt"—the period of whose birth was lost in the mists of antiquity—having been asleep for the last ten years, it was rather difficult to induce him to quicken his pace on this occasion, and thus some time elapsed before the distressed and impatient girl reached Mr. May's house. He was not at home, and she was just going to town to seek him, when he arrived at the gate. His first glance at the group which came to meet him caused him to quicken his steps, for he knew something was amiss; and when Bessy ran forward, and, sinking at his feet, sobbed out his daughter's name, a pang shot through his heart so severe as to foretell in some measure the suffering that was before him.

"My child—what of her? She is not *dead*!" he said, in the low, hoarse tones of intense anxiety.

"No, no!" said Bessy, "but two men have stolen her—carried her away in a carriage! O, hurry and go after them! O, Mr. May—I shall die if we don't find her!"

Paler than death grew the face of that miserable father; a mist passed before his eyes, and for a moment he leaned heavily against the fence beside him. It was but a moment, and then he sprang forward to order the horses put into the carriage, and, having learned the sad story more explicitly from Bessy, he took her with him to aid in finding their track as far as she had followed it. They had no difficulty in pursuing the kidnappers forty miles, to a town where they had left some horses three days before, taken in exchange others, which they had now brought back, and, ordering their own, had proceeded on their journey a few hours before Mr. May's arrival in the same place. Without losing a moment, he had fresh horses put in his own carriage, and, leaving Bessy to the care of the landlady, he hired a man to assist him, when he should overtake the fugitives, as he had now strong hope of doing. But unfortunately, only a few miles from town, one of the linchpins came out and they were overturned. Neither of them was injured, but some part of the harness was broken, and the accident delayed them an hour or two.

Once again on the way, they followed the track of the carriage, with ever increasing difficulty, for it had diverged into byways, and stopped at none of the large towns; but they went on as swiftly as possible to Hagerstown, just within the borders of Maryland. Here they found that only the night before, the object of their pursuit had been returned, with the horses, to the stable from which they had been hired several days previously, by a man whose appearance agreed with Bessy's description of the one who had seized the child; but he had been alone both in hiring and returning the carriage. By further inquiry, he ascertained that the same person had hired carriages and horses at this stable several times before and, though some curiosity had been excited with regard to him, his movements had never been watched, or any suspicions entertained respecting him. And thus the clue was lost; for the mysterious stranger was nowhere to be seen.

O, the bitter, bitter anguish of that disappointment!—the fearful perplexity and uncertainty with which, all that night, Mr. May paced the floor of his chamber, feeling that the only drop of consolation remaining for him was the thought that the beloved mother of his child had been removed beyond the reach of this woe. Again and again he groaned aloud—"Thou hast taken *her* away from the evil to come"[1]—and in the unselfishness of his true heart his own desolation was for a moment forgotten.

When morning came, his case had become known to the citizens, and many of them came to offer sympathy and all of help that could be given; but none knew what to advise, and he was equally uncertain what to do; for seven roads lead in different directions from the town, and by which of them should he seek his child? At length it was determined to send messengers along each route, and Mr. May joined one party; for, worn out as he was, he was too wretched to remain quiet. But nothing was heard of the persons they sought. It seemed almost as if the earth must have opened and swallowed them up, so completely had all traces of them vanished; and nothing was left for the miserable man but to retrace his steps to his lonely home, and offer a reward for his daughter's recovery, in the hope that avarice might induce her captors to give her up.

Poor Bessy was entirely overcome when she saw him return without the lost child, for his prolonged absence had raised her expectations, and no words can tell the dull despair of that long day during which they traveled to M——. Bessy spent it in constant tears, and frequently broke out in lamentations and reminiscences; but Mr. May uttered neither word nor groan, and his glaring and burning eyes seemed incapable of weeping. For six nights he had not slept, and only *forced* himself to swallow food, meantime, that his strength might not fail; and now his whole frame was racked with feverish pain, and his brain seemed bursting. The sun was just setting when they reached the top of the hill where the fatal deed had been accomplished; and checking his horses almost involuntarily, he looked around. Everything

---

1 Isaiah 51:1.

was the same—green and beautiful as on that morning. Could it be the sorrow in his own heart that cast a black shadow over all? As he sat, absorbed in gloomy thought, his eye fell on something white gleaming behind the fallen tree. Springing out of the carriage, and going nearer, he discovered that it was his daughter's straw hat, still crowned with the faded flowers with which her own little hands had ornamented it. With a choking sob, that seemed to suspend his very breath, he seized and pressed it to his lips, to his heart; and at the touch of that sacred relic of the lost one the torturing tension of his nerves gave way, and throwing himself along the log, he wept freely. They were the first tears he had shed, and they saved his reason or his life.

But, O! the tomb-like silence of that deserted house! O, the long days and months that followed; the feverish excitement of hope, that was indulged only to baffle and rack the soul with fresh disappointment; the wearing heartsickness of expectations that were never realized, and the harrowing fears and images of terror that haunted him like a nightmare, waking him from slumber trembling and covered with the cold sweat of agony, and making his days a prolonged torment! Handbills were issued, and scattered in every direction, offering enormous rewards for the child, or for any information respecting her; and when they were found ineffectual, Mr. May's friends urged him to believe that some fatal accident had ended alike her suffering and her life; but though this thought would have been an infinite relief, he could not indulge it. One idea, suggested by the course the kidnappers had first taken, was constantly present with him; and the knowledge of the fate to which his innocent and beautiful child would be exposed as a slave, almost maddened him. Restless and utterly heartbroken, he spent two years in traveling through the Southern States, visiting every slave market, and growing more and more sick with apprehension, as he became acquainted with the evils inseparably connected with the system in its most favorable conditions, and saw the unutterable indignities and cruelties of the slave pens and auctions.

One thing which he learned, in his search, impressed him with astonishment, and that was the *number* of children, both colored and white, that have been in various ways stolen and lost. From every direction tidings of this sort came to him, sometimes from those who, with the sympathy of a kindred sorrow, wished to console with him on his loss, and sometimes from parents too poor to prosecute the search themselves, begging him, while looking for his own child, to inquire for theirs.[1] In a few cases he was successful in obtaining information that led to the discovery of the lost ones; but of his own little wanderer he found no trace, and his hair grew gray, and his form thin and bent and prematurely old; but, however hopeless of success, he could not relinquish his weary journeyings. At length, nearly three years after Ida's disappearance, when he had spent nearly all his fortune, one of his friends in M——, received a letter from Mr. May, directing him to sell the house and grounds, and remit him the proceeds. He had heard of a little girl named Ida, who was sold in the slave market in New Orleans a year previous. True, the description given of the child was not exactly like his own Ida; but the auctioneer had noticed that there were no traces of negro blood about her, and, as this was the only clue he now possessed, he was determined to follow it. This girl had been purchased by a French gentleman, who soon after took her with his family to Cuba, and thither the father went to seek her. Letters were again received from him at Cuba, saying that the family he sought had left the island a few months before for their native land; and he was about to embark for France, in the faint hope of finding his lost darling. A few days after the date of his embarkation, one of the fearful hurricanes that sometimes visit that latitude, swept over the ocean, and the vessel in which he sailed was never again heard from.

---

1 *The Liberator* focused its review on this passage, to support the claim that this was one instance of a regular trade in kidnapped children. See Appendix B3.

CHAPTER III

"But this is a people robbed and spoiled; they are all of them snared in holes and are hid in prison houses. They are for a prey, and none delivereth, for a spoil, and none saith, Restore."
ISAIAH 42:22.

For a few moments after Ida's capture, she continued to scream violently, partly from fright and partly from anger at the rudeness to which she had been subjected, for she had no definite idea respecting the cause or duration of her forced drive in that closely-shut carriage. But when her companion, shaking her violently, told her to be still or he would kill her, and enforced his words by a tingling blow on her cheek, all other feelings, even the sense of pain, were lost in the extremity of terror, and she shrank away from him and sat silent and motionless, save for the stifled sobs that swelled her bosom. Yet, as the swift motion continued, and she became sensible that she was being borne rapidly away from home and all she loved, she ventured timidly to ask her companion why he had taken her, and where she was going.

"O, I'm only going to take you to ride a little way," he replied. "You be a good girl and keep still, and we'll see lots of pretty things."

"What made you strike me so hard for, then?" said the child; "and why didn't you let Bessy come? I don't want to go without Bessy."

"O, Bessy'll come by and by; and if you are good, I'll give you candy."

"I don't want candy, and I do want Bessy. O Bessy! Bessy! come and take me!" she cried, piteously.

"Come, now, hush!" said the man. "What are you afraid of? I'll carry you back. Hush, I tell you! I'll be good to you, if you won't cry. I'm a first-rate fellow to good little girls, and they all like me. Come, stop crying and give us a kiss. You're a mighty pretty little girl." And, as he spoke, he drew her toward him with an ill-feigned show of tenderness, and attempted to kiss her.

But the child indignantly resisted him. "Get away, you bad man!" she said; "you shan't kiss me. You have no right to take me away from papa and Bessy, and I will cry till I make you carry me home again;" and she burst into wild screams, which could hardly be stilled, even for a moment, by the fierce threats and repeated blows that were administered. At length, as they slackened their pace somewhat, in ascending a hill, the driver opened a small window in the screen behind him, that closed the front of the carriage, and said, shaking his fist at her as he spoke,

"I see something coming up over the top o' the hill, and if you don't stop that young 'un yelling, the fat'll be all in the fire. I say, Kelly, *stop her.*"

"I'll fix her, Bill," was the reply; and, taking a thick woolen scarf from under the seat, he suddenly threw it over her head and around her mouth, in such a way as completely to smother her cries, and almost to stop respiration. Thus they continued for some miles; and when it was removed, the poor child, overcome by fright and suffering, dared make no further resistance, but wept silently, and at last fell into an uneasy sleep. When she awoke, it was nearly dark, and as soon as she opened her eyes, Kelly ordered the carriage to stop; and, taking a little cup and phial from his pocket, he poured out a spoonful of dark liquid, which he diluted with water from the large bottle beside him, and then put the cup to her lips. It was very bitter, and, after the first swallow, she drew back. "Drink it!" said he, raising his hand as if to strike her; and she complied instantly.

"There, now, that's a good girl," said he; "you shall have some candy." And, as he spoke, he offered her a little piece.

"I don't want the candy, but I'm very thirsty—will you give me some water?"

"O, yes," replied Kelly; and, as she drank it, he added, "You are a little fool not to like candy. You'll have bitter enough in this world, I'm thinking, and you'd better take all the sweet you can get."

"Why will I have bitter enough?" said Ida, timidly. "What are you going to do with me?"

"You'll find that out soon enough," replied her companion, with a sardonic laugh; "you needn't be in any hurry. Little girls hadn't ought to ask questions;—haven't you been told that?"

Thus repulsed, the child sank back into her corner, and said nothing more, and soon, yielding to the influence of the powerful soporific she had taken, she fell into a deep slumber. Thus it was that, stretched lifelessly on the seat of the carriage, with her senses fast locked in oblivion, she knew nothing of their stopping at the hotel to have the horses changed, and made no sound by which she could have been discovered. The days that followed, during that painful journey, were but a repetition of the first, except that her attempts at resistance became fewer as she yielded more and more to the influence of fatigue, and fear, and suffering. The men stopped at small farmhouses to bait[1] their horses, and ate their own food in the carriage, taking turns at driving and sleeping alternately. At length, one afternoon, just after sunset, the carriage passed along a road which wound round the foot of a mountain, that was covered almost to its summit with an apparently unbroken forest, above which the gray crags, wild and broken, stood out in sharp relief against the clear western sky. Suddenly the driver checked his horses, and, opening the door of the carriage, his companion got out, and took in his arms the passive little figure beside him. Without further pause, Kelly, who was driving, applied the whip, and the horses darted rapidly away; and almost, as quickly, with the child still in his arms, Bill sprang behind the trees, and, after plunging for a few rods through a tangled maze of underbrush, he came out on a footpath, narrow indeed, but distinctly defined even in that uncertain light. Here, putting down his burden, he paused and sat down to rest. The child stood still, and looked around her. Dim shadows were on every side, in which the huge trunks of the trees stood in grim silence, like threatening monsters; but, gazing up between the branches that closed above her, she saw far away the blue, cloudless heavens, filled with softened light, just as she had seen them last when she stood with her father beside her mother's grave, and he had told her, in low, loving tones of that dear mother in heaven, and of the Infinite Father who cares for all. The recollection came back at that moment, and roused her benumbed and broken spirit to make one more effort to escape; and, springing away, she ran down the steep and slippery path—anywhere, anywhere, even to die in that black and frightful forest, so she might only be out of reach of those cruel men. But, poor little thing! Her feeble limbs had not strength in proportion to her resolute soul; and she had gone but a few rods, when a rough hand grasped her dress, and shook her with such force that the fastenings parted behind, and one sleeve was torn entirely away.

"Take that, and that!" said Bill, violently striking her bare shoulders. "And hark, now, you little fool! If you're up to any o' these tricks, I'll come nigh to kill you! Shut up, now; don't yell— it'll be worse for ye if you do." But, regardless of these threats, and thinking someone passing in the road beneath might hear her, the courageous child continued to scream loudly; and it was only by muffling her again in the scarf, and carrying her nearly all the way in his arms, that the man was able to stifle her cries

---

1 Feed.

and force her up the steep path. At length, about halfway up the mountain, they came out on a level space in front of a steep rocky cliff, more open to the light than the path had been, but still so surrounded with trees as to be hidden from the view of travelers in the road below. Here, before the door of an old log hut, sat an aged negro woman smoking.

This woman, whose name was Chloe, had been through many of the rough passages of life. Her mother, a beautiful colored girl, with eyes full of passion and a heart of fire, had been kept as the mistress, and treated as the wife of her master, a planter in South Carolina, who was really very fond of her, and would gladly have made her free. But the laws of the State rendered that impossible, unless she was sent out of its borders, and, as she was extremely attached to him, it was hard for both of them to separate;[1] and so the matter was delayed from time to time, until *Death*, that worst foe of the *happy* slave, suddenly came, and left her worse than a widow, and her children more than fatherless.[2] Chloe, the eldest child, was old enough to appreciate fully the miserable change in their condition, and to participate in her mother's grief, when the property was divided among several heirs, and they were compelled to give up various articles of valuable jewelry and dress, the gifts—now doubly dear—of their indulgent benefactor, and sent away from the home where they had been so happy, to live as slaves in another family. In all the reverses of fortune throughout the world there is none so great as this. In all other cases the sufferer has *himself* left—the slave has not even *himself*.

Chloe and her mother were both of a bold, imperious disposition, and both had been indulged to the last degree by the easy-tempered man, whose fondness had "spoiled them—completely spoiled them," as their new mistress remarked on one occasion to her friends. "The mother especially is one of the most impudent and ungrateful creatures in the world, even for a nigger—and we all know they are a thankless set enough. She made such a fuss about having her family separated, that we took a good deal of pains to keep them together, and she has never

---

1 The South Carolina manumission laws of 1820 required slave-owners to petition the legislature for each case of manumission (a historical term meaning the release from slavery); if the freed person failed to leave the state within six months, he or she would be re-enslaved and sold at auction.

2 By law, the children of a slave mother were also slaves, even though the father might be free.

seemed to be the least in the world grateful for it. She will beat her children herself, if they trouble her, but if one of us touch them, she makes a terrible time."

And so, indeed, it was; and a hard time had both mistress and servant to live along together. Elsie had so long had her time at her own disposal, and lived in luxury and ease, that the plain dress in which she was now clothed, the bare walls and scanty furniture of her mean dwelling, and the menial service required of her in her new position, were hard to be borne, and added to the poignancy of grief with which she mourned for the dead. That very grief became a source of contention; for her mistress, having been always accustomed to regard the negroes as not having feelings and rights in common with the white race, insisted that it was sullenness, and not sorrow, that made her sad, and sternly forbade her to mention her master's name in her presence; telling her she ought to be ashamed of the connection instead of making a parade of it, and loading her with opprobrious epithets, when she dared call herself his wife. Judge not Mrs. Gorham too harshly; her words were but the effect of her education, and she did not know she was cruel. It is not the least evil of slavery, that it checks and renders impossible the kindly flow of a woman's sympathies towards the suffering and degraded. Neither was Mrs. Gorham naturally a bad-tempered woman; but she had a desire for neatness and thrift, and the effort to attain these in a household of idle and careless servants, who had no ambition to excel, and evaded their work in every possible manner, had gradually worn out her patience. She could seldom bring herself to have them whipped, however much they exasperated her; but she never praised, and she often scolded them from morning till night. This was annoying even to those who, having grown up with her, were accustomed to it, and to the high-spirited Elsie it was almost intolerable, and often provoked insolent replies. Then, too, this slave-mother had been encouraged to believe that she had a right to her own children, and she found it very hard to be silent when her plans for them were frustrated, or when she saw them always blamed for any childish quarrel that occurred, and obliged to yield their rights and wishes to the caprice of their young masters. The young olive-branches that were growing up in this house were no more crabbed or crooked than others of their species; but, in a family of ten girls and boys, there is always more or less of human nature, and the apparent equality between the black and white children that played together in the yard only made more galling the real superiority that was continually assumed by the latter. Poor Chloe, who never forgot her father, and was proud to be his child, was continually rebelling against the authority of her little companions; and many were the occasions on which her mistress found it necessary to interfere, and by taunting words, or by blows, to remind her that, after all, she was "nothing but a nigger," and must learn her place.

It was at one of these times, when the child had gone crying to her mother, that Mr. Gorham overheard Elsie break out into a perfect torrent of insolent reproach, and actually by force prevent the punishment that his wife was about to administer because Chloe had struck one of the children. Stepping forward to the group, who were gathered near the door of Elsie's room, in the yard, he said, "Is this the way you talk to your mistress; and you, Mrs. Gorham, do you allow such impudence? It's enough to spoil all the negroes on the place. Here, James, Henry"—beckoning to his two sons, who stood by—"bring that girl here."

This command being obeyed without difficulty, for the whole party was struck with a sudden panic, "Now," he added, "boys, you hold her, while your mother punishes her as much as she thinks proper."

Mrs. Gorham looked at her husband appealingly. Her temper had cooled, and she did not care now to inflict the blows; but she saw that he was angry, and she knew that if she refused he would take the stick, and give Chloe a severe whipping, so she struck her a few times lightly, and then let her go. Mr. Gorham was satisfied with having established his wife's authority, and said nothing more at that time; but when he met Elsie again, in crossing the yard, he told her that if she ever used such language again, as he had heard that afternoon, he would have her tied up and whipped. "You daren't whip me," she exclaimed, in a dreadful rage; "you know I was almost your brother's wife, and these are his children, your own nephews and nieces, you are knocking round this way. It is enough to make him rise out of his grave! I dare you to whip me!"

Mr. Gorham answered not, but his face was white with passion as he turned away, and that night Elsie was sent to the city jail to be severely flogged. Desperate at this treatment, she embraced the first opportunity to run away, was pursued and taken, and locked up again in jail. "Shall I give her a good cutting-up?" said the jailer, as he received her. "No," replied Mr. Gorham, who stood by; "it's no use. I can't be troubled with her any longer, and I won't have her lamed, so as to spoil the sale of her. I'll find a purchaser that will take her out of town;" and, in pursuance of this determination, the next week Elsie went southward with a gang of slaves for the sugar plantations.

Chloe knew all this, and, not seeing the necessity of the case, or understanding how much her mother's conduct had annoyed her master and mistress, she persisted in thinking herself and her mother very badly treated, and became more sullen and ill-tempered than ever. Thus she grew up, changing masters occasionally, and with these early memories rankling in her breast, she was never a favorite or a useful servant. Then came other troubles. Everyone who has lived with the slaves, knows that deep conjugal affection and fidelity, though sometimes found, are comparatively rare among that class. The uncertainty that attends their union, and their frequent separations, universal habit, and the laws of the land, all tend to prevent it. It is not to be supposed that Chloe often felt very deeply the breaking of those *liaisons* which, at various times, she formed in common with others of her race; but the whole energy of affection in her fierce nature was centered on her children, whom she loved with a fondness that, coupled as it was with the fear of losing them, made life and love itself a torture. When the last one was taken from her she fell down in a fit, and, from that moment, no one ever saw her manifest any trace of the kindlier feelings of our nature. Compassion had no effect upon her, and harshness she returned with a wild and defiant rage, that made cruelty itself draw back appalled.

It may easily be supposed that a servant so troublesome would be often exposed for sale, and that kind masters would hardly care to purchase her; and thus, after a life of vicissitudes, gradually growing sterner and more terrible, she fell at last into the hands of a man who was connected with a gang of kidnappers. It was necessary to have some rendezvous on the borders of the free States, and she was found to be just the person wanted to guard it. Toward all of the white race she displayed a hatred that might be called inhuman, if human nature had not often showed itself capable of deeds at which fiends might blush, and even towards those of her own race, who were in happier circumstances than herself, she was willing to do all the injury in her power.

By accident these kidnappers had discovered, upon this mountain, a cave, of sufficient size to suit their purposes; and, by building a hut directly in front of the opening, it was effectually concealed from all eyes. Hither they came from the south, bringing with them provisions for themselves and their horses. Their large covered wagon was left hidden among the trees and bushes near the road, but the animals were led up the path, and driven in the cave; and here also were concealed the children that were from time to time captured, until a wagon-load had been collected; and old Aunt Chloe kept watch over all. Her wants were supplied by her masters, and she only went to Hagerstown, a few miles distant, with the willow baskets that she wove and exchanged for the necessaries of life, so as to prevent the suspicion and inquiries of the few country people who were aware of her existence in this lonely retreat. Her appearance was perfectly hideous. Her gray hair hung in elf locks over her neck, from under the dirty cotton handkerchief that bound her brows, and her face, tawny, and wrinkled, and seamed with age, was stamped with every bad passion. Her form was bent, and she was covered with a short gown and petticoat, so dirty and patched, that it was difficult to tell of what color or material the original was composed; and her hands and fingers, bony, long, and claw-like, resembled a vulture's talons more than anything human.

Such was the being who now rose from her seat beside the door, and, taking the pipe from her mouth, said, with some appearance of curiosity, "Hillo! what dat? Reckon yer done rob de white hen-roost dis time!" and a fiendish expression passed over her face, as she stretched forth her snaky fingers, and, burying them in the child's curly hair, drew her towards herself. The act, and her frightful appearance, caused Ida to cry with pain and terror. "There 't is again," said Bill, "that's just the way it's been every minute of the time the gal's been awake, since we started. Shut up, there, I tell yer!"

"Gosh! What's de good o' tellin' her to shet up?" said Chloe. "Dey allers cries dat way till you gets 'em broke in. Crying for you mammy?" she added, addressing the child; "got a mammy a'n't ye?"

"O no, no!" sobbed Ida, "poor mamma's dead, and papa's all alone. O, do let me go back to papa!"

"Sorry yer mammy's dead," said Chloe; "wish she warn't, for I knows how she'd cry!—O, wouldn't she, though?—and tear her hair, maybe. How I'd like to see her, wouldn't I? Hasn't I seed de nigger woman cry so when dere chillen was toted off to be sold?—don't I 'member when dey took my darter—O, don't I? Sorry your mammy's dead—got a daddy, though, to feel bad a'n't ye?"

"O, yes. Poor Papa! Do, please, take me home again," and the child cried piteously.

"Shut up!—there," said Bill, striking her. "Do you suppose I'll stand this yelling, much longer?"

"Gosh!" interrupted his companion, "what de use talkin'?—just give her sommat to break her sperit; dat de way dey do de young jigs when dey cries for dere mammys. I'se hearn 'em cry, and seen 'em whipped for it, many de time; and I'se hearn heaps of white buckra[1] say dere nothin' like a good breakin'-in to save trouble aterwards. Dat's what does it—breaks dere sperit and learns 'em dere place."

"Zounds! I declare, I believe 't will be a first-rate plan," said Bill, with an oath, "and it may as well be done now as any time; for, blame me, if the little jade didn't try to get away, comin' up the hill, and I'm tired of hearing her yell;" and, as he spoke, he cut from the tree beside him a long rod, which he stripped of its leaves and swayed in the air to prove its strength. "Come here," he added, seizing Ida by one arm; "I'll learn ye to mind."

But the woman interposed. "Let *me*," she said, "*O, do!* that's a nice feller—ye don't know the good 't 'll do me. Don't I 'member when de white man flog my darter, my little girl, dat cried 'cause she was sold off from me, and dey whipped us both till de blood run down, to make her let go my gown?—O, do let me do it, now—do! Ye don't know the good it do me, just to think of it!"

"Take it, then; but mind yourself what you do," said Bill, throwing down the rod and releasing his hold of the child.

"O don't whip me, don't!" cried Ida; "I'll be good, I won't cry! O, don't whip me!"

"I wants ye to cry—I likes to hear ye—it's moosic," said the hag, pausing with the rod uplifted, to enjoy her agony of terror. "Cry now—cry loud!" and, as she spoke, the rod descended on the bare, delicate shoulders. "Cry, ye white wolf-cub! cry, ye white bear-whelp! scream, ye little rattlesnake!—I likes to hear ye—cry away—I'll make ye pay for the blood of my child, where the whips cut her!" and fast and heavily fell the blows on the arms and shoulders of the victim, covering them with blue, vivid marks; till suddenly, the shrieks of the child stopped, her struggles ceased, and she fell down at the feet of her tormentor.

All this had passed in a minute, and Bill, who had stood by, half-amused and half-shocked at this burst of demoniac fury, now sprang forward, with an oath, and raised the child. "You've killed her, you she-devil, I do believe," said he; and, indeed, she lay in his arms as if dead, for this terrific ordeal had been too much for that tender frame, so unused to suffering. She had fainted. Chloe put

---

1 Pejorative slang term used by Southern blacks to refer to white men and bosses, and to poor white people more generally.

both hands into a pail of water, that stood outside the door of her hut, and, scooping some up, dashed it into Ida's face, again and again, until she gasped and opened her eyes.

"There, now," she said, "she's come to. I'se glad she a'n't dead. I don't like ter have folks *die*—dat's too good, de a'n't no pain in *dat*—I likes ter have 'em live, and moreudder, I wants dis little brat to live, so I can do it again. O, wasn't it jolly to hear her yell!" she added, with a chuckling laugh.

"No you don't, old fool!" said Bill, as she again approached with the rod, as if about to carry out her cruel desire; "no ye don't—hands off! I was mad, or I wouldn't a let ye whip her at first. 'T won't do to spile property this way, or Kelly'll be in my hair.[1] Besides, she's mighty nigh dead, now—see how still she lays."

"Gosh! Dead, I reckon!" said Chloe. "Sich a little whippin' as dat kill any young 'un! I'se seen 'em bear heap more'n dat 'fore dey faints away, down in Car'lina; and dey don't bring 'em to wid *water*, neider, I makes sure—dey takes somepun stronger'n *dat*—O a'n't I felt it?—don't de pickle[2] put life into a nigger, when he done had a cutting'-up?"

"Hold your tongue, you brute!" replied Bill. "White children a'n't to be treated like niggers, and, anyway, you never see nigger children pickled, neither. Hold your tongue."

"White chidden a'n't to be treated like niggers, a'n't dey, hey?" said the other, with a grin that showed her toothless gums from ear to ear. "Mighty sight difference dey'll be 'tween dat little brat in yer arms, and dem little niggers in de cave, when ye gets 'em in de market."

"Well, hold yer tongue, anyway; I'm sick o' yer clack," interrupted Bill, "and go into the house and get my supper, and make some gruel like you made for me when I was sick here—make it nice, old woman, for I mean it shall do this little cretur some good. She a'n't eat enough to keep a fly alive since we got her, and, after all the expense we've been at, we can't afford to have her die on our hands."

Chloe reluctantly entered the hut to obey this order, muttering to herself, and licking her flabby lips, like a hyena who has tasted blood and is driven from its prey. In a little while Bill

---

1 Our first hint that the kidnappers plan to make Ida property by selling her into the slave system.
2 The practice of pouring brine into the wounds of a whipped slave to sharpen the pain.

followed, carrying the child, who had not spoken, and hardly showed any sign of life, except by a low, quick breathing, and a convulsive shudder that now and then passed over her. Laying her on the rude bed, that stood in one corner of the hut, he began to chafe her limbs, and force her to swallow a little water, for he was now seriously alarmed lest she might die. "She'd be worth a cool five hundred to us," he said, mournfully, "beside being such a pretty little thing, as makes me most sorry for her." Indeed, it would have moved a heart of adamant to see her, as she lay helplessly on that heap of dirty rags, with her long curls wet and clinging round her face, her eyes wide open and dim, as if a mist was before her sight, and her white neck and arms bruised and disfigured with the marks of violence. She allowed herself with difficulty to be fed with the gruel; but she seemed not to know who was feeding her, or to be conscious of anything that passed beside her bed, and no threats or entreaties could induce her to speak, or to close her eyes in sleep.

Wearied out at length, Bill left her, and, seating himself at the table, where a hot corn-cake and a rasher of bacon were now smoking, he consoled himself for his fatigues and troubles by a plentiful repast. When he had finished, he stretched himself before the fire. "I wonder if I'll have time to take a nap before Nick Kelly comes," he said.

"Ye haven't once axed for de little nigs in de cave," said Chloe with a grin; "don't ye feel anxious 'bout dem de dear little cre-turs—'praps dey want some gruel, too."

"Law, no," replied Bill; "they're safe enough when they're once in your claws. A body might as well try to run away from Satan as to get away from you—no danger of the niggers."

"But 'praps dey wants some gruel," persisted Chloe. "Tell ye what, dey's cried for de mammy, much as if dey was white, and I'se had to carry in *dis ting* more'n once, and I neber see but it hurt nigger flesh just as quick as white flesh!" and, as she spoke, she took from a shelf a stout cowhide, and flourished it around.

"Get out, ye old hag!—you make me sick—ye don't seem to think o' nothing but whipping," said Bill, with an oath.

"Dat's cause I'se seen so much of it—it's been *beat into me!*" replied she. "O, gosh! down on de sugar-plantations is de place; and I'll tell ye what," she added, earnestly, "'pears like I never see white buckra, or white child, but I want to get 'em somewhar, and tie 'em up, and gib it to 'em—'pears like 't would do me good—'pears like 't would pay me for de blood o' my darter, when she was holdin' on ter my gown', and for all de blood 'ut 's been took out o' dis yer old black carcass, in some o' de cuttings-up I'se got."

"Now, I declare," said Bill, raising himself and leaning on one elbow, "I knew you was about the wickedest old hag that's managed to keep out of the fire below, but I never saw ye quite equal to this evening. What's come over ye?"

"It's dat child—dat cretur, dat's done it," said Chloe, shaking her cowhide towards the bed. "I allus feels so when I gets hold of a white young 'un. 'Pears like it bring all my whole life up afore me, to see dese little waxy tings, dat's dressed up and took sich care of, as if dey wasn't de same flesh and blood as niggers.—O, a'n't it fun to find dey feels jest de same tings hurtin' 'em, dat niggers does?"

"Why, what sets you on so against white folks?" said Bill. "I never saw as you was treated worse than other folks."

"Dat's de ting," replied Chloe, eagerly; "dat de bery ting. Ef 't was me alone, I might think, as dey use tell me, 't was cause I'se given up to Satan, and was worse'n odder folks. But I'se been in good many places, and seen good many o' my peoples, and when dey's best off, dey's no better off 'n dogs or horses, dat's fed and played wid till de massa dies, and *den sold*—and when dey's bad off, de Lord knows dat's bad 'nuff."

"But the rest of 'em don't feel so hateful and go on so—why need you? You say yourself you was ugly, and, I dare say, deserved all you got."

"No, I didn't, not *all*," she replied. "What right had den ar buckra make me work for nothin', and take my chillen and sell 'em? Tell ye what!—I'se seen tings!—I'se had tings to bear! Seven little picininnies I bring into dis yer worle o' struble, and see 'em kicked, and cuffed, and 'bused, one way 'n odder, till dey was sold away from me, or I was sold away from dem; and my heart, 'pears like 't were all tore and stuck full o' thorns, till 't last, when I knew my last child was comin', I goes out in de cane-brake—I, dat lub de little unborn baby a heap site better 'n my life, and feels as if de child's mouth suckin' at my breast would draw away de dreffle pain *here*"—and she laid her hand on her heart—"I goes and kneels down in de night, and prays de Lord dat de little cretur may neber draw de bref of life."

"*You* pray!" said Bill, with a sneer. "I reckon the Lord would be astonished to see you on your knees now. You pray, indeed! a pretty hand you'd be at it! Why didn't you kill it yourself, if you felt so bad?—I've known 'em do it!"

"I *couldn't*" replied Chloe. "I know some o' 'em does, but I couldn't. Ebery time I took it in my arms to kill it, 'pears like all de strength goed out o' me, and de little baby was stronger 'n I was."

"Then it lived, did it?" said Bill. "The Lord didn't hear ye—'t wan't no account, your prayer."

"Hear me, no!" she replied, fiercely. "Dere a'n't no Lord— dere a'n't nothin' but de debil, and he hab it all his own way in dis yer country. No fear but *he*'ll hear when anybody call him."

"Yes, I think so," said Bill. "Anyway, if there is a devil he's some relation o' yourn. What's the good o' your being so ugly? I never saw a nigger like you."

"Dey's all like me," interrupted Chloe, "ony dey keeps it in, 'cause dey's scare ob de white folks, and dey *purtends—dey purtends*—it's de ony way to get along easy, is purtendin'. But *I* neber could, more'n a little while to once't—it went agin me— somepun came up in my throat and *chocked* me when I tried to cringe, and be so might 'spectful, like de white folks wants to hab dere niggers. I *allers was* imperdent—'praps 't was cause I had too much o' my white daddy in me."

Bill burst into a loud laugh at this last sally, and, at the same moment, the form of Nick Kelly appeared in the doorway.

CHAPTER IV

"O, pity, God, this miserable age!
What horrid things, how fell, how butcherly,
Erroneous, mutinous and unnatural,
Black-hearted man doth daily perpetrate!"
  KING HENRY SIXTH.[1]

"There seems to be plenty o' *jaw* in here," said the newcomer, good-naturedly; "what's the row?"

"Nothin'," said Bill, "only we've been having a camp-meetin', and our beloved sister Chloe's been tellin' her experience."

"That's it, is it?" replied Kelly. "Well, then, what's sister Chloe's experience with young niggers? How are they in the cave?"

"O, dey's peart enuff," said she. "Young 'uns will whimper little, ye know; but dis ole nigger's de one to learn 'em shet up dere mouf."

"Come on, then, and let us look at 'em," said Kelly, shutting and bolting the door; "the moon is set, and the sooner we get started now the better. How's the child?" As he spoke he took up the candle and went to the bed; but the moment his eye fell on her, he started, and exclaimed angrily, "Who's been meddling with this child? What did you beat her for?"

"Why, you see," said Bill, rising and coming forward, "the little cretur was so obstropolous comin' up the hill, that I got mad, and set out to give her a lickin', and Aunt Chloe here took the business out o' my hands, and, 'fore I knowed it, she gave her a pretty considerable of a brakin' in, and the cretur couldn't stand it, and fainted, or had a fit, or somethin' o' that sort; and ever since she's laid that way. Do you s'pose she's shamming?"

"There's no sham about this," replied Kelly, "and it's my belief you've nigh about killed the child. Five hundred dollars jest thrown away, 'cause you couldn't keep your cursed temper. And as for you, you old hag," he added, turning to Chloe fiercely, "you deserve a good cutting-up for interfering in this way in your master's property."

---

1 Adapted from Shakespeare, *Henry VI, Part Three*, 2.5.88–91.
   The original reads: "What stratagems, how fell, how butcherly /
   Erroneous, mutinous, and unnatural / This deadly quarrel daily
   doth beget!"

"Come on, den," replied she, with a shrug of the shoulders and a malicious grin; "Come on—reckon ye better. Dis ole hag don't know enuff to hang ye both, do she?—ha! ha!"

"Know enough!" responded Kelly; "to be sure you do; but what good will that do you?—'t a'nt law for a nigger's oath to hang a white man in this country, I reckon."[1]

"Come, now," interrupted Bill, in a low tone, "she can do us considerable harm, if she wouldn't be allowed in court; she can inform about this young one here, and a pretty hue-and-cry that would bring round our ears. Don't be quarreling."

Thus reminded, Kelly stifled his anger as best he could, and moved toward the other end of the hut near the cave. Chloe, seeing the turn things were taking, followed, saying, "Sure 'nuff, what's de good o' fightin'? Dey all has to be broke in some time—*allers*—and it's easier to hab it done up here dan when you'se on de road. Must be mighty onconvenient den."

"That's true," replied Kelly; "but it don't do to whip white children like they were niggers."

"Yes," responded Bill, "white folks is white folks, and niggers is niggers."

"Niggers is niggers, is dey?" rejoined Chloe. "I neber could see, fur my part, but de nigger flesh feels jest de same tings as white flesh does. Dem two little niggers you toted in here last month, dey was mighty sight like dat white young 'un ater I broke 'em in; didn't know but dey was dead sure 'nuff, dey swine 'way so long."

"What made you beat 'em so?" asked Kelly, angrily.

"Bress your soul, I *has* to—has to make 'em '*fraid to cry*—else dey'd cry 'emselves to death fur dere mammys. Allers had to, else you couldn't do nothin' with 'em, dey's so obstropolous to git away. 'Pears like 't a'nt natural to 'em to be stolen—neber is."

By this time, Kelly had drawn away some pegs by which two or three short pieces of board had been nailed to the logs, apparently for the purpose of holding the domestic utensils that were hanging on them. This being done, showed that the wall, instead of being formed simply of upright logs, contained a large door, made of boards, ingeniously covered with unbroken semicircular strips of hemlock bark, corresponding to the construction of the rest of the building. The joints of this door were concealed by the strips of board that had been taken down, and it opened directly into the cave, which was spacious, dry, and well ventilated

---

1 Slaves could not testify against a white person in a court of law.

by a large aperture in the roof. This opening, which had evidently been formed by the same stream of water that originally hollowed out the cave, led, by a winding subterranean course, nearly to the top of the mountain, where it had a small outlet under a flat rock; and the sound of human voices, the neighing of horses, the shouts of laughter, and the screams of distress, which thus mysteriously conducted, had been sometimes heard around that spot by the solitary woodcutter or huntsman, had given the whole vicinity an evil name. There were few who ascended the mountain, even by day, without a thrill of superstitious fear, and not a man in all the country round would have lingered upon it after dark; so that the unearthly horror which had gradually invested the place was an additional shield to the perpetrators of these deeds of wickedness.

In one side of the cavern a few rude stalls had been constructed, and here the three horses of the kidnappers were tied, while, on the other side, huddled together on a heap of straw, were six negro children, who had been stolen within a few months from different parts of the country, and brought here for safekeeping, until a sufficient number were collected to fill the wagon, and make it worthwhile to proceed southward with them. It was pitiable to see the condition to which these children had been reduced by their confinement in this dark place, and the discipline that Chloe had found necessary to make them docile and fit them for the condition of slavery into which they were to be sold. True, they had been fed daily with wholesome food, and taken out separately for exercise, under the care of their jailer, who knew that her masters wished to find them in good saleable condition; but being seldom washed, they were all more or less dirty and ragged, and in their faces the careless gaiety of childhood had given place to the cowering expression of abject terror. They had evidently been well "broken in," and would make no opposition to whatever fate might await them.

"Well now, my little dears," said Bill, ironically, as he held the candle close to their faces, "a'n't ye tired of stayin' in this dark place? Won't ye like a little ride by way of variety?"

The children shrank together, as if for protection, but made no reply, until one of them ventured to ask, in a timid whisper,

"Will you take us home?"

"No, my little dears," replied Bill, "couldn't do that nohow; 't wouldn't be convenient jest now. Besides. We're goin' to do better than that for ye; we're goin' to *sell* ye to some nice man, that'll be kind enough to larn ye what yer ought to do, and take care o' yer; and yer can't think how much better off ye'll be than if yer was to be home, where ye'd have no good master, nor be nothin' but a poor devil of a free nigger when ye got growed up. Yer can't think how happy yer'll be. We be your real benefactors; 't a'n't many folks 't would take the pains we does, all for nothin' hardly but your good. Yer ought to be thankful to us, instead o' snivellin' that way. But folks is allers ongrateful in this world, especially niggers," he added, rolling up his eyes, and laying his hand on the place where his heart was supposed to be, with a gesture of mock humility and resignation. Chloe laughed aloud, but Kelly, who was not in a mirthful mood, said gruffly, "Come, now, stop your foolin'. We've got some work to do tonight, and the sooner we're at it, the better."

"Foolin'! me foolin'!" said Bill; "I never was so serious in my life. I'm tryin' to enlighten these little heathen—kind of a missionary preacher like, ye know—to show 'em the blessings o' slavery, that they've been growin' up in ignorance of. I hearn' a minister preach about it once, at Baltimore, and he proved it all right out o' the Bible—how slavery was what the Lord made the niggers for, and how them was particular lucky as was slaves in this land o' light and liberty, where they was treated so much better 'n they would be if they was in Africa, and all that. I can't remember jest how 't was done, but I know he give it to the abolitionists powerful, for tryin' to disturb 'em when they was so happy, and he proved out o' the Bible, too, how they ought to send 'em back, instead o' helping 'em away."[1]

"Out of the Bible!" replied Kelly, who had been putting the harness upon the horses, in which occupation he was now joined by his companion. "Yes, it's enough to make the devil laugh to see what some folks will try to prove out of the Bible. If there is a God, and if he made that book, as they say he did, I reckon he feels might nigh used up, when he sees some of the preachers get up in the pulpit, and twist and turn his words all sorts of ways, to prove what will be most for their own interest out of 'em. For my part, I don't believe in any such things hereafter, as they tell for; but if there is, won't some of these confounded humbugs have to take it?"

"P'rhaps they will," said Bill, laughing; "and p'rhaps some other folks will stand a smart chance o' takin it, too."

---

1 Common pro-slavery arguments. By naming Baltimore, Pike may be referring to the Baltimore Conference of the Methodist church, which was split on the subject of slavery.

"Well," replied Kelly, with a faint smile, "I believe I have a right to do as I'm a mind to, and I do it; and if I can make more money tradin' niggers than any other way, I'll do it, just the same as the wolf eats the lamb when he's hungry; it's a law of nature, and always will be, for the strong to prey upon the weak; but I tell you what, if I did believe those things, and then shut my eyes and served the devil, I wouldn't try to cheat myself and other folks into thinking the Lord would be fool enough to believe I couldn't open my eyes if I wanted to, and so let me off because 't was a mistake."

Meantime, the horses were harnessed, and the two men proceeded to change their clothes, assuming suits of quakerish gray and broad palm-leaf hats. Then, sending Chloe for a basin of water, they took off the wigs that covered their heads, to which Kelly added the black eyebrows, mustache and whiskers, he had hitherto worn, and washed their faces thoroughly with soap, thus removing from the skin some dark substance that had colored it, and showing them both to be men of light complexion. Kelly especially, whose hair was nearly red, could never have been recognized as the person whom Bessy had seen carry away her beloved charge. He laughed a little as he surveyed the altered person of his comrade, who, in his turn was regarding him. "I've worn those things so long," he said, pointing to his discarded disguise, "that I shall feel strange without 'em. But come on; go out with the horses, and by the time you get 'em harnessed and come back, I shall have the little miss ready. As for the darkies, they don't need any preparation."

Bill led out the horses through the hut, first flinging across their backs some sacks containing provisions; and, as it was now so late that he was almost sure of meeting no one, he proceeded fearlessly down the path. Kelly returned to Ida, who still lay on the bed as they had left her, and, taking off her outer garments, he cut her hair close to her head—those beautiful ringlets that had been the pride of her fond parents. He stained her skin with a sponge, dipped in some dark liquid, until it was the color of a dark mulatto,[1] and then dressed her in a suit of boy's clothing which Chloe produced at his request. Then, bringing out the negro children, he tied their hands behind them, fastening their arms together in such a manner that each might support his neighbor's steps while walking, and, passing a rope between each

---

1 An obsolete term for a child of mixed race who has one black parent and one white parent.

pair, he gave one end to Chloe and the other to Bill, who had now returned, and in this way, with the children between them, they left the hut, Kelly following with the almost senseless form of Ida in his arms.

The path was steep and slippery, but they arrived safely at the foot of the hill, where, in a little grassy nook, beside the road, stood a large covered wagon with the horses attached. In the open front was a high seat that served for the drivers; and the children being placed on straw behind, where they all lay side by side, the leather back was closely fastened down, and they drove rapidly away, leaving Chloe to return to her hut and restore things to their usual order.

They continued to travel all night, but at sunrise turned a little away from the road, and soon reached an empty barn, of which they took possession, while the inmates of the adjoining hut, who were of the lowest order of the poor whites of Virginia, cooked their food for them, and made no effort to see the occupants of the wagon. Again they started at nightfall, but the next morning they had proceeded so far southward that there was not much fear of pursuit or need of extreme caution.

If there is anything which slaveholders regard as a sacred law of domestic life, it is the precept that commands us not to meddle with our neighbor's business. With the indifferent or the cruel, this results from a carelessness respecting the amount of evil inflicted by others upon the helpless and dependent. The kind-hearted and honorable, startled at the amount of wrongs, which they cannot right, that spring to meet their gaze at the least investigation, shrink back from the ungracious task; and obstinately shutting their eyes to all without their own household, satisfy themselves with keeping things as smooth as possible there, and hug to their hearts the vain hope that, because they strive to be merciful and just, all others will do the same. Another reason is, that the negro race, inheriting our evil human nature, debased by a long course of servitude, are given to the practice of all sorts of peccadilloes and crimes, which must be kept within due bounds in one way or another; and every occurrence of life is looked upon through such a different medium, by the slave and the master, that the negro often represents things in a manner that seems to the white man willfully false and malicious. Thus, no one has any hope of arriving at the truth, or cares to interfere with his neighbor's domestic discipline; and it is considered a flagrant breach of social law for a man to listen to the complaints of any other man's servants, or, except in the most desperate cases, to make any inquiries about rumors that may reach his ears, so as to lead to the exposure of any injustice. The force of public opinion upon this point is so strong that adjoining plantations, and even adjoining houses, are generally ignorant of everything that happens on a neighbor's premises, except what the white members of the family may choose to tell. Thus it is that some good people *innocently* affirm, that in a long life among negroes, they never knew an unkind master or an injured slave; and it is perhaps because the southerners are so entirely unaccustomed to questioning or espionage, that they are so extremely sensitive to any approach to these things, on the part of their countrymen at the north, whose totally different views of this question of "not meddling" they cannot understand.

Secure, therefore, from all impertinent questioning, Kelly and his accomplice continued their way more openly than before, and with all convenient speed. Sometimes they heard of persons who had been at taverns before them, seeking for a dark-looking man, who had kidnapped a little girl; and they secretly congratulated each other on the adroitness with which they had eluded pursuit. The sufferings of the poor children during this time, though not so great as when shut up in the cave, were sufficiently severe to excite compassion. In addition to the extreme weariness of a fatiguing journey of many days in a close carriage, from which they could see nothing to amuse them, and their comfortless, cramped position, crowded together as they were on the straw, and the weary, despairing homesickness, to which they dared not give vent in tears, lest they should attract the ferocious threat, or the still more cruel lash, they were all old enough to realize that they were to be reduced to a condition of which they had, from infancy, heard tales of fear and hatred, and of which they had an indefinite horror.

Happily for Ida, during all these dreadful days, she was insensible to the heat and dust, and the constrained position from which her companions suffered, and equally oblivious of the heart-sorrows that made all minor evils seem light; for she knew not whence she had been brought, or whither she was going. If she felt the jolting of the wagon, she manifested it only by a slight movement occasionally, and lay the rest of the time quiet and apparently stupid, as she had been from the moment she sank down at Chloe's feet. When they stopped to rest, they were obliged to lift her in and out of the carriage, and feed her as they would have done a baby; and she never once spoke, or manifested any consciousness of her surroundings.

One day, as they were crossing the southern border of Virginia, they stopped to water their horses at a small stream by the roadside. The heat and dust were oppressive, and, for the first time since their journey commenced, Ida had been restless, and seemed to be suffering pain; for she moaned constantly, and sometimes screamed violently for a few moments. One of these paroxysms occurred while the horses were drinking, and Bill, after looking round at her, as she lay on the straw beside the six weary and dirty children, said to his companion, with a sorrowful shake of the head,

"'T a'n't no go, Kelly, that ar spec o' your. You might a knowd that little waxy thing couldn't stand all she'd have to take."

"She'd stood it well enough if you and that old hag had kept your hands off her, as I told you to," replied the other.

"Well, 't was too bad, I know, to spile a cool five hundred; and I don't blame ye, Kelly, for swearin' at me about it for she would a brought us every cent o' that, from somebody that deals in fancy articles. Gracious!" he added, in an excited manner, "she'd been worth over a thousand when she growed up, she was so darned pretty. But," continued he, dropping his voice with a sigh, "'t a'n't no go now."

"No," replied his companion, "she's mighty nigh dead now, and it's my belief that, if she lives, she'll be an idiot—she'll never have no sense again."

"Well, I reckon she won't," said Bill; "and, as long as the trade is spoilt, I don't mind sayin' that I'm powerful sorry for the little cretur. She did look pretty that day, settin' on the log with the posies in her hair. I wish we'd 'a had them two little nigs we went after, and then we should 'a let her alone."

His companion made no reply, but seemed in deep thought for some time. Then he said,

"I'll tell you, Bill, what I reckon we can do. I know a man up the mountain, about twelve miles from here, that has a small plantation, and I've traded some with him in these articles. I'll make him buy this gal. I reckon I can come it over him to the tune of fifty dollars; and, as it's mighty sure she won't live till we get to Wilmington, that is better than nothing. If it hadn't been for the way you used her up, I might have made two good trades on her. We could have sold her for a good price, and then gone back and given information where she was, and that would have brought us in something handsome. They'll offer a good reward for news of her, I make sure."

"That would 'a been *first rate*," said Bill, deeply impressed with his companion's sagacity. "I wonder I hadn't a thought o' that. Why didn't you mention it?—you're allers so mighty mum, Kelly. P'raps you meant to have a little private speculation out o' that end o' the trade, that I wasn't to know about, hey?"

Kelly laughed. "If I did," said he, "you've dished me completely."

"Couldn't we do it now, don't ye s'pose?" asked Bill.

"No," replied his comrade; "it wouldn't pay now to run the risk, she's broke down so. If they got her alive and well, they'd be glad enough to pass over the rest; but to find her dead, or an idiot, is another matter. There'd be too many questions asked, and we might find our trade stopped. No, fifty is the best we can hope to get out o' this job, and the sooner we get rid of her the better."

So saying, he laid the whip over his horses, and in less than two hours, they had turned up the mountain road that led to the farm of Mr. James Bell.

After proceeding for a quarter of a mile along a rough but pleasant road, bordered by noble trees, they came to a cornfield enclosed by one of those zigzag fences, which are to be found all over the States, but which seems to have been christened in Virginia. A few negroes of both sexes were at work hoeing the growing corn, whose fresh green blades waved in the faint breeze; and, seated on a stump in an angle of the fence, on the top rail of which he was cracking nuts, was Mr. Bell himself, talking to a negro who stood near. Near the fence stood a horse, with his bridle caught on the limb of a tree above him. At the sound of the wagon, the negroes stopped work, and leaned wearily on their hoes, to look on, while the overseer and his master turned round; and the latter, leaning over the fence, recognized an old acquaintance, and exclaimed,

"Why, how d' ye, Mr. Kelly—how d' ye? Quite a stranger you've been, lately, in these parts. Going up to the house? I'm coming right along."

"No, thank you," said Kelly, "can't stop now. The fact is, I've come up to have a trade with you. I've got a lot o' nigger children up from Maryland. Don't you want one?"

"Mercy!" exclaimed Mr. Bell, laughing; "carry coals to Newcastle, but don't bring any young niggers here. I stumble over them at every step, now."

"Well," said Kelly, "they're good property. Niggers are rising, and it's my opinion they'll continue to rise; and it don't cost much to raise 'em—so the young ones are a good investment, especially when you can get 'em cheap; and this one I want you to buy, I'll almost give away, for she's sick, and it's too much trouble to take care of her."

"Sick!" exclaimed Mr. Bell, again, to whose mind at that moment came the remembrance of certain curtain lectures about money matters; "what do you suppose I want of sick niggers?"

"Well, but consider what a bargain I offer you. I make no manner of doubt the child will soon get well, if she's kept quiet and nursed up; but I can't have her taken care of here in the wagon; so she'll be likely to die if I keep on with her, and I'm willing on that account to let you have her for almost nothing. You will have a chance for speculation without any trouble or risk, and I shan't lose quite so much as if she dies on my hands; so we shall both be benefited. Come, now, that's fair."

"It looks fair, certainly," said Mr. Bell, in a less decided tone than he had before used. "Let me see the young one."

"She was a mighty handsome cretur before she took sick," said Kelly, as he proceeded to unfasten and raise the leather curtain at the back of the carriage. "I tell you, it goes to my heart to have to part with her this way, for she'll sell for a thousand dollars, as a fancy girl,[1] in ten years. She'll be the handsomest gal you ever saw in the market."

"She looks like it now!" said Mr. Bell, jeeringly, as his eye fell on the emaciated and squalid form before him, her face crusted with dirt, and her hair tangled into a mass of knots, and filled with bits of the straw on which she lay. Her eyes were closed, and her breast heaved with the short, quick panting of her breath.

"You see," said Kelly, "she's dressed like a boy. Her clothes were so ragged, I put on these I happened to have, to keep her from catching cold."

"Yes, precious good care you've taken of her, no doubt," replied Mr. Bell, dryly. He was a kind-hearted man, and the miserable condition of the child so affected him that he felt willing to pay a small sum for the privilege of placing her where she could have better care. Added to this was the unacknowledged thought that, if she did live, it would be a good bargain. So, as Kelly, who did not really believe the child would live many hours longer, was anxious to close the trade, after a very little chaffering between buyer and seller, the purchase was effected, and, after receiving thirty dollars for their victim, the kidnappers drove forward to deliver her at the house, followed by Mr. Bell on horseback.

---

1 Refers to the market in light-skinned enslaved mistresses.

A few moments brought them in sight of the family mansion, which was pleasantly situated on a knoll at a short distance from the road, to which a path led from the front door, bordered with a hedge of the daily rose, and shaded by a few trees. At a little distance a broad, smooth carriage-path led by the end of the house to the stables, which, with the dwellings of the servants and the kitchen, formed a hollow square behind it. This carriage road extended some way beyond the stables, and at its termination stood a row of log huts, where the plantation "people" lived. Around each of these huts was a small piece of ground, enclosed with palings, and most of them well stocked with growing vegetables, which, with the hens and chickens about the door, gave further evidence of comfort. At the end of "the house," opposite the carriage-way, were large and well-cultivated gardens and an orchard; and the verandah that surrounded the house was shaded and nearly covered with running roses and vines of various description.

Here sat a lady reading, while two children played near her. Mrs. James Bell was of petite figure, with an abundance of fair hair, which she wore in long ringlets about her face; and although they were not always very smooth, and the children *would* crush her muslin dress, and pull her apron awry, still she was altogether a neat-looking woman, and corresponded in appearance with the general air of thriftiness and comfort about the place. She looked up from her book as the party approached; and the children, who had harnessed a little negro to a cart, and were driving him about the piazza,[1] stopped their noisy play to look at the strangers. It was with some trepidation that her husband, having received from Kelly the almost lifeless form of the little Ida, directed his steps to the place where his wife was sitting—for the little lady, though weak in some respects, had a will strong enough to have filled the breast of Goliah,[2] and invariably had fits when that will was thwarted, and thus Mr. Bell was obliged to use some diplomacy to maintain even a semblance of authority in his own family.

"Now, James Bell," she exclaimed, in querulous tones, "what have you got there—a dead nigger? Of all things on earth, couldn't you find some way to spend money but in buying such truck as that, when you knew my life is fairly worried out of me now, with the little wretches?"

---

1 Veranda.
2 Probably Goliath, the giant Philistine warrior killed by the future King David in 1 Samuel 17.

"Well, my dear, perhaps I was foolish," replied Mr. Bell, laying down his burden on the bench; "but it will be a first-rate bargain if she only lives, and I thought it was worthwhile to run the risk. I got her for a mere song."

"Her!—what's she dressed like a boy for? But it a'n't much account what it is," continued Mrs. Bell, "for I do believe it's dying now. What a fool you are, Mr. Bell! When I want anything you always say you have no money, and here you are throwing it away. I declare, it's enough to provoke a saint. I told you the last time I would not have another one bought;" and she burst into tears, and showed such strong symptoms of hysterics that her husband hastened to say,

"Well there, dear, now don't cry. I got this one for thirty dollars, or I shouldn't have taken her; and, if she lives, she'll be worth five hundred dollars in a year or two, and you shall have every cent of it. Don't cry! Venus shall take her to her quarters, and take care of her, and she shan't ask you to go and see her, if she's sick a month; so you won't have any trouble with her. Here, Venus!—where is she, I wonder?"

"O, she's near about here, you may be sure—out in the yard talking with the rest of 'em, probably. The lazy thing is always lounging round about tea-time, and I've heard Moll rattling the pans for me to give out supper this quarter of an hour past. If I'm busy reading, she's sure to be on hand to plague me; and, at other times, I might call an hour before she'd come. Here she is again"—and, sure enough, at that moment, a little dark face looked out from the hall that ran from the front to the back door through the house. "Please, miss," he said, for about the tenth time, "Aunt Mosely say, time to give out supper."

"Aunt Mosely is the torment of my life, and so are you," said his mistress, as she rose to comply with the summons. "You go and find Aunt Venus, and tell her to come here; your master wants her."

The little fellow darted off, and in another moment, his voice was heard in the yard, calling, with a prolonged drawl on the first syllable, "Ho, Venus! ho, Aunt Venus!—Massa James want you on the front piazza." In a little while, Venus appeared.

She was a dark mulatto, of about the medium height, with a full form and high, square shoulders. From long practice in carrying burdens on her head, she had acquired a habit of holding it thrown back, and the chin slightly elevated, which gave her face a queer expression, half pert and half disdainful. Her eyes were small, and her negro features had a very stupid and morose appearance, except when she smiled. It is strange to see the magical effect of a smile on a negro face. It is like sunshine breaking suddenly from a cloudy sky over a dull landscape, changing its whole aspect in a moment. In that genial light, Aunt Venus looked intelligent, and even showed that once she might have been almost handsome. But if the smile deepened into a laugh, all the sombre dignity of her appearance vanished, and her gums, garnished with broken teeth, displayed in a broad grin, her head ducked down between her shoulders, and the indescribable comical giggle that convulsed her whole figure, transformed her into something very much resembling a baboon. Her dress was the scantily-cut blue-striped cotton fabric usually worn by the slaves, and her head was enveloped in an immense red-and-white bandanna, somewhat the worse for wear. The only display of fancy in which she indulged was in the variety and multiplicity of her aprons. In this she prided herself, and four or six of different colors and shapes were the very least allowance with which she could be satisfied. All the pieces of cloth which she could beg or save were used in this way, and she was ingenious in piecing one color on another, so as to eke out the little bits that must otherwise have been lost.

On this occasion she came forward with her usual stolid gravity; but an expression of curiosity quickly followed, as she saw the drooping little figure that lay beside her master's knee. "Laws bless us!" she exclaimed, holding up both hands, "what Massa James done did now? What dat?"

"I bought the child of a man that came along," replied Mr. Bell, "more out of compassion than anything else, for she was so sick it was cruel to have her jolt her life away in that cart. Perhaps she may live, though, if you take her in hand. See what you can do for her."

Venus took the child, but she made no reply. Sad, and what, if they had found utterance, would have been called *impudent* thoughts were busy in her brain. She pressed her lips firmly together, and tears rolled slowly down her cheeks and fell on Ida's purple lips, from which faint moans of distress were now issuing.

"Don't cry," said Mr. Bell, kindly; "she'll come up, I reckon, if you take her home. You've raised many a child as sick as she is. Go along now—I have great faith in your nursing."

Still Venus answered not. She hardly heard his words, she hardly thought of the present, for the touch of that little helpless figure that lay on her breast had roused her quick sympathies, and brought up a vision of the past that made her heart bleed.

CHAPTER V

"We can tame ourselves
To all extremes, and there is that in life
To which we cling with most tenacious grasp,
E'en when its lofty claims are all reduced
To the poor common privilege of breathing."
    VESPERS OF PALERMO[1]

It was late one afternoon, three weeks after, when Ida, having struggled unconsciously with fever and exhaustion, awoke from a deep sleep, with the cool pulses of a new life in her veins. Her glances wandered around, and feebly and by degrees her brain received the impressions they conveyed. The bed on which she lay, covered with coarse but clean clothing, was in one corner of a log hut. Around the walls were hung various articles of dress and cooking utensils, and through an opening at the further end she saw a small fire burning in the clay chimney that was built outside, and, either from original misconstruction, or from the wandering propensity apparently inherent in southern property, was now leaning so far away from the wall to which it should have adhered, that it was completely isolated from the house. Through a small window near her, an unglazed opening, the wooden shutter of which was nearly closed, she had a glimpse of the sky, which was now filled with the sultry heats of July; and a sunbeam that, after glinting brightly on a branch of wild rose, which fell over the opening, came, softly and half subdued, to lighten her dull eyes and rest on her pale brow.

Near the door opposite the bed, three or four negro children were lying on the sand, or building houses of that frail material; and on the doorstep sat a tall, dark woman, with her arms folded, talking to Venus, who, arrayed in a clean gown, and with more than her usual number of aprons, was busily mending some coarse garment. The slight rustling movement which Ida made attracted her attention, and she came to the bed saying,

"Laws bless the child, she's awake! How d' ye, honey?"

Ida fixed her eyes on the face bent over her, but made no reply. It was some time before her benumbed brain could arouse itself to the activity of thought or speech; and Venus, sitting at the foot of the bed, went on with her work, after giving some

---

1 From Act 1, Scene 3 of Felicia Hemans's *The Vespers of Palermo: A Tragedy in Five Acts* (1823).

cooling drink to the invalid, who continued to regard her with an increasing expression of curiosity and wonder. At length she said, with a faint voice "What is your name?"

"Benus, honey—old Aunt Benus, my name," replied the nurse.

Again, after a pause, the child asked, "Who are you?"

"Laws bless the child!" said the delighted woman—"she'll get peart now, mighty soon; she's begun to ask questions. Who I be?" she continued, shaking all over with a convulsive giggle. "I's an old nigger-woman—don't ye see?"

Again there was a pause, and the child looked from the dark face of her nurse to her own emaciated hands, that were now returned to their original whiteness. After some moments of mental comparison, she said, "Am I a nigger, too?"

"Dono', honey," replied Venus. "Dey say you was, and mighty sick one, too. What be ye? Where was you raised?"

"What is *raised*?" asked the child.

"What, where'd ye *grow*—where ye *come from*?"

"I don't know—I can't remember," replied Ida; and her face grew anxious and troubled.

"Well, well," said her kind questioner, "you'se done talked enough now; shet your eyes and go to sleep, that's a honey;" and the little patient, weary with this brief conversation, was glad to follow this wise advice, while Venus resumed her seat by the door.

"Hear de child axing, 'be I a nigger,'" said Mary, her companion, with a low laugh. "A'n't it funny what questions de chillen will ax? T' oder day my little Pete come home and say, 'Maum Molly, why don't ye neber larn me say nothin' like dey does in de house, out o' books wid pictures into 'em?' Bless you, Pete (I say) I dono' nothin' myself—nothin' but hymns, and prayers, and sich like. 'Well, den,' says he, '*larn me dem*.' I couldn't help laughin' to hear him. Tell ye what, he mighty bright little nig—dat Pete."

"Didn't you neber larn him his prayers afore?" said Venus; "What you been about, you didn't?"

"O," replied Mary, "somehow I neber has time. Dey's allers one ting or 'noder to do, and I'se so busy, half de time 'pears like I hab to turn around five times in one place."

"'Pears like ye might find time if you jest 'deavored to," said Venus.

"Why, one ting, dey's allers so many round I'se 'shamed to," replied Mary. "One time I thought I would; and so I told 'em all to kneel down and I'd larn 'em de Lord prayers, and dey like it a heap, and larn 'em right smart; and ebery night dey tease me, 'Come, ma, larn me de Lord prayers 'g'in.' But one night

Miss Susan, she come along, and she stop and hear me larn 'em, and she say, 'Pooh! What you 'bout dere, Mary? What you know 'bout de Lord prayers? Jest tumble 'em into bed and come here; I want ye!' and den she laugh, and tells de cook I'se gettin' pious. I 'clare, I'se so 'shame I neber larn 'em de Lord prayers since, nor nothin' else."

"You needn't been 'shame," replied Venus, indignantly. "It's my suspinion 't wouldn't hurt Miss Susan, nor Mass' James, neither, to say dere prayers sometimes, demselves. De fact is, we'se an orful set on dis yer plantation—no meetin', no prayers, no nothin', but work and frolickin', 'cept when we goes to camp-meetin'."

"Yes," said Mary, "dat de fac. Mass' James say he tinks we better go to camp-meetin', and do all de religion up in a heap—dat de best way for niggers. Den dey can spend Sunday restin', and doin' de odd jobs round dere quarters and not be botherin' goin' so far to meetin' ebery Sunday. Say dancin' heap better'n prayin', any time, and puts de life into niggers, and make de work go easy next day."

"O," replied Venus, "Mass' James good massa, but he curus 'bout dem tings. Dancin' 's well enough—I used to like it myself when I'se young gal. It makes a body feel happy for little while, but de good o' dancin' *don't last*, like de good o' prayin' does."

"Dat's what I tell de cook when she laugh at me 'bout de Lord prayers," said Mary. "I tell her dere a'n't nothin; so good as prayin'—'pears like it made eberyting go heap easier. But laws! Molsey dono' nothin' 'bout it. De fac is, she's in a orful persition 'bout her soul. She says she don't believe nothin' 'bout it, and sich like."

"She!" exclaimed Venus. "It's my suspinion de less you keeps company 'long o' her, de better you'll be. I dono' where she's raised, but she do go on de most disgracefullest since she been here."

"I know it," replied Molly; "she just 'stributes herself, permiscuous like, 'mong all de men on de place. I tell her t'other day, de way she go on mighty nigh spile all de women's character. But she only laugh at me, and tells me, 'What de good of a nigger woman tryin' to be decent?' say she'll jest drink rum and do what she please, long as she live, and de sooner she die and get put in de hole, like a dog, de better; and she'll have all de fun she can, 'cause dat'll be de end ob her."

"O, the poor, impidel woman!" said Venus. "'T a'n't no wonder she don't try to be nothin' if she b'lieves dat. What has a nigger got to keep him up, if dere a'n't no world but dis yer. But dere is," she added, with emphasis, "dere *is*; and when eberyting dat's been hid in holes and corners is toted out, and shown 'fore de whole world at de judgment day—O, won't it be orful for de poor sinners den?"

"Yes, indeed!" replied Mary; and, awed by the solemn thoughts these simple words had raised, their conversation ceased, and they sat silent and thoughtful.

The next morning, Ida was better. The delicious mountain air, that stirred the vines as it came in at the little window beside her bed, touched with its light fingers a cool brow, and lips no longer parched with fever. Aunt Venus, having given her a breakfast of gruel, and arranged the simple furniture of her hut, went with light heart to "the house" to get her daily work, for she was seamstress in this establishment. Soon returning with a large bundle of osnaburgs,[1] she applied herself to cutting out and fitting, while Ida, who now began to feel some interest and curiosity, looked on. "Did I always live here?" she asked, at length.

"Laws, no, honey!" replied Venus, giggling at this question. "Don't ye see I'se an old black thing, and you's white?"

"A'n't I a nigger, then?" persisted Ida.

"Dono' 'bout dat," replied her nurse. "'Pears like you wasn't; but Mass' James say you was, and some niggers *is* white. It's my suspinion," she continued, after a pause "dat you'se kidnap."

"What is kidnap?" asked Ida.

"Laws, bless de child, she dono' nothin'!" said Venus. "Why, dey kidnaps 'em away off from dere mammys and daddys, and sells 'em to white folks. I reckon somebody done kidnap you, and dat de way Mass' James come to find you."

"Who is Mass' James?" asked the child.

"Mass' James—why he our massa, your massa and mine. He bought us, so I s'pose we b'long to him."

"When did he buy me?" said Ida.

"O, t' other day—don't ye 'member? You'se been orful sick since, and I s'pose ye don't though; but can't ye 'member nothin'—where ye come from, nor what your name is?"

The child closed her eyes, and her face grew clouded. At last she said, sadly, "No I can't remember. It seems as if something

---

1 Clothing named for its coarse, plain flax fabric, commonly used for slave garments.

dreadful had happened, something that frightened me, and then I went to sleep, and when I woke up I was here."

"Den, honey, 'pears like you'd have to stay here, if you can't 'member nothin' better," said Venus, sadly; and, from that moment, she resolved that, if the child had really forgotten the past, she would never perplex her with questions that would make her think that she had been born in a better condition of life. She knew that white children were sometimes bought from poor parents in the Southern States, and, though she suspected that Ida was the child of wealthy parents, and had probably been stolen, she had no idea that this suspicion would avail anything with the white men who might call themselves her owners. She knew the lot to which the child was doomed was a hard one, even for those who had been born in it, and educated to believe it the only one fit for them, and she felt that it would be harder still if one had the consciousness of having been born to something better.

No one who looked on Aunt Venus's inexpressive face, as she sat there steadily sewing, would have imagined her capable of the mingled train of wise and bitter reflection that was passing through her brain. She kept her thoughts to herself, and few were aware of the delicate feelings, the womanly refinement, and germs of keen intellect, that lay hid beneath that dark and unpolished exterior. She had still a little hope that with returning strength the child might regain her memory; but it was not so. The invigorating mountain air, and the judicious care of her devoted nurse, soon restored strength and health to her system; but the cloud that hid the past was not lifted from her brain. Only one trace of her former life she unconsciously retained. From infancy she had been remarkable for correct pronunciation and quick understanding of words, and she still continued to speak a pure and refined language, that attracted the attention of all who knew her, from its contrast with the jargon used by the negroes with whom she now associated. But she was the pride and delight of Aunt Venus, who was never weary of caressing her, and who gave her the name dearest to her heart, which her own daughter had borne.

As days and months went by, she grew tall, and her delicate limbs assumed the rounded contour of health; but her cheek and lips were always pale, and her step slow and inelastic, and, though kind and gentle to all, she never joined in the careless sports of childhood, and rarely spoke to anyone but her nurse, unless she was directly addressed.

"It is queer what ails that child," said Mrs. Bell, one day, when Ida left the room. "She don't seem like other children, and has a slow, dreamy manner, as if she were asleep, and yet she hears quick enough, and she isn't stupid."

"Old Molsey say," replied Rose, a young mulatto, to whom this remark was addressed, "old Molsey say dat some-body done conjur de child."

"Pooh!" said her mistress; "there's no such thing as conjuring."

"O, Miss Susan, how can you say dat?" said Rose. "I'se known heaps of folks dat's been conjur—O, laws, yes, heaps!"

"Pooh!" said Mrs. Bell, again; "you're a fool if you believe that."

"O, now, miss, dere is such tings. When any individule goes to hurt anybody, dey takes a stick, and gets some old torn bit o' dat individule's clothes, and circumwents it all round de stick, and buries it where de one dey hate will walk ober it, and den say something ober it. Den, when de individule steps on it, dey grows sick, and pines all away."

"*She* don't pine away, at any rate; she grows more healthy every day; so I reckon nobody has conjured her," said Mrs. Bell, as she took her work and went out to the piazza.

The negroes, like all ignorant and demi-civilized people, are devout believers in the powers of darkness, and have great fear of conjurers and the charm of an evil eye; and it was the general belief on the plantation that Lizzy White—as she was called—was a sufferer from this malign influence. Numberless were the charms which Aunt Venus was advised to hang around the neck of her protégé to counteract the mischief that had blighted her; but it was all in vain. She did not seem unhappy, but she was companionless, and sometimes would sit for hours with her eyes fixed on a vacancy, her hands folded idly in her lap, and her whole figure relaxed and motionless, as if in a waking dream, and, when aroused from the trance, she seemed unconscious of the lapse of time.

"Why do you call me 'Lizzy' over and over again that way?" said the child, as she sat one day at Venus's feet, in the door of their hut

The smile with which she had been regarding her faded from Venus's lips, and, bowed beneath a sudden rush of sad memories, she let her work fall to the floor, and, covering her face with her hands, wept bitterly. Ida sprang up, and put her arm around the old woman's neck. "Don't cry so," she said, "don't mauma. I didn't mean to hurt you."

"You didn't hurt me, honey; *it's the old hurt here*, that aches," said Venus, pressing her hand to her breast. "When you looked up at me den so tender, 'pears like I saw my own child—my own dear little child—that was sold away from me, when we was all toted off from Florida. O, dear! 'pears like sometimes I couldn't bear it no longer!" and she wept again, swaying herself to and fro, and murmuring in low tones amid her weeping the names of husband and children, that had long since become to her as the names of the dead. At length the paroxysm of grief exhausted itself, and she sat up and uncovered her face. "Don't cry, honey," she said to the child, down whose cheeks tears were silently rolling; "'t wasn't what you done said. It comes ober me dis yer way sometimes all in a minute, and 'pears like I couldn't bear it, noways. Dese last tree years[1] since you done stayed wid me, I'se been more comforble, so ye a'n't seen me so often, and I shan't be so 'gain, maybe. I tries to forget," she added, taking up her work, while her face assumed an expression of stern dispair; "'t a'n't no 'count cryin'. I'se a poor nigger woman, and I neber shall see 'em again—my young husband nor my chillen."

"You told me you'd tell me about 'em some day, but you needn't, if it makes you cry," said her sympathizing listener.

"Dono' how 't is," said Venus; "'pears like I wanted to talk about 'em sometimes, and yet it makes me cry. O, what a gay young thing I was when I lived 'long o' Miss Lizzy down in Florida! little I knew 'bout de strouble in dis yer world!"

"Where is Florida, and who is Miss Lizzy?" asked Ida.

"O, Miss Lizzy was an angel, one o' de Lord's angels, right out o' heaven. She was *dat* good to us, poor niggers, we would 'a laid down and let her walk over us; we'd 'a died for her, we would. O, I'se dat happy, honey," she added, dropping her work again, and taking Ida on her knee, "I'se dat happy, I neber 'spected what I'se comin' to. I had my husband and my chillen!—my *young* husband, honey, and he *so* kind, he never let me want for anything, and he work all night sometime, when he come in from hoe de cotton, so to fix things comforble for me and the chillen; and Miss Lizzy she done come in very often, and read to me, and talk 'bout the chillen—'specially 'bout my little Lizzy, dat I name for her;—used to think a heap o' *her*, she did."

"Where is she now, and where are your children?" said Ida.

"She! O, we'se all sold 'way off from her long ago, and save my life and soul, I couldn't tell where my husband and chillen is dis day;" and Venus sighed heavily.

---

1 Ida is now eight years old.

"If she was so good to you, I shouldn't think she'd let you be sold," said Ida.

"O, she couldn't help it!" said Venus. "It was dis yer way 't happened: Miss Lizzy done got married, and her husband—'pears like he wasn't quite good enough for Miss Lizzy—nobody was—but she loved him. O, how she loved him! I'se seen her eyes shine like two stars, and her cheeks flush up when he come near her; and he love her, too, and we have great times when de weddin' come off. O, my soul! de pies and de cakes and de good things dere was in de great house; and every poor nigger on the place had a new suit and a piece o' *fresh meat*, 'cause Miss Lizzy say she's so happy; 'pears like she wanted everybody else to be happy too. Well, things goes on four years more, and Miss Lizzy have two chillen, and den I sees things wasn't jist right. When I'se settin' sewin' in de house—I'se seamstress dere, honey, same's I be here—I don't hear Miss Lizzy singin' over de baby any more, but sometime I hear her talk to Mass' William long time in a low voice, like she was cryin', and sometime he gone 'way long time, and den she was *dat* anxious; and sometime in de mornin' I say, 'Miss Lizzy, you done cried last night instead o' sleepin',' and den she'd smile little, and say, 'O, no, Benus!' but I knew de strouble was comin' and sure 'nuff, it come mighty quick. One day I goes in wid my work, and I lay it down and say, 'Here, Miss Lizzy!' but she take no 'count of it, and 'pears like she didn't see me; but when I turn to go out, she say, 'Stop, Benus,' and when she turn round, I see she was cryin'. Den she tell me Mass' William done loss all de property; and the plantation was sold, and all de people, and us house servants was gwine be put up at auction, cause de man dat took the place didn't want us.

"Den, honey, 'pears like de room all swim round and round, and I *dat* blind I couldn't see nothin', for my husband—he field hand—and if I'se sold I lose him. But Miss Lizzy, she say, quick like, 'Don't you be feared, Benus, you'se allers been good girl, and Mass' William gwine look out for ye. We'se loss eberything, but 't a'n't Mass' William's fault, and you musn't blame him;' 'cause, ye see, I'se dat 'stounded I'se muttering something 'bout him in my throat, and she knew it, so she say, 'You musn't blame him; and he's gwine ask de new massa, that Joe (he my husband, honey) be sold, too, and p'raps you be sold together.'

"Well, dere little comfort in dat, but O, dis heart was sore when I go back to the chillen, and Joe; he done heard it out in the field, and he come home, and we cries, and de chillen dey cries too for company. O, dat de dark night for us all! Well, in de mornin'

Miss Lizzy come out in de yard where we all standin' talkin', and she look *dat* pale, and de red all round her eyes, 'stead o' bein' in her cheeks and lips, where 't ought to be, and she speak so sorrowful like, and say, she feel for us, dat we all set right down on de ground, and cry out loud; and Miss Lizzy, she break down, and cry too. Den Mass' William, he come out de door, and put his arm round her, where she stood leanin' up 'gainst de piazza, and lead her into the house. Den he come out and talk to us all so kind, and say what she want to say and couldn't. O, dear, dear, de Lord know what a time dat was!" She paused a long time, and her sad eyes assumed a dreamy expression, as if she was living over again that scene in the past.

"Was your husband sold with you?" asked Ida, wiping with her delicate hand the tears that were slowly dropping from that black face.

"No, honey," replied Venus, with a convulsive sob; "no, honey. Dey hoped—Miss Lizzy and Mass' Williams did—dat somehow dere'd be enough left when all was settled up dat was out 'gainst the property, for Miss Lizzy to buy in Joe and de chillen, and me and my sister Ann, 'cause Miss Lizzy and Ann and me was raised together, most like we was all sisters, and Ann was de chillen's nurse, and her husband die little while before, so she wanted us perticlar, and we was kep to be sold last. Miss Lizzy told everybody she wanted to buy us in, 'cause Mass' William say if folks knew it, dey wouldn't bid against him. But 't wasn't no 'count.

"When de time come, we'se all toted off to de courthouse, and Miss Lizzy so anxious, she and Mass' William go together in a carriage, all shut up, and wait under a tree just outside de crowd. I see de carriage, and know dey was in it, and somehow I felt more comforble. Well, de oder servants was sold, and den dey put Joe and me and de chillen up, and jist dat minute I see Mass' William get out o' de carriage and go speak to a man. Den de auctioneer done knock wid his hammer, and de sale begin. Mass' William's man bid for de lot, and for a minute everybody was still, and 'pears like I could 'a screamed for joy, for I thought we was safe. De men all look to one 'noder, like dey understood all 'bout it, and wasn't gwine bid, and we was jist gwine be knocked down to Mass' William, when somebody spoke up and offered more. O, how I feel! and de auctioneer look cross a minute, and den Mass' William's man he bid little higher. Den I breathe again; but O, de oder man he bid up too. De men dat was standin' round begin to look at him and scowl, and talk low like, and den he steps up close and jumps on a stump, and say, 'Gen'lemen, is dis a fair sale, or am it not?'

"Well, den, de auctioneer say, 'Ob course it fair;' and dey is all quiet a minute, and den somebody steps up and whispers to de man. But he swear and say out loud, 'I dono' nothin' 'bout dat. I hear of a sale o' niggers, and I come, and I see a lot that I want to buy, and I make a fair bid for 'em. I want to know if I haven't a right to do so? Certainly I has, and I won't give up my rights to any man. You may scowl at me,' he say, 'as much as you please; I can protect myself if I'se interfered with.' And out he draws a pistol. Den dey all bustle up, and some turns away, and some pulls out dere pistols, too, and dere knives; but just den Mass' William stept forward, wid his face all so pale, on'y his lips trembled a little, and his voice sounded *pressed down*, like he was holdin' on to his feelin's wid both hands, and he say—O, I can hear his voice dis yer minute, I 'members so well what was said!—says he, 'Gen'lemen, I beg there may be no blood shed or quarreling on my account. I thank you for your sympathy in my misfortunes, but if anyone chooses to take advantage of them, to distress me and my family, of course I am powerless, and the law must take its course.' Den he step back, and stood in his old place.

"Well, den, I thought I must be safe, and I bless the Lord for Mass' Williams. But 'fore I know it, de man on de stump began to bid again, and Mass' William's man he stop, and we was knocked down to de stranger. De men all turn dere back on him, and say 'Shame!' but he came up to us as bold as brass, and say he knew his rights, and he'd have 'em, and he would never be bullied out of 'em by anybody. So de folks had to let us go. Dey couldn't help us, but dey all say dey's sorry for us, and for massa and miss, too. O dear, dear, what a time it was den! De man he hurry us away, and when we go by de carriage, de door open and Miss Lizzy call me. I run up to her, and she put her arms round my neck and kiss me—de good angel—and she cry and say 'pears like 't would kill her. Den dere was great shout when de men see dat, and de boys begin throwin' pine burrs and dirt at our new massa. Den he turn round and draw his pistol again, and say he'd shoot anybody dat interfere wid him; and so we was driv away to de calaboose,[1] and shut up."

"O," said Ida, "that was dreadful! What did you do?"

"Do!" replied Venus, "we couldn't do *nothin*' but jist salt

---

1 Jail.

down our grief with our tears. Nobody could help us—we was *slaves*—and de laws is fixed so dat *folks dat wants to*, can't be good to slaves."

"But what became of your husband and children?" asked Ida, whose flushed cheek and trembling voice showed how much she was interested in this recital.

"O dear, honey, dat was de worst of all! De man dat bought us was a speckerlator; and he took us up to Savannah, and when we was sold dere, we wasn't put up together. Joe was sold to one man, and de two oldest chillen and little Lizzy and my little boy Joe to anoder, and I'se sold way from 'em all. O dear, 'pears like it will kill me to think o' dat time! O Lord, help me! O, comfort dis old broken heart!"

The child wept with her, but she could poorly understand her feelings. Impossible was it for her to know, how from out the buried past came the phantoms of husband, children, all that had once lifted her for a few short years out of the dreary coldness and darkness of her slave lot, to the warm sunshine of happiness and love; impossible to realize how the scar of that old wound yet throbbed with a keen pain, even beneath the touch of the gentlest fingers.

Suddenly Ida grasped the hands of her nurse with a quick, nervous motion. A new thought had entered her brain. In the painless and monotonous life she had led hitherto, there was little to remind her of a fact which at this moment recurred to her, startling her with a sudden sense of danger. "Venus," she said, earnestly, "tell me, am *I* a slave?"

Venus looked at her sadly a moment. That word which the negroes never use except in moments of the greatest bitterness, impressed her strangely, coming from the lips of another. "Yes," she said slowly, "you are a *slave*."

"And must I be treated so when I grow up? Can't I get away from it somehow? O, tell me, Venus! I never thought about it before;" and the child trembled all over, and looked around with a terrified expression, as if seeking a way of escape.

Venus was frightened at this overpowering emotion in one usually so gentle and calm; and controlling her own feelings by a violent effort—"Don't be frightened," she said, soothingly. "I'se heard white folks say de most o' servants was happy, so I s'pose *some is*; and p'raps you may allers be treated well. If I'd staid with Miss Lizzy, I know she'd allers been good to me. Anyway, honey, you won't allers feel like you do now 'bout it—you'll *get used* to it—we does *get used* to eberything.

O, honey, don't be frightened, p'raps the Lord'll be good to ye, and let you die while you're little, 'fore you come to any strouble."[1]

Ida made no reply. She grew calm and cold as ice in all her veins, and, sinking at Venus's feet, she leaned her head against her knees, and sadly and dreamily she repeated those fatal words, "A slave! a slave!"

At that moment the sound of footsteps and voices reached their ears, and Venus had hardly time to snatch her work from the floor, before Mr. and Mrs. Bell rode by, on their way to see one of the negroes who was sick in the "quarters." In a little while they returned. They were on horseback, and just starting for their morning ride; and, as they passed slowly, they looked complacently at the two who were sitting there together.

"They look very comfortable," said Mr. Bell. "Aunt Venus really shows some taste in the way she trains those vines over her door."

"Yes," replied his wife, "they are happy enough; but I am sorry Aunt Venus is setting her heart so much on that child, for we shall have a bad time when they come to part."

"To part!" said Mr. Bell, inquiringly.

"Yes, of course," was the reply. "We shall have to sell Lizzy, by and by, she is growing so very pretty. I believe you will make something on that speculation, after all my laughing at you so much for buying a dead nigger."

"I don't think I shall sell her," said Mr. Bell. "I've altered my mind about her. She has pretty manners, and is gentle and quiet, and I like to have such servants about the house. When she gets a little older, you can take her in to wait on the table, or take care of the children."

A light flashed from Mrs. Bell's blue eyes, and she rode her horse before her husband, turning so as completely to fill the narrow path; and, looking straight in his eyes, she set her teeth with an almost fierce expression, as she said,

"I shall do no such thing. *The girl will be too pretty.* I will have no more such scenes as I had with Ellen;—you remember her impudence. What I suffered with that girl passes the power of language. I'll have no more handsome servant girls, telling me my husband thinks more of them than he does of me!"

Mr. Bell colored slightly; and, seizing her riding-whip, he

---

1 Venus alludes to the future that Ida faces as a "fancy girl."

struck the horse playfully, and they went on again for a short distance.

"Of course," continued his wife, when their pace became slower, "I never believed her insinuations; but they were too disagreeable even at that rate. She was respectful enough when you was by and you never would believe how dreadfully impudent she was sometimes. I never shall forgive you for not having her whipped that day before she was sold—never. Why wouldn't you?"

Mr. Bell did not answer, but his features assumed an odd expression, and he cast a queer, sidelong glance at his wife's face. Then giving a long, low whistle, he spurred his horse, and they rode rapidly forward.

Far up the mountain, on the lower southern slope of which lay the Bell plantation, were the springs that fed a rivulet which came dashing, sparkling and leaping down its steep, rocky bed, occasionally spreading out for a little space into small pools, where the birds came to drink, and where the sunbeams, glinting brightly through green leaves, kissed the flowers that mirrored themselves in the smooth waters. Then hurrying on again, it played "hide-and-seek" around huge logs, the wreck of some forest tornado; or piles of driftwood that its own course had heaped; or immense boulders, preordained obstructions flung in its path by the throes and struggles of the primeval world. On it went, darkling in rocky chasms, or beneath the roots of trees, and then flashing out again to the light with a merry tinkling, like the silvery laugh of childhood; now stealing softly, with a low, musical murmur, over mossy levels, where the overhanging branches bent coyly to touch its surface, or interlocked their arms to form green triumphal arches over it, and then, with a sudden whirl, and a reckless plunge that changed it to a sheet of brilliant foam, it sped onward—downward—till, just opposite Mr. Bell's house, it came out on the road, alongside of which human hands had scooped for it a channel. Through this it ran silently and swiftly, as if anxious to perform with suitable dignity the office assigned to it, of filling a reservoir at the junction of the mountain path with the county road, where passing travelers might refresh themselves and their weary beasts; after which, as if to escape their thanks, it hid itself modestly under a narrow bridge of logs, and went on its way to lose its individuality in that of the river which at length received it.

To this watering-place at the roadside, one afternoon, at the sunset hour, there came a traveler on horseback. Throwing the reins on the neck of the animal, that he might drink, the man sat up and looked about him. Was it the lovely landscape at his feet, the purple light in the valleys that changed to a golden glory on the hilltops, the green mountainside that rose above him embowered in trees, whose leaves now thrilled with the vesper songs of birds— was it any or all of these, or was it some subtle or unseen influence, that filled his breast with such a strange and delicious sense of repose, and stilled the gnawing pain of his heart? His dress was shabby as if from neglect, his tall form was thin and bent, and his face had an expression of peering and anxious inquiry, for he was a wayworn and miserable man, to whom there remained but one consolation, but one shield against the despairing insanity that at times seemed clouding his brain. It was the belief that in some way, however incomprehensible to the weakness of mortal vision, through the infinite power of One "who maketh the wrath of man to praise Him,"[1] good would at last be evolved from this fearful evil—his own eternal good, and the well-being of one dearer to him than life. That poor heart, wrung and tortured, had taken refuge in the sublime mystery of Faith, and to that he clung firmly, albeit at times with the frozen and senseless grasp whereby the shipwrecked mariner clings to the spar that supports him amid the chilling surges of the ocean waves.

He raised his eyes to heaven and spoke aloud. "O God!" he said, "I thank thee that even unto my soul, weary and seared with woe, there come sometimes moments of peace. I thank Thee that sometimes my stern grief is softened by the sweet influences of nature, and that the sunshine, which falls alike on the evil and the good, reminds me to forgive mine enemies as I would be forgiven. O, that this long search might end! O, that my past suffering might suffice! O, that Thou wouldst give me back my child—my only one!—O God, my child! my child!"

He stretched out his arms as if he would embrace her, but they clasped the empty air, and his head dropped languidly on his breast. The horse stopped drinking, and stood pawing the ground at the bottom of the brook. The action aroused his master from a dreamy reverie. He raised his head, and saw near him a narrow road that led up the mountain, and its green shadow seemed to invite him. Half unconsciously he turned his horse towards it, but he had gone but a few steps, when a voice in the road he had left called out,

---

1 From Psalm 76:10.

"Hillo, stranger! you've mistaken the road. That's only a woods road, and it's mighty nigh night, and you'll stand a smart chance o' getting lost up there among the stumps."

"The road looks pleasant," said the man thus addressed; "does nobody live up here with whom I could stay all night?"

"Nobody, as I know of; but you'll find a good tavern two miles below here," and the traveler passed on.

The horseman paused a moment to look up the road, that had still a strange fascination for him, and then reluctantly retraced his steps down the hill. For a few rods he went on slowly, and then there came over him again the gnawing pain, the feverish restlessness, that had been for a little while allayed, and, striking spurs into his horse, he dashed rapidly along the way.

O, unhappy father! to be so near the object of all thy desires, and not to know the influence that attracted thee! O, wretched man! whose harder and duller nature was unconscious of the magnetism that thrilled over the delicate organization of thy child, rendered more impressible by her mental disease.

For, at that hour, Ida, sitting listlessly in her usual place, on the doorstep of Aunt Venus's hut, started up suddenly, her eyes flashing with a new light, her whole frame trembling with excitement, and her heartstrings vibrating even to painfulness, with the rushing of long silent emotions. "I hear! I hear!" she exclaimed; "who is it? where are you?"

"What's come over de child?" said Venus, looking round from the hoe-cake she was mixing; "dere's nobody calling, honey, as I hears."

The child did not answer, and seemed not to hear her. She stood a moment with her head thrown back, her eyes glistening, and her hands clasped and pressed against her heart; and then, swifter than a bird, she flew rather than ran down the mountain road, till she reached the high bank above the reservoir. Here suddenly the irresistible power that had drawn her along seemed to desert her. Pausing, she looked round a moment with a bewildered air, and then, sinking down on the ground, she wept bitterly.

"What was it, honey?" said Venus, when, an hour after the child entered the hut, with her usual languid step.

"I don't know," she replied. "It seemed as if somebody called me—somebody that I used to know in the time I can't remember, before I came here—and O, for a minute it seemed as if I SHOULD *remember*; but now it is all dark again;" and, overcome by the reaction of that strange excitement, she fell fainting in the arms that were fondly supporting her.

CHAPTER VI

"Full well I know
There is not one among you but hath nursed
Some proud indignant feeling, which doth make
One conflict of his life. What! think ye Heaven
O'erlooks the oppressor, if he bear awhile
His crested head on high? I tell you, no,
The avenger will not sleep!"
　　　　"Peace! peace! we are beset
By snares on every side, and we must learn
In silence and in patience to endure."
VESPERS OF PALERMO[1]

Five years Ida spent on the Bell plantation, and they were not, on the whole, unpleasant. Mr. Bell was a kind-hearted man, that liked to see those around him comfortable and happy. He would never have allowed cruelty to a horse or a dog, and on the same principle he treated his negroes well. His farm was not very large, and he took pleasure in managing it, and though obliged to delegate some authority to one or two servants, in whom he could trust, he retained a general supervision of its affairs, and was careful that his "people" had no greater tasks assigned them than could be performed by sunset; and then, if they were not too tired or too lazy, they might improve the remaining hours in cultivating their own little gardens or taking care of their pigs and poultry. In winter, wood was abundant on the mountain, and, as some of them were then employed in cutting and hauling it to market, it was easy for all of them to supply themselves, by fair or foul means, with sufficient to keep them warm. In addition to these comforts, they were sometimes allowed to go to neighboring farms, or to have a gathering on their own, and the riotous mirth that then issued from the cabin where they were assembled, might have given occasion for some of those sententious remarks upon the perfect happiness of the negro, with which the indignant charges of overzealous people at the north are frequently met.[2]

1　Hemans, *Vespers* 1.1. Pike edits Hemans to translate the play's vengeance plot into a promise of divine retribution. She selects lines from Hemans's scene, adds new punctuation and repetition, and presents the lines out of order.
2　Pike refers here to antislavery activists and, with a great deal of sarcasm, to pro-slavery apologists who made much of supposed happiness in captivity.

Sometimes, indeed, these merrymakings came to an abrupt conclusion, as, for instance, on one occasion, when a party of young men, who were acting as patrol for that night, broke into the hut where they were assembled, and, regardless of passports,[1] and not content with scattering them by blows and curses, like a flock of frightened deer, tied up one or two of them, and administered a whipping so severe as to put the victims on the sick-list for several days. One of these sufferers happened to be a favorite servant of Mr. Bell, and a man whom he had never needed to strike since he had owned him, and his master was angry enough; but nothing could be done. The patrol was a part of the system of government that could not be safely dispensed with; and if a party of lawless youth, excited by whiskey, and bent on a frolic, sometimes carried matters a little too far, why, nobody was hurt but "the niggers," and, after all, it was better for them not to get into a habit of meeting too often. They had better be at home resting themselves, than to be dancing all night, and so unfitting themselves for labor the next day. So said the neighbors, with whom Mr. Bell talked on the subject, and thus the matter ended.

Another source of enjoyment were the "camp meetings" that occurred now and then, and which many of the negroes affected even more than dancing parties. To these dark and systematically degraded minds, emotion supplies the place of intellect, and anything that can excite or arouse them from the dreary monotony of their existence is eagerly welcomed. What can do this so well and so untiringly as the awful mysteries of religion, before whose sublime heights and depths the keenest mind shrinks helpless and amazed? Thus, to them these religious meetings, with their searching appeals, their indignant rebukes, and terrific denunciations, and winning invitations, heard amid the darkness of night or the stillness of the solemn groves, and contrasting so vividly the bliss of a future state with the miseries of their present condition, supplied to their impressible natures an intoxicating stimulus, which, sometimes, no doubt, enlightened the conscience, and left behind a deep and radical change; but which oftener passed, leaving no trace save an indistinct idea of a futurity, when all wrongs would be righted, and of a sover-

---

1 Following the Negro Act of 1740, enslaved persons were not permitted to leave their plantations without a written pass. Furthermore, if the slave refused to submit to the patrol, "it shall be lawful for any such white person to pursue, apprehend, and moderately correct such slave."

eign, *somewhere*, to whom they might appeal, with prayers, that, like the inarticulate cries of animals, may perhaps reach the ear of Infinite compassion.

Five years, as we have said, Ida passed on the Bell plantation. As she grew older, the trances that at first had given indication of a diseased brain, became less frequent; but her love of silence and solitude manifested itself in the long, lonely hours she spent in rambling through the woods that surrounded her home, and it might have been some undefined association with the past that made her delight to dress her hair with flowers, and twine them into wreaths with which she ornamented the walls of their hut. Indeed, for a long time, the only interest she manifested in things around her was shown in her enthusiasm for these beauteous gifts of nature, which she was never weary of seeking and forming into bouquets, that displayed marvelous taste and skill in one so young. Very little else was ever required of her. For some reason, Mrs. Bell did not seem to like to have her about the house, and she was left wholly to the care of Aunt Venus, whose hut stood a few rods from the dwellings of the other house servants, in the rear of the garden, and had an air of neatness, and even of rustic beauty, nestled, as it was, beneath the shade of a spreading walnut-tree, and almost covered with gourds and wild vines, that had been trained over its rugged walls. Here, save for the utter want of all intellectual training, she was almost as fondly cherished as if she had been in her own home; for the simple religious instruction which she had received from her protector, was that "saving knowledge" of repentance and faith, which is the direct gift of God through the whisperings of the Divine Spirit, and worth more than all the dogmas taught in the schools. Mr. Bell was an uncommonly kind master, and his servants had all the real necessaries of life—food and clothing and fire—and the warm heart of Venus overflowed to her little charge with a pride, and a tender affection that could hardly have been exceeded.

The negro nurses are generally very fond of the white children committed to their care. They delight to dress them elegantly, and carry them abroad to attract the gaze of strangers, and will quarrel as heartily about the merits of their respective charges, as if their own children were the subjects of their discussion. What, then, must have been the eager joy with which Aunt Venus welcomed this delicate and beautiful child who had been, in some degree, given to her as her own! To her impoverished heart how priceless seemed this pearl, which the stormy waves of life had cast at her feet! She was never weary of arranging the shining tresses that had now grown long again, and hung in ringlets over Ida's brow and neck; and she mourned incessantly at being obliged to dress her lovely pet in the coarse and scanty garments provided for the other slave children. When, occasionally, by dint of selling some of her allowance of food, or by sacrificing some of her beloved aprons, or by various other expedients, best known to herself, she contrived to obtain from the neighboring town a bright pink or blue calico dress, in which to array her idol, her satisfaction knew no bounds. Some of her fellow-servants envied her, and some laughed at her for the self-denial she exercised, to enable her to gratify her pride in Ida's beauty; but it mattered little to her. She would have slaved night and day, she would have suffered cold and starvation, to obtain comforts and luxuries for this child, whom she loved as if she had been her own, and yet reverenced as belonging to a higher race, and who seemed to absorb her thoughts and her affections in the place of all those she had lost.

Venus was profoundly ignorant; she could neither read nor write; but a life of degradation and toil had not crushed entirely the native delicacy of her soul, and she could thus sympathize with the child's emotions and thoughts, and, in some measure, shield her from the rude touches that sometimes shocked the sensibilities of a nature which was now

"Like sweet bells jangled, out of tune and harsh."[1]

This care Ida repaid with a deep and exclusive affection, and she would have been happy, but for the dim, haunting memories that came over her in dreams and in her waking hours, rousing an undefined pain, as for something lacking from her life, and for the stern consciousness of her present position, which, though dimly realized at first, became as she grew older more and more the engrossing topic of thought and fear, and led her to shun more entirely those sports and that companionship with her young masters and mistresses which exposed her to the necessity of recognizing the relation in which she stood to them. Many of her hours were spent in wandering among the forest trees, and following the course of the mountain streams; and from the day when she had been so strangely drawn to the high, tree-crowned bank that bordered the further side of the

---

1 Ophelia speaks of Hamlet in 3.1.

brook, where it discharges itself into the reservoir, that was her favorite place of resort.

One afternoon, as she sat hidden from view by the kalmia[1] bushes that grew between two venerable oaks, a traveler on horseback came along the road, and paused as he saw the watering place, which was a clear, shallow pool, of a few yards in diameter, formed partly by nature and partly by the hand of man. He was a frank, fearless-looking boy, just in that golden age of dawning manhood, when the present is enjoyed with a keen zest never experienced in later years, and the brave heart, untried with sorrow, believes all things desirable to be possible, and longs to rush into the arena, and mingle in the tumult of life's battle. Patting the neck of his horse, he said, as he turned towards the brook, "Ah, Dandy, see there! Don't that make your eyes sparkle, old fellow?" and, as the thirsty animal stooped to drink, the loquacious youth continued his monologue by addressing himself to his dog—a large white hound—who, having already slaked his thirst, had improved this opportunity to lay himself down to rest, with his tongue hanging from his mouth, and his great, black, glossy ears falling forward over his eyes, as he settled his head on his outstretched paws, and prepared to refresh himself with a short nap.

"Tired, are you, Sport?" said his master, as he watched these proceedings. "Don't you wish, now, you'd taken my advice, and staid at home, instead of undertaking this tramp? I told you you'd be *awful* tired before the journey was half over—don't you know I did? You thought I'd let you ride behind! O, Sport, you know well enough I wouldn't! I told you all about that, and, if you didn't understand, it was all your own fault. You should think, now we've come on so far that you can't get back, I might walk myself and let you ride, hey? Is that what you mean when you cock up your eye that way? Why, the fact is, my dear friend, I don't believe you *can* ride. I should be very sorry to make any unwarranted assertions, but I really don't think you have the ability. I'm afraid you neglected that branch of your education. I don't believe you went to riding-school when you was young— now did you, 'pon honor? I'm afraid you couldn't carry your tail gracefully on horseback. If you didn't, you might begin now—it's never too late to learn. Is that it? Well, come, then, let's see what sort of a figure you would make on horseback!"—and, laughing aloud as the comical idea occurred to him, he dismounted, and,

---

1 A flowering evergreen shrub.

seizing the dog, managed, after some exertion, to hoist him into the saddle, and make him sit there quietly. Finding resistance vain, Sport, whose face had always been an expression of dignity, that was continually belied and contradicted by his unwieldy form, sat upright in his master's place, with the most imperturbable gravity, and submitted to have the reins placed between his forepaws, and the boy's cap pulled over his ears, out from under which his eyes blinked drolly, and his whole appearance was so funny, that the boy clapped his hands, and fairly shouted with mirth.—"That's first rate, Sport," said he. "How do you like it? Why don't you laugh? If you knew how queer you look, you'd laugh. You a'n't going to laugh at trifles? Don't you know trifles are the only things of importance in this world? You defy me to make you laugh? I'll see, then, if I can't *upset* your gravity"—and, as he spoke, he struck the horse lightly, causing him to give a sudden start that overturned the unpracticed equestrian, and down he went, with a great splash, into the water.

This feat caused a fresh burst of laughter from his gay-hearted master, who started, and for a moment, forgot both dog and horse, as he heard his laugh echoed, in clear, silvery tones, from among the trees opposite him. Conscious that his frolic with Sport had hardly been consistent with the dignity of a young gentleman of his years, and withal a collegian and a traveler, he doffed his cap in some confusion, and colored not a little as his eye fell on the face that was looking out at him, half-shyly, from behind the kalmias. For a moment he felt inclined to spring upon his horse, and gallop away from this unknown spectator, for whose benefit he had been performing; but a second glance showed him that she was but a child, and a very lovely child, too; and, in another moment, his curiosity was so much aroused to know why such a delicate and beautiful creature should be alone in that solitary place, and habited in the coarse striped garments which form the livery of servitude, that he rode his horse through the water to the spot where she was standing. She retreated a little as he came near; but there was something so cheerful and winning in the boy's fresh, youthful face, that she felt no disposition to fly from him, as she usually did from strangers.

"Come here, you pretty little girl," he said to her, "and give me some of those flowers in your basket. Come, that's a good girl."

The child drew nearer, and timidly, at arm's length, held out her basket.

"O, no!" he said, "I don't want the basket, I want only a small bouquet that I can put in my cap-band. Besides, I can't hold the basket, for you see, I have to take care of my horse; so you must sit down here and select some of your prettiest flowers."

Reassured by his kind voice, Ida seated herself, and began with alacrity to do as he requested.

"Who taught you how to dress your hair so prettily with leaves?" he asked. "Was it your mother?"

"Nobody taught me," said Ida, in a quiet, sad tone. "I haven't any mother; I live with Aunt Venus."

Astonished at her low, musical voice, and her correct language, the boy asked again, "Who is Aunt Venus?—where does she live?"

"She lives up the road about half a mile. We belong to Massa James Bell," said the child, simply.

"We?" said the boy—"*you* don't belong to him, do you?"

"Yes," said Ida, more sadly; "he bought me a long time ago, Aunt Venus says."

The boy's face flushed crimson, and he said, quickly, almost angrily, "You don't mean to tell me you are this man's *servant*; why, you are as white as I am."

Ida looked up in his face a moment, with an agitated manner, and her eyes filled with tears as she said, "Yes, I'm a servant now. But I didn't always live here, I *know* I didn't."

"Where did you live?" asked the boy, whose interest was deeply aroused.

"I can't remember," replied Ida, and her eyes assumed the dreamy expression they always wore when she referred to this subject. "Sometimes I feel as if I was just going to remember, and then it all goes away again. O, if I only could! I know something dreadful happened; I remember being frightened, and then I went to sleep; and, when I woke up, Aunt Venus was taking care of me."

"Strange!" said the boy, musingly. "Can't you even remember your old name? What do they call you now?"

"They call me Lizzy," said the child. "Aunt Venus named me; but I can't remember what my other name was. O, I wish I could! I don't believe I was always a servant."

"That's a fact," said the boy, eagerly; "your whole language and appearance tell that you wasn't; and it's a great shame for anybody to keep you so. I'll go straight myself, and talk with Mr. Bell about you; you shall show me the way"—and our young Don Quixote gathered up his reins, valorously, to begin the fight in behalf of this wronged princess; but she stopped him, by saying, earnestly,

"O don't, don't! he will be so angry! The only time he ever scolded us was once when mauma Venus told him she thought I wasn't a nigger. O, he got so mad, it frightened me! and he swore dreadfully, and said, nigger or not, he had bought me, and paid for me, and I belonged to him; and if she put such notions into my head, he'd sell her. O, don't tell him I said anything about it, for I know she'd feel so bad to be sold!"

The boy looked kindly down into the little face that gazed at him so imploringly. He felt strongly tempted to carry her away with him, and place her where she would escape the fate which awaited her; and again his face grew crimson as he thought of what would probably be the fate of one who bid fair to be so surpassingly lovely. But a moment's reflection convinced him of the impracticability of this first impulse of an honest and manly heart.

"It is a great shame," he said; "I wish I could do something for you. Can't you remember anything at all that could tell you who your own friends are? I wish I could find them."

"No, I can't remember," said the child, in a tone of the deepest sadness.

Her new friend sat thinking for a while, and then, remembering that he had yet some miles to travel before night, he said, "Well, then, I suppose I can't do anything about it; but my name is Walter Varian, and I live—really, I don't know exactly where I do live," he added, laughing; "for I have two homes, and just now I am in college; but a letter directed to the care of my uncle, Charles Maynard, Barnwell Courthouse, will reach me. You can write, can't you?"

Ida shook her head.

"Nor read?" added he.

"No; nobody ever taught me. Mass' James don't like his servants to learn such things.[1] He says they a'n't as happy if they do, and he hates to see discontented faces round him."

"Master James is a selfish, hard-hearted villain!" said the boy, with a burst of indignation; "and he ought to be ashamed of himself."

"O, no!" said Ida, "he is very kind to us all. Mauma says he is the kindest massa she ever saw, and it's only because he's *curus*, she says, makes him think that."

"'Curus,' I think!" said Walter Varian. "Well," he added,

---

1 As Walter Varian should know, it was against the law to teach slaves to read and write.

sighing, "I can't stay here any longer. I was going to say, if you ever do remember or find out anything that could enable you to regain your friends, write to me, or get somebody else to write, and I will do all I can to help you. You won't forget my name?"

"O, no, indeed!" replied Ida, eagerly; "I shall *never* forget you; and you have such a pretty name! But see, here are your flowers; you came near forgetting them."

"So I did; thank you," said her friend, placing them securely in his cap. "Now let me see if I haven't something to give you for a keepsake"—and he took from his purse a small gold coin perforated in the middle, and, producing from one of his capacious pockets a black cord, he strung the coin upon it, and hung it over her neck. "There, now, keep that to remember me by," he said, "and give me a kiss for goodbye, you dear little girl, for I must go now. Don't want to?" he added, as she drew back, shyly; "well, then, good-bye without it;" and with a lingering glance over his shoulder at the child who had so interested him, he went on his way down the hill. Ida stood looking after him as long as he remained in sight, still holding in her hand the coin he had given her. She was ignorant of its value, but she was greatly pleased with the gift, and her meeting with this handsome and kind youth seemed to her like a revelation of a new and happier phase of existence. When he was no longer in view, she turned her steps homeward, and before long she met Aunt Venus, who was coming to meet her. Ida ran towards her, eagerly showing the gold piece and relating her adventure; and thus pleasantly conversing they walked, in the growing twilight, up the mountain road.

At one corner of the field, next to the house, stood a large oak, round the trunk of which a circular seat had been constructed, and here the negroes often congregated after their work was finished, as they were returning to their quarters. When Venus and her little friend reached this spot, they sat down a few minutes, to rest, beside a group who were loitering there.

"Ki!" exclaimed a fat, hearty-looking fellow, who at the same moment came up with slow, weary steps, and threw himself at full length on the ground. "Whew! dis nigger am de tired chile! Dis yer fodder-pullin' am de very wust work dey makes a feller do. 'Pears like sometime I'd hab to run away, to get clar ob it."

"Run away! O Lor! dat a'n't sich might easy work n'other; tearin' and scratchin' ober de roots and de thornbushes, wid de dogs ater ye, may be; and starvin on berries and raw fish, or eatin' snakes, may be, and freezin' your feets walkin' in de water, may be, for fear ob leabin' de scent. O, Lor! de a'n't no fun in dat!" said one of his comrades.

"You'se tried it, Bill, may be?" said the first speaker, "yer seems to know how 't feels."

"Maybe I has, den, when I'se on de old plantation 'fore I fell to Massa Bell. O, Lor! wasn't I glad to come in and take it, and hab it ober wid? Better stay where yer is, if yer knows what's what," replied Bill.

"Well," said a fine-looking fellow, who sat astride a rail fence, "I don't want to run away, and I don't complain ob de work; what we has to do here a'n't nothin'—a'n't nothin' 't all. If I only had my wife and de chillen up here, dat lef down in Charleston, I'd be mighty satisfied; but I gets *dat* out o' sorts sometime tinkin' 'bout dem."

"More fool you, den," rejoined Bill. "Fur my part, I'se glad 'nuff my ole woman fell to Mass' James' sister, when ole massa died. I'se had tree wives, and I likes ebery one better. Take anoder wife, Jim, and don't be boderin' 'bout de ole one. Dat's what I did. I'se Mass' James' 'pinion, what he say when I ax him might I take Rosa. He say, 'Dat right, Bill—take all de wives you can get—bariety am de spite ob life.' Dat's what I tinks, de a'n't nothin' like *bariety*, 'specially 'bout women."

"O, get out—you be shame!" said two or three voices, while some others of the group seemed to agreed with Bill's opinion on matrimonial subjects; and one quite young man, rising and laying his hand on his heart, with rather an exaggerated attempt at sentiment, said, as he ogled a pretty mulatto girl who stood near,

"I'se 'zactly ob de 'pinion ob de gentlemen on de fence."

"I'se got my ole woman and de chillen," said another—when the loud laugh which this last speech occasioned had subsided—"and we'se oncommon comfortable on dis plantation, and I wouldn't complain if ony had a chance ob gettin' some larnin'. I allers did want to know how to read, and de write would come mighty handy sometime. If I ony know'd *dem*, 'pears like I wouldn't want nothin' more."

"Ki!" said Bill, "de read and write a'n't no berry easy work, neither. When ole massa live, I tinks once I'd like larn 'em—I'se house sarvent part de time den, so I hab good chance—but, O, Lor! dey's mighty sight harder dan fodder-pullin'—'t wan't no go for dis nigger!"

"Dat cause you so stupid," said the young fellow who had before spoken. "I larn all de letters once, in no time, out ob young Massa James's book."

"O, you shet up when your betters am talkin'!" said Bill. "What *you* know 'bout larnin'? Tell ye it's heap harder 'n fodder-pullin'."

"Now, fur my part," said a middle-aged, sedate-looking man, "I don't. I dono' nothin' 'bout larnin',—not de leastest ting in dis yer world—and don't neber 'spect to; but 'pears like I should like to hab my chillen larn read and write. Dere's my little Pete, now—uncommon smart chap dat Pete—and he want larn readin' *dat* bad; and sometime he get some de buckra chillen larn him little, but Mass' James, when he know it, allers swear he won't have no sich. Say 't a'n't good fur niggers. Now my Pete is *dat* bright it don't seem 'zactly right fur Mass' James say dat. Somehow tings your chillen has to take, 'pears like dey tetch ye more dan tings you has take yourself—and my Pete——"

"O, Lor! what a rungrateful set ob niggers!" interrupted Bill, snapping his fingers till every joint rattled like castanets. "Here you is, wid plenty to eat and drink, and good warm close for winter dat's comin' on, and here ye is grumblin' like yer hadn't no good massa, like Mass' James. Ef you'd only been where I'se been, and seen de holes some niggers lives in, and de cuttings-up dey gets if dey don't work the skin off dere bones—O, Lor! ef you was in some places, ye might grumble. Tell ye what, niggers, ye's dat rungrateful 'pears like ye didn't 'sarve none o' your blessings;" and, jumping on the seat around the tree, he added, with a comical grimace, "Gen'lemen and ladies, we will now close dis meetin' wid singin', after which we will disjourn home, and get supper;" and forthwith he struck up a lively air, embodying it in some incoherent and nonsensical rhymes, with a chorus of vowels and cachinnations[1] oddly jumbled together; in which many of those around him joined, with a zest that showed how easily their mercurial temperament could throw off the weight of discontent; but the older and graver men turned away, with moody faces, and sought their cabins.

The sound of their singing came, softened by distance into a pleasant melody, to the piazza where Mr. Bell and his wife were sitting. The gentleman, who was lolling in an easy chair, with his feet on the railing of the verandah, laid down the paper, which it was now too dark to read, and, after listening a few moments, he said,

"They are having a nice time down there, singing. Who says the negroes a'n't happy and contented!"

---

1 Immoderate laughter.

"Your negroes are happy enough and contented enough," replied Mrs. Bell, "and well they may be. I never saw a man get so little out of a gang of people as you do. Half the number you keep would do all there is to do on this farm, if they were only properly worked; but, there! if you won't have them whipped, you must expect them to be lazy. There never was a nigger yet would work if he could help it."

"My dear," said her spouse, with great good-nature, "the best of folks are mistaken sometimes, and you are so good that you make mistakes very often—at least upon the subject of governing negroes. Why, my love, I *pride* myself upon not being obliged to use the whip. It's a great deal easier and pleasanter to manage them in this way. Those that are good for anything will do twice as much work to be used as I use them, than they will to be driven to death; and, beside, what man would want to be always whipping? Faugh!—it's too brutal. If they won't do their work without that, why, then I'll sell 'em, and let somebody else do it. I want to get along in the world easily, and I mean to."

"Well, you must acknowledge, Mr. Bell," said his lady, "that you have a great many more hands than are necessary, now there are so many children growing up on the place. The fact is, we are literally *swarming*, and we must colonize soon, or we shall be eaten out of house and home. It wouldn't be so bad if you kept 'em in the cheapest possible way, as most persons do; but it really seems to make you nervous if they don't look just so comfortable."

"Well," said Mr. Bell, "I can't be bothered with having them complaining round me; beside, as I said, it *pays* to keep them well."

"Perhaps it does," replied his wife, "where one has only a limited number; but where a place is overrun, as ours it, it is too expensive. In fact, it has come to just this—either you must sell some of them, or your family must go without many things they need. Susy and Mary ought to have an accomplished governess, and it won't be long before Willy ought to begin to fit for college; and where is the money coming from? For my part, I think it is really wicked for you not to provide for your own children."

"I mean to provide for them," said Mr. Bell; "but you see I've held this dread of being sold as a threat over the niggers to make 'em work, and, as I do think they all do about the best they can, I don't fairly like to sell 'em as long as I can avoid it."

"They are good servants," replied the lady. "I was thinking, the other day, it was seldom one saw such an intelligent, good-looking set of people, take them all together, as ours are; but, for that very reason, it is more your duty to sell them, they'll bring so much better price in the market. Besides, what a preposterous idea for a man to think he must give his servants a *reason* for being sold! A'n't they your property? Haven't you a *right* to sell them?"

"To be sure I have," said her husband, and then, after a little pause he added, "I had an offer today for some of them. There's a trader at the tavern below here, who is making up a gang to take south. He bought six off our neighbor Elton. He gave a good price for them, too; negroes are very high just now."

"O, do sell, then!" said his wife, earnestly. "You *must* sell soon, and perhaps the market won't be so good. Come, now, go down tomorrow and make a bargain. It's a shame to have so much money lying dead, as we have on our place."

"As to that matter, I reckon you'll find it anything but *dead* when the time of sale comes. Bless my soul! what a time there'd be! I ache to think of it."

"O, they'll get over it soon! They're all so used to it, they don't mind it much after a few days. 'T isn't as if they were refined and educated, and didn't expect it. They are mere animals."

"Pooh, nonsense!" said Mr. Bell; "you know better than that. I've seen niggers manifest as much feeling as anybody could; but then they *are* mere children, and, as you say, seem to get over everything just as a child forgets its troubles. You seldom hear them say much about anything that's past, if they only get enough to eat and drink at the present moment. Well, perhaps I may as well sell now as any time; prices are so high I shan't have to part with so many, to raise the money I want, as I might at some other seasons."

"I am thankful to hear you talk sensibly for once," replied his wife. "Sell, by all means, now you have a good opportunity. If you don't want to endure the *scenes* there'll be, you can go off somewhere for a little while, after you've made the bargain, and stay a few days, and by the time you get back they will have got over the sulks, I reckon. *I* can stand it well enough. They won't make much fuss where *I am*—they are more afraid of me than they are of you. You are too soft-hearted; *I* ought to have been the *man* in this family."

"Perhaps you do wear the pantaloons," said her husband, laughing. "Well, then, whom shall we sell?"

"I don't care who goes of the field hands," Mrs. Bell replied; "but one thing I'm determined on, and that is, that Aunt Venus's Lizzy shall go."

"What do you want to sell that child for?" said Mr. Bell, in a tone of vexation. "She'll be no use to pick cotton."

"She's no earthly use here, you may make sure," the lady said, in a firm voice, "and the older she grows the lazier she is. There isn't a thing she knows how to do, except dress her hair and rig herself up with flowers. She's the vainest little minx I ever saw, and pert as you please."

"Is she pert?" said Mr. Bell. "I always thought her remarkably gentle and retiring. She has very pretty manners, I'm sure."

"O yes, no doubt you think so!" said Mrs. Bell, mockingly. "I shouldn't in the least wonder if, after a while, you should think as much of her as you did of Ellen! Mr. Bell, you're enough to provoke a saint." There was a flashing in her eye, and a quiver in her voice, that the husband knew too well; and like the "coon," who, upon recognizing the hunter, said, "You needn't fire, I'll come down," Mr. Bell hastened to avert the siege by a conditional surrender.

"Well, my dear," he answered quickly, "I don't care—she shall go. Only I advise you to let Venus go too, for she is getting old, and won't be worth much as a seamstress much longer; and her heart is so set upon Lizzy that she won't be good for much after she's gone. I heard you say the other day that Rose and Milly were very good with the needle. They can take her place well enough."

"I suppose they can. Aunt Venus don't sew as well as she used to; and I think, if her sight is failing, perhaps 't would be as well to sell her. I've always thought," added Mrs. Bell, in a mollified tone, "that I should like to know who that child is. She don't seem like common children."

"She's the child of some poor white, probably," replied Mr. Bell, carelessly; and, after some further conversation, it was settled that, beside these two, Mosley and her children and four of the field hands should be disposed of.

Venus was sitting before the fire in her hut, for it was now the middle of November, and the evenings were chilly. The pine knots cast a cheery glow and warmth over the room, and over the dusky faces that were seated in various positions, more easy than graceful, around the hearth. Lizzy sat on a low bench, with her head resting on her hand, and her eyes fixed dreamily on the fire, apparently unmindful of the conversation which Venus was holding with two of her fellow-servants.

"Did you hear how de fellers was singin' and actin' down by de big tree, tonight?" said Venus, after a little pause had occurred.

"Yes," said Mary. "I goed down to meet Joe, and dere dey was goin' it powerful. Dat yer Bill am de *actingest* nigger!"

"So he be, sure nuff," said Tenah. "Well," she added, with a sigh, "let dem sing as feels like it: fur my share, 't a'n't often I a'n't clare ober on de ober side de fence, and feels more like cryin'."

"O Lor! what de good?" said Mary. "Laughin' 's a heap better 'n crying, any time; and singin' 's better 'n either. 'Pears like singin' lifted de load right up off de heart, and made eberyting go easy. I allers sings when I feels bad."

"I don't den," said Tenah.

"We *is* a light-hearted set—we niggers, dat is de fact," rejoined Venus; "and I'se sure it's a blessin', for de Lord knows what we'd do if we couldn't throw off our stroubles sometimes, and forget 'em like. I 'clare 'fore goodness, I do believe, jist soon as de load's lifted off dere back de leastest mite, de niggers will allers dance and sing like dey hadn't no strouble in de world; but they don't *feel so*, neither."

"No," replied Mary, "dey was grumblin' powerful tonight! What dat?" she added, starting suddenly, as a slight noise at the door attracted the attention of all present.

The latch was lifted noiselessly, and the door, slowly opening revealed first a woolly head, then a face that seemed bursting, not only at the wide-open eyes and mouth, but through every feature and muscle, with astonishment and consternation; and, finally, the lithe form of a young girl glided through the doorway, and closed it behind her.

"Bress my stair!" exclaimed Mary, "what for you come dat way, Bell, stealin' in like you was some kind ob spooks? Most scare a nigger, you did."

Bell, however, took no notice of this exclamation; but, going up to Aunt Venus, and holding up both hands, she said, in a loud whisper,

"O, what you tink, Aunt Venus?—dere's gwine to be a sale!"

"A sale!" cried all three of the women together, clustering around her.

"Yes," replied the girl; "and you'se got to go, Benus—you and Lizzy, fust ob all."

Venus, who had half risen from her chair, sank back like one stunned by a sudden blow, as she heard these words; but instantly, almost involuntarily, she put her arms around Lizzy, who now stood beside her, and clasped her close to her bosom.

"O, you get out, now! You'se just tryin' to scare us! What de good?" said Mary, making a desperate attempt at jocularity.

"I be n't nother," said Bell, earnestly. "Jest as true's de stairs is a shinin' up in de sky dis yer minute, dere gwine to be a sale tomorrow; and I'se layin' down on de mat in de hall, and hear massa and miss talkin' 'bout it, and dey didn't know nobody hear 'em."

"O!" exclaimed Venus, with a groan that seemed to rend her heart. "What on airth has Lizzy and me done did, dat we'se gwine to be sold?"

"Nothin's I hears, ony miss don't like Lizzy, and Mass' James say she shan't be sold or toted off away from you."

"It's one comfort," said Lizzy, timidly, nestling as she spoke still closer to her nurse, "it's one comfort that we can go together."

"'T a'n't no count, honey," replied Venus, weeping, "'t a'n't no manner o' count. Mass' James means well, but when de speckelators gets us, dey won't mind nothin' 'bout sellin' us together. Didn't dey sell my own chillen 'way from me, and dey won't never b'lieve dat you'se anything to me. O Lord! 'pears like I should die, now, to be all broke up and toted off jest when I'se gettin' settled like, and little more comforble!"

"Who else? A'n't nobody else gwine 'cept Benus?" asked Mary, whose mind now recurred to her own danger which she had for a moment forgotten, in her sympathy for Venus.

"O laws! yes," said Bell. "Dere's Mosley and de chillen, and ole Tom, and Tabe, and Jim, and Mose Brown—dat's all."

It would have been a study for a physiognomist[1] to have watched the changing and intense expression with which those two women listened, as this list of the doomed ones was called over; and, when the last name was pronounced, Tenah, throwing up her arms convulsively, gave one prolonged, wailing cry, and sank down to the floor in a fit. Mose Brown was her husband; and she had been, for the last three months, almost frantic with grief for the death of an only child. Her master had hesitated a little, on this account, about selling Mose; but, unfortunately, there were some reasons why it was more convenient to dispose of him than some others; and Mrs. Bell had suggested that "perhaps it would be just as well to divert Tenah from her unreasonable sorrow for the dead, by changing the course of her feelings into another channel, where she might

---

1 Physiognomy was a pseudoscience in vogue in the mid-nineteenth century. A physiognomist was thought to be able to tell the character (and potentially the future) of a person by studying his or her facial features.

more easily be consoled. There were plenty of fellows about, who would do just as well as a husband for her, and she could soon supply the loss."

Mrs. Bell was a fond wife and tender mother, but it never occurred to her, while she spoke these words, that the "nigger" to whom they referred was capable of emotions as intense as any her own heart could feel under the same circumstances.

An hour passed before the wretched woman could recover sufficiently to seek her own cabin; and even then, her feeble steps were supported by Mary and Venus; for Bell, having satisfied the mischievous propensity to tell bad tidings, which seems inherent in some specimens of human nature, had long since gone to talk over the news with less interested companions.

Left alone, at length, in the solitude of her own hut, Venus abandoned herself to the tide of bitter and indignant feeling that swept over her soul. Many hours she sat before the embers on the hearth, crouching down with her face buried in her hands, motionless and silent, save for the deep groans, and the half-uttered ejaculations and prayers that at times escaped her lips. She was a Christian, and through many a severe trial she had trodden with a firm step, upheld by her faith in that which is unseen and eternal; but now in this sudden crush and ruin of all her earthly hopes and comforts, she could no longer hear the "still small voice" of the divine Comforter, and an evil spirit seemed mocking her wild prayers and tempting her to despair.

She had known deeper grief, keener heart-pangs, than those to which this change of life exposed her, but never a more severe disappointment. After her separation from her early friend—her adored Miss Lizzy—she had passed into the hands of stern men, who ignored the rights and were careless of the sufferings of their servants; and hard indeed was her bondage to them, toiling from early morning till late at night, to be repaid by the cold, miserable hovel in which she lived, the scanty clothing and insufficient food which was all that her best services could obtain; and often receiving, in case of failure, harsh words, curses and blows. After some years she had "taken" another husband, induced thereto partly by the incessant importunities, commands, and even threats, of her master, who wished her to be as profitable to him as possible, and insisted that a young healthy woman, like her, ought to be raising a family of children; and partly by the vain hope that new family cares and joys might hush that ceaseless cry of her heart after its lost ones. In this hope she was woefully disappointed. Her second choice was a worthless, drunken fellow; and though he had courted her assiduously, and hidden his vices from her sight until she became his wife, he threw off all disguise from that day, and seemed to delight to abuse and insult her to the extent of his power. Death at last came to release her from this tyranny; for a little while she enjoyed the strange quiet of her wretched hut, and busied herself in giving what care she could to her only child, a bright and active little boy, who seemed to strive to please and comfort, as much as his father had striven to oppress her. But he was not, like her first children, "beloved for the father's sake;" and though she grieved at leaving him when she was sold to Mr. Bell, it was not with that agonizing sorrow which even now, after the lapse of years, was awakened by the thought of those who had first claimed from her a mother's love and care.

These dark passages of her life made the light tasks, the comfortable home, and the quiet seclusion of her lot, since she had lived at the Bell plantation, seem like a paradise. Especially since Ida had come to nestle in her heart, and gladden that humble dwelling with the sunshine of her beauty, the toil-worn and long-harassed woman had dared to indulge in visions of peace and contentment, and of a quiet and happy old age. But now to be turned out from this pleasant place, and to leave a kind master, for the wearing labor of a rice or sugar plantation and the cruel tyranny of a heartless overseer! O, it was hard to understand how it could be right for the arbitrary will of another to subject her to this trial!—it was dreadful to feel how perfectly helpless she was, how vain must be all her struggles, how hopeless all appeal from the power that crushed her!

These and many more thoughts passed through the mind of Aunt Venus, as she sat there in the cold, dark midnight hour. Every wrong and evil she had borne, every joy she had lost, every friend she had parted from, came before her, till her brain reeled beneath the fearful excitement; but yet it seemed to her that she could have endured it all, if she could have been sure that her adopted child, the pride and darling of her heart, would continue as she had been, safe and happy, and free from any except the minor evils of her servile condition. She listened to the child's soft, low breathing, as she slumbered on the bed near her, and she thought of the probable separation that awaited them; and her whole frame quivered and shrank together as she remembered things she had known in the past, and her fancy pictured the scenes of suffering, insult, degradation and sin, which that innocent and delicate creature would be forced to undergo.

With the early dawn of morning, Ida woke from the sweet

sleep in which, for a while, she had lost the memory of sorrow. Her first thought was for the kind friend who usually lay beside her at that hour; but she was not there, and, raising herself on her elbow, she discovered Venus just rising from the floor, where her weary senses had at length found repose.

"Why, mauma," she said, "have you been sleeping there all night on those hard boards?"

"De boards is good enough, honey, for the like o' me," replied Venus, sadly; "if I on'y know'd I'd allers see you when I wake up in de mornin', I wouldn't mind sleepin' dere. Dere's things *harder 'n boards.*"

"O, mauma, don't be so sad!" said the child. "Perhaps we shall be just as well off, and I almost *know* we shall be sold together."

Venus shook her head despondingly. "Think so while ye can, honey," she said. "You dono' nothin' 'bout it, not de leastest mite in de world, and I a'n't gwine tell ye 'fore de strouble come. For my part, I don't 'spect nothin' good. I'se jist done made up my mind neber to be happy no more till de day I die."

Nothing more was said, for her words checked the child's hopefulness, and she knew not what consolation to offer. When their short and simple toilet was completed, Venus opened the shutters, and Ida, throwing open the door, let in the cool, sweet, morning air, and the golden light that, streaming up from behind the trees, gave bright token of the coming day.

"Dere's de sun gwine shine dis day, jist like he allers does," said Venus, moodily, as she came and stood outside the door with Ida. "I can't 'stand nothin' 'bout it, how de sun can shine ebery day right on, jist de same; never no hotter nor no colder, like it was dat onfeelin' it neber saw none o' de hateful things it looks at wid its great starin' eye. If *I* was de sun, wouldn't I come down wid great hot sunstroke, clap! down onto some peoples I'se seen, and kill 'em dead? But, laws! I'se an ole fool, and 't a'n't no 'count to de sun; and I'se an ole wicked sinner, too, and I hopes 'fore goodness de Lord 'll forgive me for wishin' folks was dead, and where dey couldn't bother niggers no longer, for 'pears like 't a'n't no better 'n murder I'se doin'. Well," she added, with a long sigh, "I'se *dat* wicked, I knows, but p'raps de good Lord won't be so hard onto us as de white folks is, and 'll let us off, if we *don't* mind every minute. De Lord dat merciful, honey, de good book say, like a father wid his little chillen. 'Pears like 't would be great comfort in dese times, when de debil come up so strong, if I could read dem words my own self. If I could on'y know de Lord orders eberything, 'pears like 't would be easier to bear dese yer things; but 'pears like somehow de Lord didn't have nothin' to do wid it, and den I feels *dat* savage!"

While she had been speaking, Aunt Venus had taken a knife, and, standing on a high block of wood, she had been digging the clay, which had at some former time been pressed tightly into an irregular hole, far up the trunk of the walnut-tree that stood beside the door. This mysterious proceeding had arrested Ida's attention to that degree that she hardly listened to what Venus was saying, and at this moment she interrupted her by exclaiming, "Do tell me, mauma, what you are doing to the tree!"

"Dis yer is my closet where I locks up things," replied Venus, "You know, honey, I a'n't got no trunk wid a lock onto it, so when I wants to keep things hid safe, I put 'em in some hole like dis, and plasters 'em up wid clay."

"What's in there?" asked Ida.

"You'll see in a minute, honey," replied her friend.

But the minute was rather long, for the bark had grown over the opening a little, and it was some time before Venus could manage to extract from her "closet" a small tin box, closely covered, which she opened with some difficulty, and disclosed to Ida's eyes what seemed to be a piece of old linen, compactly rolled together.

"What in the world is it?" said Ida with great curiosity.

"It b'longs to you, honey," replied Venus, as she proceeded to unroll it; "it's de on'y thing left dat you had on when you was took away, and toted down here. Now we'se gwine to be driv off south, you must take it, and take care of it yourself."

It was the upper part of a child's linen shirt, finely worked around the neck, and bordered around the sleeves with thread lace. "Is it mine? was it on me? where's the rest of it?" asked the child eagerly, with flushed cheek and hurried breath.

"Dere wasn't no more of it, honey, neber. De rest was all in rags, where it had got tore wid yer knockin' round, when ye was sick, 'fore yer come here; so I cut it off. Yer know, honey, I telled yer what a sick little creatur yer was, and how ye was dressed like a boy when I see yer. Well, when I took ye down here I took some water to wash ye, fust thing, 'cause yer was *dat* dirty, and, laws bless me! how I did jump when I find *de black wash off!* Well, den, I has my 'flections on de subject, all the time I'se undressin' yer, and when I come to take off *dis* thing last, and see how nice 't was through all de dirt, and de stain dat was on it where de rapscal done painted yer neck, to make it like you was black baby; 'specially after I see de lace 't was round it, den I say, 'Sure 'nuff, dis a'n't no nigger, nor no poor buckra child neither. Dis yer poor baby must b'long to somebody dat'll cry powerful a'ter her.' O honey, den I cry myself, to think o' your poor mammy dat had her baby stole, and toted 'way from her."

"O, Venus," said the chid, with quivering lips, while her large eyes slowly filled with tears, "you don't know how you make me feel! Can't you tell me more? Is this all you know?"

"Yes, honey," replied Venus, sorrowfully, "dat all I know, *ebery rag.*"

Ida continued wistfully turning over this relic of the past, examining the pattern of the lace, and lingering fondly over the faint traces of a leaf, with stems and small flowers delicately drawn in indelible ink; for Mrs. May, in an idle moment, had thus fancifully adorned the front of the garment which her own fair hands had made.

"What a funny little picture this is!" she said at length.

"Yes, honey; dere's where some white folks write de name, but 'pears like de wasn't any name here, on'y a picter."

And again the two examined closely this spot on which their attention was fixed; but, to their unpracticed eyes, the name, which was written in minute characters, in the centre of the leaf, seemed not unlike the other lines that shaded it.

When Ida was satisfied with looking at it, Venus took it from her, and, enclosing it in a small piece of black silk, which she had picked up somewhere, attached it firmly to the cord by which the precious gold coin was hanging, round Ida's neck. "Dere now, honey," she said, "hide dat, hide *both* ob 'em, and don't neber be lookin' at 'em where nobody is, nor showin' 'em, nor talkin' 'bout 'em to nobody, for if you do you'll lose 'em. Niggers will steal 'em, 'cause dey wants de gold, and white folks a'n't no better 'n niggers sometimes; and don't never show 'em to your massa or missis, 'cause dey'd take 'em in a minute, for fear of its telling you wasn't no nigger, and so gettin' away somehow. Some of 'em's good, I knows, but I'se noticed somehow de bery best ob 'em when dey's bought a nigger and paid for him, 'pears like dey couldn't *bear* to tell 'em go, *nohow*. I wouldn't trust no massa; but some time, if you find somebody else dat's kind to yer, and speaks pleasant, like dat young gen'leman did last night, den you jest show 'em dis yer piece ob rag, and tell 'em how you had it on, and old Benus saved it for you, and den see what dey say 'bout it.

I dono', but it's 'vealed into me[1] dat dis yer rag will be de mean o' findin' yer friends and 'lations for ye, when yer poor ole mauma's sold away off from yer."

"O, mauma, don't, don't! I can't live without you!" exclaimed the child, throwing herself on that faithful bosom, with a burst of tears, as these parting instructions caused every other emotion to vanish in the vivid fears they aroused, that she was indeed about to lose her only friend.

---

1 "I don't know but it has been revealed unto me": Venus uses biblical language and cites divine revelation in her vision of Ida's future redemption.

CHAPTER VII

"All things are weighed in custom's falsest scale,
Opinion is omnipotence, whose veil
Mantles the earth with darkness, until right
And wrong are accidents, and men grow pale
Lest their own judgments should become too bright,
And their free thoughts be crimes, and earth have too much
light."
CHILDE HAROLD[1]

The plantation of Richard Wynn, Esq., was situated *somewhere* in the green and beautiful Palmetto State.[2] After passing for some miles along the flat and sandy road, the traveler was gladdened by the neat white gateway, shaded by a splendid magnolia, that opened into a broad avenue, curving away to the south, leading toward the house which gleamed white in the distance through its embowering trees. On the other side of the gate lay the plantation, acre upon acre, stretching far away, the dead level unbroken by a single fence or tree.

A southern planter once said to a traveler, "I can't conceive how you invest your money at the north. *Here* a man's riches consist in lands and niggers." Thus, over the vast space we have described, were scattered in rows and groups, the other available property of this rich man—creatures to be bought and sold, and worked and whipped, and treated in all respects as animals in which property has been invested. As the eye rests on them, one feels tempted to exclaim with Macbeth,

"What are these,
So wretched, and so wild in their attire,
That look not like inhabitants of earth,
And yet are of it?"[3]

---

1 From George Gordon, Lord Byron (1788–1824), *Childe Harold's Pilgrimage* (1818), Canto IV, stanza 93.

2 The italics make clear that Pike does not intend to disclose the whereabouts of the likely fictional Wynn Hall plantation; however, the "traveler" in the next sentence may well be the author herself during her extended stay in Aiken, South Carolina, in 1844.

3 Banquo to Macbeth, 1.3.39–42. Pike changes the adjective from "withered" to "wretched," and revises "on it" to "of it."

See the heaps of coarse and dirty rags that cover them, or flutter about in the wind, as if they were so many animated scarecrows. Perhaps they lift their eyes a moment to gaze at you, but they pause not in their monotonous toil; for, sitting on horseback at a little distance, armed with his long whip, they know the overseer is watching them, and he is quick to mark any idleness, and they fear the penalty if their daily task be not accomplished. These creatures are not the sleek, careless, intelligent negroes of story and song. Disgustingly filthy and squalid in their attire, their faces have only a sullen, idiotic expression, and, though they are not emaciated, their skin seems hard, and flabby, and wrinkled, as if the juices of their bodies had been dried up by the corn meal on which they are fed. If you should visit that row of whitewashed huts, under the trees, half a mile distant, you would see no gardens around them, no poultry crowding the doors, for Mr. Wynn never interferes with the government of his overseer; and the overseer is a shrewd, thrifty man, who will allow the negroes no such excuses for neglecting their work. All the strength they have to labor they owe to the master who has bought and paid for it at the highest market price; and all the time they spend in care for themselves is so much stolen from him. And as for the negroes, they have plenty of corn to eat, and they may sleep as soundly as they please from late in the evening till dawn, and they have two suits of strong clothes a year, which *ought* to keep them comfortable, and if they will be careless and improvident they ought to suffer from want, but their masters must not be blamed. And, indeed, who shall in any way blame Mr. Wynn's trusty and well managing overseer? If one of the wealthiest men in the state can, with impunity, starve his negroes nearly to death, in an economical attempt to feed them on cotton-seed,[1] and if the governor habitually disregards the law that provides to each negro four pounds of meat weekly, and only

---

1   Pike cites Theodore Weld's *American Slavery as It Is*
    (1839), Chapter 1: Food. General Wade Hampton, a wealthy
    Charlestonian, "undertook to entertain the company with the
    relation of an experiment he had made in the feeding of his slaves
    on cotton seed. He said that he first mingled one-fourth cotton
    seed with three-fourths corn, on which they seemed to thrive
    tolerably well; that he then had measured out to them equal
    quantities of each, which did not seem to produce any important
    change; afterwards he increased the quantity of cotton seed to ·
    three-fourths, mingled with one-fourth corn, and then he declared,
    with an oath, that 'they died like rotten sheep!!'"

allows them meat during the festivities of the Christmas holidays,[1] who can expect public opinion to lean so far towards benevolence and indulgence, that its voice shall call upon any merely private individual to recognize his negroes as carnivorous animals—especially while bacon is growing higher in the market every year?

But, leaving these wretched beings, whose present condition and whose future fate, both as regards themselves and their country, it is alike painful to contemplate, let us proceed along the avenue towards the spacious and elegant family mansion. How cool and pleasant is the shade of the lofty trees on either side, and how gracefully their trunks and branches are overgrown and festooned with the wild rose—now past the season of its blossoming—the ivy and the bullace vines, whose ripe berries gleam amid their green leaves! Passing the end of the house, where they have attempted to atone for the inhospitable southern custom of turning the chimney out of doors, by covering it with running roses, some of which have climbed even to the roof, we follow the sudden sweep of the path round the corner, and find ourselves in front of a large building, two stories high, and shaded above and below by a double piazza, which surrounds it on three sides. At the further end, but hidden from view by a high, vine-covered lattice, are the kitchen and other buildings that make up the domestic *ménage* of a wealthy southerner, and from the front piazza the land slopes gently, covered with its primitive growth of the lofty pines, beneath whose shadow may be seen, here and there, a specimen of the Black Jack—a kind of dwarf oak, whose smooth shining leaves, just putting on their autumn livery of golden brown, deserve a more dignified appellation.

The season was now far advanced; the sultry heats of summer had given place to that delightful temperature when the mild sunshine and the delicious airs seem to woo man to a perpetual holiday, and make the simple sensation of life a luxury. The smoldering embers in the fireplace showed that the early morning had been cool; but the windows and doors were all open, and idly lounging on the "jiggling-board,"[2] that stood upon the

---

1   James Henry Hammond, Governor of South Carolina from 1842 to 1844, gave a speech in 1850 defending the parsimonious diet of his 300 slaves.

2   Pike refers to an iconic piece of outdoor furniture local to Charleston, South Carolina, known as a "joggling board." This long, thin bench, suspended between two posts with rockers at the base, bends and jiggles in the middle when sat upon.

piazza at the end of the house, might at this hour have been seen the form of Walter Varian. In fact, he *was* seen by all who were near enough to see him; for, though it must be confessed he was *lounging*, there was about the boy a restless activity, both of mind and body, that made itself manifest wherever he might be, and seldom allowed his tongue or his limbs to remain so long quiet that anyone could become oblivious of his presence. And few would object to this consciousness; for there was such a bright and genial air about him, such a nobleness in his lithe form and his irregular but handsome features, such a fearless light in his clear brown eyes, such kindly independence in his firm voice and his ringing laugh, and such careless grace in his movements, and even in the waving of his soft, luxuriant chestnut hair, which was never smooth for five consecutive minutes during his whole life, that Walter Varian's presence was like sunshine in any house, carrying life and animation wherever he went.

Near him, just inside the window, where the sunlight, which was flickering down on the piazza through sprays of rose-leaves and vines that shadowed it, might not fall too *frowningly* on her fair face, sat his cousin, Mabel Wynn. She was at this time just entering the "teens;" and though girls at that age are usually in the transition stage, when hair that has always hung down revenges itself for being turned up and imprisoned in combs, by making the neck seem long and ungraceful, and the shoulders high, and when hands and feet are useless encumbrances, which it is distressing to be obliged to take care of in company, still the heiress of Wynn Hall, conscious of beauty and wealth, carried her haughty little head as high, and moved with as much grace, as one could desire to see. She was, indeed, very beautiful, with features of faultless symmetry, eyes of the deepest and most celestial blue, fringed by long, dark lashes; and the broad mazarine blue ribbons, that fastened the silken braids of her light hair, served to set off the alabaster[1] purity of her complexion. She was dressed in a light plaid silk, that left bare her snow-white neck and arms; and, as she leaned back in the depths of a large easy-chair, her delicate hands were idly playing with, and pulling to pieces, a large bouquet of late-blooming roses.

"See there, now, how you are tearing the flowers I took so much pains to gather and arrange for you this morning!" said Walter, as he saw her employment.

---

1 A fine-grained translucent white gypsum used in European homes for ornamental sculpture.

"Well, I have nothing else to do," replied the little lady, with a slight toss of her head; "and roses are not so great a rarity that I should be so very choice of them."

"Roses! no indeed; but to think that *my gift* should be ranked with common flowers! Beside, see what a heap of them you are scattering on the floor," added he, with a little confusion at the smile that curled the lip of his uncle, who heard his attempt at gallantry.

"O, that makes no matter!" replied Mabel; "Rose can sweep them up again; she has nothing else to do. But I thought you and Uncle Charles were going shooting this morning."

"So we are, if he ever gets ready. He went some time ago to order a lunch before we started, but neither Charles nor the lunch seems to be forthcoming. O, I mistake! Please consider that last sentence retracted, taken back, never uttered, for, lo! in the distance I see Alfred approaching—Alfred the Great—and, behold, he beareth cakes that are *not* burnt,[1] and wine that maketh glad the heart of man, and bread the staff of life, and bacon which in this southern country may be called the terra firma on which that staff is supposed to rest. Come, Alfred, draw the little table out here, and set your waiter[2] down, and then go tell Master Charles that his presence is requested on the south piazza."

These last words were addressed to a tall, handsome mulatto boy, whose intelligent, good-natured face and neat attire at once prepossessed the beholder in his favor.

"Yes, Mass' Walter," he said with a smile, as he proceeded to do as he was told, "Mass' Charles wouldn't let me clean the gun, and he say he be done cleaning himself by 'leven, but the clock done struck 'leven some time ago, and he hard at work yet."

"Go tell him the luncheon is waiting to be eaten, and the partridges are waiting to be shot, and, what is more important than all, *I* am waiting, though neither to be shot nor eaten," replied Walter, laughing; "and say to him, also, it is my humble opinion that if he spends all day in cleaning his gun, it will be dark before he will be able to use it."

---

1 Allusion to a legend about the English king Alfred the Great (849–99). When fleeing a Viking invasion, Alfred took refuge in the home of a peasant woman, who did not recognize him. She asked him to watch cakes she had cooking in the fire. Distracted by affairs of state, Alfred let the cakes burn and was scolded for his negligence.

2 A small tray.

Alfred gave a quick glance of intelligence and affection at the pleasant face that was turned towards him, and withdrew noiselessly, to carry the message. The smile faded from Walter's lips as he looked after him, and he said carelessly, as he turned again to his cousin,

"Alfred is a handsome, bright-looking fellow. It's almost a pity he isn't going to be a *man* when he grows up."

Mabel lifted her head, and opened her large eyes in a kind of wonder. "What in the world *will* he be, if he isn't a *man?*" she said.

"O, a chattel personal, a *boy,* an animal—anything else you please, but never a *man.* Old Homer says,

'Whatever day
Makes a man a slave, takes half his worth away;'[1]

And it is true now as in the days of the glorious old Greek, that a slave can never be a *man.*"

"You should have given that quotation in the original; it would have sounded more *learned,*" said Mabel's father, scornfully, without looking up from his book; and Mabel herself replied, with a pretty indignation,

"I don't think Alfred would thank you, if he heard you calling him *that.* If you could only know how fond he is of us all, and so proud of belonging to our family! It is really laughable to see the scorn with which they all look down on a family of free negroes in the neighborhood. Beside, you have no right to call them such names as you have whenever you have spoken about them since you came back; papa says that isn't the proper term at all. They are servants—servants held to labor—that's what they are called in the constitution of the United States, and that's what they are; and it's only the vulgar Yankees that call them anything else." And the girl sank back in her chair, and folded her hands, as if she had settled the question, and there was no appeal from her decision.

But Walter replied, with more irreverent nonchalance, as he carved the bacon, "Because they are not called by the right name in the constitution, is no reason why I should not use the right

---

1 *The Odyssey,* Book 17. Thomas Jefferson (1743–1826) used this quotation in his discussion of race and slavery in *Notes on the State of Virginia* (1785), and added this comment: "But the slaves of which Homer speaks were whites." Pike was possibly considering this distinction when she placed this unlikely conversation here.

term in speaking of them. They *are* slaves, and what's the use of mincing the matter? If a man isn't free—if he don't own his wife, or his children, or even his own hands and feet—he's a *slave*; and that's quite a different thing from simply being a servant."

"Free, indeed!" replied Mabel, her ruby lip curling in great scorn;—"how ridiculously you talk, Cousin Walter! How fine it would be to send off the plantation people into the free States! They don't know how to take care of themselves a day, and as for the house servants, they wouldn't be free if they could—you may ask any of them."

"Ask *them*!" replied Walter. "That would be equal to the farce of taking Daniel Webster[1] to a certain plantation, where everything had been prepared beforehand, and telling him he might ask any questions he pleased, and find out for himself just how the negroes were treated. There isn't a mother's son among them but has wit enough to know what answer to make to anybody his *master* allows to question him."

"What an absurd, vulgar manner you have acquired of talking on this subject!" said Mr. Wynn, laying down his book, and drawing his chair nearer to the window, as he saw his daughter was at a loss for a reply. "One would think you were some ignorant northern abolitionist, instead of having been born and raised at the south, and well acquainted with our domestic institution from your infancy."

"Your pardon, uncle; but it is we, who are born and raised among servants, that are ignorant, and not the northern abolitionists. I dare affirm, that a person who sat down intelligently to think what human nature is, and who remembers how, throughout all history, unlimited power has always been abused, and who reflects on the degradation and deceit of the one class, and the pride, and impatience, and evil passions, that may with impunity be exercised by the other class—I say, such a man, if he had never seen or heard of a slave, would have a more correct idea of what slavery must be, than the most of those who are educated to believe themselves born to a state of society that *must* continue, and accepting it as it is, to see, and hear, and know as little about it as possible."

Mr. Wynn had been fidgeting in his chair, with difficulty re-

---

1 Celebrated statesman and orator (1782–1852). A powerful senator from Massachusetts, Webster helped to broker the Compromise of 1850, a package of congressional bills intended to avert a civil war over the issues of slavery and states' rights.

fraining from interrupting his nephew. Now, however, he broke out in a tone of scornful anger:

"O, yes! no doubt you *dare affirm* a great many other things on the subject as foolish as this last wild proposition has been; but I beg you won't make my house the scene of such nonsense."

"I will not insist upon offensive epithets," said Walter; "but pray, uncle, allow me, before you seal my lips in silence, to tell you how it happens that I, born and raised among servants, as you say, have so suddenly changed my sentiments in regard to them; and if I am wrong, do convince me of it, for I assure you I find my present feelings most uncomfortably at war with my pecuniary interests. In truth, when I first went to college, I was the most surprised and indignant youth alive, at the stories poured into my ears respecting the relation between master and servant—horrible stories of cruelty and tyranny, such as it would make your blood run cold to hear. But to my surprise I found, after the strictest inquiry, that, as far as human evidence can establish anything, the most of these stories were *facts*—yes, and some of them had occurred in this very State, but I had never heard of them before. Then I insisted that these were but isolated instances, and that the great majority of masters were kind, and the servants generally perfectly contented and happy; and to this there came a reply drawn from the sensitiveness of the whole south in regard to this subject;—the anger with which we repel the slightest injury into our domestic management; the care we take that our servants should not converse with strangers, either those of their own color or white men, or even talk with our own neighbors about home affairs; the vigilance committees we establish, and the strictness of our laws, and the insult and even personal injury which those have experienced to whom suspicion has attached of coming among us with sentiments inimical to our beloved 'institution.' One day, in a general conversation, a man said to me, 'It is not possible that such a state of things should be, if you did not all know that this is a magazine that must not be entered with a lighted lamp. Depend upon it, my dear fellow,' said he, 'if there was not something everywhere to conceal, there would be somebody who would be willing to come to the light; and, though I have no doubt you are ignorant of it, there have probably events happened in your home neighborhood, or perhaps on your own plantation, that would not read well in a newspaper, even with the fairest construction. I mean no offense,' he continued, 'but human nature is the same everywhere, and though there are noble exceptions in which *man* is better than human nature, generally speaking tyranny is and must be the result of unlimited power; and, for my part, I don't see why you don't acknowledge it. I could never understand,' said he, 'why southerners, who are determined to keep their slaves, and make the best of it, don't say right out that they make stringent laws because they are afraid to give the negroes the least liberty, lest there should be an insurrection; and they will not have them talked to by strangers, because they don't wish them to get an idea that anybody regards them otherwise than as slaves, lest it should increase their present discontent. This would at least command respect. But it is an insult to common sense to be told the negroes are perfectly content and happy, and well treated, and yet forbidden to have anything to say to them upon their own condition.'"

"The insolent Yankee!" exclaimed Mabel, with flashing eyes; "why didn't you shoot him, Walter, on the spot?"

"I did try to," replied her cousin, half laughing, and with heightened color in his cheek. "That is, I was angry enough to do it; and, taking the best means I then knew to revenge the insult I thought I had received, I sent him a challenge."

"You did! Did he accept it?" asked Mabel, leaning forward with great interest and pride in her cousin.

"No; he meant nothing personal—he was only talking. But I was unused to free discussion; we haven't much of it down here, you know," he added, with a sly, momentary glance at his uncle.

"But how could he refuse a *challenge*?" said Mabel. "The coward! I supposed he didn't dare fight!"

"Not so fast, coz—he was no coward. I had always liked him before that, and he is a splendid fellow; you would like him your-self, if you knew him;—he ranks 'number one' in the class."

"He was a coward, for all that, if he wouldn't fight," replied Mabel; "and it's strange you don't think so. I hope, at least, you horsewhipped him—the poltroon!"[1]

"I am sorry to disappoint your ladyship," said Walter, smil-ing; "but though, regardless of Dr. Watt's advice, I let my 'angry passions rise,'[2] he was as cool as the coldest ice-cream you ever tasted, and as sweet, and proved as efficacious in cooling the fe-ver of my blood. You will laugh when I tell you how he answered my challenge. It was not ten minutes after I had sent it, before

1 Coward.
2 From a hymn for children, "Let dogs delight to bark and bite," by British hymnist and poet Isaac Watts (1674–1748).

George Hunter himself—the very man against whom I had been breathing out slaughter—entered the room."

"Was it George Hunter, the friend you have been writing about so enthusiastically for the last year?" exclaimed Mabel.

"The very same," replied Walter. "He came in, and walked straight up to the side of the table against which I was leaning with both elbows, and, speaking in a pleasant and yet dignified tone—for he has a great deal of dignity—he said, 'I am sorry, Varian, that you should have thought I meant to insult you in my remarks this morning.'—'That is nothing here or there,' said I, fierce as a turkey-cock; 'I did think you meant to insult me, and I still think so, and now the question between us had better be left to others. I have sent my friend to your room, and I suppose you have referred him to yours,' I added pointedly. He smiled a little. He was some years older than I, and I know must have been a little amused at my vehemence," added Walter, to whom the year that had elapsed since the time referred to had brought so much wisdom and knowledge that he was able to smile at his boyish folly.

"He had no right to laugh at you," said Mabel. "I don't see how you could bear it, after his other insult."

"O, he didn't laugh at me; he was perfectly respectful," replied Walter; "and there was something in his manner that calmed me in spite of myself. For a moment, he did not answer me, and then he said that he had rather peculiar notions about fighting. If I insisted upon it, he would try to give me all the satisfaction it would afford me to shoot at him, but he had not the least desire to shoot me, so that it was not at all necessary for him to consult any friend upon the subject. Well, this was rather a novel way of putting it, and I was a little puzzled what to say, for I had been with him in the shooting-gallery, and I knew he was a better shot than I was—so the advantage was on his side if he had chosen to fight. As I did not answer, he went on to say that he might be mistaken about it, but it seemed to him quite likely I could talk with him upon the subject in dispute as rationally and satisfactorily with my own lips as through the mouth of a pistol, and he was sure my arguments would be quite as well received; and though knock-down arguments were some times conclusive, he hardly thought the fact of having shot at him would be admitted in the debating-club as proof that I was right and he was wrong. Well, you know I am good-natured enough when the first flash is over; and there was no great need of a quarrel, after all, for I couldn't help owning to myself that he had as much right to his opinion as I had to mine; and so we talked a while, and then shook hands upon it, and have been good friends ever since."

"That is a pretty story you have been telling!" said Mr. Wynn, in a tone of careless scorn. "I don't wonder, after hearing such a confession, that you are not ashamed to have adopted that young man's opinions."

Walter bit his lip, and cast down his eyes a moment. He had a habit of blushing when strongly excited, and now his cheek and brow were flooded with the crimson tide that welled up from his loudly throbbing heart, for he was just at the age when the imputation of cowardice is felt deeply, and those taunting words had wounded. "I did not adopt his opinions," he said firmly, after a little pause, "until I had become convinced that, on most subjects, he judged rightly, and I think, when thus convinced, I showed full as much wisdom in adopting them as I should if I had murdered him for differing from me."

At this retort Mabel gave a start, and a half-frightened glance towards her father, for he was a man to whose reproofs his family were not accustomed to hear bold replies. A quiet and scholarly gentleman, spending most of his waking hours in his library, he could, when he chose, be delightfully gracious, and even, at times, familiar with those around him; but let anything happen to offend him, and he was positively awful. He did not *say* much, but he used immediately to retire behind his spectacles, and through them, as through the embrasure of a fortress, he sent such glances as were more powerful than any argument in silencing and confounding the daring rebel, or the rash opponent. He was a very tall, angular-looking man, and his German descent might be traced in his large bones, his firmly-set jaw, which a long thin red beard covered, as with a fiery halo—his square face, light hair and light blue eyes; but every peculiarity of form or feature as lost to one who endured that stony gaze, and all his six-feet altitude seemed covered and concealed by those spectacles, behind which he had impregnably entrenched himself. The story of the Gorgon was no longer a myth to the unfortunate offender in such times;[1] and self-possessed, indeed, must he be who could retain the power of speech, or remember what he wished to say, many moments after those cold eyes had assumed that peculiar and fixed expression.

But Walter was now aroused, and, secure in his consciousness

---

1 The three Gorgon sisters (the best known is Medusa) had the power to turn to stone anyone who looked directly at them.

of right, he found himself on this occasion, almost to his own surprise, enduring, unmoved, the petrifying glance that was now bent upon him. Turning to Mabel, he said calmly, and with a secret delight at thus defying the relative whom he had always feared, rather than loved, "To return from this digression, it was in consequence of what I heard at the north, from sober and sensible men, that I determined to open my eyes and see for myself. Last year I was prevented by that fever I went through with; but this year I carried out my intention as far as possible, which, to be sure, is not very far, for all imaginable impediments and deceits are thrown in the way of an impartial inquirer. I made the tour on horseback that I might be able to diverge into the byways and small towns; but I often met with suspicion, and sometimes almost with insult. It was decidedly the 'pursuit of knowledge under difficulty;'[1] and once it was only by being able to satisfy the hotel-keeper that I was a Carolinian, and had the honor to be connected with the Wynn family, that I escaped being ordered out of town, as the penalty of my imprudence."

"Served you right, too," said Mr. Charles Maynard, who had joined them in time to hear Walter's last remark, and saw, by a glance at the face of his brother-in-law, how matters stood. "Served you right, Sir Spyall," he repeated pleasantly, as he seated himself before the table, where stood the untasted luncheon, and then, half turning to Mr. Wynn, he added, with a comical twist of his features, "We mustn't be too severe on him, though, brother Richard. You know he's *young*."

"He's old enough to know better than to talk such arrant nonsense," replied Mr. Wynn, gruffly.

"O, young men of his temperament always pass through a fever of enthusiasm! It is a necessity of their nature, as much as the measles, or the chicken-pox. He'll get over it; there's nothing like age and experience, and, above all, some personal interest in having the established order of things continue, to reconcile a man to the existing mode of life. He'll be a violent conservative, as soon as he gets hold of the plantation at Oaklands; see if you don't sir!" he added, nodding with twinkling eyes at his nephew.

"It may be so," replied Walter, good-naturedly, "but I don't

---

1 Proverbial phrase taken from the title of a book by George Lillie Craik (1798–1866), a Scottish writer and literary critic. *The Pursuit of Knowledge under Difficulties* was first published in 1831, and revised and enlarged editions appeared in subsequent decades.

believe I shall change my sentiments on this subject if I live to be as old and gray as the most venerable rat about the premises."

"Well, come now, eat your luncheon," said Mr. Maynard, "or those partridges will get tired of waiting, and fly off before we get ready to shoot them. You've lost an hour here now."

"*I've* lost it?" replied Walter, laughing; "I was waiting for you. Now we are on the subject, I just want to tell you one thing, to show how ignorant the whites are of the manner in which the negroes are treated, even in their immediate neighborhood, or else how shamefully they will lie about it. I had been told, everywhere through Virginia, that *whipping* was an almost unheard-of thing; and at last one man told me that he hadn't known of a nigger being tied up and whipped for ten years, anywhere about there. Well, the next day I had a good chance to examine the whipping-post in that very town, and just for curiosity I touched it with my fingers, and instead of being dry ash rusty as they would have been if unused for any length of time, the irons, where the wrists are fastened, and the front of the post where the body presses, were all smooth and greasy with the sweat and fat of the poor fellows."

"Ugh!" exclaimed Mabel, with an expression of disgust, "how can you say such things? How horribly vulgar!"

"How horribly wrong!" rejoined Mr. Maynard, half seriously and half in fun. "Why, Walter, you've come to be a second edition of Paul Pry,[1] enlarged, if not improved. What right have you to poke your sacrilegious fingers into the bleeding wounds of your country, and tear them open in this way? Don't you know you are endangering the Union? Eat your luncheon, boy, and don't get puffed up with the idea that you were born to correct all the abuses in Christendom, for I don't believe you have any such mission. Eat your luncheon, and then acknowledge that you never thought of being so philanthropic till you fell in love with that pretty little girl on the mountain."

"What nonsense!" said Walter. "But she was a little beauty, and I say, it's a shame—"

"Hush now! No more of that," interrupted Mr. Maynard, throwing a tiny piece of bread across the table, directly against his nephew's lips. If Charles Maynard had lived to be a hundred years old he would always have been something of a boy.

"Well, I *will* say, she was too pretty for a servant," persisted

---

1 A meddlesome busybody, the title character of a popular 1825 farce by English playwright John Poole (c. 1786–1872).

Walter, laughing; "and yet it wasn't so much her face as her musical voice and her grace of manner that interested me.[1] Sport knows—don't you, Sport?" he continued, addressing the dog, who lay on a mat near him.

"If Sport does know, he won't tell," said Mabel, desiring to turn the conversation from a subject that had so offended her father. "He has grown to be terribly lazy since he came down with you. He won't move unless he is compelled, and he sleeps day and night."

"He is mighty still, indeed," said her Uncle Charles. "It was so bright, last night, that I expected certainly to have heard him; but he seems to have even given up his favorite habit of 'making night hideous,'[2] by baying at the moon."

"Poor fellow!" said Walter, patting the dog, who, finding himself the object of remark, began to rub his nose with his huge paws, and stretch himself, and cast side-glances from the corners of his eyes, in a manner that caused a general laugh from all the group except Mr. Wynn, who rose and retired to his study, deeming this the more dignified way of withdrawing the artillery that had for once proved ineffectual to silence the offender. Sport was the most affectionate animal ever known; but it was impossible to see him endeavor to return caresses, without thinking of the fable of the donkey that would be a lap dog. "Poor fellow!" repeated Walter, "he is completely tired out. The journey was too much for a gentleman of his years, and it has fairly given him the rheumatism. His joints are so stiff he can hardly move."

"I shouldn't think the rheumatism would affect his voice," said Mabel. "Pinch his ears, Walter, and make him say something. I should like to hear one of those long, musical howls that used to run through all the notes of the scale."

"Howl! You don't mean to say Sport *howls!*" exclaimed Walter. "Why he is a splendid singer. I pretend to be a judge of music, and I'd put him against any 'Tenore' in the world. If you could only have heard him sing 'auld lang syne' on the college green at the last commencement. He completely drowned the voices of the graduating class, on the chorus. Can't you give us a specimen now, old fellow?" he added, pulling one of the dog's silky long ears. But Sport only replied by an expressive glance, and, giving an immense yawn, turned over, as if to compose himself to sleep.

---

1 Ida was ten years old at the time of their meeting.
2 Phrase taken from *Hamlet* 1.4, when the prince first sees his father's ghost.

"It's no use; he won't display his acquirements," said Mr. Maynard, shrugging his shoulders; "and if he has the rheumatism he ought to be excused. It is not a musical disease."

"I don't know about that; it is apt to *bring out the chords*,"[1] replied Walter; at which his uncle laughed, and, as Alfred just then came along the piazza with their guns, powder flasks and other accoutrements, the two gentlemen arose, and leaving the dog, who could not be enticed from his mat, they sauntered forth down the path that led into the valley.

The beauty of the day, and the hope of finding game, tempted them to spend several hours in wandering beneath the green forest arches, and over the levels and hollows where their feet trod softly upon fallen pine leaves and the dry silver sands that everywhere cover the surface of that ancient sea-border, and from which, by some unknown and wondrous alchemy, these lofty pines draw the rich and odorous gums with which they overflow. But the covey of partridges, which, the day before, when he walked without his gun, had persisted in tantalizing him by keeping directly in his path, now very provokingly refused all further acquaintance with Walter, and, after a circuit of some miles, they were returning homeward, when suddenly Dash, a little spaniel who had followed them from the house, stopped, and commenced barking furiously at the foot of a large pine, which was nearly bare of branches for thirty feet from the ground.

They were weary with their long ramble, and it was late in the afternoon, so they tried to call off the dog; but no—he would stay there, and he would bark; and he kept it up so long and so pertinaciously, throwing himself nearly off his feet in the violence of his demonstrations, that their curiosity was aroused, and Walter proposed that he should "shin" up the tree, and see what there was there to justify Dash's extreme excitement.

"The tree is a pretty tall one, and hard to climb," said Mr. Maynard, measuring it with his eye; "but I see a hollow up there between the lower branches, and if you choose to risk your neck to gratify your curiosity, I won't object to sitting down on this log to rest myself while you do it."

"I'll try it, anyway; there may be something worth having, and, at any rate, Dash seems to think so. Come on, then, Dash, I'll climb, and you bark, and see which of us will get tired of the

---

1 Walter has evidently made a pun concerning arthritis, though its meaning is now obscure.

tree first;" and, as he spoke, he threw off his shooting-jacket and made a dash at the sturdy old monarch of the woods.

After infinite toil, and not a few slips and scratches, he managed to reach the lower branches, and, seating himself astride one of them, was about to thrust his hand into the hole to ascertain what might be there, when a slight movement within arrested his attention, and he drew his face suddenly back, as a huge black snake darted his head out with a loud hiss at the intruder. "Confound the dog!" he exclaimed; and then, instantly recovering from the first shock of surprise, before the creature had time to withdraw itself, he seized it firmly by the neck, and, with a quick motion, jerked it from its nest and flung it down to the ground. "There, Dash," said he, "if that is what you were making such a fuss about, take it."

His uncle could not hear his words, but he saw the motion, and sprang up in amazement as the snake fell at his feet. Then bursting into a laugh, at the idea of taking so much pains for such a prize, in which he was joined by Walter, from his elevated seat, Mr. Maynard set the dog on the snake, who was gliding quietly away, and Dash revenged himself and his master, by shaking and biting it until it was dead. Having reached the ground in safety, but with no very exalted opinion of the sagacity of his canine companion, Walter was just putting on his coat, when they were both startled by loud screams, that seemed to come from a spot not very far distant.

In some parts of Carolina there are rounded and elongated hills of slight elevation, which it is easy to see were once islands, by the worn pebbles and *débris* with which their steep sides are sometimes covered, and by the cliff-like shapes in which the retiring waters have in other places worn the clay, which lies many feet in thickness beneath the sand that covers their flattened tops, and has been washed down into the shallow vales that wind between them. In these valleys and bowl-shaped depressions are many clear springs of water that, during the short course they run before losing themselves in the loose soil, moisten the roots of various kinds of hardwood trees, oaks, elms, and walnut, that are usually overrun with various luxuriant flowering or fruit-bearing vines. In the spring, especially, while the woods are filled with the delicious fragrance of the yellow jasmine, one can hardly imagine a more beautiful picture than these valleys present, filled as they are with a soft, green light, and bright with flowers, and echoing with the songs of birds; and if the vista can be enlivened, as usual, with a group of negro women, singing, or talking, or scolding, over their washing around the spring, and children, most picturesquely primitive in their habiliments, bringing broken branches and pieces of "fat-wood"[1] to feed the fire beneath the large kettles where the clothes are boiling, nothing seems wanting to complete the picturesque effect.

Through these woods, feeding plentifully upon fallen nuts and the "mast" of the pine burrs,[2] there wander droves of swine, of all colors and sizes. Their roving life renders them almost as swift and agile as goats; and sometimes the males will resent any annoyance most fiercely. They have often been known to attack smaller animals, or children, who came in their way, and the tusks that have been taken from some of them are long enough and sharp enough to have graced the heads of their ferocious ancestors, the wild boars of Europe.

The shrieks, which Mr. Maynard and his nephew still continued to hear, directed their steps to the brow of the elevation whereon this little scene of the snake hunt had occurred and, looking down into the valley, they saw plainly the cause of the outcry. One of these wild swine had attacked a little girl, who had escaped him only by springing upon the rugged stump of a tree that had been blown down. There she was one or two feet above his reach, but the stump was old and rotten, and the standing-place insecure. The enraged animal had already with his tusks torn into splinters the bark around the root, and was now tearing off long pieces of the decayed wood, and, though the child still balanced herself, her footing was every moment growing fearfully uncertain.

Without waiting for a moment's thought, Walter, who had left his gun at the foot of the tree he had climbed, seized a stick, and, leaping down the steep bank, ran to the spot, followed by the valiant Dash and Mr. Maynard. Fortunately this gentleman had his gun in his hand when he was first startled by the child's screams, and, still retaining it ready loaded, reached the scene of action in time to take an unerring aim directly into the face of the boar, who, diverted from his first charge by their approach, had killed poor Dash by piercing him to the heart with one blow of his tusk, and, having snapped in pieces the stick which Walter defended himself, might have injured him severely, had not Mr.

---

1   Resin-impregnated pine heartwood, commonly used for kindling due to its flammability.
2   Reference to both the seed, or "mast," found in pine burrs, and the "mast pine" or tall, straight pine used in shipbuilding.

Maynard come to the rescue. The charge of small shot, with which the gun was loaded, of course did not kill the animal, but it blinded him so completely that it was easy to keep out of his way till the piece could again be loaded with a bullet, which soon laid him on the ground in a death struggle.

This being done, Walter hastened to the place where the child, half-fainting with terror, had sunk down at the foot of the stump. She was dressed in soiled and torn clothing, and, as her head rested on her hands, a coarse muslin sun-bonnet hid her face. Laying his hand on her shoulder, and stooping down, he said, kindly, "Are you hurt, little girl? Look up and tell me your name."

At the sound of his voice the child started, and, looking up, eagerly seized his hand, exclaiming, "It is you! O, how I did hope we should find you!"

"Is it possible?" exclaimed Walter, at the same moment. "Why Lizzy, can this be you? Are you a witch or a fairy, child, that you thus appear to me all alone in the woods? If your adventures with the pig had not been so entirely human, I should be almost afraid of you," he added, laughing.

But Lizzy did not laugh in return. Her large brown eyes filled with tears, and, still grasping his hand in both her own, she said, "O, Master Walter Varian, we have been sold, and we are going to some dreadful place, and you said—" The words died away in a convulsive sob, and the tears ran down over her pale cheeks; but those wild, melancholy eyes were still fixed imploringly on his face, as if to remind him of the promise she hardly had the courage to claim.

"I said I would help you, and I will if I can—don't cry," replied Walter, cheerfully, and, returning to his uncle, who had stopped to look at Dash, and was now approaching, he added, "Whom do you think we have saved? It is my mountain maid, my woodland nymph—it is the little girl I told you of. Come and see her."

A change had come over Ida during the few weeks that had elapsed since their first meeting. The excitement and variety that had so suddenly succeeded to the monotony of her former life had roused her mind to unusual vigor. Her face had lost its quiet and dreamy expression, and her eyes had a restless, searching glance of inquiry and fear. Yet, despite the poverty and disorder of her attire, she was still uncommonly beautiful, and, from the moment he saw her, Mr. Maynard was as much charmed with her appearance as his nephew had been. She still retained her hold of Walter's hand, and now, half-sitting, half-crouching, at his feet, she looked searchingly into the face of the newcomer, as if to read what influence he might exert on her future fate.

"She is a delicate-looking child—too delicate to bear rough usage. How came she here?" asked Mr. Maynard, after a moment's silent scrutiny.

"She says she has been sold from her former master," replied Walter. "Tell us about it, Lizzy. How came you here?"

"They are over on the other side of the hill," answered the child, reassured by his kind manner, "and Maum Venus was so tired and thirsty I came down to the spring to get some water. Then I saw those pretty red berries"—pointing to a holly-bush not far distant—"and, when I came to get them, the pig chased me."

"And you were frightened, and jumped on the stump—poor child! Well, you were in some danger," said Walter. "But tell me, how happened you to be sold, and where are you going?"

"I don't know," replied Ida, simply. "They said Mass' James wanted to raise money, and so he sold us—Maum Venus and I, and seven more niggers. A trader bought us, and we've come ever so far. O, I'm so tired, and so is Venus!" and she sighed heavily.

"Poor child!" said Walter, pityingly, "did you walk all the way?"

"No," replied Ida. "Maum Venus walked, but sometimes he let me ride. The children took turns in riding with him in the wagon. The wagon got broke today, and that's the reason we 'camped so early."

"And are you going much further?" asked Mr. Maynard,

"I don't know," replied the child, her tears again flowing. "Maum Venus says we'll all be sold again before long, and she thinks we'll go to some dreadful sugar plantation, or somewhere else, where I can't be with her."

"Poor child! Don't cry; I'll see what can be done," returned Walter; and then, addressing his uncle, he added, "It will never do to let this child be exposed to the chances of a public sale. There is probably a large gang of them, as they have been driven so far, and I don't doubt the trader will be glad to sell this one."

"And you mean to buy her?" asked Mr. Maynard, musingly.

"Yes, I want to," said Walter; "that is, of course, with all due deference to you as my guardian. I know I am not rich, but I must be allowed this piece of extravagance."

"You can't afford it," replied the uncle; "but I have never denied you anything since the night you cried for the moon, when you were a 'two-year-old,' and I suppose it's hardly worthwhile to begin now. I will make the bargain with the fellow, who I see is coming after his stray goods. I can do the thing better than you can."

Walter looked up the valley as his uncle spoke, and saw the driver approaching. He was a short, thick-set man, with a brutal expression, and his bloated face gave token that he sometimes indulged in beverages stronger than water. The child shrank closer to her protector as she saw him coming near, and exclaimed, in a frightened whisper, "O, see, he's got his whip in his hand—he's angry because I've been gone so long! Don't let him whip me, will you—he beats them dreadfully sometimes, when he's angry—see there!" and, raising her arm, she showed a cut, several inches in length, where the lash had fallen, through her torn sleeve.

"Did he whip you?" cried Walter, with flashing eyes.

"No," replied Ida, "but he whipped Mauma, cause he said she was always lagging behind; and I put my arms round her, and so he hit me. Poor Mauma was sick, and *couldn't* walk fast."

Walter bit his lip to keep down the indignation he felt; and the driver, coming up at this moment, put out his hard hand to seize the child, saying, as he did so,

"Here you are, then, you little runaway; what you been gone so long for?—come along now!" But Walter, by a quick movement, placed himself between the slave-driver and his trembling victim; and Mr. Maynard, touching his arm, drew him a little aside, and demanded what he would take for the child. It made little difference to the man where or when he sold, provided he could get a good price for his slaves, and as Mr. Maynard was acquainted with the market value of such articles, it was not long before a transfer was effected; for, having determined to buy the child, the worthy purchaser felt no disposition to hold long parley with the man, whose coarse jokes and allusions to what Ida would soon be worth as a "fancy girl," aroused disgust and anger.

Meantime, Walter had remained beside Ida; and soon his uncle returned to where they were standing. "I have bought her for you," he said; "but you will have to pay five hundred dollars for her."

"So much!" returned the nephew. "Well, it will be worth that to be able to do what I want for her. You belong to *me*, now, Lizzy. You shan't be treated badly any more."

"O, how good you are!" cried the child, her expressive face glowing with thankfulness and joy. "And Venus too! have you bought Mauma, too?" she added, eagerly.

At that question, Walter looked rather blank, for, as he had said, he was not rich, and he felt that he had already reached the extent of his ability. But Mr. Maynard said, with an expressive shrug of his shoulders,

"Venus too!—O no, indeed! Where were you raised, child, that you have so little idea of the value of money? A man can afford to expend five hundred dollars' worth of generosity, upon a rare occasion; but a thousand or fifteen hundred, that's a tune of another metre. You must be satisfied with being well off yourself, and let Venus go."

At these words a shadow fell over the child's beaming face, and, after a moment's silence, she slowly dropped Walter's hand, which she had not released until now, since she first seized it, and turning slowly away, with her eyes fixed on the ground, she began to walk up the valley.

"Where are you going?" cried Walter, a little disappointed at this movement.

At the sound of his voice, the child turned round, and still walking slowly backwards, she said,

"I'm going back to Maum Venus. Perhaps somebody else will buy us together."

"And won't you go with me unless I buy Maum Venus too?" said Walter, a little piqued.

His tone touched the feelings of the sensitive child, and running to him again she seized his hand, and, pressing it to her lips, she exclaimed,

"O, yes! Don't be angry with me. I shall always think you are the best man that ever lived, but I *can't leave Mauma*. It won't make much difference to you, but I am all she has got in the world; and she says she will die if I'm sold away from her. Don't be angry with me. I *must* go back to Mauma."

"No, you don't do no such thing!" said the driver, now coming forward and laying his hand on her shoulder. "I a'n't going to have you kicking up such a bobbery as ther'll be if she finds you're sold. I don't 'low no such fooling. A bargin's a bargin, and now the gents has bought you, they must keep you."

"You might at least allow her to go back and say goodbye, and get her clothes," said Mr. Maynard. "She must have something more decent than these rags, hasn't she?"

"No she ha'n't, nother," replied the man. "I don't 'low my niggers to tire themselves with carryin' such a bundle o' truck as them gals of Mr. Bell's brung with 'em. The clo'se they has on, gen'ly lasts 'em till they gets to market, and then them that buys 'em must give 'em somethin' to put on. So I allers takes away their clo'se and sells 'em 'fore I start. Sometimes these 'Ginia niggers has fust-rate clo'se, and brings me in consid'able."

"Well, well," said Walter, impatiently, "it will do no harm for her to bid Maum Venus good-bye."

"Yes 't will, *too*!" replied the driver. "I never 'lows no sich things as good-byes. If the niggers gets an idee that you're goin' to look out for their feelin's the least bit, why, they're all over your head in a minute. You jist has to *put 'em down*, and *keep 'em down*," he added, stamping his foot heavily on the ground, as if he were crushing something. "You see, gents, it is very different with us traders from what it is with you that lives on plantations. The niggers gets kind o' settled down like, and feels at home, and is more contented, so you can 'ford to let 'em have feelin's if they wants to. But us that jist buys and sells, we can't 'low no sich nonsense, for they nat'ly makes a fuss 'bout leavin' their old masters, and their 'lations, and children; and if we 'lowed 'em to make a fuss, they wouldn't be fit to travel. Now be patient, gents, and I'll tell you," he added, as Mr. Maynard was about interrupting him. "You see that 'ar Venus is powerful tender on that child, and if they bids each other good-bye, and all that stuff, she'll make sich a devil of a fuss, that she won't be fit to travel tomorrow, and she'll lag behind and hender the whole gang. But if she finds it out gradual, and don't see no more of her, she won't realize it so much, and I shan't have no trouble with her. That's the way with niggers. While a thing's happenin' they makes a powerful fuss, but when it's over and they know it's did and it can't be undid, why then they settle down quiet, and a'n't no trouble."

"Nevertheless," said Walter, impatiently, "the child wants to see her mauma again, and I say she shall—come Lizzy." He took her hand as he spoke, and was leading her away; but with a brutal oath, the trader sprang before him in the path, exclaiming,

"I say she *shan't*, then. She belongs to you, but Venus belongs to me; and now I should like to know how you're going to help yourself?"

Walter was about making an angry reply, when the discussion was cut short by the approach of the object of dispute; for Venus, becoming alarmed at the child's prolonged absence, had managed, unobserved, to leave the group of slaves, who were sitting and lying together beneath the trees on the other side of the hill, guarded by one of the traders. The moment she saw her, Ida dropped Walter's hand, and, like a bird darting to her nest, she threw herself upon the bosom of that faithful friend, and, clasping her hands around her neck, burst into a flood of passionate tears.

"O, honey, I'se powerful scared 'bout you—where ye been?" said Venus, gazing with surprise at the two strangers, the angry face of her master, and the dead animals that lay near.

"There now, I telled you so," said the driver, as he saw this act; "ther'll be an awful fuss to get 'em apart now!" Then, turning to Venus, he raised his whip, threateningly, and said, "Look here now—you jest let go o' that gal, and go back where you came from. You a'n't no business here; and that gal's sold to these gents, and you a'n't got nothin' more to do with her."

With a deep groan, Venus staggered back, and would have fallen to the ground but for the tree that stood directly behind her. Her arms dropped helplessly from that little clinging form, and her face fell forward on the child's head that lay on her breast. The blow, which for three weeks she had been fearing, had fallen at last, and for a moment all was darkness and blindness. In a little while the faintness passed away, but she made no further outcry, and shed no tears. Her sorrow was too stern and crushing for any such outward demonstration; but it seemed to her that an iron had had seized her heart, and was wringing thence the last drops of her life-blood. Sinking slowly down against the trunk of the tree, as if her limbs had lost their strength, she drew the child down to the ground with her; and, sitting there, she rocked her body to and fro, as she bent over her, and uttered a low, inarticulate, murmuring sound, so expressive of anguish that it touched even the obdurate feelings of the slave-trader, and, dropping the whip he had raised to strike her, he stood gazing at her in silence.

"I can't stand this any way," exclaimed Mr. Maynard, impatiently, after a painful pause of a few moments. "Either you must take back the child, or you must sell me the woman. I won't be instrumental in such cruelty as this."

The trader was not so far overcome, but that he was as much on the alert for "a trade" as ever. Moreover, he was a little frightened. One, who seemed to know every phase of human feeling, has said,

> "The grief that does not speak,
> Whispers the o'er-fraught heart and bids it break;"[1]

and this man had once before seen just such an exhibition of intense agony, on the part of a mother, whom he had parted from

---

1 *Macbeth*, 4.3.209–10. Malcolm's advice to Macduff here begins: "Give sorrow words."

her only child; and in *that* case, the sale being completed, and the child taken away, the mother dropped dead at his feet. Is was, therefore, with no little pleasure that he found the prospect of a like disastrous issue for his present speculation averted by this proposition of Mr. Maynard, and he quickly replied by asking what he would give for Venus.

"She looks like an old woman," replied Mr. Maynard, "you could not get more than five hundred dollars for her."

"Say six hundred, and you shall have her," said the trader quickly. He had discovered Venus was nearly blind of one eye, and he thought he was making a good trade. Mr. Maynard was careless about money, and too much excited now by his compassionate feelings to make any very particular examination of the "article" he was purchasing; and, using the top of the stump for a table, he gave his note for the amount, and then hastily went towards the place where they were sitting, for he had drawn a little aside in concluding the bargain.

Venus looked up when he touched her shoulder, for she thought he meant to take away her darling, and, clasping her yet closer in her arms, she said in low, husky tones, "Who is it honey, that's bought ye?"

"It's Master Walter Varian, the good young man I told you about," replied the child. "O, ask him to buy you, too!"

"'T a'n't no use," said Venus, shaking her head, despairingly; "but, O, honey, 't a'n't quite so bad to have you go, if he'll only treat you well!"

"Don't you understand," said Mr. Maynard, "that I've bought you? And you shan't be separated from the child."

She had, indeed, been unconscious, deafened by misery, while this change in her fate was being effected, and now she seemed unable to realize the great and sudden joy. "*Me!* Did you say *me?*" she cried in a shrill voice. "O, God! Did he say he'd bought me too? And may I go with Lizzy? O, massa, you wouldn't be joking with a poor old nigger woman that has her heart almost broke!" she added, looking earnestly in his face.

"No, I am not joking," said Mr. Maynard, kindly. "Come, get up and come along now, for it's getting late, and we've had no dinner."

Venus rose from the ground at these words, with the child still clinging around her; but, as her new master was about turning away, she threw herself at his feet, and, clasping her hands as if in prayer, she exclaimed, "I calls down de blessing ob de Lord on you, out of heaven, and 't will do ye good, if 't is a poor old creatur' brings it. You shan't neber have 'casion to be sorry for this thing you've did, massa—neber. I'll work for you mornin' and night, and if ye a'n't got nothin' for me to do, ye may hire me out—ye may do any airthly thing ye want to wid me, massa, if I can on'y see my Lizzy ebery day, and know how she's comin' on. O, massa, de Lord bless ye! Ye can't tell nothin' 'bout what dat child is to me. I'se lost husband, and chillen, and everything, and she's instead ob 'em all."

"Well, that'll do now. Come on, we're getting late," said Mr. Maynard; but the tears stood in his eyes as he turned away, and, linking his arm in his nephew's, they went up from the little valley in the path that led homeward, with Venus and Lizzy following at a little distance behind.

CHAPTER VIII

"Now, the soul alone is willing,
    Faint the heart and weak the knee,
And as yet no lip is thrilling
    With the mighty words, 'Be free.'
Tarrieth long the land's good angel,
    But his advent is to be."
    J.G. WHITTIER[1]

"I don't know but we have done a foolish thing," said Mr. Maynard at length, to his nephew, as they walked along. "What shall we do with these new possessions of ours, I wonder? The fact is, I do hate to feel badly, and I can never see anybody in distress without doing all I can to help them. It's foolish, I know."

"It is a folly which becomes a wise man more than all his wisdom," said Walter, pressing his uncle's arm affectionately.

"Thank you, but it's a folly nevertheless, and a misfortune too; for there is so much distress in the world that one can't relieve, that the little one can do seems of no use. For that reason I make it a rule never to go where people are in trouble, if I can help it. I can't even live on my own estate. I tried it awhile; but, as I said before, I hate to feel badly, and there were so many troubles always occurring, that I couldn't help, that I gave it up."

"You didn't give up the plantation!" cried Walter, in amazement.

"No; but I gave up living at home. After your poor mother died, the place grew too lonely, so I got an overseer, whom I knew I could trust, and, having made such a calculation, and found how much the place would bring in yearly, with the negroes well fed and moderately worked, I told the overseer I wanted so much, and he might have good wages, if he'd carry on things just to suit me, and take the whole charge."

"It seems to me that you place great power in the hands of your overseer," replied Walter, gravely. "What if he is a dishonest man, and, giving you only the sum you fixed upon, works the people to death, to make as much more for himself?"

"O, he don't, I reckon," said the uncle. "I run down upon him when he least expects me, and take a gallop round the place to see that the general aspect of things is right. I won't have any

---

1 From John Greenleaf Whittier (1807–92), "At Washington" (1845).

cruelty, and he knows it; but otherwise I don't interfere with the plantation discipline."

"But you are here at Uncle Richard's much of the time. You must see some things here that go wrong, as well as on your own plantation," persisted Walter.

"No, indeed, I don't," replied the other. "I know no more about the state of his negroes than the man in the moon. I never go near them, and I ask no questions. It is the only way for a man to live easy under this troublesome domestic institution of ours. One must either think of the negroes only as brutes, and be perfectly careless of their feelings, or else one must shut one's eyes and ears, and let things slide as smoothly as possible. Beside, if I do see any wrongs here, I don't feel any responsibility about them, and that is a great weight off one's shoulders."

"Still," said Walter, "I don't see that by running away from your plantation, you get rid of the responsibility that attaches to the possession of negroes. The only way to do that is to free them."

Mr. Maynard shook his head, and almost groaned. "I can't do that," he said; "conscientiously, I couldn't. I wish I could. If I thought they would or could take care of themselves, I'd free them tomorrow, and thank the Lord for being rid of them. You look as if you didn't believe me, Walter, but I would. Do what you will, as long as you keep men and women in slavery, you can't satisfy them or make them happy; and I'm sick and tired of trying to do it, and meeting only complaints. People are always saying negroes are ungrateful, and I don't know but they are, for they can have but little idea of the dilemma their masters are in. I wish that the ships that brought the first ones over here had been sunk in the sea with all on board. They are the plague and the curse of the country, and nobody knows it better than their owners."

Walter was astonished at this outburst of feeling, for he had never heard his uncle speak so decidedly upon the subject. "If you think so," said he, "why don't you free them?"

"I can't—I ought not to. They are not fit to take care of or govern themselves, and least of all to do it in a republic like ours. They have been so debased by generations of ignorance and ill-usage, and kept so long in a depressed and dependent state, that the best of them are mere children, and haven't the least idea of self-government. I really think that if I were to send mine to the free States, each with a hundred dollars in his pocket, to start in the world with, in five years they would every one be vagabonds and paupers; and I certainly have no right to inflict this burden on those States."

"But why not educate them, and teach them to conduct themselves like men that have an object in life, and let that object be their ultimate freedom? If the old and infirm must always be what they now are, the children and the grandchildren might become worthy to receive their rights as men."

"I would willingly do it, but it is impossible. The laws of the State positively forbid education, and that lies at the foundation of any preparation for freedom.[1] My dear boy, I've thought of this matter in every possible light, and I find my hands completely tied. Neither public opinion nor the laws would allow me to do anything to arouse in the minds of my own negroes the idea of liberty; for the spark which I kindled on my own hearth might spread till it made my neighbors homeless. I happen to be so situated that I could sacrifice great pecuniary interests without wronging anyone, but very few of my acquaintances are in like circumstances. Their negroes are all their property—for the land is worthless without negro labor—and if the negroes are freed, their wives and children must be plunged in poverty. I cannot blame them that they thus dread to have the subject agitated, when they are so utterly unprepared to meet the sure result of that agitation, and I cannot feel it right to disturb the peace of the community in this manner. No, I am completely fettered. I cannot do the good I would, either to myself or my negroes, and 'the evil I would not,' somebody else does."[2]

"Still," replied Walter, "it seems as if *something* might be done. With an evil in our midst, that is our curse at home and our disgrace abroad, it seems unmanly for those who realize it, to sit supinely mourning over their lot, and doing nothing else. If you cannot move one step towards extricating yourself from this dilemma till there is a change in public opinion, why not endeavor now to correct public opinion? We need not be ashamed of evils which we have inherited, if we do all in our power to remedy them; but we are—we must be—responsible, if we neglect the duty of at least commencing a reform; don't you think so, uncle?"

"Walter, my boy," replied Mr. Maynard, "you left home so young, and have resided at the north so much of the time since,

---

1 Walter evidently doesn't know that it was illegal to teach slaves to read and write; see also above, p. 110.
2 Romans 7:19, "For the good that I would I do not, but the evil which I would not, that I do."

that you seem to have forgotten that 'the trail of the serpent is over us all.'[1] The fact is, there is little freedom of action, and still less freedom of discussion, in this glorious old Carolina, of which we are so proud. It is the working of the curse—the negroes are not the only slaves. A man may do what little he can, *secretly*, to instruct his people, but if he do so much that the neighboring negroes get discontented from the contrast, he is pretty sure to have the laws enforced against him by somebody. There are always enemies enough around a man, who are glad to thwart his favorite plans when they have an opportunity. And as to talking with my neighbors, and spreading free opinions, it won't do, my boy, it won't do. What little light I have I must hide under a bushel,[2] in the midst of this evil and adulterous generation. Men will agree with you in general terms that slavery is an evil, and the negroes are a plague, and it is a pity we can't get rid of them; but once seriously propose to them to commence the work of reforming the laws that sanction the abuses of slavery, or in any way to take the first step towards its abolition, at a period however distant, and you'll see how sincere they are. You will be lucky if you escape being mobbed as an abolitionist, and, from that moment, you will be a suspected person, whom it will not do to be too intimate with. I don't mean that *all* are insincere; but the majority have too much at stake to really desire any movement that will affect their pecuniary interests. We don't live in the age of martyrs, my boy, and nowadays men carry their hearts in their pockets and their principles in their purses. 'Great is Diana of the Ephesians!'[3]—we'll worship her fervently, lest the hope of our gains should be gone."

"How in the world then, shall slavery ever be abolished?" cried Walter, "if nobody has any power to agitate the subject in any way?"

"It never will be abolished!" replied his uncle, "*never!*"

They were near the house, and, at this moment, Sport who had condescended to come a little way to meet them thrust his cold nose into Walter's hand, which hung by his side.

"Hillo, old fellow!" said he, "were you lonesome today with-

---

1 Popular quotation from *Lalla Rookh* (1817), an oriental verse romance by Thomas Moore (1779–1852), referring to the loss of innocence of Adam and Eve in Genesis 3.

2 English proverb derived from the preaching of Jesus, as reported in the gospels according to Matthew, Mark, and Luke.

3 Acts 19:28.

out me? Did they treat you well while I was gone? I really hope you were able to sleep a little, you've been so broken of your rest lately. See here, Lizzy," he added, turning to the child who was now close behind him, "here's Sport—a'n't he a fine old dog?"

Lizzy laughed, for seeing him brought to remembrance his comical appearance as he sat on horseback by the mountain brook. "You haven't learned to ride yet, have you, Sport?" she said.

"Ah, you remember that, don't you?" said Walter, laughing also.

Then, seeing she carried a bundle in her arms, wrapped in her old sun-bonnet, he asked her what it was; and, unrolling it, she showed him the dead body of poor Dash.

"I didn't like to leave him there for the pigs to eat," she said.

"And you were the only one of us that remembered him! You are a good little girl," said Walter, touched by this proof of kind feeling at a moment when the child might have been excused for thinking only of herself.

"You know he got killed in trying to help me," she replied simply; "and I thought, perhaps, if I brought him here, you would let me bury him."

"So I will," replied he. "We will have Dash buried with military honors."

They went on to the house, where they found Mabel and her mother waiting for them on the piazza, a little uneasy at their long absence, and wondering greatly to see them so attended on their return.

"This is a new purchase of mine," said Mr. Maynard, in reply to the inquiring glances directed towards him as he came near— pointing as he spoke to Venus, who, with her arms folded, stood meekly at the foot of the steps—"and that little thing clinging to her, is a chance acquaintance of Walter's, a pearl that he found cast before swine[1] in the wilderness, and he has redeemed it from the hand of the spoiler!"

"What do you mean? Where have you been detained so long?" asked Mrs. Wynn.

"In plain prose, then," resumed her brother, "we have been, as one has said, 'through scenes and unscenes;'[2] and, moreover, Walter and I have made a purchase this afternoon, the reasons whereof we will give you some other time. Now, having brought

---

1 English proverb derived from the Sermon on the Mount, Matthew 7:6.

2 Source uncertain; later attributions include to "an old woman" or an "old darkey."

home our merchandise, as you see, we would crave the gracious lady's permission that they may be well taken care of for the present. But, first of all, where is the dinner we should have eaten three hours ago? For our inner man groaneth, yea even fainteth, for lack of nourishment. Verily, at this moment I could, like Esau of old, sell myself for a mess of pottage."[1]

"I wouldn't advise anybody to buy you," said Walter, laughing, "For, according to the sentiments you have been expressing, you would not be very safe property."

"Hush! Remember that is strictly *entre nous*," said his uncle, in a low tone, turning round to say it, as they followed Mrs. Wynn to the dining room, where a plentiful repast awaited them.

Leaving them to discuss the viands she had provided, Mrs. Wynn returned to the piazza, where she found Venus still standing with the weary child leaning against her.

"You may sit down," said Mrs. Wynn, kindly; "you must be very tired."

Mabel had been asking her questions, and eying the shrinking child from head to foot, but it had not occurred to the little lady that either of them were fatigued.

"Thank you, missis," said Venus; and at this permission she seated herself and took Lizzy on her knee.

The poor woman had been somewhat awed by Mabel's haughty glances. She did not as yet even know her new master's name, and she felt the keenest anxiety to learn the character of the female influence to which she and her precious little one should be subject. At Mabel's manner she was somewhat disconcerted, but Mrs. Wynn's kind voice reassured her. A few moments sufficed to answer the few questions Mrs. Wynn cared to ask, and then, calling a young girl from the yard, she bade her tell Maum Abby to come to her.

Giving one curious glance at the strangers, the messenger hastened away. Passing round the corner of the house, she went to the end of the piazza, which, as we have said, only surrounded it on three sides, the fourth side being shaded by six or eight very large and widely-spreading trees, that made quite a little grove, into which the sun's rays could hardly penetrate, and which completely hid the yard and kitchen offices from the view of persons passing along the avenue that led to the house. Under these trees stood a small frame building, neatly painted outside, and con-

---

1 Refers to Esau of Genesis 25:29–34, who sells his birthright to Jacob for a bowl of lentil pottage (i.e., soup or stew).

taining two rooms. It was close to the piazza, though concealed by the angle of the building, for here lived Maum Abby, a valued servant, who had once reigned supreme over the corner bedroom, when it was Miss Mabel's nursery, and who was now expected to be always within the sound of Mrs. Wynn's voice, if she should need her there at any time. This corner room, no longer needed as a nursery, Mrs. Wynn herself occupied, and, though there was a younger and more sprightly damsel who claimed the honor of being her maid, the gentle lady liked better to be waited upon by Maum Abby, whose refined manners, correct language, and quiet demeanor, might have graced a higher station in life. She was a quadroon,[1] of a tall, slender form, with mild black eyes, and regular features, which always wore a pleasant and winning expression. She was a great favorite with the whole family, and Mrs. Wynn loved her more as a companion than a servant; for she had been her playmate in childhood, although ten years older than herself, and had also shared her studies in some measure. Thus Abby had learned to read and write, and by improving every opportunity for reading and study she possessed far more general information than was suspected even by those who knew her most intimately. When her young mistress was married, she removed with her to Wynn Hall, accompanied by her husband and four children, as bright, as happy, and most as much delighted with her new home as was the young bride herself. But after this change the sunshine of her life departed. Mr. Wynn was fond of his wife, but he had not the genial disposition of the Maynard family, and Abby was made, in various ways, slight indeed, but noticeable to one so petted as she had been, to feel that the favors of her lot were *favors granted*, not *rights received*; and that, despite all her advantages, she belonged to the inferior race. Then, after some years, in one sickly season she lost her three eldest children, and before the next spring her husband died. This accumulation of troubles, which she felt most keenly, combined with long and wearisome watching over the sick, broke her constitution and saddened her whole nature, and she would have pined herself into the grave, had not Mrs. Wynn watched over her with a sister's sympathy, and with Christian love poured into her heart the blessed consolations of religion. It was long before her deep and bitter sorrow could be alleviated; but, as

---

1 An obsolete term for a person of mixed race whose enslaved parent was also of mixed race. Abby is one-quarter black—and three-quarters white—by descent.

time went on, her heart recovered power to receive the precious promises which the Scriptures offer to the afflicted, and then her mistress felt the satisfaction of seeing that her cares had not been in vain, and that the words which had apparently fallen on deaf ears, had been silently, and almost unconsciously, acting as a healing balm for the sufferer. She resumed by degrees her maternal duties to her only remaining child, and the various light employments to which she had been accustomed; and at length no trace remained of the storm through which she had passed, except the subdued and chastened expression which she wore, instead of her former gay and buoyant manner. She was deeply grateful to Mrs. Wynn and warmly attached to her, and she had no wishes ungratified except those connected with her boy.

Alfred had inherited his mother's thirst for knowledge, and early gave promise of uncommon intellect, and she longed for and appreciated the advantages of education for him. She could not bear to think that her handsome and precocious boy should grow up ignorant and degraded like most of his race are, or be content to dwarf the mind, and debase the soul, and regard the condition of the fawning and petted servant as the highest and most favored to which he might aspire.

O, how she longed—that poor slave mother—for the advantages of schools, and books, and teachers, which are within reach of the most destitute of white children in the free States! Her heart seemed to die within her when she looked forward to his future, and saw him growing up to manhood amid the trammeling and deforming influences that now surrounded him. With great care and secrecy, lest Mr. Wynn, who angrily opposed such things, should know it, she taught him to read and write, and by slow degrees she resigned herself to the idea that when he became a man she would in some way manage to effect his escape from bondage, though that act would most probably separate them for the remainder of her life. The chains of servitude to her had been golden links, worn lightly and easily, but they became iron fetters when she saw them laid upon her son, and she could endure to be left alone, provided she could know he was free.

She was sitting by the window of her room when the messenger from Mrs. Wynn came to seek her. Everything about her was neatly and tastefully arranged, and on her lap lay some fine embroidery, upon which she had been at work; but it was now too dark to sew, and she was leaning her head on her hand absorbed in deep thought.

"On'y think, Maum Abby," said the girl, "that ar' young Mass' Walter be the spiletestest feller! What you reckon he done fetch home dis time?"

"I have no idea; what is it?" said Abby, looking up.

"Why, nothin' else but two niggers—a black one and a white one. A'n't that powerful queer? Miss wants you to come and take care of 'em; so do come 'long, for I'm dyin' to know how he come to catch such like in de woods!"

Abby rose, and, laying her work aside in a pretty workbox, followed the girl to the piazza, where Mrs. Wynn still remained.

"Here, Mauma Abby," she said, "is Venus, a new servant that Mr. Maynard has brought home. I wish you would take her and the little girl, and get some clean clothing for them both, and let them have Alfred's room for a few days. He can sleep somewhere else."

"Yes, Miss Emma, I'll attend to them," said Abby; and Venus arose and followed her. She was quite surprised, when ushered into Abby's apartment, to see the neat carpet on the floor, the tastefully arranged curtains at the windows, and the painted furniture. She had never before seen a servant's room so richly arrayed, and, simple and inexpensive as was everything there, she was almost afraid to sit down amid what seemed to her so elegant, or to feel herself on an equality with the delicate-looking woman who conducted her. After leaving her alone for a few minutes, Abby returned, and led her into the adjoining room, which her son usually occupied. "This will be your apartment for the present," she said.

"We must have some water, and get washed up—Lizzy and me—before we can get into dem nice clean sheets," replied Venus. "O, it do seem mighty good to have a roof over a body again, when night comes, and a bed to sleep onto! We'se most fagged out, Lizzy and me is, sleepin' on the ground dis three weeks. We a'n't been used to it."

"You had a comfortable home, then," said Abby.

"Yes, mighty comforble," replied Venus. "Not so fine as dis yer, but comforble for niggers. I done guv up entirely, when we was sold, and thought de Lord done forget all 'bout us."

"The Lord never forgets," said Abby, speaking in a low tone, as if rather to herself than her companion. "His ways are dark and mysterious, and he covers the path with clouds along which he leads us; but he never forgets us, *never*, and at last he will bring us where all is brightness. Let us trust Him through all, for the end will come at last."

"I reckons you'se got larnin', somehow, you talk so nice," said Venus, gazing at her with unfeigned admiration.

"Miss Emma has always been very kind to me, and I have had many advantages," said Abby with a slight blush. "But I must not stay here talking, while you are tired and hungry. I see the poor little girl looks like she would cry from weariness. You will find plenty of water here, and some clean clothes, and you had better bathe her and put her in bed, while I get you something to eat, and she can take her supper lying down."

"I 'clare, you'se too good. We didn't think o' being sich a heap o' strouble," replied Venus. Abby smiled, and left the room, "on hospitable thoughts intent."[1]

The next morning, notwithstanding her fatigue, Venus rose early, that she might be ready if called upon by her new master. But she saw nothing of either Mr. Maynard or Walter, for they were occupied with company which had arrived the previous evening, and, as Mr. Wynn had invited several gentlemen to dine with him that day, the whole household was busy, and Abby was left alone with the newcomers, nearly the whole morning. Walter had privately requested that the little girl might not be dressed in the coarse clothing usually provided for the servants, and so Mrs. Wynn had given Abby a cast-off merino dress of Mabel's, which she was busy over all the morning, making it, with Venus's help, into quite a handsome and well-fitting garment. Meantime, Lizzy, who was not literally of the *sans culottes* class in society,[2] was "making a business" of resting herself, and was quite refreshed by the time she was permitted to arise. Great was Venus's delight at the child's appearance, when, having washed her, and carefully arranged her glossy curls in the most becoming manner, she arrayed her in the bright blue dress, whose soft folds seemed so much better suited to that delicate form than anything she had previously worn.

"I 'clare, honey," she exclaimed, "'pears like you wasn't a nigger, now! These is powerful good folks we'se got amongst dis yer time. Dere's Miss Emma comed in to call Maum Abby just

---

1   John Milton (1608–74), *Paradise Lost* (1667), Book 5.

2   In the late eighteenth century, *sans-culottes*, or those without silk knee-breeches, referred to the lower classes of French society committed to the democratic and egalitarian ideals of the French Revolution. Pike insinuates here that Ida was born to leisure, and not to the working class.

now, and she axed for you, honey, and spoke so pleasant. I 'clare, I loved her de fuss minute I sot eyes onto her!"

Venus had been improving the opportunity, while they were working together, to acquire some knowledge of her new surroundings. Abby was never weary of talking about the Maynard family, and she had given her companion a history of each member. Perhaps the reader would enjoy being equally enlightened.

Charles, Mabel, and Emma Maynard, were early in life left orphans. But the sorrow of this bereavement was greatly lessened to the two young girls by the watchful love and care of their brother, who was twelve years older than themselves, and who, receiving them as a sacred charge from their dying mother, devoted his whole time to them afterwards, for many years. They were all of peculiarly refined natures, and affectionate dispositions; and thus, happy in each other, they passed many pleasant years, growing up to womanhood in the seclusion of their fine old family seat at Oakland. After a time, Mabel, the eldest, married; but her husband proved to be dissipated, and a spendthrift. Two infant children she laid in the grave, and then one of those terrible steamboat explosions, so common on the southwestern rivers, suddenly deprived her of her husband, and four years from the time she left her home as a bride, she returned there, ruined in fortune, and broken-hearted, to give birth to a son, and then to die. This child, which she lived long enough to see christened with his father's name, Walter, she commended to her brother's care, beseeching him to adopt him as his own; and well and faithfully had that request been fulfilled. A year or two after Mabel's death, his other sister, Emma, had given her hand to Mr. Wynn. Many wondered that a woman so gentle and timid should have fancied one so cold in manner, and of a disposition so unbending, as characterized Richard Wynn. But people are often attracted by their opposites, and there is something akin to magnetism in the influence by which a man of strong will compels the assent of a woman of feebler organization, and less marked individuality. Emma Maynard was a pretty little creature, with one of those characters that expand into beauty, and acquire use and strength, only when constantly surrounded by an atmosphere of love. She was dependent and affectionate, inclined to take a low estimate of her own acquirements or abilities, frightened at a frown, and silenced by a look. Her husband was undemonstrative, and not very warm-hearted. He liked his wife better than anybody else except himself, but he had an almost morbid horror of sentiment, and did not think it at all worthwhile to indulge her in any such weakness. He was, moreover, extremely opinionated and self-reliant, and had an imperious manner, so that, almost unconsciously, his wife lost her sprightliness and gaiety, and subsided into a very quiet, unobtrusive woman, beloved by her servants, for whom she contrived many indulgences, but possessing little influence over either her husband or her daughter, and depending for her happiness almost wholly upon the society of her brother, who, since her marriage, had spent the greater part of each year at her house.

Walter, growing up under these influences, and inheriting all the genial and impulsive qualities of his mother's family, had always loved his aunt, who knew little difference between her feelings for him and those with which she regarded her own daughter, and felt for his uncle Charles Maynard the same affection and respect he would have cherished for a father. But for Mr. Wynn, who, though he treated him kindly enough when he happened to think of it, took little notice of him usually; he experienced an indifference that was tinged with dislike; and he had, by turns, quarreled with and petted the little Mabel, who, with advancing years, was developing a disposition composed of both parents, but containing the best qualities of neither.

Venus, who was a great talker, was detailing to the child a lengthened account of the various events and character of which the morning's conversation had given her information, when Patra, the girl who had been sent to call Abby the night before, thrust her head into the window of the room where they were sitting.

"How d' ye, s'mornin," said she, good-naturedly.

"Thank 'ee, we'se rested some, Lizzy and me is, and got clared up might comforble," replied Venus.

"I reckoned you must be 'siderable 'freshed by dis time," said Patra, "I'd been in to see you 'fore, but we'se gwine have a dinner-party today, and we'se all been dat busy. Got de table done sot now, though, and it do look mighty fine. Wouldn't you like come look at it, 'fore de dinner's toted in?"

This is what Venus had been longing to do, for she began to be tired of staying all day in one room, and it was now three o'clock in the afternoon. So she eagerly accepted the invitation.

"Come, den, and I reckon you never see sich like in all *your* born days. Sich powerful heap ob plate! My stair! De silver and de glass do shine so! We'se got more den things in dis family 'en anybody all roun' here, and Maum Abby, she does *derange* 'em most beautiful. Miss Emma always leave all *dat* to Ma'am Abby, she got such powerful taste at deranging de tables when we has company. You may bring the little girl, too."

Venus held out her hand for the child, but she drew back. She preferred remaining alone, rather than encountering so many strangers; and, having given a hasty glance in the glass, to see that her new turban was tastefully folded, and, from the force of habit, given her dress the smoothing touch she usually bestowed on her aprons—the beloved aprons which had, alas! fallen victim to the cupidity of the slave-trader—Venus departed with Patra, who felt a personal pride in displaying to her astonished and delighted companion the riches of plate and glass with which the tables were ornamented. Afterwards, in speaking of it to Lizzy, Venus acknowledged, "You know, honey, I never did see nothin' half so splendiferous in all my life, but I warn't gwine to tell *her* so—the nigger!—'cause for fear she'd think I'se some poor cretur' t' hadn't been used to de fust fam'lies." Therefore, under the influence of this not unnatural desire to make an impression, and keep up appearances, she restrained her surprise as best she might, and affected a nonchalance equal to that of the most fashionable leader of the "ton."[1]

Patra was a little disappointed when she saw the indifference with which Venus seemed to regard the glittering display before her; but one's *manner* has a great effect in imposing upon the darker as well as the more enlightened circles of society, and it was with her respect heightened, by several degrees, that she conducted her companion to the kitchen, and introduced her to the servants there. Venus was willing to make herself useful, and anxious to acquire a reputation in the family; and, as there was plenty to do, she was soon deeply engaged, under the superintendence of the cook, who was really quite a culinary artist, in the mysteries of taking up and preparing the dishes for the table.

More than an hour had passed away, and the child was still alone, amusing herself with watching from the window the various groups in the yard, when suddenly she saw Venus approaching with a pace so rapid, and a manner so agitated, that she hastened to the door to meet her. Tears were running down her cheeks, but the expression of her face was anything but sad; and her appearance was irresistibly comical, as she trotted along, with her head thrown back, her mouth distended, her small eyes twinkling, and her whole figure, even to the tips of her fingers, shaking with a universal giggle.

---

1 I.e., *le bon ton,* or the upper crust of society.

Seizing Lizzy's hands, she exclaimed, "O, honey, I'se found him! You *must* come now, for I'se found my son John, dat I lef a little feller, when I was sold way to 'Ginia. Come and see him, honey. On'y think how he 'membered his ma' Benus all dese twelve year I a'n't seen him; and I 'clare 'fore goodness, honey, he's growed so handsome, I'se clar shamed of him."

As she poured forth her overflowing joy in these words, she drew the bewildered child along to a room adjoining the kitchen, where the servants of the guests were assembled, and here she found the boy whose unexpected recovery had nearly made his mother crazy with delight. He was the son who had cheered her last unhappy marriage, and, left alone as he was when his mother was sold, he had had abundant cause to remember her fondly, as the only being from whom he could claim the unselfish kindness and care which every human being longs to receive from *someone*. He was now a tall stripling of seventeen, black as a mulatto could be, but with good features and a pleasant expression, which might justify his mother's opinion of his beauty. Learning from the servants the incident of the day previous, which was by this time generally known, and finding that the woman was named Venus, he made inquiries which led to a mutual recognition.

The child fully sympathized with her friend's delight, but she hardly knew what to say to the boy, who was himself somewhat embarrassed at attracting so much observation; for the news had spread rapidly through the yard, and the door and windows were now crowded with heads of various sizes, shapes, and colors, all with eyes wide open and eager to see the meeting between Col. Ross's John and his mother. For a little while Lizzy endured this battery of eyes, and gestures, and exclamations, in common with Venus and her son; but at length the crowd dropped off in various directions, and the child, glad to escape observation, slipped away quietly, and was returning to her room, when her attention was attracted by some pots of rare and beautiful flowers, which had been removed from the conservatory and placed for ornaments on the piazza, opposite the dining room windows. The most common flowers had a magical influence over Lizzy's mind, and she was lost in admiration of these, which surpassed everything she had ever seen. Forgetting everything else, she walked before them, touching them gently with longing fingers, and bending over them to breathe the delicious fragrance which they exhaled.

While she was thus occupied, some of the gentlemen who had finished their dinner, and were sitting talking over their wine, began to turn their chairs a little from the table, preparatory to joining the ladies in the parlor. In doing this one of them noticed the child, and remarked to Walter Varian who sat near him, that he was not aware Mr. Wynn had a daughter so young.

"That child is not Uncle Richard's daughter," said Walter, laughing. "*I* have had the pleasure of owning that dainty bit of flesh and blood since yesterday evening. Yes, sir," he added, as he met his companion's astonished gaze, "I bought her and paid for her, to a man who claimed to own her, and so I suppose, by all the laws of the country, I may say she's *mine*."

"Still, I am astonished," replied the gentleman, "for she is so delicate in appearance, it hardly seems that she can be a servant, or come of that lineage. She is beautiful enough to make *some* father's heart glad. How can she be a servant?"

"I have no doubt she is of white parentage," replied Walter. "You notice that though she is not very fair, her skin has the clear darkness of a brunette, and not the yellowish tinge which marks the lighter shades of the negro race. Her features, her whole form and mien, show that she is wholly of the Anglo-Saxon lineage; and if you should hear her speak, you would see, by her correct pronunciation, that she has at some time in her life been taught by refined and educated persons. See, there she goes, gliding out of sight. She has heard our voices, and I have noticed that she is very shy."

"How comes she here—where did you get her?" asked his friend.

"I found her yesterday in the woods, and bought her from a gang who were being driven southward; but I saw her first a few weeks since, while traveling through North Carolina, just on the northern border of that State. It was in quite a romantic spot, and she had dressed herself with leaves and flowers, and looked like a little fairy. I talked a little with her, and became quite interested in her, and so when I found her again yesterday, in such a forlorn situation, I couldn't refrain from purchasing her."

"She will be well treated here," remarked the other, as Walter paused.

"I shall advertise, and see if I cannot find her parents," replied he, quickly. "Of course, such a child as that must have friends who will be glad to claim her. She was doubtless stole from them."

"It may be so," said another gentleman; "but she may be one of the poor whites, and in that case, she would be much better off to be a servant here than to live at home. It may be, too, that she was sold instead of being stolen. I have frequently seen white children who were thus thrown into the market. These miserable 'clay-eaters' often sell their children, and I suppose the Virginia 'crackers'[1] do the same; and in my opinion, it is the best thing they can do for their children."

"Do you really think so?" said Walter, "Can servitude—*slavery*—be in any case the proper condition for a parent to force a child into? I know they are miserably poor, but, still, is not liberty the greatest of all blessings, man's immortal birthright, which none should willingly give up?"

"In some cases it may be and undoubtedly is, a birthright which should be kept sacred as life!" replied his companion; "but there are many cases where servitude is much more for the real good of a person, or a class. These poor whites among us are an instance of how utterly impossible it is that all men were born to be equal. They are lower even than our negroes, and if they were all to come under negro laws tomorrow, it would be far better for the next generation than it will be for them to remain as they are. It has always been so, and always will be. There *must* be two classes in every society. The learned, the cultivated, the wealthy, must be the *patricians*; and the laboring class must be the plebeians, and it makes little difference whether they are black or white."

"*Simply* because a man is poor, you will reduce him to the condition of a serf!" exclaimed Mr. Maynard, joining the group, who were now sitting near a window; "we must take care, then, how we become bankrupts."

"Not simply because he is poor, but if he be ignorant and degraded, the best thing one can do for him is to place him under guardianship. The lower classes are not fit to govern themselves, and it is a false philanthropy that insists upon their having the right to do so. Society would be much better, and government established on a firmer basis, if they did not have it."

"Would it not be a better plan," said Walter, "to establish schools, where they could be educated, so that they might rise in the social scale, instead of enacting laws that would keep them forever degraded. Some of our most renowned countrymen had parents and grandparents that were poor, and ignorant, also, as compared with what you call the patrician class."

"They were exceptions," replied the gentleman. "There are exceptions to every rule, you know."

---

1 Pejorative terms for poor white Southerners; Pike explains "clay-eaters" on p. 319.

"True," replied Walter; "but nobody can tell if these would have been exceptions, if their parents had lived under the 'negro laws' which you propose to make for the poor and ignorant of our day."

"I cannot think it right," resumed the first speaker, "to impose negro laws upon the whites. The negro is an inferior race, and was evidently intended for the position of servitude which he has always occupied; and though the 'clay-eaters' may envy the happier position of our negroes, it will never do to place them in a similar state, because it will break down the distinction of races, which ought always to be strictly observed."

"How unfortunate they are!" said Mr. Maynard, ironically; but his friend went on with perfect gravity.

"Yes, their situation is indeed deplorable; but it is a pity that they will sometimes sell their children to the traders; not so much, perhaps, on their own account, for no doubt the children are benefited, as that this fact, being known, serves as a shield for those vile men who kidnap children born to a better condition of life, as I have no doubt has been the case in regard to the little girl we saw on the piazza."

"I agree with you perfectly in that last observation," said another gentleman, who had not till now joined in the conversation. "I shall never forget one poor man, whom I met in New Orleans three years since, searching for his child that had been stolen from him. I never saw a man so bowed and broken with anxiety and sorrow. He said she was his only child, and his wife had died a few months before the daughter was lost. He had traced the kidnappers into Maryland, and there lost their track, and since then, had been all over the south and west seeking her in vain. Poor fellow! His face haunted me for weeks afterwards. I never saw such a picture of despair. It was dreadful to think what he must have suffered."

"Did he tell you the child's name?" asked Walter, anxiously, for he felt a deep interest in the story.

"Yes, I asked him particularly, that I might know in case I ever heard anything about such a child. The name was Ida—Ida May—rather a peculiar name, too—"

He paused suddenly, for with a faint cry the child sprang through the open window and stood before them. When, finding herself the object of remark, she had glided out of view, she had not left the piazza, as they supposed. Between the windows of the dining-room there was a low seat, and here she had placed herself, that she might still gaze on the beautiful flowers, and also hear the voice of her kind friend Walter, for whom her young heart beat with an enthusiastic admiration and love. There she had lingered, listening to the conversation, until, as the last speaker began his simple story, her attention became aroused and fixed. The stirring events of the last few weeks, which had so painfully broken the monotony of her existence, had excited in her mind a dim and confused memory of scenes and events in the past which had likewise brought fear and suffering, and something in that recital seemed to clear away the thick haze that clouded her mental vision, and when at length the name—*her name*—was mentioned, the "electric chain"[1] was touched, and vividly, as with a lightning glare, all the long hidden years were visible before her.

Standing in the midst of the startled circle, with her head bent forward, and her small hands clasped imploringly, she threw around one quick glance of agonized inquiry, and exclaimed wildly, "That's it, that's my name—*Ida May!* I remember it all now, and poor papa, and my dead mother's grave, and Bessy, and the flowers and those dreadful men, and O, that dreadful woman that whipped me so! O, I remember it all now! Where have I been so long, and where is papa, and dear, dear mamma—where is she?" and with these words she fell down insensible on the floor at their feet.

Almost petrified with surprise, they had listened to her, and now Walter, springing forward, lifted her in his arms and carried her into the open air, while Mr. Wynn, whose *sotto voce* conversation, with a few politicians at the other end of the table, had been thus interrupted, hurried forward with his guests to see what was the matter.

It was some time before the child could be revived from that long and death-like swoon, and then it was succeeded by a burst of weeping so violent and hysterical, that Mrs. Wynn was obliged to withdraw her entirely from the excited group which had gathered round her.

The sense of sorrow and of loss, which, through long years, had been mercifully hidden from her by her mental disease, now came over her with the intensity of a recent occurrence; and she turned with a child's wild and unreasoning homesickness from

---

1　Paul Gilmore, in *Aesthetic Materialisms* (Stanford, CA: Stanford UP, 2009), explores the concept of "Electric Chain" popular with British and American Romantics. This phrase originates in *Childe Harold's Pilgrimage*, Canto IV, stanzas 23 and 172.

the strange faces around her, although those faces expressed but kindness. It was only after an opiate had been administered, and Mrs. Wynn, taking her in her arms as she would have taken an infant, had soothed her with low-breathed words of hope and promise, that Ida became calm, and yielded to the gentle slumber which was now stealing over her. Having attained this point, she had her removed to a small room adjoining Mabel's, and, undressing her with Venus's help, she laid her on a cosy little white-curtained bed. While doing this, she discovered the gold coin which the child wore around her neck, and the little roll of silk which Venus had attached to the same cord.

"What is this?—a charm?" she asked of her assistant.

"Laws, no, missis!" replied Venus. "'Pears like it's a charm, but 't a'n't. You see, missus, I knowd from the very fust dat dis yer child never wasn't no nigger, and so thinks I, I'll just save dis yer, dat I reckoned she had on when she was kidnap, and maybe some day somethin' would turn up 'bout her."

"Why didn't you show it to your master?" asked Mrs. Wynn, regarding with great interest the little roll that lay in her hand.

"Well, missis, I didn't 'zackly know how he'd take it. I don't want to say nothin' 'gainst Mass' James, but you know, missis, what some folks is 'bout dese yer things," replied Venus, with a wary fear of committing herself by any obnoxious candor.

Mrs. Wynn smiled at her caution, and, thus encouraged, Venus went on.

"I did tell him I thought she was kidnap, one day, when he comed in to ax how she's gettin' on; but he telled me shut up, 'cause, if she was kidnap, she was some poor buckra child, and 't wasn't none o' my business. So, den, missis, I see perhaps 't would be jist as well to take care of it my own self, and so I did. But when we was sold, I tied it round her neck, 'cause I'se scare dat she'd be sold 'way from me some time, and den you know she done loss it altogeder."

Commending her care of the child's interest, Mrs. Wynn left her to watch by the bedside, and, detaching the roll from the cord, she took it with her to the parlor, where her guests were busily engaged in discussing the unexpected event. The child's words and her earnest, artless manner had struck an instant conviction of her truthfulness through the heart of each one that had listened to her, and they had obtained from Walter every particular of his first meeting with her on the mountain, and from the gentleman who had seen her father, all he could remember of that incident. Mrs. Wynn produced the fragment of linen, which she had extracted from its silken cover. "Here," said she, "is a piece of the child's dress, which Venus had the good sense to save, in hopes it might, at some time, lead to a discovery. She says there is no name on it, but you see it is very prettily and fancifully marked."

As she spoke she handed it to her brother, who, after a moment's careful examination, exclaimed triumphantly, "There is a name traced here in the centre of the leaf, but so delicately that it is almost impossible to read it."

"Give it to me," said Walter, seizing it eagerly. "You know, as you told me yesterday morning, I am *younger* than you are, and perhaps my eyes will prove better. Yes, here is a name—*the name*—Ida May! What further proof is needed?"

CHAPTER IX

"With warmer faith let woman's lips
  Whisper the child whom they caress;
Learn from the hand that shelters thee,
  In love, to succor, pity, bless.

"For all the brave world is given to us,
  For all the brave in heart to keep,
Lest thoughtless hands should sow the thorns,
  Which bleeding generations reap."
    PASSION FLOWERS[1]

A month after the events related in the last chapter, one afternoon, Walter Varian, with Mrs. Wynn and her brother,
were seated together near the windows of the south parlor. A
wood fire was burning in the fireplace, and the room, with its
brightly-flowered carpet, and damask curtains, had assumed
a very different aspect from that it wore in its summer dress.
But the cool matting and the muslin hangings at the windows
would hardly have suited this time of year, for it was now past
Christmas, and even to the "sunny south," winter brings many a
cold and dark and gloomy day.

They were sitting together, but they were not conversing; and
every few minutes, as Mrs. Wynn glanced her eyes up from her
sewing, or Mr. Maynard looked over the top of the book he was
reading, their gaze sought the window, which commanded a
view of the avenue for a short distance, as if expecting the arrival
of someone. At length, Mrs. Wynn looked at her watch, and said,
"He ought to have been here half an hour ago; what can have
delayed him so long?"

Walter threw down the scissors, with which he had been cutting a skein of thread into little bits, and exclaimed, "Here he
is, at last. Now for news, for we shall certainly get some reply
today."

At this moment a horse came galloping furiously up the avenue, and a little woolly-headed negro, who rode him, throwing
himself off in a manner to impress the beholder with admiration

---

1 Julia Ward Howe (1819–1910), "From Newport to Rome" (1854).
   Pike misquotes her contemporary, which suggests that she may
   have encountered this poem not in the published edition but as a
   copy circulating in manuscript.

for his skill in "ground and lofty tumbling,"[1] brought the animal's career to a sudden close, by a jerk of the bridle, that nearly threw him on his haunches. Then, throwing the bridle over the limb of a tree, the boy bounded up the piazza steps, and Walter, opening the glass doors which communicated with the piazza, took from his hand the calico bag, which contained the treasure he had brought from the post-office, half a mile distant.

"Reckon I'se done fotched it dis time, Mass' Walter," he said, pulling a forelock that hung down directly over his eyes, as if cultivated for purposes of civility, and making a scrape of the foot that would have done honor to any dancing-master, as he gave the bag into Walter's hand. "Reckon I'se fotched it dis time; heap ob letter in dere."

Walter closed the door again, and, opening the bag, looked anxiously over its contents, until he found a letter with a Pennsylvania postmark, which he gave to his uncle. Mr. Maynard read it aloud. Part of it was as follows:

"But the pleasure with which the news your letter contained was received through our village, where every heart had thrilled with a painful sympathy for the sufferings of the lost child, was damped by the recollection that there was not one of her relatives left to rejoice at her recovery or provide for her future wants. Her father's parents were both the only children of their respective families. Mr. May had one sister, who died young, and his wife's brothers and sisters had all been carried to the grave by the same pulmonary disease that caused her death. Thus the lost child had, except her father, no relatives but some young cousins, whom she had seldom seen, and who, being now minors, are not in a condition to take care of her. Her father, whom you mention as having been seen by a friend at New Orleans, did, indeed, go there, after he had spent nearly the whole of his moderate fortune in searching for her, all over the States, and hearing while there of something which encouraged his hopes, proceeded from there to Cuba, in order to find her. All the property he had left he turned into money, and took with him, and that is the last that was ever heard of him. He wrote that he was going from there to France; but as he has never returned, or sent any report of himself, it is supposed that he was either lost at sea in a hurricane that occurred about that time, or died with the island fever; for he was there at a sickly time of year, and his health was much impaired by his suffering and anxiety.

---

1 A phrase commonly used to describe acrobatic entertainments.

"These are painful details, but I thought it right that you should know them. You have been kind to the little girl, and perhaps you are the best friend she has left on earth. I have communicated with her mother's two brothers-in-law, but they are in poor circumstances, and do not offer anything more substantial than congratulations on her recovery. There is a young woman here, who took care of her when she was a baby, and was with her picking flowers on the day she was stolen, who is very truly delighted to hear from her again, and offers her a home at her house. She is married to a small farmer, and has two children of her own to provide for, but I have no doubt she would do the very best she could for the child, if you will bring her here; but she has no means to send for her traveling expenses. Indeed, the five years that have elapsed since she left here have somewhat changed the population of our village, and there seems to be nobody in particular to propose any plan for the child, and I hardly know what to advise. I enclose a letter for Ida, from the woman I spoke of, who seems really anxious to have her once more under her care, for she has always blamed herself bitterly for leaving the child alone with strangers, and thus occasioning her loss. Hoping to hear again from you on this subject,

"I remain, &c., &c."

There was a general expression of dissatisfaction on the faces of the listeners, which was in unison with Mr. Maynard's own feelings, as he closed this letter; but for a moment, neither spoke. Walter was the first to break the silence. Shrugging his shoulders, and shivering all over, as if with cold, he said, "I wonder how low the mercury gets, about this time of year, up among the hills in Pennsylvania? Judging from this specimen, which hasn't lost its frigidity in coming all this distance, I should imagine the thermometer must have indicated forty degrees below zero the morning it was written."

"I don't like the tone of it at all," replied his uncle. "The writer is evidently determined to avoid all responsibility respecting the poor little orphan. Shame on it! I'll burn the letter;" and flung it indignantly towards the fire.

But Walter sprang forward, and, taking it carefully with his handkerchief, as if afraid of being frozen if he touched it, he laid it on the mantelpiece.

"It won't melt, even in so warm a place as that," said he, his eyes twinkling mirthfully, "and Aunt Emma can keep it and put it into the refrigerator next summer. She won't need to buy any ice."

Mrs. Wynn smiled, but her face grew grave again, and she colored a little, as she turned to her brother, saying, "It is a very strange combination of circumstances, by which this little girl is left so forlorn."

"Very strange indeed!" replied he; "but no doubt such things do sometimes occur."

"I should be happy to keep the child myself," pursued Mrs. Wynn, with a little hesitation. "Indeed, I had spoken to Mr. Wynn about a plan I had, of adopting her as our own, in case it seemed advisable; for, from what Col. Vance said, that day of the dinner-party, I felt it was doubtful if her father was alive. But you know, Mr. Wynn is peculiar in some things," she added, casting down her eyes as she spoke, "and he did not think it would be advisable—he thought it might make trouble hereafter, and his ideas of our duty to our own child would not admit of it. Indeed I did not insist upon it as I should if I had consulted the dictates of my own heart, for Mr. Wynn said he was sure Mabel would not like it; and, though I blush to say it, I had myself seen some traces of jealous feeling on her part."

Mr. Maynard's lip curled with a pitying smile, as he looked at his sister's glowing cheek, and listened to the timid and deprecating tones of her low voice. The idea of the little woman having the courage to *insist* upon anything, after her lordly spouse had pronounced his dictum upon it, had been dismissed from his mind long ago. But he did not tell her so. He only said, in reply, "I am sure the impulses of your heart are all generous, my dear sister, and you will do all you can for the child who has interested us both so much." Then he seemed to fall into a reverie, from which he was aroused by Walter, who, after a few moments, stopped drumming on the mantelpiece, an occupation he had been diligently pursuing since he laid down the letter, and, pressing his hands together so firmly that the blood left them, he threw himself heavily into an armchair, exclaiming, "How convenient it would be, just now, to be rich! Uncle Charles, if I had Oakland now in possession, which you are so continually promising me, I know what *I'd* do."

"Would you?" said his uncle, his face brightening. "Then I'll have no further doubts about *my* plan. Having given you a thing so often, I didn't really want to take it back, and yet, the final result of my purposes would demand a little sacrifice from you, and also some help from your Aunt Emma. To be short about it, I should enjoy, amazingly, to adopt this child; but, in order to do it, I must curtail your pocket-money a little now, and you must spare a reasonable slice off the Oakland estate by and by, so that my adopted child may be well provided for. It won't be felt much *now*, or for some years to come; but I find every year my income grows a little less—the lands are all wearing out, in fact, under our ruinous system of cultivation—and, by and by, when you want to spend money like water, as all youngsters do when they are traveling, as I mean you shall do, after you leave college, you will have to economize a little. Think a minute—count the cost, my boy."

"I don't need to think," said Walter, eagerly; "how kind you are, uncle! It was what I was longing to propose, but I didn't want to seem generous with what wasn't really mine. You shall never suffer, if the land does wear out. I can work!" and he stretched forth his young, elastic arms, and clenched his fists, as if he would defy the world.

His uncle looked at him a moment, with proud and tender expression. How he loved the boy! How he felt his youth renewed, as he looked on that vigorous form, and that fine face, glowing with enthusiasm! If there were weak places in that character, which had never yet been tried by a single cross, if there was danger in those impetuous impulses, he was not the one to see it. No! At that moment he would have matched his boy, Walter, against the universe; and all on account of—what? Because he had consented to an act of generosity that would give him only pleasure at present, and from which he did not seriously believe he should ever suffer any perceptible loss. So fond and blind is love!

But it is something to have the boy's impulses on the right side! O, yes, no doubt Walter was a very nice young man; but not quite, not quite so perfect as Mr. Charles Maynard at that moment imagined.

Turning, then, to his sister, he went on to say, "Perhaps, then, I am the only selfish one in the room; for Emma, I must acknowledge that I have lived this pleasant, wandering, desultory life so long, that I shrink from going back to my old home, there to fix myself, permanently, with a respectable housekeeper and all the steady retinue which the education of a little girl requires. Can you help me? I think brother Richard must get interested in Ida after a while. She will be no care to him, and she certainly cannot be an annoyance; and I am not afraid but Mabel will love her, too. She has been so long the only pet of the house, that it is not strange she is a little jealous, now, of the extreme care and attention we have all been lavishing upon the little orphan for the last month. The child will claim nothing from you that can affect the most partial estimate of your duties to Mabel, and I think brother Richard cannot object to having her board in the house, and be under your care. You see I have not once spoken of the additional labor I throw upon you. I know your heart, Emma. It will be a labor of love."

"You do me but simple justice, brother," said Mrs. Wynn. "Most gladly will I undertake the charge, if Mr. Wynn consents. I don't think he can have any objection. Poor little Ida!" she added, after a pause; "I wonder how she will bear to know that she is an orphan?"

"She will not feel so badly now, as she would to have known it when the memory of her past life first came back to her," said Mr. Maynard. "During the last month she has become attached to us, and new associations and new surroundings will soon dim that glowing picture of her old home, which at first filled her brain. She is such a mere child that she must soon be comforted, as all children are."

"And she is so interested in learning to read!" said Walter, "What a bright child she is! When she came here she didn't know her letters, and now she can read very well in short words."

"You began with her the day after we found her out, didn't you?" asked Mr. Maynard.

"The very next day," replied Walter. "I asked her if she would like to know her letters, and she learned them all in an hour or two. It is a perfect pleasure to teach such a scholar. It is as if her mind had just waked from a long lethargy, and every faculty seems eager to acquire and to understand."

"What a pity that she has lived so long, without even the first rudiments of knowledge! She will be so mortified, when she comes to associate with girls of her own age," said Mrs. Wynn.

"She'll come up with them—I'll risk her," replied Walter; and then, as if impressed with a sudden thought, he added, "But what reason and justice is there in the difference we make between her condition, now we know she is the child of white parents, and the treatment she would have been considered entitled to if we had not made that discovery? Why wouldn't she have needed knowledge as much then as now, and been as capable of receiving it? Who knows how many children sold in the slave market, as she was, have minds equally susceptible of cultivation? What sense is there in making the color of the skin, or the difference of lineage, outweigh every other indication?"

"Stop, O, stop!" cried Mr. Maynard. "You are asking questions that have puzzled wiser heads than yours—"

"Hush!" interrupted Mrs. Wynn, laying her hand on her brother's arm, to arrest his attention. "I hear the children coming downstairs. I will go and talk with Mr. Wynn. It will be better to say nothing about the letters we have received, until we can tell decidedly what will be done with her." She gathered up the letters and her work, as she spoke, and vanished through the door leading to the library, just as Mabel and Ida entered the room.

Mr. Wynn opposed but few objections to the proposed plan. In his secret soul he regarded it as foolish and Quixotic, and thought that Ida had much better be sent back to her friends at the north; but he saw how much his wife was interested for the child, and he knew that his brother-in-law would never give up the scheme. He had none other to urge, and moreover, he did not wish, by any unwarrantable opposition, to deprive himself of the pleasure he derived from the society of the good-natured and merry-hearted Charles Maynard; for plantation life is dull, unless there be cheerful faces and merry voices to make light and music in the dwelling, and, except during Walter's brief visits, the pleasant old bachelor provoked nearly all the noisy mirth that was heard in this household. Mr. Maynard had great facility in adapting himself to the disposition and habits of those with whom he lived. He held his own opinions quietly, and he had great tact in never hitting them carelessly against the sharp corners of other people's theories. Therefore it was, that, almost unconsciously to either, it had become quite necessary to Mr. Wynn to retain him in his family, and, provided he was not called upon to give money, or time, or care, to the orphan girl, he was willing that his wife and her brother should take such measures as suited them respecting her.

Happy in this permission, Mrs. Wynn went back with a light heart to the parlor, where her brother still remained with Walter and the children, and by a word and a gesture signified to him her husband's acquiescence. Then, drawing Ida to her side, she told her, very gently and tenderly, of the news they had received, and that she was now alone in the world, with none to love her as they would love her, who were anxious, from that moment, to adopt her as their own. The child wept bitterly at this disappointment of her hopes, but it was impossible for her to help being consoled by the kindness of those around her. She had a warm heart, and she had already learned to love dearly those who had been the means of rescuing her from her abject situation, and who had done so much to make her happy.

The letter which the same mail had brought for Ida, from her old nurse, Bessy, was full of the warmest expressions of interest and affection, urging her to come and share her humble home, and promising to secure for her every advantage in her power. Ida's eyes overflowed again, as it was read to her, but she expressed no inclination to accept the invitation. Ties later formed were stronger, and, placing her hand in Mr. Maynard's, she said, as she wiped away her tears, "I will stay here and be your little girl, Uncle Charles—yours and Aunt Emma's."

"And mine, too!" cried Walter, who was sitting on a low seat, beside her.

"Yes, and yours, too, if Mabel will let me," said Ida, looking up appealingly to Mabel, who was leaning over the back of her mother's chair.

"I! I'm sure I won't hinder you!" exclaimed she, a little roughly, while the roses deepened their crimson on her cheek.

Mr. Maynard looked from one to the other and laughed heartily. Mrs. Wynn looked up, also, and, apparently, a new thought suddenly crossed her mind for a shadow passed over her face, and she withdrew her arm from the little form it had encircled. In another moment, however, she pressed the child to her bosom again, and kissed her with great tenderness, as if to atone for an involuntary wrong.

It was settled, then, that Ida should remain in her present home, receiving instruction from Mabel's governess, who, patient soul, was glad at last to have a pupil that really desired to learn, and with the proud and delighted Venus to be still her "mauma." This latter personage was now, indeed, in a state of perfect beatitude, at the change which had come over the fortunes of her little pet. She made herself glorious with aprons of every shape and hue, and tired everybody with her ceaseless repetitions of her own sagacity and Ida's merits, and made everybody laugh by the convulsive giggle that invariably ended the story.

From that day Ida's memory was awakened, and her mind recovered its tone, there had been a change in her appearance. Instead of the slow, dreamy, and listless manner that had formerly marked her, her eyes now sparkled with life, and her step became quick and buoyant. As she became aware of her own ignorance, she seemed not for a moment to relax her eager craving for knowledge, and the readiness with which she seized upon different studies, and the retentiveness of her memory, equally astonished and delighted Mr. Maynard.

Thus passed some happy years, over which "let the curtain drop."

CHAPTER X

"At the summit of her dominion, in the depth of her luxury, her Titanic institutions in full action, and her appetites surfeited with indulgence, we see that it is all a vision of death. Inarticulate prophecies of lamentation are in its music, spectres sit around its banquets, and the grim genius of destruction sits and laughs in its strongest places."

ANON.[1]

The curtain rises. Eight years have passed.[2] It is Christmas Eve at Wynn Hall.

The air is soft and still, but the sky is clouded and the night is dark, and the flood of light, that streams from every window of the mansion, falls in long lines through the misty atmosphere far in among the stately pines that have kept solemn "watch and war" over so many succeeding periods of Christmas festivity. Lights are flashing also in yonder grove, which may be seen far away across the cotton field; and beneath the glare of the flaming torches, a joyous multitude of the "field people" are here, around a well-spread table, gorging themselves with meats of different kinds, which they taste now for the first time in a year. This is a commencement of the yearly holidays, and every servant had today received a new suit of clothes, and blanket, and a piece of meat, and has been dismissed from all work for a week; for Richard Wynn, Esq., is proud of his descent from the land where Christmas is observed most joyously, and he as strictly forbids work, and encourages unrestrained liberty among his people, at this time, as he enforces the contrary rule for the remainder of the year. O, how delightful is this season of rest! They have looked forward to it with such longing. The ordinary restraints are removed; they have plenty to eat, new and clean clothes to wear, and all the liberty consistent with their circumstances. Now the dull, brutalized faces begin to light up with a more human expression of hope and desire, and the careworn, furrowed brows assume somewhat the air of content. Christmas Eve their master likes to have them gather in this grove, which

---

1 Taken from a review of Thomas De Quincey's (1785–1859) works, *The Christian Review*, vol. 19 (1854): 93. The anonymous reviewer responds to De Quincey's volumes on "Caesars" and "Essay on the Philosophy of Roman History."

2 Ida is now 18.

is well lighted for the occasion, and devote the hours to hearty mirth; and, though not much accustomed to this mood, it is not long before the stimulating influence of unfamiliar food, and the beer with which they are plentifully supplied, raise their animal spirits to the requisite height, and the old woods re-echo with laughter and song, and the mingling of many voices in all sorts of discordant sounds.

The remainder of the week each individual passes according to his inclination. Those who have wives or families on distant plantations are allowed at this time to visit them provided they may be trusted out of bounds for more than twenty-four hours at once. The remaining servants fish, set traps in the woods, or repair their houses and fortify themselves in various ways against the ensuing winter; or, more frequently, preferring the *dolce far niente*,[1] lie all day in the sun and sit longingly around the cabin fire, enjoying the unwonted luxury of full repose after the exhausting toil of the summer. Some there are who vary these enjoyments by getting drunk, *ad libitum*,[2] which they are now allowed to do if they can procure the means, although temperance is very strictly enforced at other times. In short, this is the season when they may enjoy themselves "to the top of their bent;" and that these enjoyments are so wholly animal gratification, is only what may reasonably be expected of these degraded beings, chattelized through long generations.

It is Christmas Eve in the cabin. It is Christmas Eve in the hall. Everywhere lights are flashing, and merry voices ring out on their air. Above and below, through the spacious parlors, and over the broad piazzas, light footsteps are falling and graceful forms are flitting, for the hospitable old hall is crowded with guests, and old and young are eager to enjoy the gaiety that reigns everywhere. In the drawing room are gathered the grandfathers and grandmothers, looking on while the blooming young matrons and their husbands, the elderly spinsters, the antiquated bachelors, and the young men and maidens, mingle in a social dance, their airy feet keeping time to the lively strains that proceed from a fiddle held in the hands of "Uncle Ned."[3] Everybody

---

1 Italian phrase for idleness, or pleasantly doing nothing.
2 At one's pleasure (Latin).
3 Perhaps taken from a folk song popular in the 1840s, "Old Uncle Ned." Refrain: *Den lay down de shubble and de hoe—o—o / and hang up de fiddle and de bow. / No more hard work for poor old Ned. / He's gone wha de good niggas go.*

feels like dancing when Uncle Ned fiddles, and he knows it, and rejoices in his power, as he sits on the piazza, just outside the open window, nodding his head, and rolling his eyes, and opening his mouth so that every one of his white teeth glistens in the light that streams over him; and if anybody could stop gazing at the dancers long enough, they might almost discover what he had for supper, they can see so far down his capacious throat. Some of the dancers do smile as they glance at him in the pauses of the dance; but he rolls up his eyes a little higher and bends his head sideways a little nearer his beloved instrument, and his elbow shakes a little faster, and soon the observers find they have enough to do to "face the music" without attending to the queer looks of the musician.

In the south parlor, Mr. Wynn with a few of his grave and quiet compeers were cozily seated around whist tables, discussing, in a dignified undertone, the affairs of the state and nation, or pausing now and then to look through the open doors into the adjoining rooms, when a fresh burst of music, or a shout of mirth, attracted their attention.

In the dining-room the tables had been cleared and set against the wall, and the boys and girls, together with a few "children of a larger growth," who had wearied of dancing were exercising themselves in the time-honored games of "hunt the slipper" and "blind-man's-buff;" while all along the piazza, the house servants, dressed in all their finery, were crowding in at the doors and windows, with a keen sense of enjoyment at seeing the fun, and many sententious remarks respecting the merits of the different performers. Their children, neatly, and in some instances tastefully dressed, had gathered in the corners and angles of the dining room, whispering and laughing, and now and then darting across the floor and joining in the game, as if they found it impossible to resist the temptation. But their interference was generally received with a good-natured remark, or a pleasant jest, and at length the most of them were mingling unrestrainedly in the sport. Children are usually true cosmopolitans.

Near the glass door, that opened upon the piazza from this room, a group of women were standing. One of them might readily have been recognized as our friend Venus; for the passing years had touched her lightly, and she seemed to have renewed her youth instead of growing old. A great improvement was perceptible in her dress. Her turban was of the finest cambric, and her bright plaid dress was of nice woolen material, while her aprons, which, in defiance of all criticism, she still persisted in wearing one above another, were made, one of black and the other of green silk, and abundantly ruffled.

She turned to one of her companions, and the happy look which she had hitherto worn faded from her face, as she said, with a sigh,

"Laws bless us! Patra, how Mass' Charles would 'joy heself ef he was ony here now! 'Pears like de Lord might a found somebody dat needed gwine up to heaven more 'n Mass' Charles, and lef him down here wid us a little longer."

"Dat was mighty onhansome ting in de Lord, takin Mass' Charles dat way!" replied Patra. "O, ef you'd ony been here when de news come! Reckons dere was powerful heap ob tears shed den. Poor Miss Emma! she was in de most awfullest perdition all dat night; 'pears like she die, or be 'stracted, or d'ranged, or some such like, she feel so bery bad. An' Mass' Richard, too—tell you what, it do take somethin' to take him down—an' he was took down *dat* time, sure 'nuff."

"Must been mighty hard for Mass' Walter, too," said Venus, "'way off dere in strange country. Must overcome him powerful."

"Well, 't is as 't is, and can't be no 't iser," replied the mercurial Patra, throwing off the recollection of grief with a prolonged sigh, and turning to the gay group within the room. "We was dat 'stounded for one while we didn't none ob us tink ob notin', but we'se got ober it now some, so 't a'n't worthwhile 'flectin' 'bout it. Look at Miss Mabel! She do look powerful handsome in dat white satin gown, don't she?"

"Dat she do," replied Venus, in a tone slightly acidified, "handsome clo'se does set off some folks mighty powerful."

"Handsome clo'se!" replied the other, indignantly. "Dat jest you ugliness, Aunt Venus. 'Fore I'd have sich a jealous despumsition! You allers was jealous, 'cause Miss Mabel was heap handsomer 'n your Miss Ida—allers."

"Me jealous!" retorted Venus. "What for I be jealous? A'n't no need o' bein' jealous, 'cause a nigger like you don't know 'nuff to tell who you ought to 'mire most. You a'n't no judge who's handsome."

"Hush, girls!" said Maum Abby, who was just then passing, and overheard these last sentences. "You have no need to quarrel about your young ladies—they are both beautiful," and her eyes rested with a long, melancholy gaze upon the two maidens who stood in the doorway opposite them.

"Dat fact, Maum Abby," replied Venus, in a calmer tone; "but 't won't neber do for Miss Ida to stan' dere no longer. She'll be gettin' chilly 'fore she knows it. De draft o' wind from dis yer door, has clar intercourse all ober her." Away she hurried to give a timely caution, but before she reached the spot where they were standing, Walter Varian had joined them.

"Here you are, then, young ladies," he said, gaily. "I have been looking for you. Our guests in the drawing-room are tired of dancing, and have been asking for a little music; and I am a committee of three sent to inform you of it."

"We are tired of dancing, also," said Ida, "and came out here to look at the children a few moments. I like to see them playing. How careless and happy they seem! How entirely they give themselves up to their mirth!"

"And how well those dark butterflies, with their crimson trimmings, serve to set off the radiant complexions of their playmates!" said Walter, pointing to a group of gaily-dressed negro children, who were clustering around two fair patrician girls, busily engaged in an attempt to "thread the needle."[1]

"Yes, they serve very well as foils," said Mabel. "I have often noticed that white children never look so pretty as in the arms of their colored nurses; and the good souls are so proud of them, too!"

"Your father spent that winter in Germany, to some purpose," said Walter, addressing her. "This is quite equal to Christmas in the 'Fader-land,' only you have no Christmas tree. I wonder at that omission."

"We had one last year," replied Mabel, "but it was so much trouble that we concluded to dispense with it this year.[2] Maum Abby was the only one who had any taste in arranging it, and now she has a lame wrist so that she can do but little; and, after all, they are childish affairs. It is hard for grown people to have much faith in Kris Kringle."

"O, it does us good to be children sometimes!" said Ida—"to go out of our conventionalisms, and our starched-up proprieties, and sympathize a few moments with the simple joys of childhood.

---

1 Children's game dating to colonial times. A row of children hold hands, raising them as high as they can to allow the leader of the row to pass under, with the whole line following through. The game ends when the "chain" is broken.

2 Christmas trees, a German tradition, were not commonly seen in the United States in 1854. The tradition began gaining traction by the late 1850s and was a firmly established practice by the end of the nineteenth century.

For my part, I should much enjoy playing with the children here a while tonight. Suppose we join the game a few minutes."

"Simple tastes do well enough to talk about," replied Mabel, with a slight curl of her rosy lip; "but children always savor too much of bread and milk to suit my fancy."

"We will join them, perhaps, by and by," said Walter, laughing, "if Ida wishes. I don't object to a good boisterous game now and then. As Ida says, it brings back our youth, and *mine,* you know, is rapidly departing." His eyes gleamed with mirth as he ran his fingers carelessly through his wavy and abundant hair, which as yet certainly gave no token of age. But he dropped his voice a little, as he added, turning expressively to his cousin, "I am old in the heart's calendar, at any rate—we don't reckon *that* time by months and years."

"They are calling us from the parlor," said Ida, whose attention being thus turned in another direction, she had only imperfectly heard these last words.

"Yes," said Walter, "they will call me a dilatory messenger, if I allow you to stay here longer. Let us go and have some music. Come Ida; Come Ma-belle."

There was something in the tone with which he thus pronounced his cousin's name, that caused Ida to look up earnestly into his face. His eyes were bent upon Mabel's with an unmistakable expression, as he offered her his arm; and for one instant he touched, with a quick, nervous pressure, the white jeweled fingers that rested there.

There was a slight flushing of Ida's cheek, and a dropping of her eyelids for one moment—nothing more, no other sign of feeling or change of demeanor; and yet, in that one moment, the secret and fondly cherished romance of her whole life died out in Ida's heart, and she felt the cold, sharp stab of the sword-like thought, that she was cut off from the sympathy on which she had counted to aid her in the prosecution of a great work, and that she was alone in the unsympathizing and distrustful circle, in which for a while she was compelled to remain.

Ida May had only that day arrived at the hall, after a prolonged absence. For three years after her adoption by Mr. Maynard, she had remained under the care of Mrs. Wynn, daily improving in health and pursuing her long-neglected education with an avidity that at the end of that time had advanced her as far in her studies as is common with girls of her age, who have had much better advantages. Then came a general overturning of the sober routine of domestic arrangements. By one of those mysterious changes of climate not uncommon at the south, this part of the district which had hitherto been remarkably healthy, had been gradually becoming infected, during the summer months, with a sickly miasma.[1] Mr. Wynn began first to fail beneath the poisonous air, and then others of the family being affected, it was reluctantly decided necessary to remove during the warm season to another location. Walter had by this time finished his collegiate course, and Mr. Maynard determined to fulfill a long-cherished plan, and take his nephew with him on a lengthened tour through foreign lands. Mr. Wynn, for whom a sea voyage had been prescribed, accompanied them with his wife through England and Germany, having just placed the two girls at boarding school in Baltimore. In making these arrangements, it had been a question of much debate what should be done with Venus. Ida longed to take her with her, but if she left the State she could not return again,[2] and it was as yet uncertain how long the girls might remain at school. Finding that she must be separated from her nurse, Ida, in accordance with Venus's private request, had begged of Mr. Maynard that she might be hired somewhere in the neighboring city, and that she might be allowed a certain percentage on her wages, which would in the course of a few years enable her to buy her freedom.

To this plan Mr. Maynard readily agreed; but, when Mr. Wynn was informed of it, he made many objections, and, finally, ended the discussion by declaring, that if his brother-in-law chose to be so foolish, and set so bad an example, he would secure himself against being injured by it, for, from the day she was free, Venus should never enter the boundaries of his plantation. He would have no free niggers exciting improper ideas among his servants. Therefore, though Venus had in three years amassed the sum fixed upon as the price of her freedom, she had refrained from taking any further measures to secure it, lest it should be the means of preventing her from visiting Wynn Hall during the vacations when the young ladies would probably return home. This

---

1 In the heat of a wet summer, South Carolina lowland swamps and marshes were thought to emanate an infectious air, known as miasma (Greek for "pollution"), as plant matter rotted and decayed, contaminating the air and spreading diseases and epidemic fevers. Those who could afford to do so removed to the coast and cities during particularly hot or humid summers. Germ theories of contagion were not generally accepted until the late 1800s.
2 South Carolina's slave code restricted the movements of enslaved persons "abroad" to other states.

was not so much an act of self-denial as appears at first sight, for, previous to his departure, Mr. Maynard had assured her that his will was made, and, in case any fatal accident happened to him in his journeyings, she would become the property of Miss Ida.

After a year's residence abroad, Mr. and Mrs. Wynn had returned home much improved in health; but the young ladies had continued at school, only returning to the hall once a year, at the Christmas vacation. Mr. Maynard and his nephew, after traveling in Egypt and Palestine, had returned to Europe, and leisurely explored every country that contained things venerable, or curious, or rare, in art, or picturesque in natural scenery. Perhaps there was no part of his life which the genial, happy-hearted man enjoyed so entirely, as the three years thus employed. "He that carries much, brings much away,"[1] saith the proverb; and, having pursued a course of reading with special reference to this plan, through many previous years, he knew where to look for things, and was fully prepared to understand all the antecedents and associations connected with them, when found, and to impart these to his companion.

They rested, at length, from their wanderings, at the University of Gottingen,[2] where it was determined that Walter should remain a year or two to complete his law studies. It was in accordance with his own wishes that he studied a profession; but, even had he not desired it, his uncle would have advised it. He knew that though he should not need it as a means of livelihood, he would be much happier, and more useful, to have some steady employment, and some object of ambition; and that Walter's restless temperament and active mind, could not with impunity be trusted to the pleasant idleness amid which he had glided dreamily down the stream of time. Here, then, he intended to leave Walter, and, after going home for a visit to Mrs. Wynn, who incessantly begged for his return, he would perhaps induce her and her husband to try another voyage across the Atlantic, taking with them Mabel and Ida, for a little tour on the continent, and then they would all return home together when Walter's studies were finished.

But, "man proposes and God disposes."[3] A week from the

---

1 No attribution found for this proverb.
2 University in central Germany founded in 1737, known in the nineteenth century for its law faculty.
3 An adage derived from Proverbs 16:9: "A man's heart plans his way; but the Lord directs his steps."

night on which these delightful plans had been proposed and discussed, while Walter, for the first time, did the honors of his own room in the university, the warm heart of Charles Maynard had ceased to beat, and those lips, on which had ever dwelt words of kindness, were still and cold in death. He had passed through many perils in his journeying by sea and land, to die of a rapid and fatal fever, in a strange country, with none to weep over him of all whom he had loved and blessed, except his grief-stricken and almost heartbroken nephew.

Compelled to make his uncle's grave in a foreign soil, Walter relinquished the purpose of returning home, which he had formed in the first shock of his sorrow. The sods that covered that form made a foreign soil seem like his native land. They did more. The living presence of that honored and beloved relative would have been a shield between him and the temptations of vice. The sight of that grave, bringing with it, as it did, so many pure memories of youth and home, always aroused the better principles and the refined instincts of his nature, and kept him from falling into the gross dissipation which too often accompanies a student's life abroad.

Meantime, Mabel and Ida had continued at school together during three years, associating as of course they must in that connection, but not with much strengthening of affection or intimacy, as time went on. Mabel had from the first been jealous of the attention which her uncle and cousin bestowed on the orphan girl, and she was naturally too selfish to sympathize with their benevolent plans respecting her. As they grew older, and it became evident that Ida was greatly her superior in intellect, and was, moreover, gifted with a quiet perseverance, by which she was enabled to so surpass her even in those superficial accomplishments to which the spoiled child of fortune had chiefly devoted her attention, this jealousy deepened into a feeling of positive dislike, which was only partially concealed from its object, though most artfully hidden from others. By insinuations, and words dropped with seeming carelessness, she contrived to misrepresent many of Ida's actions and sayings, in such a way as to prejudice her father and mother against her; and though Ida kept up a constant correspondence with Mr. Maynard, there were several causes operating unknown to him during his long absence, to alienate from the rest of his family this child of his adoption and love.

Mrs. Wynn was generous and kind-hearted, and she had faithfully discharged the duties she had promised her brother to perform for Ida. But she was human, and, therefore, not quite perfect; and, as Ida's presence in the family might thwart her favorite plans respecting Mabel and Walter, though she never encouraged Mabel's half-uttered communications, and always took Ida's part in any question that arose between them, it must be confessed that there were many times, after the girls had nearly attained to womanhood, when the anxious little lady felt that it would be a great relief to her mind if Ida should find some other home until Walter was safely married to his beautiful cousin. But she struggled conscientiously with these thoughts, and imagined she kept them strictly concealed from everyone, and most of all, from the orphan girl for whom she really had a warm affection, and who had been committed to her as a sacred trust by the brother she was never to see again. Perhaps they were not noticed by others, and might not have been visible to one of different nature, for Mrs. Wynn was invariably gentle and kind; but Ida, though a clear-headed and strong-minded girl, had one of those delicate organizations that can be impressed by the "sphere" of those with whom it comes in contact, and interpret correctly the latent meaning of a word or look.

She had never been much attached to Mabel, and, making many warm friends at school, she did not so much notice her growing coldness, but it was with deep pain that she became sensible of the gradual change which she noticed in Mrs. Wynn. It was nothing of which she could complain, nothing sufficiently palpable even for remark, but, nevertheless, it was there, and when she found that all her efforts could not charm it away, she began to shrink away from them a little; her letters to Walter grew shorter and more infrequent—for a word and a gesture, which had been made when she at one time received some letters from him, had spoiled all her pleasure in the correspondence; she began to spend her vacations more frequently at the north, with her friend Bessy; and thus it was that, during the two years following the death of her benefactor, she had not visited the place where he supposed he had secured her a permanent home.

Fortunately for the poor girl, whom Death seemed to pursue so relentlessly, she had renewed her acquaintance with the devoted friend of her infancy, and was at her house when she received the dreadful tidings of Mr. Maynard's sudden death. The passing years, that had worked so many changes, had left bright tokens of prosperity to Bessy. Married to the proprietor of a small rocky farm among the hills, she was content with her toilsome lot, and thought she wanted no other treasure than she possessed in her husband and two children. But one day there came to the mountain farm, a stranger with a book and a hammer. He sauntered about for a while and then went away. The next day he returned with two others, and the whole party seemed bent upon prying into every nook and dingle,[1] and examining the texture of all the rocks, at which Mr. Morton (Bessy's husband) had so often threatened vengeance. At length they made an offer for the farm so greatly above its seeming value that the sagacious farmer was startled. They told him a plausible story, but he was not put off so easily, and, at length, they were obliged to let him into the secret, and admit him to a share in the profits. The little rocky farm covered a coal-mine of untold value, and Bessy was the wife of rich man.

They removed to Harrisburg, and the first day that could be devoted to that purpose, Bessy set out for Baltimore, to claim recognition from her long-lost pet. Ida had heard of her good fortune, and knew she was coming; but she found it difficult to see in the richly-dressed and lady-like woman who stood before her, any traces of the trim little maiden whom she only faintly remembered. But Bessy knew enough to support her position with dignity, and Ida found at her house always a cordial welcome, and in its hostess a devoted admirer and untiring friend.

Mabel had left school a short time before her uncle's death, and Ida, who was two years younger, was to remain a year longer. But when she could arouse herself from her deep grief at that unexpected loss, Ida determined to remain at school until she was eighteen, which was the time fixed for her majority, in Mr. Maynard's will. This change in her position involved new duties and responsibilities, and gave her a new motive for acquiring a thorough education. Her only means of support was the property which that will secured to her. It consisted of a portion of the estate at Oaklands and a number of negroes, and she was to take possession when she should be eighteen. Until then Mr. Wynn was to be her guardian. The value of this property was sufficient to secure her from want during her life; but Ida looked back on the five years she had passed before she knew Mr. Maynard, upon scenes she had never forgotten, upon conversations which, dimly understood at the time, came back with clearness of import that startled her as she recalled them, and she said to herself, "Better toil, better suffer, if need be,"[2] than by word or deed to coun-

---

1 Valley.

2 Attribution lost, based on 1 Timothy 4:10: "For therefore we both labour and suffer reproach, because we trust in the living God...."

tenance in any way the system whose blighting curse she had known so well. Until the power was in her own hands, she could only keep her purpose a secret, and prepare herself as much as possible for its fulfillment, for she knew that Mr. Wynn would defeat it, if he suspected it while he had control of the property.

Mrs. Wynn and Mabel had been greatly in hopes that Walter would return home some months previous to the time when it would be necessary for Ida to visit them, in order to take possession of her estate; but the young gentleman seemed to be in no haste to comply with their wishes, which, to be sure, being unexpressed, he might be pardoned for not regarding. It was late in October, and they had returned from the mountain retreat, where their summers were now spent, before the wanderer was welcomed to his native land.

Tearful, indeed, was that welcome at first, for it brought back too vividly the memory of one whom they still mourned; but time had chastened their grief, and in their hearts green grass was growing over the grave whereon once had fallen only the cold, wintry rain of despairing tears.

Walter Varian was ignorant of his aunt's purposes respecting him; but if he had known them, and been disposed to act the good boy, he could not have obeyed with a more dutiful alacrity; for, almost from the first day he saw Mabel, he had been completely fascinated and enthralled by her beauty. The fair promise of her childhood had been more than fulfilled, and she was now, at the age of twenty, most radiantly and peerlessly beautiful. Words fail to describe her queenly form and mien, the perfect contour of her face and head, her classic features, her blue eyes that hid themselves beneath long, dark lashes with an expression of dignified repose, the purity and brilliancy of her complexion, which mocked at the commonplace comparison of alabaster or Parian marble,[1] the delicate bloom which tinged her cheek and mantled into brightness on her curved lips, and the glossy wealth of her light brown hair, which she usually wore simply knotted in the Grecian style, or braided and disposed like a crown around her stately head.

When, in his daydreams, he had contemplated the possibility that he might one day be married, Walter had always imagined that she should require not only personal beauty, but also a heart and a mind, in the woman who should be his wife. But, bewil-

---

1 A fine, semi-translucent pure white marble prized by the Greeks for classical sculpture.

dered and dazzled, he had not stayed to consider of this now, and perhaps it was natural that, when those beautiful lips opened, an ardent and impressible young man should mistake the pebbles that fell from them for pearls.

Walter had been two months at home, and he was already privately betrothed to Mabel Wynn, and had only waited for her father to return from a journey, which had detained him some weeks from home, in order to claim publicly the fair hand of his cousin, and to beg that she might speedily become his wife. Mrs. Wynn was kept too much in awe of her husband to make him a confidant of the purpose which so long had agitated her gentle breast with contending hopes and fears; but she had no idea that he would oppose it, and great was her surprise and consternation, when, the night after his return, in the privacy of their own room, she told him of Walter's wishes, and found that he was averse to the union. The proud father looked higher for one with whom to mate his peerless child. He liked Walter very well, but Mabel's husband must be far more wealthy or far more influential than her cousin was likely to be, at least before many years; and after rejecting innumerable suitors, in obedience to his commands, it would ill become him, he said, to allow her to marry Walter, whose whole fortune was very moderate, and whose talents and future position in society remained to be established. In addition to these objections he urged the fact that Col. James Ross, whose plantation was a few miles distant, a widower and a millionaire, had lately been fluttering round Mabel, like a moth round a candle, and there was no doubt he would soon propose for her.

Mrs. Wynn cried bitterly with disappointment, and even ventured to remonstrate, which so astonished her husband that, for a while, he could hardly answer her; but he continued inflexible, and the only concession she secured was a half promise that, if Col. Ross did not propose, he would not forbid Mabel's union with her cousin.

The next morning, without betraying all that had passed, Mrs. Wynn convinced Walter that he had better, for a while, defer asking his uncle's permission to the marriage, and thus the parties were situated when Ida arrived at the hall. She intended to have been there earlier, but was detained by the impassable state of the roads, and some business delays on the part of the gentleman under whose protection she traveled. She found the household in a bustle of preparation for the festivities of Christmas Eve, but she was received with great cordiality by Walter, who had always remembered her with deep interest, and by Mrs. Wynn, who, now that the chief fear of her soul was removed, felt a return of the unselfish affection she had first entertained for the orphan.

In the excitement of her arrival, and meeting so many old friends—above all in again meeting Venus, whom she had not seen for two years, and who laughed and cried over her by turns, in the excess of her joy—in the preparations going on throughout the house to entertain the numerous guests, some of whom must remain all night—and finally in dressing for the party, there had been no opportunity for Ida to observe the new relation in which Walter stood with his cousin. But the little scene I have described had revealed to her the secret, revealed it with lightning power, that for a moment left her stunned and blinded; and though, by the habit which is like a natural instinct to most women, she walked calmly into the drawing-room with her companions, and listened while Mabel sang, and then seated herself at the piano, choosing mechanically the gayest songs and the most noisy and rapid music, there was going on all the while within her soul one of those unacted, unwritten dramas, of which the world is usually profoundly ignorant.

But she was a brave girl, and, though startled and disappointed, she was not dismayed. In the secret chambers of her heart, the death sentence was read over hope of whose existence she had been unaware until that moment revealed them; there was a self-reliant lifting up of her head, a glancing of her thought heavenward, and Ida was strong again, and calm of soul.

That night, when Mabel and she retired to the little dressing-room, where they were to sleep together, having given up their beds to their guests, Mabel came behind her as she stood before a mirror smoothing out her curly tresses, and, passing her arm round her waist, said—fixing her eyes the while on the face in the glass before her, in order to perceive any change of countenance—

"I will tell you a great a secret, Ida. I am engaged to my cousin Walter!"

"I thought so," replied Ida, and she could not help adding mischievously, "I congratulate you on your success."

Mabel was quite taken by surprise, and a little annoyed at this playful rejoinder. She had always fancied that Ida had a secret fancy for Walter, and the thought of triumphing over her had been a powerful stimulus to her desire to number Walter among her own suitors, and added zest to the pleasure with which she received his addresses. She had hoped to see confusion and pain in the face of one she deemed her rival, when the fact was known, and therefore had chosen a moment when the lights were so placed that every emotion could be detected.

"What do you mean?" she asked, half angrily.

"O," said Ida, already repenting of her words, "they say matrimony is a game at which we women play, and some win the prize, as you have done. You have been successful, I congratulate you."

"And you have lost!" returned Mabel, half maliciously, for she suspected a latent sarcasm in her companion's first remark.

Ida laughed merrily.

"That cannot be, for I did not enter the lists," she said, and then added more gravely, "now let us be sober. I deserve to have my nonsense recoil on my own head, for I should not have answered you thus. The love of Walter Varian is not a thing to laugh about. If you have the happiness of his life in your hands, you have a high and precious trust, and I think you must feel the responsibility, Mabel."

"Mercy! Don't go into heroics, I beg!" cried Mabel. "I'm not going to trouble myself about his happiness, I assure you. I shall expect him to make it his business to look after mine."

"And does he agree to this one-sided bargain?" said Ida, who knew that her companion was not jesting, but simply expressing the feelings of her heart.

"O, he'd agree to anything I proposed. I never saw anybody more in love than he is with your humble servant—he is completely blinded—it is really funny. Don't you remember how much he used to think of you—how handsome he thought you was? Well, his head is so completely turned now, that he actually thinks you have grown homely."

"Is it possible?—poor, infatuated youth!" exclaimed Ida.

"It is so," repeated Mabel, provoked that she could not annoy Ida. "He told me, tonight, that he never saw anybody whose face so much disappointed him, he expected you would be so pretty."

Ida looked on the reflection in the mirror before them. She was not so beautiful in her womanhood as she had been when a child. Her figure was slight, and rather under the medium height, and her face, now more than usually pale and sallow from the effects of a recent illness, could bear no comparison with the perfect and radiant beauty of Mabel's. Ida saw it, and she was conscious of a faint feeling of mortification that Walter should have made the comparison so much to her disadvantage, and have remarked upon it to one who never had neglected any opportunity to gall and wound her. But the next instant she put down the emotion proudly, and replied in the same playful tone she had hitherto maintained.

"Everything is by comparison, and Walter was very unfair to expect me to devote my whole time to the business of growing handsome, as you have done. Even for the sake of pleasing him, it would hardly have been worthwhile to sacrifice everything else, and spend these last five years *à la grand Lama*,[1] in reflecting upon and worshipping myself. He should not have compared me with you, and you may tell him so when he is inclined to do so again."

"He didn't compare us; he said there was no comparison," said Mabel, bluntly.

"I honor his discrimination," replied Ida. "When he becomes still further acquainted with us, I suppose he will come to the conclusion that there is no more comparison between the inside than there is between the outside of our heads."

"And what there is will be all in my favor, if he is judge, you may be sure," replied Mabel, turning away with a faint blush and an air of vexation. "Do come now, let us stop this nonsense and go to sleep. You are so uncommonly bright tonight, that I find I shall gain nothing in a war of words. Suppose we rest our weapons until tomorrow."

"Suppose we conclude a treaty of peace for all coming time. I did not mean to offend you, Mabel dear," said Ida, following her, "but I felt a little mischievous. I do sincerely congratulate you."

"Perhaps you think I am the only party who is to be congratulated in this union," replied Mabel, petulantly.

"Perhaps so," rejoined Ida, with an arch glance into Mabel's eyes, as she kissed her fair cheek; and thus the conversation ended, leaving Mabel uncertain, as her companion meant she should be, whether her intended triumph had not after all been a mistake arising from her own misconception of Ida's feelings.

---

1 I.e., the Dalai Lama.

CHAPTER XI

"When shall I breathe in freedom, and give scope
To those untamable and burning thoughts,
And restless aspirations, which consume
My heart in the land of bondage?"
        VESPERS OF PALERMO[1]

The next morning, while the servants were yet engaged in the early sweeping, and general "putting to rights," which followed the Christmas party, Venus, who was making herself useful with a broom, was surprised to see Ida descending the stairs.

"A merry Christmas, Mauma!" she said, "and here is your Christmas present. Isn't it handsome?" and she unfolded a warm, soft, woolen shawl, woven of the bright colors which Venus most affected, and playfully threw it over her head.

"Bress de honey!" exclaimed she, extricating herself from its folds, and surveying it with admiring eyes; "how she do allers 'member her ole mauma, and know what she want most uncommon! Dis yer shawl now *dat* hansum, 'pears like I'se gwine look powerful pretty in it. Bress de child! she done got up mighty airly and dress herself. It be merry Christmas sure 'nuff for ole Benus, when she see her young miss' dis bright mornin'. How d'ye, honey?"

"O, I'm well, and quite rested after my journey," said Ida, as she threw her arms around the neck of her old friend, and kissed her heartily. That dark face, with all its uncouthness, was always pleasant to her.

"'Pears like I neber see you 'gain, honey," said Venus. "Dis old heart done long for you dis heap o' days. What for made her stay 'way from home so long?"

"No matter now, Mauma," replied Ida, "we won't be separated again. You shall always live with me if you want to, and go with me wherever I go."

"Dat ar' good news, dat am up and down fact," replied Venus, in a tone of great complacency. "But run 'long now, honey, for dat ar' Patra she dono' no more 'bout sweeping dan tree-toad know 'bout singing, and she do make such powerful dust you'se getting all covered. De nigger! she a'n't neber been edicated 'bout sweepin', dat gal a'n't. Now, when I sweeps, 'pears like you neber'd know it. De a'n't one speck o' dust. But some folks is *dat* stupid."

---

1 Hemans, *Vespers* 1.3.

This latter sentence was lost to Ida, for she had retreated from the clouds which "cast their shadow before"[1] Patra's vigorously-handled broom, as she approached the parlor door. Stepping out on the piazza, she stopped a moment to caress the dog, who had stretched himself there on a mat. Sport had grown old and feeble, but he did not forget old friends, and, after rubbing his nose most expressively in reply to her affectionate greeting, he even aroused himself to the unwonted exertion of following her, as she went towards the garden.

Ida had never forgotten her early passion for flowers, and now she sauntered along the well-known walks, stopping now and then to speak to the gardeners, or to gather some buds and blossoms, that were lifting themselves up to the sunshine as joyously as if most of their companions had not perished beneath the chilly touch of approaching winter. She seated herself, at length, in a sunny spot, beneath the hedge of wild orange that surrounded the garden, while Sport stretched himself at her feet, and, after shaking his ears over his face as though under a pretense that the sun hurt his eyes, but really because he was a little ashamed to have his ultimate intentions known, gave himself up to a gentle doze. Ida watched the dignified old dog with a quiet smile, and her thoughts went back to the first time she had seen him, to her hiding place among the trees, and to the brave and handsome boy who had then appeared to her braver and handsomer than aught[2] of mortal mould. She thought of the kind friend who had adopted her when she was a forlorn orphan, and whose care and love had never failed her, until death had torn him from her forever;—thought of him with a tender longing, and not a few quiet tears, that fell like dew-drops upon the roses she was twining together; for, since last evening, she had felt that Walter was entirely lost to her. Mabel's husband could not even be her friend; and with Walter her last hold on the family of her protector seemed gone.

From this reverie she was aroused by the sound of voices on the other side of the hedge, and, looking through a small opening beside her, she saw that near the angle of the hedge where she sat, was the gate of the fruit garden, which was immediately behind the other. At this gate a man and a woman were standing. The man had his back toward her, and seemed to have just opened the

---

1 Proverbial phrase derived from the poem "Lochiel's Warning" by Thomas Campbell (1777–1844).
2 Anything.

gate that his companion might pass out. She had laid her hand on his arm, and was looking up in his face with an eager, imploring expression. She was evidently quite young, and was very pretty, with soft, sad eyes, and a timid air that suited her girlish figure.[1] "You will be sure to come *once*, at least," Ida heard her say, in tremulous accents.

"Yes," replied her companion, in low but firm tones, "I will certainly come, though *when* I can't tell you. He watches me like a cat does a mouse; and even now, when all the rest are at liberty for a week, he has given me some plans for a summerhouse to draw, and has told me to draw on them every morning in the library, so that he may be sure I am not with you—curse him!"

The woman looked down a moment, and her lip trembled. "It is too bad!" she said; "and now the baby is growing so pretty and cunning—I've learnt him to say a mighty heap of words since you was there."

"It won't last much longer," said the man; "even the worm turns when he is trodden upon. I am no worm, but I will turn, too."

"It is all because I am *free*, you say," replied the woman. "O, how often I have been tempted to sell myself for a servant, *that* we might live together in peace as the other servants do!"

"Don't say that, Elsie," said her companion, in a more cheerful tone. "The only thing that has kept me up at all has been the thought that you was out of his power, and that our boy was free. O no, Elsie dear, there's an easier way than that to set things straight."

The woman gave a slight shudder, and said, mournfully, "Maybe so, but I haven't been able to sleep nights for thinking, what if you should get lost in the woods, and starve to death, or get bitten by rattlesnakes, or drowned in some of those dreadful swamps, or torn to pieces by dogs when they are hunting for you." She grew deadly pale, and dropped her voice almost to a whisper, as she uttered these last words.

"Don't be afraid of *that*—*that last*," replied the man. "Listen, Elsie; I have a pistol. *I will never be taken alive.* I will never be torn by dogs. I will die like a man—like a *free* man."

"That's what you've often told me. That's what I'm afraid of, that some way you will be killed, and I shall never see you again. Awake or asleep, it's never been out of my mind a minute for a week, and at last I got so frightened I had to come all the way here, for fear you might have gone without saying

---

1 Note that Pike does not disclose their race.

MARY HAYDEN GREEN PIKE

good-bye, though you promised me you wouldn't. O, Alfred, don't go!"

She threw herself into his arms, as she spoke, with a wild burst of tears. He clasped her to his bosom, tightly, convulsively, and his whole frame heaved and trembled; but, after a few moments, he mastered his emotion, and said, sadly but firmly,

"Don't say that again, Elsie. You know how long I have waited, because I could not bear to leave you. It almost kills me to see you crying—don't dear."

She made a strong effort to control herself, and lay quite still on his breast, as he went on, more cheerfully, but always in a tone so low that Ida could not have heard, only that she was close beside them, though unseen.

"You need not distress yourself with these fears," he said. "A body wouldn't think you had courage to walk all night alone through the woods to come here and see me, if they saw how you tremble at the idea of my traveling alone in the woods. I shan't be in any danger of losing my way, for I have a compass; and, as for being hunted with dogs, a good horse will take me out of their reach in one night, and it will go hard if *somebody* don't miss a horse the morning I'm missing;—he owes me more than the worth of a horse, for all the years I've worked for him. No, Elsie, I must go *now*; it's been getting worse and worse for the last year and I can't bear it any longer. I want to own myself; I want to be where I can live with you in freedom, and educate my children;—they say colored people can do all that in the Northern States. O, Elsie, it is hard for you now, but we shall be so happy by and by! I shall find ways of letting you know where I am, and then you can come to me with our boy."

"I wish I could go with you," said Elsie, plaintively, "I feel as if I should never be able to find you when you get so far off, even if you live to get there."

"It wouldn't do, anyway," replied Alfred, shaking his head with a sad smile. "It would lessen the chances of my escape; and then, though I don't mind being tired, and torn, and wet, and hungry, myself, I couldn't bear to see you enduring all that, and I know the boy couldn't live through it. But we mustn't talk here any longer, Elsie. I shall be missed, and you may be seen. It was a little imprudent for you to come at all, for I have no doubt he would get you taken up for stealing, as he did before, if he should catch you about here."

"I couldn't help coming," said Elsie, submissively. "I felt as if I must see you, or I should certainly die."

"Poor dear!" said Alfred, with a fond caress. "I'm glad you came, for it seemed as if I could never get away again long enough to go to you."

There was a long, silent embrace, and then Elsie turned away, turned back again, and, throwing herself into his arms, exclaimed, "Remember, you've promised me you won't go without saying good-bye—you will come and see me once more."

"Yes, I will certainly come," replied Alfred; and then, with lingering steps, often turning and looking back, she went away.

Ida had listened to this conversation, at first, involuntarily, and then with an undefined alarm and astonishment. When she found she was becoming possessed of what might be a troublesome and delicate secret, her first inclination was to glide silently away; but a second thought determined her to keep watch lest the servants at the other end of the garden should come too near, or some ear, less friendly than her own, should overhear them. She knew nothing of their circumstances, but she could not help sympathizing with their feelings. She had not seen Alfred at her last visit at the hall, and now, when, as he stood gazing after his wife, he turned his face towards her, she was surprised to see how he was changed from the animated, happy-looking boy she remembered so well. He stood a long time at the gate, after Elsie's slight form had disappeared among the pines, with his arms folded, and his face set with a stern and gloomy expression. Then a deep, deep groan broke from his lips.

"Poor Elsie! poor little Elsie!" he murmured, as slowly he took his way towards the house; and then Ida also left her seat, and, with loitering thoughtful pace, retraced her steps.

As she reached the garden gate, she met Walter, who was surprised to find her abroad so early.

"They must have accustomed you to very singular and primitive habits, up there in the northland, where you have been sojourning so long," said he, when the usual Christmas greeting had passed between them; "and I see you have even enticed Sport into the same practices."

"Yes," replied Ida. "Sport and I were always good friends, and I was glad to find that he had not forgotten me. *All* my old friends are not here to greet me," she added, mournfully.

"No," replied Walter, who understood this allusion to his uncle; "and I don't wonder you miss him who is gone. The house seemed so strange to me without him, when I first came home, that I hardly knew what to do with myself."

"He was such a kind friend, such a generous protector!" said Ida, with much emotion. "I was doubly orphaned, and the world looked dark, indeed, when he died."

Walter did not reply. Any allusion to his uncle touched his tenderest feelings, and her emotion affected him.

"These calm, bright mornings always remind me of Uncle Charles," said he, at length. "He loved the sunshine, and there was a sunny, genial warmth about all his moods of feeling, that seemed the reflection of everything calmly bright in the outward world. The last words he spoke were to ask me to open the shutters that he might see the sunrise, and then, turning towards it, he prayed. The light from a brighter world broke over him then."

There was another pause, and then, taking the flowers she had been gathering, Walter said, in a more cheerful tone,

"You are true to your old loves, I see—flowers, flowers always, where you are. They have often reminded me of you during these years when I have not seen you. I shall never forget how like a wood-nymph, or fairy, you looked the first time I ever saw you, peeping out from behind the kalmias; do you remember it?"

"O, yes," replied Ida, "I remember it very distinctly, and your tricks with Sport, and his fall into the water; I thought it was *so* funny then."

Walter laughed, and stooping down, he pulled the dog's ears, saying, "We don't frolic so now, Sport, do we? We've grown older and wiser and more dignified now; haven't we, old dog? *You* were always dignified. O, yes, I dare say! But you don't mean to insinuate that I wasn't, do you? O, Sport, don't grow slanderous in your old age!"

"Sport scorns the accusation, and thinks it unworthy of reply," said Ida, as the dog bounded suddenly through the open gate, near which they were standing.

"Recurring to his old adventure reminds him of water," replied Walter; "he seems to be going towards the well. What is the matter there, I wonder? Old Aunt Judy seems to be scolding at the top of her voice."

The well was near the kitchen, and, as they approached it, a savory odor of baking and stewing, coming from the open window, told that breakfast was in active preparation. Over the fire, one or two servants were engaged in culinary operations, while in the yard, Aunt Judy, with her head enveloped in a red turban, was fretting and fuming like an enraged turkey-cock.

"What is the matter?" Walter repeated, as he came near. "What ails Aunt Judy? A merry Christmas to you, aunty!"

The little, short, fat woman turned her head as she heard his pleasant voice, but her face did not relax a muscle.

"'T a'n't merry Christmas," she answered; "here de folks 'most ready hab breakfast toted in, and a'n't a drop o' water left for boil eggs, and de bucket a'n't nowhar, an' all dese yer lazy niggers say dey can't fin' it. De lazy creters, dey's allers circumlogin' roun' when nobody don't wan't 'em—why don't 'y come find de bucket?"

"The bucket is probably down in the well, for I see the chain is broken," said Walter, taking hold of it. "There is old Bill Gray cutting wood—make him go down and get it."

"I done axed him heap o' time, but he won't do nothin' for me—de cantankerous ole nigger!" said Judy, shaking her fist wrathfully at an old fellow who was at work at a little distance, and whose gray wool, sticking out in all directions, and a white bristling beard that nearly covered his face, had obtained for him the soubriquet of Bill Gray.

"I reckon he'll go down if I ask him, though," said Walter, laughing at the odd faces she made in her indignation. "Here, Bill Gray! Ho! Uncle Bill! come here, I want you to go down the well and see if the bucket is there; Aunt Judy can't find it anywhere else."

The negro prepared to obey, with sundry angry gestures towards Judy, and muttering all the while to himself. "Put eberyting on ole nigger now; think *ole* Bill do eberyting. Ole Bill a'n't young nigger no more; he got rheumatiz in ebery one he joints. Ole Bill can't go down de well all time, find bucket. Ole Judy want *drown* dis nigger, *she* do. Mass' Walter no hold rope, let he down, all 'lone."

"Don't you be afraid," said Walter. "For our own sakes we shouldn't care about dipping you in the water. You don't look as if you would improve the taste of it much," he added, with a smile, as he surveyed the soiled and tattered clothes of the negro.

After some delay the rope was adjusted, and Walter held it with the help of some young boys, who, by this time, had clustered around. They were inclined to make a joke of the matter, and Ida was greatly amused, as she stood looking on, to see them rolling up their eyes, and making all sorts of faces, as they swayed themselves backward, pulling on the rope, and shouting, "Nigger down de well! nigger down de well!"

In a few moments after Bill's gray head disappeared down the narrow opening, his voice was heard calling out, "Dat 'nuff—hole on now—I see him—he down here—pull up now!"

In obedience to this request, they began drawing up, and slowly old Bill emerged from the well.

"Where is the bucket? a'n't it down there? you said you saw it," cried half a dozen voices, as he climbed over the curb and stood before them empty-handed.

"Yes, he down dere; me see him," replied Bill, with an air of stupid composure.

"Why didn't you bring it up, den, you cantankerous ole fool?" cried Judy. "Here de breakfast time mos' come, and de water for boil de eggs down in de bottom de well, and no bucket to tote it up wid."

"*Mass' Walter no tell me bring he up*—say, *see he down dere*," replied the negro, looking round with an expression of injured innocence.

Walter could not help laughing heartily at this ridiculous blunder, in which, however, he suspected a spice of malice, and he was about ordering the old fellow down again, when suddenly Alfred came up from the fruit garden. As he saw the group around the well, he paused in his rapid walk, and came towards them.

"What is it?" said he; "the bucket down there? O, yes, I remember, I broke the chain myself, and then somebody called me away, and I forgot about it. I'll get it in a minute;" and, as he spoke the last words, he sprang down the slippery stones, disdaining the aid of a rope, seized the lost bucket, and, reappearing above ground, gave it to Judy, and walked hastily away.

Something in his manner arrested Walter's attention, and made Ida's heart throb quickly. His face was clouded, and no smile relaxed its gravity, though all around were laughing at Bill Gray. He seemed to perform the deed mechanically, as if his thoughts were elsewhere, and he had not the deferential glance and smile with which the servants, even in their most hurried moments, acknowledge the presence of their masters.

Walter looked after him a moment, and then followed Ida She had retreated to the piazza, and was now relating to some of their guests, who had joined her there, old Uncle Bill's amusing misconception of Walter's command.

Ida told a story well. When she was amused or excited, the most beautiful color flushed her cheeks, usually so pale, and her clear dark eyes flashed and sparkled. She had one of those faces whose chief attraction consists in their power of expression. At times she might have seemed to a casual observer simply as a delicate-looking girl, with an intellectual expression and a finely-formed head; but once she let that face become animated, and it arrested the eye, and stamped itself on the memory; when many others, more perfect in regularity of feature, or purity of complexion, had faded and been forgotten.

Now, as Walter looked at her, animated as she was by the conversation, and glowing with the bloom she had caught from the fresh morning air, he was surprised at his own blindness in having been disappointed in her appearance, when, after so long an absence, he had first met her the day before. He looked from her to Mabel. There was no comparison between the two, in regard to feature or complexion, but there was something—some intangible expression of beauty about Ida's face—that Mabel's seemed to need, and while he was trying to think what it was, the bell rang, and they all went in to breakfast.

The whole family, with their guests, were driven to church in carriages. It was a neat little church, tastefully trimmed with oak wreaths intermingled with the pearl-like berries of the mistletoe, and the holly, with its thorny leaves and shining fruit, red as coral. But, as they entered the door, Ida saw Maum Abby, who had come with them, kneeling apart in one corner, and she noticed that, instead of the usual simple invocation, she was praying and weeping bitterly; as if, now she was in the house of God, she were hastening to throw off the weight of some secret grief, at the feet of the merciful One who has bidden the weary and heavy-laden to come to him and find rest. The sight recalled to Ida Alfred's pale, sad face, and the scene she had witnessed in the morning, and, plunged in serious and perplexing thoughts, she hardly noticed the whisperings of her merry companions, or the kind greetings all around her; and it was not till there was a sudden hush in the assembly, and the sublime words of the service fell upon her ear, that she was reminded of the preoccupied manner in which she was listening to solemn worship.

Immediately after dinner their guests departed, and then, as they drew their chairs around the fire, in the deepening twilight, Ida said to Mabel, "What has Alfred been doing with himself all these long years that I have been at the north?"

"I was going to ask the same question," said Walter. "I have noticed he has entirely lost the polite manners and bright, happy look, for which he was distinguished when a boy. I remember I liked him better than anybody about the house; but he won't talk to me at all now."

"O, we have had a heap of trouble with Alfred," replied Mabel, "and I call it too bad in him, and a downright shame in his mother, Maum Abby, to encourage him in it as she does, after all ma' has always done for them both."

"What has he done?" asked Ida.

"Well, in the first place, he wanted to marry a free girl, named Elsie, one of a miserable family of free niggers that lived a mile from here. It was a most obstinate fancy of his, for he knew from the first that papa is decided against having any of his servants mingle with the free negroes in any way; and he never allows one of them on his premises if he can help it. Then, when he asked leave to marry her, of course, papa was angry at his impudence in thinking of such a thing, and told him so."

"He didn't allow it, then," said Ida.

"No, indeed; of course not; but Alfred was angry about it, and so was his mother. She talked to ma' about it, till she almost made her think it was unreasonable, though papa had explained to her that he was conscientious in the matter. At length there was so much trouble about it, that papa found he must take some stern measures, for Alfred kept going there slyly; and one night, when the girl had come here secretly, as she thought, to see what had become of her beau, whom papa had kept quite close for a day or two, he had the girl arrested, and accused her of stealing some little thing that had been missed from the house, and threatened to send her to jail, where she would have been whipped for it, you know. She was dreadfully terrified, and begged, and prayed, and so, after papa had kept her locked up all night alone, he let her go; for he did not really suspect her, and only wanted to frighten her. But he went down there that day, and told the girl's father he might move ten miles away in any direction he pleased, or he would prosecute her for stealing. Of course they could not help themselves, and were obliged to move; for, even if they were innocent, they were too miserably poor to do anything at law with a man in father's position; and so we got rid of them nicely."

Walter winced a little at the triumphant tone in which this little story was concluded. He looked up quickly to see if there was not some expression of face, to contradict the feeling the tone would indicate. But no. That blue eye was calm and cold, and those beautiful lips wore a smile of exultation, as she turned to him, as if expecting his sympathy. For the first time, since his return home, his cousin's smile did not make him supremely happy, and there was a very perceptible bitterness in his tone as he said, "It is almost a pity you did not let Alfred marry the girl, as he wanted to. What harm could have come of it?"

"O, it would never have done at all!" replied Mabel, warmly.

"You have no idea how ugly and discontented the servants get if they associate much with the free negroes. Papa always said so, and declared that he would not have one of them about here. They don't belong together, and ought not to be together. I am sure it has proved so in Alfred's case, for ever since that time he has been as sulky and as discontented as possible. He is downright ungrateful and so I tell Maum Abby, who is always in the dumps if he can't have everything he wants."

"He is her only son, you know," said Ida, gently. "It is not strange she should sympathize in his feelings."

"But he has no business to have such feelings," persisted Mabel. "You have no idea what ridiculous notions he has about himself. It is not only that he couldn't marry Elsie—though I do believe the deceitful fellow has managed to keep company with her ever since, but papa don't choose to take any notice of it—but he is always teasing papa for leave to buy his own freedom. Papa took all the pains to send him to Columbia[1] and have him learn a carpenter's trade, so he is now a superior workman, and he has really a genius for architecture—you should see some of the plans he has drawn—and now, after all that, he isn't willing to stay here and work! He thinks the little things we have for him to do are quite beneath his dignity—the proud puppy!" she added, with a sneer. "He says if he could go to some city, he could earn enough in a few years, by working out of hours, to buy himself. As if he'd be any better off, then! It is very annoying."

"It must be exceedingly so, to have a servant get into such an unwarrantable frame of mind," said Ida. "It is *very* strange, considering all the circumstances, that Alfred can't be happy and contented here."

"It is indeed!" replied Mabel, unconscious of the sarcasm intended. "And to think he should turn out so, after we have done so much for him! I'm sure he was treated almost like one of the family, till he began to be so obstinate, and, even then, papa did all he could for him. He told him he might marry any one of the servants he pleased, and should have a mighty fine wedding—a perfect jubilee—and be married by a minister, too; but the ungrateful fellow didn't so much as thank him."

"What an instance of human depravity!" exclaimed Ida, mockingly. "I wonder at your father's forbearance! It seems to be a great mistake, in the economy of nature, that this Anglo-African race are possessed of a mind and a will."

---

1 The state capital.

"I agree with you there," replied Mabel. "There is nothing that spoils a servant like having a will of his own. He has no need of it. It don't belong to the station for which he is born, and there is nothing to be done but to put it down at once; for one can have no further peace in a house where a servant has set himself up in opposition to his master. But papa has been unwilling to resort to harsh measures, because mama feels so badly whenever anything happens to make Maum Abby sorry."

"Yes," said Mrs. Wynn, who, as she sat in her armchair in the corner, had quietly listened to the conversation this far, "I am very much attached to Maum Abby, and I can't help feeling for her. Alfred is her only son, and it isn't strange she should think he ought to be indulged, even if he is a little unreasonable. Beside, Mabel, you know that Alfred always does what he is told to, and does it well; and it seems a little hard to punish him for being sulky, when we know he is very unhappy."

The gentle little lady spoke in a timid, apologizing manner, as if she thought her kind feeling was a weakness which required excuse. But Mabel only replied, "He ought not to be unhappy—he has no cause. If he would be less obstinate, and get rid of these foolish notions of liberty he has got from associating with the free negroes, he would be happy enough. I think some discipline, that would take down his pride a little, would be the best thing that could happen to him, and make him far more agreeable to us that have to endure his sulky moods so often now. As Ida says, it is mighty inconvenient to have them have a will of their own."

Ida had determined to be very calm and discreet. She had many reasons for avoiding whatever might offend or wound those around her, but she could not longer endure to be so misunderstood.

"Is it possible," she exclaimed, "that you did not understand me, Mabel? O, think what are Alfred's real circumstances—think what trials of feeling he must endure! No doubt he loved this Elsie, with a deep and true affection, and she returned it. Think what an insult to every right feeling it is to offer him another wife, and compel him to abandon Elsie, simply to gratify the arbitrary wish of his master! O, Mabel, what if it were yourself—how would you feel in like circumstances?"[1]

"Nonsense, Ida—don't go into heroics! I did give you credit for having gained a little common sense since I saw you last, but it seems I was mistaken," replied the beauty, with a scornful laugh.

---

1 Mabel is in like circumstances, as she suspects her father will forbid her to marry Walter.

"I am talking common sense," persisted Ida, "I am appealing to the best feelings of your heart. Don't dismiss the subject with a sneer and a laugh. Try to learn compassion for him by thinking how you would feel—"

"I shall do no such thing," interrupted Mabel; "and I don't thank you for the comparison. There is a vast difference between Alfred and myself."

"O, no doubt you reckon yourself composed of the porcelain of human clay!" replied Ida, almost bitterly; "and yet, I read in my Bible that 'God hath made of one blood all men that dwell upon the face of the whole earth.'"[1]

She paused a moment. The firelight, which fell over her as she bent forward a little, and raised her hand in the earnestness of her speaking, showed her face animated with a noble and pure expression, and her eyes almost flashed with indignation, as she continued, "There is nothing, nothing in all the wrongs and woes which this system of domestic servitude is heaping higher and higher continually, nothing that seems to me such a fraud upon humanity, such infidelity towards the Creator, as this attempt to crush and root out that God-given thing—the human will. I know this dominion over the will of the servant is essential to his value as property—I know the master could not live in peace without it—I know the public tranquility depends upon this utter subordination; but all that, instead of reconciling me to the fact, deepens my abhorrence of a system that demands so horrible a sacrifice. Think what incredible strength there is in the human will!—what noble, what mighty deeds it has achieved! to what heroism it has nerved the feeble and the timid!—what tortures men have endured with smiles, because this innate principle triumphed over the quivering muscles and the fainting frame! O, what a prolonged agony—prolonged through many generations—it must be, which crushes and destroys the will! The old torture of the *peine forte et dure*[2] was nothing in comparison with it!"

She spoke rapidly, and with an energy that bore down all interruption, and, when she had ceased, a thoughtful silence

---

1 Abolitionists read Acts 17:26 as scriptural justification for racial equality.

2 Hard and forceful punishment (French). A form of torture also known as pressing, or placing increasingly heavy stones and weights on the outstretched body until death or confession, was reserved for those who chose not to speak a plea of guilt or innocence.

succeeded. Mabel was the first to break it. She did not like the expression with which Walter's eyes were fixed upon Ida's face.

"Come," she said, "let us have some music, and 'drive dull care away.'[1] The world may be spinning round the wrong way, but, if it is, my head is spinning in the same direction, and I fail to perceive the confusion."

Her words were mirthful, and *carefully* toned to the gentle accent she knew he most liked to hear; but they jarred upon the ear that was yet echoing with Ida's grave and earnest utterance, and upon thoughts which, after lying dormant in his brain, seemed now rousing themselves to a new and startling power. She perceived this, and, leaning forward, she placed her warm, soft hand on his, and, looking up into his eyes, said, softly, "Come, Walter."

She *knew* that touch, and that tone, would thrill every nerve in his frame, like an electric shock; and she cast backward upon Ida a quick glance of triumph, as he led her to the piano.

Ida looked after them in silence. She saw the lingering pressure with which Walter relinquished Mabel's hand; she heard the low tone in which words, indistinct to her, were spoken; she marked the rapt and entranced attention with which he listened to her singing, and a keen pain wrung her heart. Walter, from whom she had hoped so much—who had been from childhood her *beau idéal* of all that was noble, and generous, and manly—was he, after all, no better, no wiser, no more unselfish, than the rest of mankind? Had he forgotten the grand schemes of benevolence that had been the dream of his boyhood? Now that the time for action had come, was he about to repress his first fresh impulses, and adopt ideas less at war with his pecuniary interests? He, the hero—the all-conquering—was he about to sacrifice to mammon,[2] or, for the sake of a blind love, bind himself to a course he had once abhorred? It must be so, else why had he not spoken one word in token of sympathy with her, when he saw her combating alone against a host of prejudices? Her eyes filled with tears of bitter disappointment; for, of all the trials of womanhood, there is none greater than that which so many have to endure, in discovering the idol of their youthful imagination to be made only of common clay, and its grand proportions dwarfed to the common standard of humanity.

---

1 Refrain of a popular folk tune.
2 Money, sometimes personified as the god of money, from the Sermon on the Mount: "Ye cannot serve God and mammon" (Matthew 6:24).

CHAPTER XII

"This is sad! this is piteous! but less would not have sufficed the purposes of God. The future is the present of God, and to that future he sacrifices the human present. Therefore it is that he works by earthquake. Therefore it is that he works by grief. O, deep is the ploughing of earthquake! O, deep is the ploughing of grief! but less than these fierce ploughshares would not have stirred the stubborn soil."

THOMAS DE QUINCEY[1]

It was a clear, frosty night. The moon was sinking slowly to the western horizon, but the first faint light of dawn had not yet appeared, and the stars were looking through a thin, misty veil down where deep shadows lay over the landscape. Through the darkest of these shadows, keeping as much as possible among the trees and along the fences and hedges, a man was walking with a quick, light step through the Wynn plantation. Pausing a moment now and then, as he came nearer the house, to hush some one of the numerous dogs that at various points started up with a bark to meet him, but who, upon recognizing him, slunk silently away, he went on till he reached the yard, crossed it, and, pushing open the door of Maum Abby's room, entered and threw himself heavy upon a chair.

The little room was, as usual, in perfect order, but it was evident that the bed had not been occupied through the night, and the dim candle that burned on the table showed a face anxious and pale with watching, as Maum Abby rose from her seat by the fire. Going to the man, who was now leaning his head on his hands, she removed the hat which was pulled down over his brows, and, smoothing back the damp curls of glossy dark hair, she pressed her lips repeatedly upon them, upon his forehead, and the hands that covered his face, her features working convulsively all the while, as if it was only by a strong effort she could refrain from tears.

The man sat silent, making no token of reply to her caresses, for some minutes, and then his head sank lower and lower, till it rested on the table before him; a shudder passed over his whole frame, as if all its cords and muscles were giving way, and sobs burst from his bosom, thick, gasping, as if the tempest of grief would break the strong heart it was convulsing.

---

1 From "Finale to Part I—Savannah-la-Mar" of De Quincey's *Suspiria de Profundis and Other Writings* (1845).

Maum Abby made no further endeavor to restrain the expression of her own sorrows, but, sitting down beside him, with one arm over his neck, she leaned her forehead upon his shoulder and wept silently. At length they both grew calmer, and, as the violence of his emotion became exhausted, she raised herself, and, lifting his head with a gentle force, she drew it down till it rested on her bosom, and with a trembling hand she wiped his tear-wet face, and stroked his hair with a low murmuring sound, as one would soothe a child.

"I shall tire you, mother," he said, at length attempting to rise.

"No, Alfred, no," she replied, in a tone of quiet sadness. "You have found comfort for many sorrows in resting them upon your mother's heart, and it will not fail you now. Rest, my boy. You must be very weary, and this may be the last time my bosom can be your pillow."

Her voice choked again, but she shed no more tears. There was a long pause, for Alfred was exhausted in body and mind. After a time, however, he raised himself, and then his mother asked,

"Did Elsie bear it well, at last?"

"Better than I expected," replied Alfred; "and in fact for her sake I am glad this parting is finally over. Ever since she was here last week—Christmas day, you know—she has been in a perfect fever of anxiety and expectation. I expect she will be sick; perhaps she will die. She hasn't much constitution, and I can see how dreadfully the trials of the last three years have worn her. It won't take much now to kill her."

He said this with a gloomy calmness, that was more painful to his mother than tears.

"Poor boy! poor boy!" she said softly, "how she loves you!"

A convulsive sigh swelled Alfred's breast, but he restrained all further demonstrations of grief, and after a few moments replied in a quiet tone.

"Yes, she loves me, and that love has been the curse of her life. It has caused her to be persecuted by Mr. Wynn, and has eaten up her health and strength with anxiety for me. It would have been better had I minded what you said from the first, and by attempting this escape long ago, as you wanted me to do, left her free, while she could perhaps have loved somebody else who could have made her happy. And yet"—he added, lifting his head, and speaking in a more earnest, animated tone—"and yet, what a blessing, what a comfort she has been to me, in spite of all! O, mother! I have often thought, for a little while, that I was richer and happier than *he* is"—and he pointed towards the room where Mr. Wynn was then sleeping—"in the possession of this feeling that made me forget everything else. O, mother! nobody can tell, but those who have known from experience, the strength of the tie that binds *us* together, who have no other joy, no other comfort, nothing else to make life bright! It is stronger than the love of freedom, stronger than the hatred of servitude; it makes us indifferent to everything else, and contented if we can have that one thing we love! If I could have lived with Elsie in peace, I would never have tried to be free. Mr. Wynn is a fool!" he added, rising, with a bitter laugh; "he has strained the bow till it has broken."

Maum Abby looked at her son as he walked to and fro in the narrow room, and her heart swelled with contending emotions. She knew how deep was his affection for his wife, and the struggle it had cost him to repel her fears and resolve to leave her. Yet she felt that the sacrifice of present comfort to future good, which the husband and wife were making, was nothing in comparison to that required of her. Elsie was a timid, girlish little creature, and she had a thousand fears as to what might become of herself and her boy, in case Mr. Wynn's vengeance should alight upon them, when he found Alfred was gone. She had also a deeper and more unselfish anxiety, which was wearing out her life, lest the hardships and perils of his long and venturesome journey towards the land of freedom, should prove too much for her husband's strength and life; or that some of the numerous enemies, that would beset his path behind and before, should force him to a combat where escape was hopeless, and a speedy death from his own hand, the most merciful fate she could anticipate for him.

But, if he succeeded—if he reached the blessed land where his powers would no longer be fettered, where his mother fondly dreamed he would acquire wealth, and education, and all the advantages of freedom—there Elsie might go to him; she could live with him in happiness the rest of her days, and be proud of his prosperity. But his mother had no such hope to cheer her. After the setting of another sun she should never more behold the face that had been dearer to her than the daylight—more precious, more fondly cherished than her own life. It was her right, her duty, to secure liberty for her son; but she felt that the ties which bound her to her mistress were such as could never be broken. Mrs. Wynn depended upon her for much of society, and for assistance in the cares of housekeeping; and gratitude and love alike forbade her to leave one who had always been to her like a younger sister. To these duties she must devote herself so long as Mrs. Wynn lived. She might hear of her son's success, and rejoice in it, but she could never see him again. It was under the influence of this train of thoughts that she said,

"Mr. Richard has been harsh and cruel to you and Elsie, I know; but even if he had not, it would have been impossible for you to have been contented to be always a servant. You have powers of mind which must expand; and the little education I have been able to give you has given you a taste for more. You already know an amount which is considered dangerous."

"Yes," said Alfred, smiling; "they will have reason to consider it so, when I get far enough away to emerge from the swamps, and travel in the public conveyances. I have papers and letters enough to prove to anybody, that never saw me, that I am a free negro, moving north from Alabama."

Alfred was very handsome, notwithstanding his dark skin; for he had straight, well-formed features, and silken, wavy hair. His mother gazed at his face, lighted now by a smile of hope and triumph, and she almost groaned aloud as she thought how lonely her home would seem when he was gone.

"O," she exclaimed, "it was for this I taught you to write, for this I stimulated your thirst for knowledge, and used every means to procure books for you to read! It was for this I rejoiced when I saw you quick to learn, quick to remember, ingenious, active in body and mind! It was for this I mourned when I saw how your love for Elsie diverted you from the intense desire for freedom, after I had educated you to know your rights as a man, and to long to claim them. O, Alfred, it was for this, for this very hour; and now it has come, my heart fails me! When you reach the north, you can have Elsie and your boy; but O, my son, you will never see your mother again—never!"

Her voice died away in a low moan, and she bowed her head despairingly; but Alfred was now aroused from the extreme depression and the violent grief which parting with his wife had caused him, and hopefulness had taken the place of despondency. He comforted his mother with tender words, and bright pictures of the future; and though she shook her head sadly, when he spoke of having her with him in his northern home, she was half persuaded to believe that by and by, when she was old and feeble, so that she could not longer be of service to Mrs. Wynn, she might go to live with him. In the meantime, he would write to her. Some way would be found by which they could correspond, and she would be far happier to know he was prosperous and happy at a distance from her, than to have him with her, and see him coerced and threatened like a dog. The more he talked to her, the brighter his own hopes grew, and it was with hearts comparatively light and happy that they sought their respective beds, just as the day was dawning.

That morning, as the family was sitting around the breakfast table, after their morning repast was finished, Mr. Wynn said to Ida, "Now that the Christmas frolics are over, and we have come back to the sober routine of life, I suppose you will expect me to give an account of my stewardship, and deliver to you the title-deeds of Miss Ida May's estate."

Ida smiled, and said she was in no hurry to assume responsibility and care.

"Nevertheless," replied Mr. Wynn, pleasantly, "since it must be done, you may come to the library after dinner, and I will endeavor to be ready for you." Then turning to Walter, he added, "You remember I advised you, some weeks since, to sell your plantation and stock, and yesterday I heard of a gentleman who, I think, will purchase. He will probably also buy the negroes, if you wish to sell. It would be better, I think, for you to sell all who are too old to change their habits; the others it will be more profitable to hire out. They will bring you in quite a revenue; and if you are to live in the city and practice law, you won't want the care of a worn-out plantation. If you like, we will drive down to Col. Ross's place, where I met the gentleman who talks of purchasing."

Ida glanced wistfully at Walter while his uncle was speaking. She had longed to know what disposal he meant to make of his property; but the change that had taken place in him, and the slight restraint that had sprung up between them, had prevented her from recurring to a subject on which she feared they would have no coincidence of opinion. Walter looked thoughtful and grave for a moment, and then he said quietly, "I should prefer thinking of the matter a little first. I have hardly been over to Oaklands since my return and I know little of the state of affairs there. Is the gentleman going to leave immediately?"

"Not that I know of; a few days will make no difference," said Mr. Wynn, a little coldly.

"And he cannot go today, at any rate," said Mabel gaily, "for he has promised to go out with me to try my new pony—your Christmas gift, papa." The beauty laid her hand on her father's arm, and looked up at him with her bright eyes. She was the only person in the house who was familiar with him. There seemed to be a perfect sympathy between them.

Her father smiled, but made no objection. He had confidence in Mabel. He understood her quite well, and he had no fear that she would balk his schemes for her through any foolish sentimentalism. So long as she did not entangle herself with any engagement, Walter might pay her any attentions she chose. Just then the door opened, and a woolly head was thrust into the room, and the voice of a young negro waiter said, "Please, Miss Emma, you'se done finished breakus, ole Uncle Billy want see you mighty bad. He not so bery well heself dis mornin'."

"Tell him I will come soon," replied Mrs. Wynn, and the boy disappeared; but returned again in a few moments, saying "Uncle Bill say you *must come right 'way now.* He done hurt he sore toe, and it do ache powerful."

Mrs. Wynn rose to this second summons, and went out. She was surgeon and doctor to most of her servants, as, indeed, the mistresses of plantations usually are. When Ida and the rest followed, a few minutes after, they found her bending over the negro's huge, dirty foot, and, with her soft white hands, cleansing and binding up the wounded part. As Ida stood by looking on, Walter remained a moment beside her.

"What you said the other night," he said, in a low voice, referring to it, abruptly, for the first time, "was very true; and yet there is another aspect in which to view the subject. Look at this instance. What northern woman, of Aunt Emma's station in life, would perform these menial offices for a sick negro?"

"Many would, I trust, if it were necessary," replied Ida. "There are kind-hearted and charitable women there, as well as here. But it is a disgusting business, in itself considered."

"Yes, indeed," said Walter; "and yet it is a part of the duty which every lady owes her servants, and pays them without a murmur. Ah, Ida, the cloud may have a silver lining, after all!"

"God forbid that it should be all darkness when there is so much light in human homes! But, Walter," she added, with an arch glance from under her long eyelashes, "if this man had always been free—if he had not always been treated as a child—he would probably have known enough himself to take care of so simple a wound as this; and he would, perhaps, have had the means to procure medical attendance, or ointment and soft linen to wrap it with; and he might have had a wife and a child, who would have been capable of performing this office; so that the delicate ladies, like Mrs. Wynn, might be relieved from employments so repulsive. Ah, Walter!"

Walter laughed, and ran his fingers through his hair. How that gesture always recalled to Ida the days when she first knew him! "The same trenchant little Ida as of yore!" he said. "I believe you have changed less than anybody."

"Is that intended for a compliment?" replied Ida; "because, if it is, I will endeavor to behave properly under the infliction;"—and she cast down her eyes with a comical expression;—"but it won't do to throw away my blushes, if you mean that I am the only one who has not been improved by the lapse of years."

Walter was about to make a merry rejoinder, when his attention was attracted by seeing one of the plantation people peering round the corner of the house near them. He had come up the steps of the front piazza, and, hearing voices, had ventured near.

"What a wicked-looking face!" exclaimed Ida, in a low voice, as her eyes fell on him.

"Yes," replied Walter; "that is a specimen of the class that puzzle philanthropists." Then, raising his voice, he added, "Ho, boy! what are you looking for here?"

"Want see massa," the man mumbled out, after some hesitation.

"Go to yonder door, then, and you will find him," replied Walter. "I hear him talking in the hall."

"Want see he 'lone—got somethin' tell," muttered the negro.

"Go then and see him 'lone," replied Walter. "Here you, Dick"—beckoning to a small scion of the colored race standing near—"go show this boy to your master."

The fellow went after his guide, with downcast eyes and a shuffling gait; and through the open door they saw that, after a few words, Mr. Wynn led the way to the library the negro following.

"Now, then, what is it?" said Mr. Wynn, as he closed the door behind them, and seated himself in his study chair. "I warn you, beforehand, that I will listen to no complaints."

"'T a'n't no complaint, 'zactly, I'se gwine make, massa," said the man, his small eyes glancing around the room with a cunning and treacherous expression.

"What is it, then?—be quick!" said Mr. Wynn.

"I'se got somethin' for tell massa, maybe massa like know," replied he, in a low tone, and with the same restless glances.

"Here you!—what's your name?" asked Mr. Wynn.

"A'n't got no name, 'zactly; dey calls me 'Number Tree,'" replied he, with a grin.

"No name.—how happened that?" exclaimed his master.

"See, massa, I'se mighty little when I'se sold, and de auctionee he forgit my name, so he calls me 'Number Tree,' and dat be my name eber sence. Do jes' well, massa."

"Well, then, 'Number Three,' look right at me, and tell me what you've got to say, and waste no more time about it. Do you hear?" said Mr. Wynn.

"O, yes, massa, me hears; me allers hears powerful quick; me got mighty long ear for hear, else me neber hear dat I'se gwine tell massa, las' night."

He paused, and again Mr. Wynn exclaimed, impatiently, "What is it?"

"Massa know 'bout den mis'eble free nigger, live down by de branch tree four year 'go—dem dat ar Alfred boderate massa 'bout, 'fore massa tote 'em way off. Massa 'member?"

"Yes, I remember them. What of them?"

"I'se down dar whar dey lib, las' night, massa, and I'se creepin' long under de bush, cause I'se so scare de patrol, and I sees—"

"What were you there for?" exclaimed Mr. Wynn, angrily; and then, as the man hung his head in a disconcerted manner, he added, "Stealing corn, I suppose. But go on; you didn't come to tell me of *that*, of course. You saw—"

"Ki, massa," said the fellow, scratching his head. "'T *warnt dat*, 'zacly, I come for tell massa. I sees bright light shinin' out under dar door, and bimeby a man come and open it, and a woman jump right in his arms; and de light shine all over him when he was huggin' her, and I sees 't was Alfred. Well, massa, I a'n't nothin' but a nigger, but I'se hearn tell a heap 'bout Alfred and dat wench, so t'inks I, Number Tree'll watch and catch what he can, and maybe massa give him *button*."

He looked up slyly, and Mr. Wynn replied, "Yes, you did right; I will reward you. What did you see?"

"Well, massa, de fire he crack and snap so, I didn't 'zacly hear much when he was in dar, ony somebody cryin' some de time; but when he come out to go home, den I hear de wench talk to him, and he talk to her. I can't tell 'zacly what dey say; but I hear 'nuff for know dat ef massa don't look mighty sharp, he lose he nigger 'fore tomorrow mornin'."

"Lose him, how?" exclaimed Mr. Wynn, excitedly.

"Yes, massa, done loss he entir'ly; he be gone goose 'fore to-morrow mornin', ef massa don't grab he dis very day. He say he steal de swif' hos, and ride like a streak ob lightnin' all night."

"Zounds!" exclaimed Mr. Wynn, letting his hand fall heavily

on the table before him. "I should hardly have thought that of him, sulky as he has been of late. He was going to steal a horse, and ride off to parts unknown, was he?"

"Yes, massa, dat jis' it; and when he done *settle* dar what he gwine go, den he gwine send for de wench and de baby."

"I'll settle him!" said Mr. Wynn, as his brows grew dark with anger. "You are very sure—you are certain it was Alfred, are you?"

"No, massa," replied 'Number Tree,' again resorting to his favorite manipulation, and, rubbing his wool with great violence, "No, massa, I can't say day I'se 'zacly *certain*, but I'se *right sure*."

Mr. Wynn sat a few moments buried in thought. He had sent Alfred and one of his fellow-servants some distance that morning, with some plants from his conservatory, which he wished to present to a neighbor; and, at first, he feared Alfred might seize that opportunity to escape; but, after a little reflection, he felt convinced that the plan the negro had mentioned was the most feasible, and would, therefore, most probably be tried; and that his best course would be to keep his discovery a profound secret until Alfred's return, lest something should transpire to give him a hint of it, and thus induce a premature flight. Telling the negro, therefore, that he would come down to the quarters the next day and reward him handsomely for his fidelity, he charged him to mention the matter to no one, and to return to his work without delay, and thus dismissed him.

The morning wore slowly away. The sun, which had arisen so brightly, shrouded itself in clouds, and suddenly there poured down one of those incessant, deluging rains, that mark a southern winter. There could be no riding party that day, and the horses, that had been brought round, were ordered back to the stables; and Mabel, whose brow always grew cloudy with the sky, was making up her beautiful lips to pout a little at the prospect of staying indoors all day, when a carriage drove to the door, and Col. Ross was announced. This was fortunate for Mabel, who was delighted to tease Walter by a little flirtation with the gallant widower. But the young gentleman was less pleased. He had hardly had a moment of quiet conversation with his cousin during the past week, as they had been constantly visiting, or entertaining guests, and he did not like it that she should be so evidently flattered by Col. Ross's attentions. He began to fear that Mabel was more artificial, less content with home joys and quiet pleasures, than he should like his wife to be; that she had less intelligence and discernment than he had imagined, or she would not have frowned at the idea of a quiet morning with him, and she would not have welcomed that old fop, who was now whispering compliments in her ear, as they stood together beside the flowers at the window opposite him. Yes, he was sure that was a compliment—it was just so she had cast down her eyes and blushed bewitchingly, when he had told her, the day before, in that very spot, that she was fairer and more stately than the calla lily, whose pellucid cup they were now admiring. He thought he was only scornful of such coquetry, but he was in fact dissatisfied with himself for thinking she could be less than perfect, and at the same time intensely jealous of her.

Meantime, Ida, after going into her room to lay aside her riding habit, had not returned to the parlor. She felt nervous and restless. A vague presentiment of coming evil oppressed her, and she dreaded the meeting with Mr. Wynn, which had been appointed for that afternoon. She knew he would oppose her with harshness, and, though she was not afraid of him, it would be very disagreeable. She sat for a while thinking about her future course, and then went down to find Maum Abby, and have a little chat with her. She longed to tell her that she knew her troubles, and sympathized with them, but whenever she had attempted to converse with her, since her return, Maum Abby had pleaded the constant occupations of the busy week, as a plea for leaving her, evidently because she did not want to talk of Alfred.

This morning she was sitting sewing in her neat little room. She looked worn and weary, and Ida saw that she had been weeping; but she was not disposed to be talkative, and, after a few fruitless efforts, Ida left her, and returned to the parlor.

Mabel and Col. Ross were sitting in the bay window, playing backgammon, and apparently carrying on an animated conversation. Walter, at the centre-table, was looking over the plans for the summerhouse, which Alfred had completed with great neatness and elegance. It was to be a tiny Gothic temple, placed in the centre of the garden, not much in keeping with the other edifices truly, but very tasteful in itself and planned to suit Mabel's fancy, whose ideas upon architecture were rather peculiar.

As Ida entered the room, Walter placed a chair for her beside him, and turned over the drawings for her inspection. As she did so, and saw the taste and talent displayed in them, she said, almost unconsciously thinking aloud,

"I don't blame Alfred for wishing a wider scope for his powers, and greater remuneration. It is a great shame that he is not allowed to buy his freedom."

"Treason! treason!" said Walter, in a low voice, playfully, and then added, more gravely, "After all, would he be happier then?"

"If you had spoken those words five years ago, they would have been transposed a little, and the question would have been an affirmation," said Ida, looking up archly.

Walter colored slightly, as he met her glance. "Ah! perhaps so," he said; "I was young, then, and enthusiastic. Now I have grown older and wiser, and am inclined to let the windmills of society turn in peace, secure from any Quixotic attacks of mine."

"You now prefer to employ yourself in grinding your corn at the mill, rather than in fighting it," replied Ida, in a playful manner.[1]

"I understand you; you think I have grown selfish," said Walter, quickly. "Perhaps I have. Selfishness is the grand conservative element in society. People always outgrow their early enthusiasm, and it is well that they do, or the world would be strangely turned upside down."

"If you mean the enthusiasm which is the result of mere animal spirits, the effervescence of youthful ignorance and thoughtlessness, I agree with you," said Ida; "but the enthusiasm for truth and right, which is the first instinct of a noble soul; the scorn of wrong that yet contains no Pharisaical contempt for the wrongdoer—should this abate as years move on? Should this grow so cold, that a man can at length do that which once he would not allow in another?"

"I know to what you refer," said Walter, gravely; "but other men have done this—wise and good men—statesmen, lawgivers, and clergymen have done this, and justified themselves in it. Why should I affect to be wiser or better than they? Why should I not do as others do?"

Ida raised her clear, dark eyes to his face, and the flowery crimson of her cheek deepened, as she replied in a low, earnest tone, "Because 'every man shall give an account of *himself* to God!'"[2]

Walter was startled by this unexpected and solemn reply. He was not willfully irreligious, but he was thoughtless, careless, as are most young men of his age, and these few simple words

---

1 The idealistic hero of *Don Quixote* (1605) bravely fought windmills, under the delusion that they were giant enemies. Ida playfully jabs that Walter now casts windmills in their more natural (but material and lucrative) role, in processing grain.

2 Romans 14:12.

seemed to put the whole subject in a new light before him. Instinctively he glanced across the room to see if they had been overheard; but Mabel and Col. Ross were talking so gaily over their game, that they evidently had no thought for anyone but themselves.

Ida had spoken from the first impulse of her own thoughts, and was half afraid the next moment that he might be offended; but he was not.

"I acknowledge the reproof," he said, as he met her inquiring look, "and henceforth I will try not to measure my duties by another man's conscience. But this is a perplexing maze in which I find myself involved. I do not think just as I used to about holding servants—honestly, I do not. The subject has its shadows, I know, in some cases, but it seems to me that, with kind and just masters, the lot of our servants might be made a blessing to them, as well as convenient for us."

Ida smiled. "It is the old story—'we first endure, then pity, then embrace.'"[1]

"No, it is not that—it is not the callousness of familiarity with evil. It is merely choosing the less dangerous horn of the domestic dilemma. I see what is wrong, and hate it as much as ever; but I am uncertain what to do in my own case. *I* should not be a hard master; my servants will be happy—perhaps more so than if I free them."

"Dare you trust yourself with the possession of absolute power over the lives, and persons, and destinies, of your fellow-men? Dare you incur the temptations which follow in the track of this usurpation of authority, which God never meant one man to have over another? Who ever did so and came out from the trial unscathed? If you dare do it, I dare not. I shall free my negroes as soon as they become legally mine."

"I supposed you would do so," replied Walter; "but what will you then do?—you will be left penniless. Pardon me the uncivil question," he added, coloring violently. "I shall, of course, be most happy to have you share my home, when I get one in which to receive you," and he glanced towards Mabel.

"Thank you, Walter," said Ida, quietly; "but I shall be dependent upon no one. I have already made arrangements to teach school. I have some warm friends at the north, who will assist me in providing for my servants when we arrive there. I suppose the

---

1 From Alexander Pope (1688–1744), *An Essay on Man* (1733–34), epistle 2.

sale of the land will be sufficient to establish them, and then, with health and education, I do not fear but I can support myself."

Walter looked at the slight form and youthful face of the speaker, and was half astonished at her energy, half annoyed at the idea of anyone in whom he felt interested being compelled to work for a living. He had been brought up in the false ideas on this subject which prevail everywhere in a slave country, and he had yet to learn the dignity and beauty of labor.

"Yet it will be a great sacrifice," he said. "Do you think you have given sufficient thought to the subject, to know all it will cost you?"

"O, yes!" replied she, and her tone was a little sad. "I have counted the cost, and the only part I shall dread to pay is the risk I encounter of losing the friendship of this family, who have been so kind to me. I know I shall offend their strongest prejudices."

"Not mine!—you surely do not fear losing *my* friendship, by this act of self-sacrifice!" said Walter, in a tone so earnest that Ida's heart thrilled with a strange emotion.

"I will not fear, after this morning," she replied; "and, perhaps, I shall be glad to have your aid in the matter. I do not expect much help from Mr. Wynn."

"No, he will only cast obstacles in your way," said Walter, "and if you escape serious annoyance you will be fortunate. It will be 'braving the lion in his den.'"

"I know it—I dread it a little. Mr. Wynn is formidable when he is offended."

"And, after all, Ida, it is doubtful if those miserable creatures will be able to take care of themselves, or happier for the change."

"Perhaps the oldest and most degraded will not be," replied Ida; "but you must remember that it is not these few alone whom I shall benefit. I am giving liberty, and a chance for improvement, to their children, and their children's children, to remotest generations!" and, as she spoke, her eyes kindled and dilated, as if she was already looking, through the coming years, upon the countless host who should arise to call her blessed.

"Still," persisted her companion, "the benefits are distant and uncertain, and it is with the present you have to do. The same results may be brought about in some other way, if you wait; and you seem so young and fragile, to cast yourself so boldly on the world, and to brave 'the slings and arrows of outrageous fortune."[1] You are treading a toilsome and dangerous path, and you must tread it alone."

"O, no!" said Ida, roused by this continued discouragement, "O, no, I am not alone! Those who tread this pathway may be so few and far between, that each one may seem to be the first; but yet, many have preceded me, and many units make a multitude, you know, Walter. I suppose that in some places, at least, we each of us leave 'footprints on the sands of Time,'[2] though the work of each one seems so little. It is a comfort to know that, though *individual* traces may be lost, the tramp of passing generations will wear a broad and permanent pathway, on which those who come after may march into the 'new kingdom, wherein dwelleth righteousness,'[3] that, we are assured, shall one day be established on this globe of ours. You see," she added, smiling at her own earnestness, "that I have great hopes of our race, and for myself I do not fear. I can work, if I am little."

Walter's eyes were beaming with admiration, as they rested on her. Her self-abnegations, her earnest faith, her courage, impressed him deeply. Her words seemed to melt the ice of worldliness and selfishness that had gathered about him, and awaken to new life all his heart's best impulses.

But, unconsciously, she had raised her tone a little, and attracted the attention of the occupants of the bay-window.

"Your little friend seems to be very much in earnest," said Col. Ross, in a low tone.

"Yes," replied Mabel, raising her voice that her words might be audible to Ida, "Miss May has a habit of inflicting little speeches and sermons upon her particular friends. They are very eloquent, I can assure you."

"And extremely edifying, I have no doubt you meant to add," rejoined Ida, pleasantly.

Mabel laughed—one of her short, malicious laughs, that expressed more than words—but Walter, shooting an indignant glance from under his frowning brows, retorted,

"No doubt Miss Ida, like all generous persons, sometimes forgets the ancient proverb—which I will not repeat, since it is more forcible than elegant."

---

1 *Hamlet*, 3.1.58.

2 Henry Wadsworth Longfellow (1807–82), "A Psalm of Life" (1838).

3 2 Peter 3:13: "Nevertheless we, according to his promise, look for new heavens and a new earth, wherein dwelleth righteousness."

"About casting pearls before swine, I suppose. Thank you," said Mabel, haughtily, with a withering glance.

"*Lest they turn again, and rend you*,"[1] added Walter, with emphasis.

"What is this all about?" exclaimed Col. Ross, looking from one clouded face to the other, with great astonishment. He was not very quick-witted, and not very familiar with the book whence this allusion was drawn.[2]

"Walter seems to be annoyed with my innocent remark," said Mabel, recovering herself.

Just then Mr. Wynn entered, and the conversation afterwards became general, until they were called to dinner.

Dinner was ended, and Col. Ross, having ordered his carriage was about to depart, when a messenger came to say that the boys sent with the plants had returned.

"Where is Alfred?" asked Mr. Wynn.

"Alfed say, massa, he done come back; say, ef dere a'n't nothin' else, he like mighty well go to bed, 'case he a'n't so very well."

"Tell him I want to see him a moment in the library, and then he may," was the reply; but Ida noticed an ominous compression of those thin lips, and an unwonted sternness in the tone with which those simple words were uttered, and her fears were at once aroused. In an instant she thought of the bad face of the man who had been closeted there with Mr. Wynn in the morning, and she was impressed with the idea that Alfred's secret was discovered. As soon as she could escape from the room unnoticed, after Col. Ross's prolonged leave-taking, she hastened to Maum Abby's room. But it was empty. Alfred was already in the library, and Ida returned just in time to see Mr. Wynn enter, and shut the door carefully behind him.

Locking the door as he shut it—an action that startled Alfred not a little—Mr. Wynn walked to the fireplace, and, turning round, put his hands behind him, straightened himself firmly on his feet, and fixed his eyes, without speaking, upon Alfred, who was standing near him, by the table. We have before said that few could endure the particular stare with which he expressed displeasure; and, least of any, could the man who now stood before him, burdened by the weight of a secret that involved all he held dear in life. He cast down his eyes, shifted himself from one foot to the other, changed his position, played nervously with

---

1 They quote Matthew 7:6.
2 I.e., the Bible.

the cap he held in his hand, and, at last, unable longer to endure this silent torture, he said, respectfully, "Dick said you wanted me, sir."

"I did want you. Give an account of yourself. Where were you last night?"

Alfred started visibly at this question, and, through his dark skin, it was easy to see that every particle of blood receded from his face. Twice he essayed to speak, and his lips seemed too rigid to form the words he would have said. He knew, from his master's whole manner, that disguise was useless—that, through some unknown channel, his secret plans had been conveyed to the ear that should never have heard them; to the heart that would know no pity. Nerving himself at length to meet his fate, he looked up, and, with an effort at calmness, he replied, firmly, but still respectfully, "I went to see my wife, sir."

"Who is your wife?" said Mr. Wynn, with a sneering emphasis on the last word.

"Elsie Nellore," replied Alfred.

"Did I not command you, three years ago, to have nothing more to do with her, or any of her family?" said Mr. Wynn. And then, as his companion did not reply, he went on, with increasing excitement. "And now is not this just what I told you would be the consequence of associating with them? You have grown sulky and discontented, and full of notions that ought to have been whipped out of you long ago—but I have been foolishly indulgent—and tonight you were going to steal my best horse, and run away, were you? You ungrateful dog! Is this the way you pay me for all I have done for you?"

Alfred was proud and high-spirited, and, in the desperation of his circumstances, he could no longer restrain the burning words that were struggling for utterance, like the lava in a pent volcano.

"What have you done for me?" he exclaimed, lifting himself proudly. "A mighty debt I owe you, sir, but not of *gratitude*! What have you done for me? You made me a plaything in childhood! You fed and dressed me well, because you like to see fat and neat-looking servants about you! You educated me just enough to suit your own purposes, and then rudely checked my craving for further knowledge! What more did you do? You persecuted the girl I loved, and insulted me by offering me another woman in her place—"

"Silence!" thundered Mr. Wynn, stamping his foot on the floor.

"I will not be silent!—I will speak now, if I die for it!" cried

Alfred. "Twenty-five years I have served you faithfully; and because your oppressions at last made me sad and gloomy, you have scolded and threatened me. You did not like it because the man you had wronged would not sing and smile, as well as work for you—because I had a human heart in my bosom, because God made me with the same wishes and powers that he gives the white man—"

"You insolent puppy!" exclaimed Mr. Wynn; "dare you talk that way to me!—to me! your master? *You* talk of being *wronged*! You'll find I have a way to take these notions out of your head, you impudent nigger! You shall be tied up and flogged before all the people in the place. I'll take the conceit out of you, if I take all the skin off your back first."

Alfred shivered from head to foot as if with deadly cold. He knew this was no unmeaning threat. But his eye quailed not as he answered: "For your own sake, sir, be careful what you do to me. I cannot bear what some can. I have not been degraded quite to the condition of beast, and I have the feelings of a man. I tell you I could not bear it, though I know some can. It would ruin me. I should be either an idiot or crazy."

"You had better be crazy or an idiot, than such a rebellious, impudent, scoundrel as you are now!" said Mr. Wynn. His voice was terribly calm and cold. His anger had reached the point where all outward demonstration ceases.

Alfred made a step forward, and raised his hand a little.

"Twenty-five years I have served you," he said, "and never a lash has fallen on my back; and, mark me, sir, never a lash shall fall there! I have escaped that disgrace and torture, and I never will endure it—never!"

As he spoke these last words, Mr. Wynn also stepped forward, and, seizing a small riding whip that lay on the table, struck a sudden stinging blow directly across Alfred's face, cutting the skin slightly from his eye to his chin. Alfred caught it in his hands, as it was descending a second time, and, twisting it from his master's grasp, broke it in three pieces, threw it over Mr. Wynn's shoulder into the fire, and sprang to the window. There was a momentary delay in undoing the lock, which was fastened; and, seizing an oaken chair, Mr. Wynn made one bound across the floor, a heavy blow descended, and Alfred was stretched senseless on the carpet. At the same instant, a wild shriek ran through the house—a prolonged cry of anguish and despair, which curdled the blood of every listener—and Maum Abby rushed through the half-opened window into the room. Stooping down she raised the lifeless form and laid the head tenderly on her bosom.

"My boy! My boy!" she said, in a low tone; "it is ended then at last—it is all over—and it has come to *this*!" and, after those words, she spoke not again during all the scene which followed.

The heavy fall, the scream, the crash of the breaking glass, brought all the family to the spot. Mr. Wynn heard them coming, and he unlocked the door and threw it open. Mrs. Wynn was the first who entered. Starting back at the sight which met her view, she gave her husband a look of terrified inquiry. He answered it as if she had spoken.

"It means that I had discovered Alfred to have been pursuing a course of deception and disobedience for three years, and I taxed him with it. He was impudent, and I struck him. He attempted to escape, and I felled him to the floor with the same blow which you see has demolished my window."

"Is he *dead*?" exclaimed Ida, pale with horror.

"No, he is not dead," said Walter, who was bending over the senseless form. "He is not dead—he is stunned and hurt; doubtless; but his heart beats yet. Bring water—take off his neck cloth and loosen his clothes. Aunt Emma, you had better take his mother away. This is no place for her."

His rapid commands were obeyed, but Maum Abby silently refused to leave her son, and none insisted that she should. Some time elapsed before life and reason came back to Alfred's benumbed senses and bewildered brain; but at length he breathed freely, and sat up on the floor unaided, save by his mother's arm, that lightly supported his head as she stood behind him. Then, as the servants and the ladies withdrew a little, Mr. Wynn came forward from the fireplace where he had looked on without speaking, while they were endeavoring to restore him; and, standing directly before the helpless man, he said, glancing to the servants and pointing to Alfred as he spoke:

"You all see this fellow—you all know how little cause of complaint he has had, for he has been treated better than any of you. Now, listen. This fellow was not content with being sulky and disobedient, but was intending tonight to steal one of my horses, and run away from this place. I tell you this that you may know what an ungrateful dog he is, and I command every one of you to go down to the quarters tomorrow morning, and you will see how he will be punished. Let it be a lesson to you all. If you do your duty you shall be treated well, but if you are impudent and disobedient you must suffer the consequences, as he will have to do. You remember what I told you," he added, turning to Alfred, and shaking him a little by the shoulder—"*I will do it!* You dared to brave my power. You will find it can *crush you.*"

He spoke in the same tone of deadly vengeance he had used in addressing his victim just before he struck him, and all present felt that this was no time to appeal for mercy. The servants drew near each other, and looked with an air of terror from their master to their offending companion. Walter leaned against the window with his arms folded over his breast and his lips firmly compressed, but his eyes were fixed on Alfred. The ladies had withdrawn a little into the recess, and Maum Abby alone remained with her son. For a few moments none spoke or moved. Every one of the group seemed petrified, and Mr. Wynn enjoyed his victory with a stern and cruel triumph.

Then, motioning three of the strongest negroes to approach, he told them to take Alfred and carry him upstairs to the attic, where was a large dark closet, in which he was to be confined through the night. They obeyed, and Alfred, tottering feebly to his feet, allowed them to grasp his arms and coat. Maum Abby made no useless opposition. Only once, as he was rising from the floor, she bent down and pressed her pale lips to his forehead, and gazed a moment into his face with an unutterable expression, and then quietly followed as they led him away.

Mr. Wynn followed also. As they passed the hall door Alfred made a violent effort to free himself from their grasp; but those who held him were strong, and their master's eye was upon them, and after a short struggle they conquered him. Slowly they ascended, until, at the head of the stairs leading into the attic, they came to a strong oaken door, that opened into a large closet, containing no window—no other door—no chance for escape. Alfred looked into it, and felt that his doom was sealed.

None of the family knew for what purpose this place was first constructed, and it had rarely been used during the present generation; but a more secure dungeon for a prisoner could hardly have been made. The door was very thick, and secured by a ponderous lock that creaked savagely as Mr. Wynn turned the key. As they thrust Alfred into this cell, his mother attempted to enter, also; but Mr. Wynn, with his own hand, drew her back, shut the door, and locked it. Then, withdrawing the key, he said, sternly, "Go down, now, all of you. If I find a person lingering about here, I will have him served as Alfred will be served to-morrow. Do you hear—*go down!*" he added, turning to Maum

Abby, who remained leaning against the wall after the others had disappeared.

"Can you have a heart to bid me go? I am his *mother!*" she answered, clasping her hands over her heart, and lifting her eyes to his, with an expression that touched even his stern nature in its angry mood, and, without another word, he left her.

The short twilight of a winter's day was fading, and through the small windows everything looked dim and indistinct in the large garret; and as the heartbroken woman felt herself left there alone in her great sorrow, she gazed upon the walls of the closet as upon a tomb, where her son was immured alive. Sinking down on the floor, she placed her lips to the crack at the bottom of the door, and called in a loud whisper, plaintive and thrilling—"Alfred, my son! my dear son!—I am here. It is your mother, Alfred!—speak to me! I will never leave you, my son—never! O, Alfred, speak just one word to me!" And so on into the night were breathed out those yearning cries of a mother's heart. And he answered her once. The cold lips that pressed the door were warmed a moment by a fevered breath from within, and a low, hoarse tone, that she could scarce recognize, said faintly, "O, mother dear, pray for me—pray for me, for I feel that I am going mad!"

Amid the gathering shadows of evening, Walter and his companions returned to the parlor. Mrs. Wynn was weeping violently, but Ida was too indignant for tears. Walter was stern and silent, and neither of them felt inclined to talk about the scene they had witnessed, except Mabel, who gave a sigh of relief as she threw herself back in her cushioned chair, and glanced, with a surprise half real and half affect at the gloomy faces around her.

"Why are you all so still?—has papa frightened you out of your wits?" she said, laughing. "I declare, he frightened *me*, though I am pretty well used to his moods. Don't cry, mamma. For my part, I feel relieved that the fuss is over. I've been expecting it a mighty long while. Alfred has been so cross and sulky that I knew he was planning some mischief, and I told my papa so some time ago."

"*You did!*" exclaimed Walter, his lip curling with indignation and scorn. "Did you advise with your father about the punishment too?"

"Really, Cousin Walter, you are getting to be a perfect bear!" said Mabel, pouting her lips. "When you first came home, I thought you had become quite civilized and tame; but for the last week you have shown as much *brusquerie*, as in the days of your youth, when you and I were always quarreling. What do you mean, sir, by going on so—and to *me?*"

She dropped her voice a little with a tender accent on the last words, and gazed at him out of her fine eyes with a grieved and reproachful expression, that would, a short time since, have melted his heart within him. But now he was almost startled to find that her power over him was gone. Her careless and heartless words had shocked him too severely, and, without answering her, he turned to speak to Ida. But Ida had vanished, and he sat down by his aunt, with whose grief he felt great sympathy. Mabel looked after him with a sly smile, and a strange expression. She was beginning to weary of Walter. His grand airs and abrupt expressions did not accord with the admiration and flattery she expected from her admirers, and the respect with which he listened to Ida's absurd opinions suited her still less; but she was determined he should not withdraw from her until she saw fit to cast him off, and therefore she assumed an anxious, grieved look, whenever her eyes met his, and played the amiable so perfectly, that his feelings changed, and he began to hate himself for the severity he had manifested towards her.

Mr. Wynn had stopped a moment at the parlor-door, as he descended from the attic, to say that he wished his tea sent into the library, and to request that none of the family would go near the closet where Alfred was confined. Mabel had no disposition to disobey him, and Mrs. Wynn was afraid; but a gloom hung over the whole household; the tea was almost untasted, and at an early hour they separated.

Walter, having gone to his chamber for a book, returned to the deserted parlor, and trimmed the fire, but he could not read. In vain he strove to divert his mind from the serious and perplexing thoughts that filled it; and, after a while, he gave up the effort, and, walking slowly across the floor, he reflected deeply—more deeply than ever before—upon his present position and future life. As he paced to and fro in deep reverie, the door opened, and Ida appeared. The light which she held in her hand showed her pale, troubled face, and her eyes red with weeping.

She set the lamp upon the table, as he came near, and looked up at him as if about to speak, but he interrupted her.

"O, Ida!" said he, with a sigh, "it is from *this* you are going to redeem your servants; from this you are going to free yourself. I envy you. This is a dreadful life—so beset with temptations, so full of responsibility!"

"And *you*—you also may be released from it," replied she.

"I! Ah no! I am not decided in purpose, as you are," said Walter. "I am not free to act. I am completely trammelled. Mabel would never consent to it."

"And you love her!" said Ida, almost inaudibly.

"I am *engaged* to her," was the reply.

Ida looked down in confusion. The words had fallen from her lips unconsciously, and his engagement with Mabel was not a subject on which she wished to converse with him. Recovering herself in a moment, however, she said quietly, "It was not of this I came to speak, and we have not time to talk of it now. O, Walter! cannot something be done for Alfred? It will kill him, and his mother, too, if that threat is carried out. I have urged your Aunt Emma to intercede for him; but she is too much afraid, and despairs of availing anything. Perhaps she would not do; but cannot you?"

The color went and came in Walter's face, as he replied, "I am the least likely to succeed of any in this house; my uncle has always delighted to oppose me in everything. I should only make matters worse by my interference."

"Are you sure?" urged Ida.

"The fact is, *I dare not*," replied he. "Not that I fear my uncle, but I fear myself. When I am excited, I cannot control my words; and I feel now that, if I opened my lips, a torrent would flow forth. And O, Ida!" he added, after a little pause, "what am I, that I should reproach him? Am not I, too, 'verily guilty concerning my brother?'[1] Have not I, these three years, been leaving my people in his care, and in the hands of a hired overseer? How many such tragedies may have been acted, of which I know nothing? No, Ida, it will not do for *me* to talk with my uncle on this matter."

"Then I will go myself," replied the girl, drawing up her slight figure, while her face lighted with a sudden courage and hope.

"Go, and God be with you!" said Walter, as she turned away. His eyes rested on her, as she left the room, with a strange feeling of admiration and pain. He could not avoid comparing the earnestness and purity and sweet womanly grace of her character, with the cold selfishness which Mabel had continually manifested where he had seen her brought in contact with others. Among the many thoughts which had burdened him

---

1 From the story of Joseph and this brothers, Genesis 42:21: "And they said one to another, We are verily guilty concerning our brother, in that we saw the anguish of his soul, when he besought us, and we would not hear; therefore is this distress come upon us."

that evening, not a few had been of this connection with Mabel. Among the many faults with which he had taxed himself, he was not least severe upon the hastiness he had shown in his rapid wooing, and the fickleness of which he might be accused, could anyone know how the fervency of his love had worn away within the last week; how the glory that surrounded his idol with a dazzling halo had paled and faded, until, now, her very beauty no longer charmed him, so plainly could he see the deformity beneath. He had accused himself of harshness and inconstancy towards one whose faults were, perhaps, only the effect of her position and education, and, in a repentant mood, he had checked even his purest impulses, lest they should become sins against one to whom he considered himself pledged in honor; nonetheless that, by her own desire, he had refrained from obtaining her father's consent to their union.

"In what a maze of perplexity have I involved myself!" exclaimed he, as he resumed his restless pacing to and fro. "Fool! fool! that I was! A fair face and a tender voice have made me mad and blind!"

Ida tapped once or twice at the library door, and when a voice said, "Come in," she entered. The close wooden shutters were fastened over the broken window, and the heavy curtains drawn tight, to keep out the cold air. A study lamp burned on the table, and a bright fire of pine knots and oak wood flared in the chimney. The air of cosy comfort, the warm glow that pervaded the room, contrasted strangely with the scene enacted there a few hours before. Seating herself in the chair to which Mr. Wynn pointed her, by the table opposite him, Ida remained a few moments without speaking. Then, although her heart was burning with grief and indignation, she said, in a very respectful and submissive tone, "I have ventured to intrude upon your quiet, that I beg you to abate Alfred's punishment—"

"I beg you will desist from this entreaty," interrupted Mr. Wynn, waving his hand with a courteous gesture. "I never threaten in vain. He must endure his punishment."

"O, Mr. Wynn, I fear it will kill his mother!" said Ida. "If he has done wrong, he has surely suffered for it. Can you not be persuaded to relent?"

"I have been foreseeing this crisis for some time," replied her companion, "but have delayed provoking it until the last possible moment, through consideration for his mother, who has been a very faithful servant, and to whom Mrs. Wynn is much attached.

But, now, it has come, it must be gone through with. It will be better for him—"

"O, sir," exclaimed Ida, "think of the disgrace and the torture!"

"Still," persisted Mr. Wynn, in the same calm manner, "still, I say, it would be better for him. If I yield one iota while he is but half subdued, I shall lose the benefit of what is past, and he will grow refractory again, presuming upon my forbearance. I must go on firmly, and break down his absurd feelings of independence. It is painful and annoying to all of us, and I should hardly have expected that Alfred would have subjected my family to this trial; but, after it is once over, I do not fear a repetition of it. I seldom have more than one trouble of this kind with my servants. You spoke of the disgrace; but, my dear young lady, it is no disgrace to a negro to be whipped, and is not considered so by any of them who have right ideas respecting themselves. It might disgrace a white man, but it is the proper punishment for a colored person."

"What makes the difference?" asked Ida, quietly.

"The difference is, that white men, not being held as property, are amenable personally to the laws of the State, and can expiate their crimes by imprisonment. But we have no such recourse for our servants. It would ruin us to lose the time it would take to imprison them in punishment for their offenses; and, beside, the lazy dogs would not mind confinement that released them from their accustomed tasks. So we have no alternative but to whip them; for we *must* keep them in subjection. You see it makes quite a difference."

"Quite a difference!" said Ida.

"For that reason," continued Mr. Wynn, "whipping has always been the established punishment for servants, and they all expect it; indeed, they rather like it. They always seem to think more of a master who keeps them up pretty well. Of course, I don't mean one who is too severe—who—"

"Abuses them," suggested Ida, as he paused an instant.

"Yes, that's it; they don't want to be abused, of course; but no negro, who is not above his place, thinks it a disgrace to be whipped; and the very fact that Alfred thinks it so, and spoke of it in that way, only confirms me in the opinion that it will be the very best thing for him to have. There is no kindness in allowing them to have too high notions; it only makes them discontented."

"But think of how dreadful it will be! O, Mr. Wynn, I don't believe he can bear it! He is of more excitable and nervous organization than some; and I don't believe he will go through with it without losing his reason or his life."

"Let him lose them, then!" said Mr. Wynn, with emphatic sternness. "A dead nigger is better than a disobedient one."

"After all, what has been this man's crime?" exclaimed Ida, too much exasperated to retain her calmness longer. "He loved a woman whom he was not allowed to live with openly, and so he met her clandestinely. Is that such a very dreadful sin? Would you not have done it yourself? Would not any man of right feelings have clung to the woman who loved him, in spite of all persecution? He was never unfaithful to you; he did all your work, and would have done it cheerfully, if continued opposition to his wishes had not made him unhappy. O, sir, he is your servant; but is he not also a human being, and has he not rights on which you have trampled?"

"I beg you will desist from this language," said Mr. Wynn. *"A servant has no rights,* except such as his master chooses to allow. Alfred's connection with that woman was not his only offense. He was planning to escape to the north. That is a design which I can never pardon. The severest punishment is not too great for it."

"But you know, Mr. Wynn, that he has repeatedly asked you to allow him to buy himself. He tried every honorable means before he came to this last desperate resort. O, sir, can you blame him that he desired to be free? It must be hard for a man like him to realize that he must spend all his powers of mind and body for the service of another; that he is to be continually restrained in the exercise of his will and his affections by the wishes of another. What man of Alfred's energy and intellect could endure it? And yet, for this, you say he must be punished!"

Mr. Wynn had risen from his chair while she spoke, and now, from his six feet altitude, he looked down upon the daring little being, who was uttering such incendiary doctrines in his ears, with a sort of angry astonishment.

"It is vain to talk to me on this subject," he said at length, after keeping his eyes fixed upon her for some time. "What I have said, I will do. No human power shall interfere with my family discipline. Alfred has been impudent and refractory, and he shall be punished, if I knew he would die under the lash."

Ida looked earnestly in his face as he spoke these words. He did not seem excited. During the whole conversation he had not raised his voice, but nothing could be more hopeless than its cold, quiet monotone, and there was no sign of relenting in the stern features where every muscle seemed rigid as if carved of stone. But Ida did not quail beneath those petrifying eyes. Rising from her chair, she came near him, and said, with great earnestness and solemnity,

"You are about to commit a great sin. Pause, I beseech you, before it is too late! Think what it is to take the life or destroy the reason of a fellow being. O, what right have you to torture him? Do you not fear?"

Mr. Wynn half turned on his heel, with a short disdainful laugh. "Fear what?" he said. "That the skies will fall?"

"No, but that the hour of *revenge* will come," said Ida, trembling at her own words. "Do you not fear that all this anguish, all these wrongs, will hasten an hour of retribution, when the fearful debt shall be paid which has been accumulating through so many generations? What shall hinder its coming soon, if men like Alfred are driven to desperation with persecution and torture?"

For reply Mr. Wynn crossed the room slowly and deliberately, and opening the door pointed into the hall. "*Go!*" he said; "you have spoken words that if you were a man you should take back at the point of the sword. As you are a woman, I have no alternative than to bid you leave this room, and beware how you dare attempt such things in this house. Go!" he repeated, in a tone of such deep and concentrated wrath that Ida dared not resist, and silently she left him.

In the hall she met Walter, who had anxiously awaited the result of the conference, though he had little hope that she could effect anything.

"I see by your face that you have not been successful," he said.

"I hardly hoped to be," she replied, "but I could not rest till I had tried to help him. O," she added, wringing her hands in bitter self-reproach, "why was I so faint-hearted—why did I not warn him to be more careful?"

"Have you known of this before?" exclaimed Walter.

"I knew something, and I could guess the rest," replied Ida; and then she told him of the scene she had witnessed and the words she had overheard the day after her arrival, the week before. Walter was deeply affected. In their excitement it did not occur to either of these young persons, that all this sympathy with a refractory servant was highly dangerous and improper, and subversive of long-established institutions.

Leaving Walter after a short time, Ida returned to her own room. Maum Venus was sitting before the fire, soundly sleeping, with her head on the table, and the light footsteps of her young mistress did not waken her, as she hastily wrapped herself in a large, thick shawl, and, taking another on her arm, again left the chamber, and stole softly upstairs to the place where Maum Abby was still keeping watch by her son. All was dark and chilling in the large, damp garret, and as the light Ida carried fell over her figure, bent together as it was, and her face hidden in her hands, she was frightened by the stony silence and immobility of her appearance. A slight movement and a low moan, which came from the bowed form as Ida wrapped around it the shawl she had brought, gave a token of life and reassured the trembling girl, and she sat down on the low step beside the afflicted woman. Looking up when she felt the pressure of Ida's arm around her neck, Maum Abby fixed her eyes upon her in a stern and gloomy manner.

"It is you, is it?" she said, abruptly. "What are you doing here? Go down."

"Yes, it is I," replied Ida, gently. "I have come to stay with you; won't you let me? I could not bear to think of you here alone."

Maum Abby gazed at her a few moments absently, as if she was trying to comprehend those simple words, but the gloom of her countenance did not relax.

"Put out that light, then," she said, at length; "I can't bear it—it hurts me. There should be no light anywhere; all the world should be dark, dark and cold, like my life!"

Her eyes were still fixed and stony, and her long, thin finger pointed to the lamp with an air of command. Ida gave a half-terrified glance into the gloom around her, which to her excited fancy seemed peopled with indistinct forms, that moved and glided with the rapid beatings of her heart; but she obeyed the request and extinguished the light. Those slow-moving, solemn, distressful hours! They haunted her dreams, for years after, with even more of horror than she felt while they were passing. Thoughts of all that the strong man armed with power has dared to do, and all that the helpless have been compelled to suffer—of all the fearful histories that might be connected with that very spot—crowded upon her brain, until the darkness appeared to grow tangible and gather around her with a cold, stifling pressure, like the hands of spectres. The pattering of the rain upon the roof above them seemed like the trampling feet of the vast multitude who might one day come crying for vengeance on this house, where, through long generations, man had enslaved his fellow; and low voices of wailing sounded in an undertone through the monotonous murmur of the elements. Ida shuddered and drew nearer to her companion, exclaiming,

"Speak to me, Maum Abby; it is frightful to have you so still and cold! Don't feel as if you were forsaken and had none to help you; for One who is stronger than the mightiest will not forget you, even now. Who knows but he will deliver your son from his pitiless master? Let us pray to him, let us call upon him with tears, for he has promised to hear the cry of the needy and the oppressed."

She would have said more, but Maum Abby checked her, not harshly, but with a frigid quietness, as if she felt the powerlessness of words, the fallacy of hope.

"*You* can pity me, *you* can pray for me!" she said, "but this is no time for talking. My soul is dried up within me. I have wept over the graves of my children, but I have no tears for this woe. This is the hour of my trial, and God sends no angel to comfort me, only you, poor, kind little girl, that cannot help me. He works no longer by miracles, and nothing but a miracle can save Alfred. O that I should have lived to see this hour, when I have no longer any faith in God!"

"'Like as a father pitieth his children, so the Lord pitieth them that fear him,'" replied Ida, softly. "'He knoweth our frame. He remembereth that we are but dust.'"[1]

Maum Abby bent her face again to her knees without replying, and took no further notice of her companion, who, pressing close to her side, kept silent watch in prayer for her. That brave, full heart was conscious of its own deep sympathy, but it availed little to the stricken mourner. Too stern was the grasp of her pangs for such solace. Her soul sat veiled in its agony, blind to all without, and conscious only of its crushed hopes, and a sickening, shuddering sense of the torture to which her son was doomed on the morrow. Afterwards, when the sad drama had been played to its close, and her first fierce woe was past, the gentle touch of Ida's hand upon her brow and neck, her few low-toned words, her tears and her uttered sympathy, came back upon the memory of the sufferer with a soothing and healing influence, and she recognized the angel whom God had sent to her; but now, through these long, fearful hours, she was scarcely conscious of her presence.

An hour or more had passed, when a faint light was seen glimmering though the dense darkness below them, and a figure robed in white swiftly glided up the stairs. It was Mrs. Wynn. She knelt down before Maum Abby, and strove to clasp her hands, but she drew them hastily away.

---

1 Psalm 103:13.

"O dear, dear Maum Abby!" she said, sobbing, "I do pity you so! I do feel for you! I stole away the moment he was asleep. He told me not to come, and I didn't dare to, lest he should hear me, while he was awake. O, I do pity you so! This is terrible, terrible!"

Maum Abby raised her head with the same stern look she had fixed upon Ida.

"Go back to your bed, Miss Emma," she said, authoritatively. "I know you feel for me, but you can't comfort me; nobody can. I am a poor, desolate, old woman, and tomorrow my only son is going to be whipped to death. *He* said so. I was listening at the window and heard him, and you know he *never* relents." She threw her arms wildly upward, and cried out, "O Lord God, hear me! How long, how long shall the wicked triumph?"

"Don't curse us! O, don't curse us!" exclaimed Mrs. Wynn, seizing her hands and trembling violently. "It is the fault of our false and cruel position; of our laws that give men unlimited power over their servants. *He* would never have been what he is but for that. O, Maum Abby, pray for us! pray for him! Don't curse him!"

"I will try to pray for him," she replied, relapsing into her former stern, despairing calmness; "but O, it is hard to do it now—now, when the devil is tempting me to curse God and die. Go away, and pray for him yourself, pray for us all. You can do no good here. I don't want to talk. When I talk I can't hear my son's breathing, and that is all I have of him now. Go away, you come between me and my son!"

She spoke these last words almost petulantly, and, deeply grieved, Mrs. Wynn turned away. Again silence and darkness reigned around them. The rain fell with a continuous, dull, heavy plashing on the roof above their heads; and from below there came up through the murky air the faint ticking of the hall clock. No other sound was heard, save, from the closet behind them, the labored breathing of the prisoner, panting and broken, like the gasping of one in mortal pain, and often interrupted by a heavy sob, or a low moan, or faintly-spoken prayers. Thus the night wore away.

Just before the first gray dawn of morning, Ida returned to her own room, and threw herself on her bed, completely chilled and exhausted. Soon a deep and dreamless slumber stole over her wearied senses; and it was long after the usual breakfast hour, when she awoke. Great was her surprise when, on descending to the breakfast room, she found the servants just bringing in the dishes for the morning meal, and Mabel, with a frowning brow, walking to and fro, and giving directions in a tone indicative of no slight degree of vexation.

"What's the matter with you, Ida?" she exclaimed; "you look like a ghost. Couldn't you sleep last night? How mighty hard it rained!—it kept me awake some time."

"I didn't sleep much," replied Ida; "but it wasn't the rain that prevented me."

"What! are you out of sorts too, with all the rest of the household? I believe papa and I are the only sensible members of the family. Here ma' has cried till she has brought on one of her dreadful nervous headaches, and can't leave her bed, and Maum Abby, who knows just what to do for her, is sitting there moping about Alfred, and won't come and take care of her, or see after the servants; and so everything has gone wrong this morning. I declare this is a world of trouble."

"It is, indeed," replied Ida, with a sigh, her thoughts reverting to Maum Abby and her son with such intensity that she was almost unconscious of Mabel's selfish application of the trite remark.

"Let us have breakfast, and then I will go away somewhere. This is getting intolerable!" exclaimed Walter, impatiently, coming forward as he spoke from the window-recess, where he had been sitting behind the curtain unobserved.

"*Et tu Brute!*"[1] said Mabel, laughing and coloring a little—"which, being interpreted, means, have you been there all this time, Walter, listening to my scolding of the servants? If so, I expect you have a most exalted idea of my housekeeping abilities. Confess, now, you had no idea that was one of my accomplishments. Don't you think I could manage a household finely?"

"Excellently well, I have no doubt, as far as the discipline of your servants was concerned," said Walter, dryly.

"That is rather a doubtful compliment, uttered in that tone," replied Mabel, somewhat disconcerted; "but I will impute its deficiencies to the *mauvais esprit*[2] that possesses us all this morning; and, as I see papa coming, we will have breakfast, if you please."

They gathered round the table, and Mabel, taking her mother's place, performed the honors gracefully; and made an effort

---

1 From *Julius Caesar*, 3.1.77. Latin phrase meaning, "and you, Brutus?" These dying words of Julius Caesar signify the ultimate betrayal of friendship.
2 Bad spirit (French).

at conversation, for which she was rewarded by an approving glance from her father; but Walter continued absorbed and silent, and Ida was waiting, in suppressed excitement, the moment when Alfred would be brought forth to his punishment.

Suddenly the footsteps of several men were heard in the hall, and in a few moments, little Dick came into the room where they were sitting, with a message for Mr. Wynn.

"Please massa, de overseer done come, wid de niggers and de handcuff, for tote Alfred off."

Mr. Wynn took the key of the closet from his pocket, and handed it to the boy. "Give him this," he said, "and show him where Alfred is. I will see him on the piazza when he comes down."

The boy disappeared, and a dead silence fell upon the group around the breakfast-table. Ida leaned back in her chair, so sick and faint with the violent throbbing of her heart, that it was with difficulty she sustained herself. Walter's eyes were fixed on his plate, and he was apparently unconscious that he was gnawing his lip, instead of the piece of meat he was nervously cutting and re-cutting into the most minute bits. Mr. Wynn sat like an iron statue of decision, and even Mabel looked a little pale and excited.

Some moments elapsed, and then there was a little confusion heard above stairs, a quick step descended, and Dick again threw open the door, exclaiming, "O massa! come dis minute up star. Dat ar' Alfred done kill heself!"

"What did you say?" said Mr. Wynn, sternly, his face growing a little more rigid and white as he fixed his eyes on the child.

"Fact, massa," repeated he; "dat ar' Alfred done kill heself—cut hole in he troat and let out all de blood. Done shirked he whippin' *dis* time, massa, anyway."

Mr. Wynn rose quickly and left the room. Walter lifted his head, and his chest heaved with a deep inspiration, as if a load had been lifted from it, while he exclaimed fervently,

"Thank God for that!—he is *dead!*"

"Why, Walter, a'n't you ashamed to say so?" said Mabel. "For my part, I'm really sorry, for now who will we get to build our summerhouse? My heart was set upon having that before another year, and there isn't a workman anywhere around who was equal to Alfred. I'd rather have nothing at all than one of those common things. I say it is a downright shame for him to kill himself, when it is so inconvenient to lose him."

Walter listened to her with an expression of utter astonishment, which gave way to indignation as she completed this last sentence, and, with the bluntness that characterized him when excited, he exclaimed, "Cousin Mabel, if you were empty-hearted as a soap-bubble, one would think you could not speak this at such a moment as this;" and, giving her a reproachful glance, he followed Ida, who had already left the room.

He found her standing beside Maum Abby, in the midst of the whole household, who had by this time gathered around the spot where Alfred lay across the threshold of the closet door, with his head supported in his mother's arms. Through what intense disappointment, through what utter despondency, through what anguish of mind and heart, that excited brain had grown delirious, only God can know. But he, who gives the fullness of a boundless sympathy and pity to the weakness of our human nature, will pardon that wretched man, who, left thus alone to wrestle with a crushing tyranny, and finding himself cut off from all other refuge, had dared with his own hand to open the gates of death, that through them he might escape from the oppressor.

This thought was a comfort to the bereaved mother, who sat silently bending over him. It was no shock to her when the men, who, imagining Alfred asleep or sulky, were dragging him roughly forth, suddenly loosened their hold, exclaiming that he was dead. For two hours she had listened in vain for the panting breath which all night long had given assurance that he was still alive; and, after the first involuntary heart-thrill the knowledge thus gradually attained brought with it a sensation of relief; and, thinking of all he had endured in the past, all he must have endured in the future, more fervently than she had praised God at her child's birth, that mother gave thanks that her only son was dead.

As they stood around her silently, even the garrulousness of the negroes being checked by the pitiful scene, a slow decided step was heard on the stairs. It was Mr. Wynn; and, as the sound of his footsteps drew nearer, and the group, scattering apart, left him face to face with the dead, Maum Abby unclasped her arms from the lifeless form she had been holding close against her heart, and, laying it down tenderly upon the floor, arose and stood before him. There was something almost majestic in the solemn reticence of her manner—something awful in the utter desolation in which this tragedy had involved her, that hushed the very breathing of those who listened, as, pointing with one hand to the corpse at her feet, and raising the other a little to demand her master's attention, she said to him—"Look! there is my boy!—he is dead, and you, *you* have murdered him! Do not start back—do not frown on me—my son is dead, and you cannot harm me now! It is not for *me* to curse you—not for me! I know now why God has permitted this wrong to be done. I know not, blind worm that I am, how my child's death can cause the wrath of man to praise Him, or my own misery advance the purposes of His holy will; and yet I trust Him—O, I will trust Him though he slay me!" she added, raising her clasped hands high above her head, and looking upward. For a moment she stood thus, her lips moving inaudibly, as if she prayed, and then gradually lowering her arms and fixing her eyes again on Mr. Wynn, she continued: "I will not curse you, that you have robbed me of what was more to me than my life; that you drove him to desperation and insanity, that ended in death. God will pardon *him* that deed; but, when He maketh inquisition for blood, will He not require it at *your* hands?—you, who could not pity—who would not forgive! What will you answer, when One who judgeth righteously shall ask you, 'Where is thy brother?' O, Master Richard, beware! Learn, while it is yet time, that these whom you are crushing, are *men*, and repent before God of the evil you have dared to do. Repent!"—and here her voice rose like the pealing of an organ swell—"Repent! for, behold, the day cometh that shall burn as an oven, and all the proud, yea, and all that do wickedly, shall be as stubble, and the day that cometh shall burn them up saith the Lord of Hosts."

She paused. There was a lurid light in her eyes, and with her pale, stern face, her tall figure elevated to its utmost height, and her hand raised with a prophetic earnestness, she looked like one inspired. Self-possessed as was Mr. Wynn, and firmly as he had braced himself against any manifestation of the feelings that secretly agitated him, he had quailed before the influence that acted like a spell upon those around him; but when she ceased speaking, he recovered himself, and, stepping a little aside, said half aloud, "These are but the ravings of insanity. Take the woman away."

She bent forward a little, and laid her hand lightly upon his breast, but he shrank from her touch with a slight shudder. "I go, I go," said she. "I have no more to do here. Bring my son after me—bring him to my room for a little while—a few hours, and then the earth must cover him. He will sleep there in peace, and I—God help me!—I shall be *alone*."

Her words, changed now in tone and manner, had a melancholy and touching pathos, as if they came from the depth of a broken heart; and she tottered as she descended the stairs slowly, with an uncertain step, like that of one who walks in the dark. Moved by a simultaneous impulse, Walter and Ida sprang to aid her. Her hands were clenched together, and her eyes glazed and dim. The reaction from that unnatural and desperate calmness was commencing, and in a few moments she was seized with strong convulsions that for many hours threatened her life.

CHAPTER XIII

"I tell thee that a spirit is abroad,
Which will not slumber till its path be traced
By deeds of far-spread fame. It moves on
In silence, yet awakening in its path
That which shall startle nations."[1]

During several days which succeeded the events that had disturbed, in a manner so painful, the peace and happiness of this family, Ida found herself placed in a very unpleasant situation, by the marked and studied coldness with which she was treated by Mr. Wynn. The funeral services for Alfred had been performed, in a very quiet manner, the evening of the day on which he died; and, after that, each member of the family instinctively avoided any allusion to the subject, in his presence. Maum Abby secluded herself in her little dwelling, and refused to see anyone except her mistress and Ida; who spent many long hours there, in the vain endeavor to

"Minister to a mind diseased;
Pluck from the memory a rooted sorrow;"[2]

and all things seemed to go on in the usual routine, except that Mr. Wynn entirely ignored Ida's presence in his mansion. Since the evening when she had so daringly offended him, he had never spoken to her; and when, in his intercourse with his family, he addressed those who were near her, or engaged in conversation in which she had borne a part, his eyes looked above her, around her, *through* her, but never once seemed to rest upon her, and his ears manifested a like insensibility to any sound that might issue from her lips.

Finding at length, that she must take some decided measures to overcome a course of conduct which, from its pertinency, was becoming vexatious as well as embarrassing, and also desiring to take possession of the property left her by Mr. Maynard, that she might be enabled to accomplish her purposes respecting it during the winter which was now passing, Ida determined to venture again into the library, where her stern guardian spent his mornings, and thus render an interview unavoidable.

---

1 Adapted from Hemans, *Vespers*, 1.2.
2 *Macbeth*, 5.3.40–41.

It was a mild, bright morning in January, when she left her room for this purpose. In the upper hall she met Walter, booted and spurred, and twirling Mabel's riding-whip in his hand, as he waited for her appearance. As he saw Ida, his countenance fell, and he exclaimed,

"Why are you not dressed for riding? I thought you told Mabel you would go with us this morning."

"So I did, in fun. She was only joking when she asked me," replied Ida. "You don't suppose I would be *Madame de Trop*,[1] do you?"

"Nonsense!" said Walter, impatiently. "*I* wasn't in fun when I asked you, and neither was Mabel; so you shan't have that for an excuse for breaking your promises."

"It is only telling a little bit of a white lie—so white and transparent as to be almost invisible—to break such a promise as that was," said Ida, laughing. "I thought you both understood me."

"Lay no such flattering unction to your soul,"[2] replied Walter. "I depended upon your words, and have ordered your horse, and hurried Mabel away to dress, that we might have time for a long ride. It is so pleasant this morning it will do you good, and I'm sure you need the exercise. So please go and get ready now—won't you?"

"I can't," said Ida, shaking her head and blushing a little, beneath the earnest eyes that were fixed on her.

"Don't say so," persisted Walter; "don't shake those ringlets with that positive air, as if that decision were final. Only think how long it is since you have been out with us. I know," he added, in a graver tone, "that you have spent your mornings with Maum Abby, and I honor you, Ida, for your kindness to that poor woman, for your courage and your sympathy with her trouble; but your own health will suffer if you continue this kind of life much longer. Come to ride with us this morning—*do*."

"I can't, indeed," replied Ida, resisting by a mighty effort the influence of his pleading voice, and braving with a mirthful glance, the eyes whose peculiar expression thrilled her frame magnetically. "I have devoted this morning to a less pleasing

---

1 "De trop" is a French expression meaning one too many. Ida suspects she will be the third wheel—unwanted and unwelcome—on their date.

2 Adapted from *Hamlet*, 3.4.152–53: "Lay not that flattering unction to your soul / That not your trespass but my madness speaks."

employment. Like Esther of old, I am going to venture into the king's presence, unasked, and request an audience."[1]

"May he hold out the golden sceptre, if such is your rash purpose!" replied Walter. "But why can't you wait till tomorrow? I am unavoidably engaged to ride with Mabel this morning, but tomorrow I will remain at home. Uncle Richard has treated you with positive rudeness lately, and I confess I dread to have you encounter him alone. You know how severe he can be."

"I dread it also, and therefore, I won't talk any longer about it, lest I lose my courage. Why don't you talk in a more encouraging strain? Fie, Walter! A gentleman five feet six inches high, who has *experienced* Europe, Asia and Africa, and come home bearded and mustached like any Russ,[2] to talk of dreading any other mortal man! O, fie!"

"Don't be saucy, Ida," replied Walter, with a smile, and an expressive glance. "You know it is only *for you* I fear. You are very brave, but it goes against my ideas of chivalry to leave a woman to fight her battles alone, especially where the right is on her side."

"Thank you," said Ida; "but Heaven forbid that I should draw *you* into my quarrel with your uncle! What trouble it would make! Your aunt, Mabel, what would they think of me? No, Walter," she added, sadly, "it is as you told me: I am treading a difficult path, and I must tread it alone."

"Perhaps not entirely alone," replied Walter, earnestly. "My feeling and my ideas have changed somewhat since that morning. That awful tragedy shall not be all in vain. I shudder when I think that perhaps it was needed to arouse me thoroughly from the indifference that had crept over me regarding this matter."

"Then you were indifferent?" said Ida. "Knowing how you felt once, I thought perhaps you assumed it."

"No, I was indifferent. I had come to regard it as a necessary evil, partly from having been away from home so long that everything connected with home was clothed in the softened light which mantles distant objects, and partly because my patriotism was aroused to the highest point by the slurs and sneers I heard cast upon my country when I was in foreign lands. I was forced so often to explain and extenuate and defend our social system,

---

1 Jewish queen married to a Persian king, whose timely intercessions delivered her people from massacre and ruin, now celebrated by the feast of Purim. The golden scepter signifies the king's approval (Esther 5:2, 8:4).

2 Russian.

when I was among foreigners, who are glad to make it a byword and a reproach, that I almost made myself believe, at length, that all was as right as I wished it to appear."

"And now?" asked Ida.

"Now we will go to ride, if *M. le chevalier*[1] pleases," said a voice behind them; and, turning, they saw Mabel standing near.

How beautiful she was at that moment! The closely-fitting bodice, and the sweeping folds of her riding-habit showed her queenly form most advantageously, and her black velvet hat, with its flowing plumes, heightened by contrast the pearl-like purity of her complexion. And yet, as Walter Varian looked at her, there was no smile on his lip, no triumph in his eyes. He did not say to himself, exultingly, "This radiant, this peerless beauty is mine—she loves me." Instead of this, a strange pain shot through his heart, a feeling half of disappointment and half of remorse, and his soul whispered within him, "I am bound to her irrevocably, and yet I know that between us there is no sympathy of thought, and there can be no concord of action."

He had felt this at times before, when her words had jarred harshly against the emotions which recent events had awakened, dissipating the fascination which her wonderful beauty had first exercised over him. But never had he been so conscious of it as now—when the admissions he had made to Ida half committed him to a line of conduct which Mabel would regard with indignation and contempt.

"Really, I grieve to have interrupted so interesting a *tête-à-tête*,"[2] she said; "but I must be excused, since it is quite time for us to go. Ida, I see, is not dressed. Didn't you know that Walter ordered your horse?"

"I did not know it until he informed me just now," replied Ida. "I thought he understood that we were joking, when I said I would go."

"I was afraid that was the case," said Mabel; "but since it is so, I think we shall not be able to wait for you. Come, Walter, it will be too warm by and by."

"What shall be done with your horse?" said Walter, as they descended the stairs.

"O, leave him there in the shade. If I feel like it I will ride out to meet you on your return."

---

1 Knight (French).
2 Conversation, literally "head-to-head."

She watched them canter away. Mabel rode finely, and her commanding mien and figure never appeared to better advantage than on horseback. Since the morning when her heartless speech had so irritated Walter, and he had turned from her to Ida, she had begun really to fear that her power over him was growing less, and her pride, the strongest passion of her nature, was startled, lest Ida should win the love which hitherto she had held so lightly. Accustomed as she was to receive the homage of all who came near her, and see suitors bowing at her feet, she had accepted her cousin's devotion very much as a matter of course, and replied to it favorably, without a very definite idea of holding herself bound by the promise; but now she was becoming more interested in a game which began to be difficult, and all her powers of pleasing had been exerted to charm back her half-revolted fiancé, and, as is often the case, her own feelings were excited and enlisted in the effort.

Mr. Wynn looked up in surprise when Ida entered the library, but he placed a chair for her with a frigid politeness, and then, retiring behind his spectacles, he continued to gaze at her without speaking.

"I beg that you will not regard me with such fixed displeasure," said Ida, with an embarrassed manner; "I am very sorry to have offended you."

The expression of his face softened a little, and he bowed his head slightly, in token that her apology was accepted. Then, laying his hand upon a quantity of books and papers, which were piled on the table, he said abruptly, "These documents are ready, and should have been in your possession before now. I suppose you will hardly care to look over the accounts yourself; but it will be necessary for you to select someone to manage your business, and I think you will find I have done all that could be done with your property during your minority."

"I have the utmost confidence in my guardian," replied Ida, pleasantly, "and am sure it will be quite unnecessary to go over the records. But, since you have referred to the subject, will you please tell me briefly what is the present state of the property and its amount?"

"With pleasure I will do so," said Mr. Wynn. "The income, above the expenses, since I have had the care of the estate, has been about four thousand dollars, which I have placed in the bank at your disposal. The portion of Oaklands, which Mr. Maynard gave you in his will, is, as you know, that small detached farm which is separated from the rest of the plantation by a strip of worthless black jack."[1]

"Yes, I know it," said Ida. "I rode over there once with you and Mabel, when I was here three years ago. Uncle Charles used to call it, 'the Triangle.'"

"He gave it that name, I believe, from some slight resemblance in its shape to that mathematical figure," continued Mr. Wynn; "and also, because, having a very trashy set of negroes on it, he found it difficult, with his peculiar notions, to manage them. He used to say facetiously that they *tried* every *angle* in his disposition."

"Poor Uncle Charles!" said Ida, with a thoughtful smile.

"It was unfortunate for my brother-in-law that he was totally lacking in the firmness necessary to plantation discipline, and consequently his fine estate has been suffering from poor management for many years. Oaklands may come up in the hands of a skillful cultivator, if Walter concludes to sell it; but I regret to say that the Triangle, which was never as valuable land as the other, is now entirely worn out, and would bring nothing of consequence in the market. There are about twenty negroes connected with the farm, and you will probably find it for your interest to sell them. But, of course, all that can be arranged with the person whom you shall choose as your agent in business matters. If I might advise, I should recommend you to authorize Walter to act for you. He will take an office in the city, before long, and, I have no doubt, will make the best possible settlement for you."

"Thank you," replied Ida; "but Walter will hardly get established before spring, and there is but one way in which I can allow my negroes to be disposed of, and I wish that arrangement to be completed during this winter. I shall have free papers made out for each of them," she added, her heart beating a little more rapidly than usual, "and send them to the free States. Four thousand dollars will be sufficient to locate them there comfortably, I think, and make provision for those who are too old or too ignorant to take care of themselves."

"I am not surprised by this folly," said Mr. Wynn, his cold courtesy of manner instantly relapsing into sternness; "but I think you will find, after you have wasted your fortune in this

---

1 Black jack oak trees grow in the poorest soils, often in an area that has suffered a fire. Mr. Wynn refers to the strip of land itself, rather than the oaks standing there, as worthless.

way, that the people, whom you have thus placed in a false position, will hardly thank you."

"Perhaps not," replied Ida, smiling; "but I think their children will; at any rate, I shall have a clear conscience, and that, you know, sir, is worth more than a heap of money."

"But it will hardly give you a livelihood, nevertheless," said Mr. Wynn, scoffingly. "But that will matter little, I suppose. It is the way with these pseudo-philanthropists, to make themselves notorious by some needless sacrifice, and then to be a burden on their admirers ever after."

"I am afraid your acquaintance with philanthropists has not been very extensive," remarked Ida, quietly; "but, even if it is so, your observation hardly applies to me, since a simple act of justice ought not to be called philanthropy."

She paused, but Mr. Wynn deigned no reply, and she saw that she had again offended him. "I beg you will not be angry because I claim the right to exercise liberty of conscience," she continued, in a deprecating tone. "I have received much kindness from all your family, and I know it was the wish of one, who was dear to us all, that we should always be friends, and it grieves me inexpressibly to be compelled thus to offend your prejudices. Believe me, nothing would induce me to risk incurring your displeasure, and forfeiting the friendship of your family, except a strong conviction of duty."

"Duty! Nonsense!" retorted Mr. Wynn. "Your abolitionist friends at the north have instigated this movement, and you are carrying it out for the sake of effect."

"You are entirely mistaken, sir," said Ida, respectfully, but with great dignity; "and I assure you that it is no northern influence, but what I have seen and heard here in the south, that has made me an abolitionist. Our views of right differ so much, that it is plain we should not prolong this conversation," she added, rising from the chair. "I thought it most proper to inform you of my intentions in respect to this property, before taking any legal measures; and I wished also to ask your permission to order the carriage and drive over to the Triangle. I want to see for myself what is the state of affairs there."

"I shall give no such permission, or, in any way, countenance these absurd proceedings," said Mr. Wynn, angrily.

"Perhaps, then, you will allow a servant to ride after me," persisted Ida, whom this sort of opposition only served to render more cool and decided.

"No servant of mine shall go with you. I tell you, I will not countenance such proceedings," said Mr. Wynn. "If you go to the Triangle on such an errand, you must go alone."

"Then I will go alone," replied the undaunted girl; and she turned away suddenly as she spoke, and went to her own room.

Her heart swelled with indignation and pain. She had really desired peace, and she had met with the most unreasonable and unreasoning contention. She had only desired liberty to do quietly that which her conscience demanded, and she found herself subjected to the most imperious despotism. As she went up the stairs, she saw her horse, still saddled, standing where Walter had left him, and the thought occurred to her, that now, better than at any other time, she could accomplish her purpose of visiting her plantation, without being obliged to call upon anyone for assistance.

"I will go this very day. The breach is rapidly widening that sunders me from this family, and the sooner the business is accomplished now, the better it will be for us all," she said to herself, as she entered her chamber, and began to put on her riding habit.

While she was thus employed, Mrs. Wynn entered the door.

"Where are you going, Ida?" she asked, with a quiet surprise, as she marked the girl's flushed cheeks and hurried movements.

"I am going to the Triangle," said Ida.

"To the Triangle! Why dear child, it is eight miles away— sixteen miles you will have to ride! You won't be back before dinner."

"Perhaps not," replied Ida, "If I don't return, you will please not say anything about it at table. I think Mr. Wynn may not like it."

"Mr. Wynn! What has he to do with it? And who is going with you?"

"Nobody; I am going alone."

"Alone! Why, my dear girl, you mustn't think of it. Mabel and Walter rode away some time ago; but you shall have a servant to go with you, if you are determined to take so long a ride."

"I had rather not, dear Mrs. Wynn," said Ida, gently.

"But you *must*. Who ever heard of a young girl like you riding so far alone? It will be very improper and unsafe."

"Not exactly according to conventional rules, I know," replied Ida; "but still not really unsafe. Don't urge me, for, indeed, I must go alone. To tell the truth, I have spoken to Mr. Wynn about it, and he refuses to allow me an escort."

Poor Mrs. Wynn sat down at these words, as if the allusion

to her husband had taken away all her strength. "O," said she, "it seems as if we should never know the last of that sad trouble connected with Alfred! You are a brave girl, Ida, and a great comfort to Maum Abby; but sometimes I wish you had not tried to intercede for her poor boy. It frightens me to see how Mr. Wynn looks at you ever since! I do so dread any quarreling, and now it seems as if we were never to be at peace again."

"I fear there will not be peace again while I remain here," said Ida, her eyes filling with tears, "but, dear friend, you won't blame me, will you? No one can tell the bitter sorrow it has cost me to take this offensive position; but, with my convictions of duty, I cannot do otherwise; and since it must be done, it had better be done quickly, and then I can go away, and you will be happy again."

"Don't speak so sadly, Ida," said kind little Mrs. Wynn; "it is not you who have made the trouble, and something more than your departure is needed to restore happiness, to me, at least. Here is poor Maum Abby, who seems to me now like an accusing spirit haunting the house, though, God knows, my heart aches as if it would burst every time I think of her," she continued in a dejected tone; "and that unfortunate girl, Elsie—it distresses me to think of her. She was found this morning again stretched senseless on Alfred's grave. This is the third time she has been found there, and once she was completely drenched with a soaking rain, that fell during the night, and she has been in a high fever ever since. I can't have a heart to be cross with her, and tell her she shan't come here; but I shall not be able to keep it much longer from Mr. Wynn, and I know he will be angry. O, dear Ida, you don't know what trouble and anxiety I see before me for years to come; and then to think that it is all because we are upholding a terrible wrong! O, Ida, what shall I do?"

"There is but little that *you* can do, dear Mrs. Wynn," replied Ida, with an affectionate glance into the face that was clouded with perplexity and grief. "You have the power to render your servants much assistance, and make them far happier than they would be otherwise, and in that you must find comfort, and not distress yourself about those things wherein you are fettered by the authority or the action of others. *Impossibilities* are never *duties*, as I told you when we were talking yesterday on this subject. I trust Maum Abby will grow more resigned and cheerful by and by, and as time goes on, she must feel your kindness; and I think that poor little Elsie will not live long to trouble or offend anybody. But I must not stand here to talk any longer, or I shall not have time for my ride."

250 MARY HAYDEN GREEN PIKE

"I will not urge you any more," said Mrs. Wynn, "for young as you are, you seem to be better capable of guiding me than I am of directing you; but I do dread to have you go alone, and certainly you must have something to eat before you go. Come with me, and take a snack."

Ida willingly complied with this friendly suggestion, and, having thus fortified herself against the demands of hunger, she sprang lightly on her horse, who, tired with waiting her pleasure so long, darted away the moment he felt the touch of her whip. As she passed the library window, where Mr. Wynn was sitting, he looked up, and his lip curled till each "separate and individual hair" of his thin red beard seemed bristling with wrath at the audacity with which she had braved his displeasure.

Imperious and arbitrary by nature, it was not strange that education and the influence of his position should have so habituated him to a tyrannical imposition of his own will upon those around him, that he was totally unprepared to view with equanimity the course Ida was pursuing. That one of his family should assume the right of self-guidance and oppose his expressed wishes or question the propriety of his actions, seemed to him a monstrous and unheard-of act of rebellion. Alfred's death had shaken him for a few hours, only to leave him more firmly rooted than ever in his habitual self-will. It was an accident, he said to himself, owing entirely to the obstinacy of the servant, and for which he was in no way responsible; and it irritated him to know or to imagine that any of his household thought otherwise.

For a mile or two, Ida rode rapidly. It was a clear, sunshiny day, and the swift motion, the brightness all around her, and the pleasant air filled with the aroma of the budding pines, raised her spirits and nerved her energies for the duties that lay before her. But, as the sun rose high in the heavens, and the heat grew oppressive, and the flat sandy road became wearisome, doubts, fears and discouraging thoughts again perplexed her, as she reflected upon the difficulties that must be encountered, and the responsibility she was assuming, and on her own youth and inexperience, and the loneliness of her position, without one friend to aid her, except Walter Varian. The idea of being obliged to involve him in her troubles, or to depend upon him for help, was worse to her than all the rest.

It was, therefore, with a slower pace, and a somewhat saddened brow, that, six miles from Wynn Hall, she turned away from the main road, and entered the narrow and shady one, which she recognized as leading to the Triangle, by a tall dead pine-tree, of peculiar shape, that stood at its entrance. It was a pleasant winding path, but intersected by many others which crossed in all directions; and, before she had ridden a mile, she began to be puzzled, as many another traveler has been in those pine lands, to know which of the various roads, all looking exactly alike, converging, diverging, running in parallels, or meeting in circles, she ought to pursue, in order to reach her plantation. After making several turnings, she began to fear she had lost her way, and seeing at a little distance a deep shady hollow, where an old woman was washing beside a spring, she rode in between the tall, straight trees, which here rose like the pillars of a cathedral, supporting a roof of closely-woven branches, through which the sunshine came, softened into a dim, green light, that suited well the cloistered stillness of the place.

The woman who was pursuing her labors in this secluded spot seemed to be between sixty and seventy years of age. She was bent and wrinkled, and the hair which showed itself under her scanty turban was literally "white as *wool*."[1] She wore a sack or short gown, of very thick gray cloth, which came a little below her hips, and the rest of her person was covered by three or four ragged petticoats, which, mingled in a picturesque confusion of tatters, hung from under this upper garment; and her feet and ankles were bound about with strips of rags in place of stockings, while on the ground, under her washing-bench, was a pair of cowhide shoes, of the rudest and strongest construction. She looked up from her work, as Ida drew near, with an expression of sullen curiosity; but after a momentary glance at the fair vision, she seemed to regard her presence as an annoying interruption of her work, and though she answered the questions addressed to her, in a respectful manner, she was evidently little disposed to the loquacity so common among the negroes.

While Ida was ascertaining the route she must take to gain her plantation, and its distance, certain sounds, which, for the last fifteen minutes, she had heard at intervals, became louder and more frequent, and, as she paused and looked with some alarm in the direction whence they proceeded, a pack of fierce-looking bloodhounds, of the largest size, burst through a low coppice of laurel that grew on the edge of the stream at a little distance, and, with their noses close to the ground, pursued a straight course through the hollow, and disappeared in the woods beyond. Ida

---

1 As in Elsie and Alfred's meeting, when speaking from Ida's point of view, Pike does not discuss skin color.

drew back, with involuntary dread of the ferocious creatures, who seemed strong enough to have dragged her from her horse and devoured her, if they had chosen to notice her presence. But, to her surprise, the woman manifested no alarm, and made no effort to hide from them, but stood looking after them, without speaking, until the sound of their hoarse baying grew faint in the distance.

"Are you not afraid?" said Ida.

"No," said she, with a short, bitter laugh, while the gloom of her face deepened, "no, I a'n't scare! *I* a'n't de runaway nigger! Dem creturs knows what dey 'bout! Dey on de track now, yer see! I know 'em! I'se seed 'em go 'traight t'rough a hull gang, workin' in de fiel', an' neber tetch one!"

"I've heard of these things before," said Ida, speaking rather to herself than to her companion, "but it don't seem as if dogs could be so well trained!" .

"Dem a'n't *dogs*—dem's *debils!*" said the woman, in a sharp, angry tone. "De a'n't nothin' hunts niggers like dat ar' gang do, 'thout de debil is in 'em. Dat de reason why de nigger so scare when he hear 'em. He know de debil a'ter him, he can't git 'way, no how. Ki! dem a'n't dogs!"

Just then two men, on horseback, armed with guns, and ferocious-looking as the dogs they were following, came through the coppice, and passed along near them. They half stopped, and looked at Ida suspiciously, as they saw her talking with the woman, and their rude, lawless gaze made her glad of the presence even of one who could afford little protection; but they did not speak to her, and, though they often looked back, they offered no molestation.

"The dogs belong to those men, I suppose," said Ida, breathing more freely when they were out of sight.

"Yes, dey all brongs togeder—they all sarve dere massa," replied the woman, sententiously.

"Do you know who they are after?" asked Ida.

"I reckon!" replied she, "I hearn massa tellin' somethin' to den ar men las' night, when I'se up de house, payin' my wage. I reckon dere a'n't many *he's* niggers run far 'thout habin' dese yer debils after 'em. Yeller Sam done ketch it, 'fore dis day done shed, I tell yer." .

"Who is your master?" said Ida.

"Name Massa John Laikin," answered her companion.

"Are you washing for his family? Why do you bring your work so far from the house?" said Ida, who knew where the gentleman referred to resided.

"O, I'se ole woman, yer see, and so he let me hire myself, and I live little piece down here by de wood, and gets de washing from de folks in de tavern. Sometimes heap o' folks dere, and den I does mighty well."

"What do you pay your master?" Ida asked.

"Five dollar, and find myself," replied the woman.

"Five dollars a month! that is more than a dollar a week!" exclaimed Ida. "How can an old woman, like you, earn enough to pay your master so much, and find food and clothing for yourself?"

"I doesn't allers," said the woman, with a half sigh; "but den Mass' John keep de 'count de week when I don't bring de whole dollar, an' I pays him up when I gets it. Mass' allers manage some way come out square when de month come roun'."

"But how do you get your own food and clothes?"

"O, I jest does de best I can. Sometimes I gets little guv me. De ladies guv me all dese petticoats, long time 'go," she answered, taking hold of her accumulated rags; "and sometime my chillen send me little. My son, down in Charleston, he skinch heself o' trousers,[1] and send me de cloth for make dis nice warm sack, keep me warm in de cole days and nights."

"I am glad your children help you, for you must find it rather hard to get along," said Ida, compassionately.

"Well, missis, what wid all den tings, and getting my little 'bacca, and my little tea, and my little 'lasses, and my little bit o' bacon, it do come pretty hard, sometime, on a poor old cretur. Nobody knows, but de Lord, he knows," she added, with a heavy sigh.

"But if you can go to Him with your troubles," said Ida, "and ask Him to give you strength and patience to bear them, and to make you good, so that you can go to heaven when you die; and, if you can have a sure hope that you are a Christian, you have one comfort that nobody can take away from you."

It was strange to see how the gloom and the sullen expression faded from the old woman's face, as Ida was speaking, and in its place there came a smile of interest and of hope. Those words had touched the chords of a spiritual life, which, wherever appealed to, whether in the breast of the high or the lowly, the educated or the ignorant, send forth the same unfailing strain of joy and triumph.

---

1 He scrimps, using the fabric needed to make his own trousers sparingly, in order to send a portion to his mother.

"Dat it!" she exclaimed, "dat it, missis! It am de sure hope o' de odder worle dat helps us when dis worle am all dark. Sometime it look hard, and jest when I tink, now I'se done 'pented, an' de Lord, he done forgive me, an' I'se mighty good Christian, den de debil come, and it all go 'way, an' I don't see nothin but a heap o' sin all roun' me. Den I pray—pray much—pray all night, may be—and den de hope all come back, an' I mighty glad 'gain. But 't wont be allers so, missus, I *feels* 't wont! In de odder worle de debil won't have no chance to upset us, like he do now; and den how happy we will be! O, de sufferin's o' dis yer time a'n't nothin'—*a'n't nothin'*—'pared to de glory dat's gwine be 'vealed inter us den!"

"That is a blessed promise to the tired and the suffering," said Ida. "Only think how great that glory and happiness must be, which will outweigh all the sorrows we have to endure in this world! And God gives us a great deal to enjoy, even in this world, in thinking of those things which he has in store for us in heaven."

"Dat it—dat it—'pears like we'se rich when we has dis sher, ef we don't have nothin' else!" exclaimed the woman, eagerly.

"Yes," replied Ida; "and to the poor and the suffering God often gives more of the consolations of his grace than he does to those who are rich, and have other things to make them happy."

"Dat it!—dat it!"—repeated the woman, holding up both hands with a solemn gesture. "O, miss, you'se *rich*, and you'se *white*, and you'se *free*; but de Lord, up in heaben, he care for de poor and de lowly, *jest de same* he do for you; an' ef it wan't for de good probidence o' de Lord, I dono' what de poor nigger would do."

The earnest manner in which these simple and touching words were spoken, affected Ida deeply. Nothing had ever so convicted her of her own want of faith and submission; for, in her heart, she had been murmuring at the Providence which had ordered for her such a changeful and lonely life, and made her so early fatherless and motherless. She had shrunk despondingly from the trial and the task before her, and almost arraigned the wisdom which had appointed such a duty for one so helpless and so friendless. "O!" said she to herself, "if this miserable woman, aged and destitute of all that makes life a blessing, can have such faith in God, and such submission to his will, how much more should I!" And it was with a humble and chastened heart that, after having given her companion a small sum of money, she pursued her way, meeting with no further adventure, until she arrived at the entrance of the narrow road that led through the plantation.

Here she paused a moment, to collect her thoughts, and to survey the scene before her. The whole extent of the farm was visible from the place where she stood; its level surface, unbroken by fences, and now destitute of vegetation, showing the brown soil formed from the trap-rock,[1] which once yielded such abundant crops, but which had now, by that very means and by subsequent bad management, become thin and exhausted. Scattered over the field, in the distance, were a few negroes at work, beating down the old cotton-stalks with clubs; but no one was near, and Ida rode slowly along, towards a group of log huts, that stood under the shadow of the black jack oaks that skirted the treeless expanse. Her heart sank within her, as she stopped before each door, and looked within the miserable dwellings, which presented only a picture of discomfort and filth, and reflected that, though they seemed hardly fit habitations for cattle, they were the homes of human beings, at the expense of whose poverty she had been living in luxury. Knowing Mr. Wynn's views on these subjects, and his treatment of his own field-hands, she had not expected to find more than the bare necessities of life, in its lowest estate; but she was unprepared for such utter destitution. In fact, Mr. Wynn himself was hardly aware of it. He had left everything to the overseer, and thought his duty as a guardian was fulfilled in obtaining the largest possible income for his ward.

At the door of one hut an old woman, evidently blind, was sitting, holding a wretched-looking baby, while two others lay on the ground before her. A little further on, several children, no one of them having sufficient clothing to answer the purposes of decency, were playing and quarreling together. Appalled and disheartened, Ida passed them all without speaking, and proceeded some rods further, towards a low building, used for storing cotton and other products of the plantation. As she came near, she heard the sound of voices raised in anger and entreaty, and then a swinging blow, followed by a shriek. Hastily dismounting from her horse, she pushed open the door and entered.

A short, ruffianly-looking man stood before her, with a long, heavy whip raised in his hand to give a second blow to the quivering, naked creature who was tied to a beam on one side of the shed, his hands drawn so high above his head that only the points of his toes rested on the floor. Near them a woman was crouch-

---

1   Dark igneous rock, such as is commonly used for railroad beds.

256   MARY HAYDEN GREEN PIKE

ing on the floor, her scanty dress half torn from her shoulders, and her face bowed on her knees in a posture of fear and despair.

At the glare of light which streamed in upon them on the opening of the door, the man turned, and started with astonishment at the unexpected vision that was revealed.

"What is all this about? Why do you whip that man?" said Ida, coming forward with an air of dignity and authority, which compelled respect. The man stared at her a few moments, and then she repeated her question. He answered in a tone half sullen and half insolent,

"I don't know what business you have interfering, but I ha'n't no objections to tellin' you that this sher wench desarved a floggin', and I told this boy to give it to her, and 'cause he wouldn't I've tied him up, and after I've given him a first-rate cutting-up, I'm going to give her another. I'll larn 'em to tell me they won't, the impudent niggers!"

He shook his fist at the kneeling woman as he spoke, but she crept forward a little, and, seeing compassion in Ida's face, she said tremblingly,

"O, miss, he be my husband—he couldn't b'ar to beat me!"

Ida laid her delicate little hand on the woman's head, as if to shield her, and turning to the overseer, whom she had seen once before, and whose name she now remembered, she said,

"Mr. Potter, take that man down immediately, and send him to his work. I won't have either of them whipped."

The woman gave a stifled exclamation of joy at these words, and pressed the folds of Ida's dress with both hands to her forehead, as if performing an act of worship; but the overseer uttered a brutal oath, and, bringing the leaden end of his whip-handle heavily down on the floor, exclaimed—

"Who are you? Go about your business, and leave me to manage mine!"

"Your business is mine also," said Ida, kindly but firmly. "I am the owner of this plantation, and of these negroes. I am Miss May!"

There was something in her manner that enforced the truth of her words; and, knowing that if they were true it was for his interest not to offend her, he muttered, in a half-respectful tone,

"If you be Miss May, they be your'n sure enough; but how came you here this time o' day? Why didn't Mr. Wynn come with you?"

"I chose to come alone," said Ida, with a gentle dignity that repressed further questioning. "Do you not remember me? I saw you at the hall Christmas day. You were just leaving as I arrived there. Mr. Wynn paid you some money as you stood on the piazza, before the library window."

"Beg your pardon, miss," said the man, gruffly, now fully convinced of Ida's identity. "I does remember somebody comin' that day, and I see you knows all about me. But this sher boy and gall does deserve a whippin' powerful, an' if I'm goin' ter have the care o' the plantation, yer see 't won't do fur ye to interfere. That's what Mr. Wynn allers tells his niggers when they complains 'bout his overseer."

"We will talk about that some other time," said Ida. "At present I want to see that man taken down."

Mr. Potter obeyed this request without further parley, but with evident reluctance, and he shook his whip threateningly at the man and woman as they crept away coweringly before his angry glance, thankful for their release from the impending punishment, but half doubting if their deliverer had power to ensure them against his future vengeance. Left alone with him in the vacant and dusky building, Ida felt half afraid of the rude nature whose savage propensities she had restrained. Standing in the doorway, she said,

"I saw a woman standing on the piazza of your house. If you will allow me, I will go up there and rest a while, for I am very much fatigued with my long ride, and, meantime, we will talk a little about the state of things here. Mr. Wynn tells me you have managed the place admirably since you have been here, and I thought you would be able to give me more direct information about it than anyone else."

This compliment, which was intended to conciliate, had something of its desired effect, for the angry brow cleared a little, and lifting his hat to scratch his head—an operation for which his long black fingernails seemed expressly adapted—Mr. Potter said, with an awkward effort at politeness,

"'T a'n't much of a place, my house a'n't, but such as 't is you'r welcome to go and sit down there if you're tired. If I'd 'a known you was comin', I'd 'a told the wench to tidy up a little."

The house referred to stood a few rods distant, and its occupant had told but the sober truth when he said it was not much of a place. It was a small wooden building, containing four rooms, two on the ground floor and two above. The unfailing piazza surrounded the lower story, and the windows were secured with thick wooden shutters, which were closed in every room except now, thus giving the house, from which the rain had long ago washed every trace of paint, a desolate and jail-like aspect, enhanced still further by its position in the bare open field, destitute of a garden or of any tree or shrub to enliven its dark exterior. In Mr. Maynard's time there had been trees before the house and a garden around it, for the overseer who then presided was blessed with a wife and children, and had some regard for the amenities of life; but he had quarreled with Mr. Wynn soon after Mr. Maynard left the country, and Mr. Potter, who took his place, was a different sort of man. So the trees had been felled, that he might be enabled while walking on the piazza to view all parts of the extensive field, and the garden fence had been burned up for fuel, and the garden ploughed up.

When they reached it, a bold, slatternly-looking[1] mulatto girl, who was sitting on the piazza, engaged in mending some of her master's garments, rose from her chair, and, with a curious stare at Ida, retreated slowly within the house. She took the vacant seat, and Mr. Potter perching himself on the section of a pine log, that lay on the floor, she proceeded to ask him questions about the farm, and to ascertain the ages and the capacities of the different negroes whom she was proposing to transform from "chattels personal"[2] into men and women. He told her what she desired to know with a sort of surly good-nature, and she found him to be a shrewd man, with common-sense ideas of business matters, priding himself greatly on his capability for saving money, and caring for little else in this world. The conversation lasted for some time, and Ida was surprised, at length, on looking at her watch, to find that it was nearly four o'clock in the afternoon. She rose hastily, and at the same moment a vivid flash of lightning seemed to fall from the heavens above them, and a crashing peal of thunder was heard. Ida sprang down the steps and looked up. The house faced the west, where the sun was shining in the cloudless blue, and thus she had been wholly unconscious of the thick and heavy clouds which had risen from the opposite quarter, and now, towering high in the zenith, and piling themselves up in a formidable array, covered nearly half the sky.

"What shall I do?" exclaimed she, in perplexity. "If I wait for the shower to be over it will be too late to reach home before dark, and yet there is no hope of escaping it if I start now."

"That's a fact," said Mr. Potter, who now stood beside her,

---

1 Slovenly, untidy.
2 Term used in property law to refer to movable personal property, including slaves.

and cast a weatherwise glance around. "This season[1] has come up mighty sudden, but we're goin' to have a stunner before it's over. I shouldn't wonder if it rained all night."

"I shouldn't care so much for getting wet," said Ida; "but my horse is afraid of the lightning, and it is really unsafe to be among the trees in such a storm."

"If you wait, perhaps Mr. Wynn will send the carriage. If I may speak my mind, you'd 'a done better to come that way in the first place, but 't a'n't none of my business, I 'spose."

This remark, which, by recalling to Ida her morning conference with Mr. Wynn, reminded her how entirely she must now depend upon herself, decided her what to do; and, springing upon her horse, she said,

"I must trust to Providence to delay the storm until I can get to a place of shelter."

"There is a tavern down in the village, three miles or so from here, taking the fust right hand road after you cross the branch;[2] but I don't reckon you could even get there, 'fore the storm. It'll rain ploughshares and hoe-handles in five minutes."

"I must try it, nevertheless," said Ida, who shrank instinctively from spending the night where she was; but, as she turned her horse's head towards the road, she was astonished to see little Dick in a wagon standing halfway between the house and the entrance of the farm, from which Venus was just alighting, bearing in her arms a large carpet-bag. Riding rapidly up to them, she heard, as she came near, the old shrill tones of Venus, exclaiming,

"Now I say you *shall* stay till I can speak to Miss Ida. P'raps mought be she like to go home with yer."

"No," said Dick, "you don't coach *dis* chile stopping for nothin' in *dis* place, when Mass' Richard tell him not, wid *dat ar' look* on he face. Let go de hos head, yer old fool!" and, giving the animal a cut with the whip, which also fell partly on Venus's hand, the stable Jehu[3] wheeled around and drove away.

"What can be the meaning of this?" thought Ida, with a sudden faintness of heart, that was not at all alleviated by the expression of Venus's face as she turned to her.

---

1 [Pike's note:] In Carolina "season" is the common term for a shower of rain.
2 [Pike's note:] That is, brook.
3 A king of the Jews who, in 2 Kings 9:33, orders Jezebel thrown down from a castle window and runs her over with his horse and chariot, killing her.

"What ar' all dis sher 'bout?" she exclaimed; "what yer been doin' to make Mass' Richard mad? Bress de honey, I'se do wish she let de brack folks 'lone, not be all time gettin' into scrapes!" she added, in a tone of vexation. "'Spose it's sumthin' about Maum Abby, a'n't it?"

"I don't know what it is, mauma. How came you here?" replied Ida, feeling ready to cry, at the dilemma to which she was reduced.

"How cum I here? Mass' Richard send me," said Venus, "He looked like thunder cloud, and say, 'Go put up Miss Ida's night-dress, and get ready to ride with Dick.'—'What ar' she, massa?' I say. Den he scowl, and say, 'No matter;' and tell me give you dis note, and tell Dick leave me here and go right straight home."

She handed Ida a note, as she spoke; and, opening it with trembling hands, she read the following brief epistle:

"Having left the premises of her guardian, in the most unlady-like and contumacious manner, Miss May will see the propriety of not returning until she shall be requested to do so by some member of his family."

"Cruel! tyrannical! What shall I do?" she exclaimed in distress; and a few hot tears fell on the paper as she crushed it in her hand, indignantly.

Meantime, swift as winged messengers of wrath, black as Tartarean gloom, the clouds had spread over towards the west, and the sunlight was growing dim. The air had become heavy and oppressive, and an ominous, death-like stillness brooded over the earth, like the calm with which a brave soul awaits the stroke of doom. There was a distant flash, a long, low peal of muttering thunder, and then, from directly above them, there darted a blinding, enveloping glare, and a tree, which stood by the gate a few rods distant, fell to the ground shivered into a thousand fragments. Ida's horse reared and plunged violently forward, and it was with great difficulty that she mastered him, and retained her seat; but the sudden shock, and the violent, physical exertion, restored her self-possession, and, beckoning to Venus to follow, she rode back to the house.

She sprang from her horse, who, snorting wildly, dashed away the moment he felt himself free, and, running up the steps of the piazza where Mr. Potter was standing, who had been an amazed spectator of her meeting with Venus, she said to him, hurriedly,

"You see, we must stay here tonight. It would be wild to brave this storm."

"Is that your servant with the big bag?" the man asked.

"Yes," replied Ida. "You can accommodate us in some way, I hope."

"You'll have to put up with what you can get, I reckon," said the man, with a short, insolent laugh. "I don't feel right sure that you're what you pretends. It looks powerful strange for one o' Mr. Wynn's young ladies to be comin' here this way, and he as proud as the devil. Likely story you b'long to him!"

"I assure you," said Ida, earnestly, concealing her fear of his rude manner as well as possible, "I assure you it is as I have said. I had no idea of remaining when I came, but now I must stay, and you surely will own my right to a lodging in my own house."

"If 't is yourn, you're welcome to the whole on 't, rats and all," he answered, with another of those disagreeable laughs, that made his listener tremble, while they angered her. "But how am I to know it's yourn? Here you come fust, and then your gal with this truck," he added, kicking the bag which Venus had now laid on the floor beside her. "It looks mighty like you'd been turned out of doors, neck and heels; and I reckon you'll find yourself mistaken, if you think I'm goin' to have any impostors comin' here orderin' me round and interferin' and askin' questions."

Ida was ready to sink with chagrin and fear; but, controlling herself, and speaking firmly, though her face was white as marble, and her lips seemed stiffening, she answered,

"Your language is somewhat rough, but I think you cannot mean what you say. You surely would not turn away anyone from your door in such a storm as this; and you must know, that, even if Mr. Wynn has refused me his house, I am no less the owner of this property, and of that fact I can bring abundant proof."

In his excitement, Mr. Potter had not thought of this. He had so long regarded Mr. Wynn as the director of affairs, that it was hard for him to realize the ownership of another; and, puzzled as he was respecting his unexpected guests, he bit his lip, and turned sulkily away, while Ida and Venus entered the house.

It was a wretched-looking place. The hall was half filled with pine knots and sticks cut for firewood, and though the mulatto girl, apprehensive that Ida would enter, had hastily swept up the floor of the only room inhabited, and made some slight attempt at order, she had not succeeded in hiding its dreary discomfort. But there was little inclination to note this now. The lightning had become incessant, and the unnatural darkness of the house was lighted with a lurid glare that clothed everything within the room, and all the landscape without, in a weird purple light, indescribably awful. The thunder rolled and reverberated, coming continually nearer with its loud, heavy crashing, until the whole house shook, and the very earth seemed to tremble; and then, suddenly, swiftly as if the foundations of the firmament were broken up, down came the deluging rain.

The overseer had followed Ida into the house; but, as the storm increased, he could no longer disguise his fears, and, after one or two attempts to swear at the mulatto girl, who was trembling and moaning in the darkest corner of the room, he threw himself down on the bed that stood on one side of the fireplace, and, burying his face in the pillow, remained silent and motionless.

Seated opposite the window, at a little distance from it, Ida viewed the scene. She had been harassed and distressed when she entered the room, but soon all that passed away. Her hands, that lay in her lap, were clasped unconsciously, and with her head bent a little forward, her eyes dilated, her lips apart, she gazed in silence; but she was pale from excitement now, and not from fear. All the enthusiasm, all the poetical sensibility of her nature was aroused; but what moved her more than all was the appeal to her religious feelings. The lightnings, whereby it seemed as if an invisible hand was writing mysterious truths, in sharp jagged characters, on that dark wall of cloud; the livid radiance, that quivered through the air, and ran along the ground, amid the dashing of the fast-falling rain; the shock of the thunder, sounding and re-echoing from every part of the heavens; all this tumult and strife of the elements spoke to her of God; and before this display of his power her soul exulted and expanded with a sublime faith. She felt his presence. She heard his voice. In the rushing tempest he addressed her, and as she listened she was no longer afraid. That God, whose will alone controls these agencies, beneath which the gigantic products of nature, and the mighty works of the human race, are cast down and destroyed, and at whose lightest touch man shrinks and shrivels like a leaf, was he not able to deliver her from the snares that had been laid for her, from the dangers and evils that beset her path? Her whole being was bowed in adoration, as the glory of his majesty was thus revealed, and her heart was filled with confidence and peace. Half unconsciously, she chanted, in a low voice, those words that were sung in clarion tones of triumph, long ago, among the hills of Judea:

"Then the earth shook and trembled
The foundations also of the hills moved and were shaken,
Because He was wroth.
There went up a smoke out of his nostrils,
And fire out of his mouth devoured.
He bowed the heavens also and came down,
And darkness was under his feet.
He made darkness his secret place.
His pavilion round about him were dark waters
And thick clouds of the skies.
The Lord also thundered in the heavens,
The Highest gave his voice; hailstones and coals of fire.
At the brightness that was before him his thick clouds
        passed;
Hailstones and coals of fire.
He sent from above, he took me,
He drew me out of many waters,
He brought me forth also into a large place,
He delivered me, because he delighted in me."[1]

After an hour of incessant fury, the storm abated a little. The lightning became less vivid and incessant, and the house ceased to rock with the violent concussion of the thunder peals. The overseer rose from his bed, and stretching himself as if he had been asleep, though no one could have slumbered in the midst of that noise, he came to the fireplace, where a few embers were still burning, and laying his hand with no gentle touch on the shoulder of the girl, who was still crouching there, he said, with an oath,

"Why don't you get up and go about your business, you hussy? Don't you see it's most dark? What you scared at? There's been a devil of a row, to be sure, but we've all lived through it, and I reckon we shall."

"I be n't scare," said the girl, as she lifted her head. "I was, to de fust, but I be n't scare now;—but dat 'ar miss am lookin' out de winder, and she won't want it shet."

"Well go out and bring in the wood for tonight, then, and we'll see," replied the man. "I reckon I'm master here, yet."

The girl did as she was commanded; and meantime, a few low-spoken, rapid words of explanation passed between Ida and Venus, for the latter, knowing that her mistress liked to be left to

1 From Psalm 18, "The Lord is my rock."

her own thoughts unmolested, at such a time as this, and having learned from example a certain fearlessness of the electrical phenomena, very unusual with persons of her class, had refrained from the questions she longed to ask, and sat silently on the floor at Ida's feet, until Mr. Potter's coarse voice broke the spell, and called her thoughts back from the high regions where they had wandered.

CHAPTER XIV

"It gives me wonder great as my content
To see you here before me. O, my soul's joy!
If after every tempest come such calms,
May the winds blow till they have wakened death!"
 OTHELLO[1]

When the mulatto girl had brought in quite a quantity of wood from the hall, she locked and bolted the outer door, and then entering the room, closed that door also carefully behind her, securing it with two wooden bars, which crossed it at the top and near the floor, fitting into iron sockets in the casement. Somewhat startled, and wondering to see such precaution that seemed excessive, Ida asked Mr. Potter why he had his door so securely fastened; but he was stooping down over the fire which he was kindling, and pretended not to hear her.

The girl then lit a yellow candle, which she placed in a battered brass candlestick, and then, approaching the window, she put out her hand to close the shutter.

"Don't you do dat," said Venus, interposing. "Miss Ida allers likes to look out when de lightnin' shine."

"It dark," said the girl; "we allers shets 'em at dark."

"Leave it a while longer," said Ida, gently. She felt an undefined dread of being barricaded thus in this small room with such companions.

"It dark now!" persisted the girl. "*Dey* allers comes and looks in ef we leaves 'em open ater dark."

"*Dey*! who *dey* be?" asked Venus, still keeping hold of the window.

"*Dey* looks in, I say," repeated she. "Let me shet 'em."

"Who be *dey*? What harm dey do when dey looks in?" said Venus.

"*Dey*! why de *ghosts*, you stupid nigger!" retorted the other, bluntly. "Dey allers comes 'bout dis time, ef I don't shet 'em."

Venus retreated a little, and looked with a bewildered air at the window and then at the girl; but she rallied in a moment, and said,

"Ghosts! de a'n't no such. My miss say dere a'n't, you fool!"

"Dey *is*, too!" replied the girl, with an earnest air, as if she

---

1 Othello greets Desdemona after surviving a stormy voyage, 2.1.186–89.

fully believed her own words. "Dey all 'bout dis yer house nights. O Lor! we hears 'em de whole time, trampin' and poundin'. O Lor! you wait!"

"But did you ever see them?" asked Ida. "Are you sure it is not the rats you hear?"

"See 'em! O Lor! miss, yes," replied she. "Many time, ater dark, I'se seed 'em come an' flat dere noses 'gainst de winder, lookin' in. Dat de reason we allers shet de shetter when come dark. O Lor! I'se seed 'em heap o' time!"

"I reckon they won't come tonight, anyway," said Ida, who could not help laughing at the ludicrous idea of a ghost flattening its nose; "and I prefer to have the window left open. The room will be very close with it shut."

The girl looked round at her master in perplexity, but he broke out with a string of oaths, and bade her shut the shutter and not stand there fooling, but come and get supper. He never commenced a sentence without swearing, but his profanity seemed more than ever horrible in contrast with his craven fear during the hour previous.

Having closed and barred the window, as she had done the door, the girl brought forth a few broken dishes, from a small closet over the fireplace, and proceeded to get the supper ready. Mr. Potter sat smoking a short pipe in dogged silence, fortunately sitting so near the wide chimney that the draft carried most of the offensive smoke out into the open air. Ida addressed one or two remarks to him, but he would not answer, and kept his eyes fixed on the floor. The girl seemed to take the cue from her master, and her bold, insolent replies were even more offensive than his taciturnity; so, after a few efforts, they gave up the attempt at conversation, and looked on in silence while the girl fried some bacon and made some tea, and placing on the table some black, hard-looking corn cakes, announced that supper was ready.

The man drew his chair up to the table when he heard this, and turning to Ida said gruffly,

"If you want some supper, you better move up. Now you're here, I 'spose you may as well eat."

Before Ida could reply, Venus, whose wrath had been gathering at the various insults offered her mistress, started to her feet, exclaiming,

"*Dat* de way you talk to my miss? You old cantankerous creatur', don't you know she *your* miss too? You set down fust 'thout waiting for her! You'd wait till she got through 'fore you'd eat a mouthful, ef you know'd what's manners. You s'pose my miss eat sich trash as dat! 'Nuff to make a nigger sick to look at it!"

"Hush, Venus, do," exclaimed Ida, greatly distressed as she saw the effects of these rash words.

"O, let her go on! let her! she better try it! She better stick up her nose at me! I a'n't going to play second fiddle to no woman, while niggers is round, and I a'n't noways sure neither of yer is what you pretend to be. Yer better not provoke me; I can manage both of yer."

Venus was going on with her defiant anger, but the expression of fear and trouble on Ida's face restrained her, and she sat down again abruptly, turning her back to him.

"Don't mind her," said Ida, who, feeling herself wholly in the power of this rude being, was anxious to conciliate him. As she spoke, she drew her chair nearer the table, and endeavored to eat something, that he might not think she disdained his surly hospitality, at the same time forcing herself to talk of events connected with Mr. Wynn and his family, both to divert his attention from Venus and also to impress him, in this indirect manner, with the idea that, in spite of the circumstances that had aroused his suspicion, she was really the owner of the farm on which he lived, and it would be for his interest to treat her well. But, as he rose from the table after finishing his meal, he reached over towards her to take a piece of bread from a plate beside her, and she discovered that this breath smelled strongly of some intoxicating liquor. Her heart sank within her. This, then, explained the reason why he had grown increasingly rude; and here she was, far from all help, shut up with a half-tipsy savage, and a girl who seemed capable of being his accomplice in any wickedness, with only Venus to aid her in any scene that might ensue.

A wild fear thrilled her soul. She rose from her chair, with a sudden determination to go forth into the darkness and the night storm, rather than remain where she was; but, as she stopped to whisper to Venus, a peal of thunder burst from a cloud so near that the reverberation shook the house as if a heavy ball had been rolled against it, and everyone in the room stood breathlessly, half expecting the walls to fall to pieces around them. The tempest had returned upon them in greater fury than ever, and though they were too closely shut in to see the lightning, they could hear the hissing and howling of the storm in momentary pauses when the thunder grew more distant. It would be death to go abroad then, on foot and unprotected as she was; but to remain all night where she was seemed impossible. Compelling herself to assume a calmness of manner she was far from feeling, she approached Potter, who was sitting before the fire with his elbows on his knees, and his face covered with his hands, and said to him, "Is there no other room in this house where your servant or Venus can build a fire, so that I can stay there tonight? You told me that there was no furniture anywhere but here, but you can spare me a chair and a light and I do not care for more. I shall not sleep any tonight."

"No I reckon all the sleep you got wouldn't amount to much, with the creatures ther is up there mutterin' and crawlin' round yer, and puttin' their hands on ye—ugh! cold as ice," he added, with a shudder and a half-terrified look round the room.

"I'm not afraid of that," said Ida, impatiently, though in spite of herself, a thrill of superstitious fear stole over her at his words. "Let your girl show me where to go, and Venus and I will take care of ourselves."

"She shan't do no such thing!" said the man, looking up. "Nobody don't open them doors this night. If you'd thought on't afore dark, I'd 'a let you gone where you was a mind. If you like the company o' them creatures, you might 'a had it for all me; but now you've got to stay here, an' that's the hull on't, and afore morning' I reckon you'll be glad you're where they can't come in, if they carry on like they gen'ly do these times."

Ida could not help an involuntary shudder at his look and manner, although, of course, she had no faith in the existence of the things he believed in. She was about to urge the point again, but he prevented her by saying, abruptly,

"'T a'n't no use to talk. I won't have the door opened, and that is the up and down of the matter. They're all round the house by this time, and you'll hear 'em muttering and moaning and creaking the stairs going up and down, 'fore long. If the doors open they'll all rush in here to 'oncet, and maybe I couldn't get 'em out again. They driv me out of all the rest of the house, but I fixed this room so the a'n't even a key-hole for 'em to get into, and shets all up tight at dark, and keeps a fire all night, and snaps my fingers at 'em. No, marm. You may be mistress o' this house, but I'm master, and I won't have no doors opened out o' this room tonight."

Having thus delivered himself, he resumed his position with an air of surly determination. The girl, after putting away the few dishes unwashed, had sat down in the corner opposite him, and, leaning her head against the bedclothes, shut her eyes as if intending to go to sleep. In the back part of the room, Venus was resting her arms on the table, and, with her chin reposing on them, was gazing at the two with mute defiance.

There was nothing more to be said—there could nothing more be done. The iron circle of necessity pressed hard and close upon Ida, and she sank beneath its weight. Her nerves had been too long and too severely tried, and they were yielding to the pressure. The glow, the ecstasy of feeling that first sustained her, had departed. The eye of Faith grew dim. A sense of her helplessness, of her loneliness, of her powerlessness, in contact with these rude, coarse natures—of the insults she had received, of the unknown wrongs she feared, a feeling of isolation, as if she were cut off forever from human love or succor, as if she were a worthless thing, flung forth to buffet the cold waves of life, only to be overwhelmed and sink at last—all this came over her in the moments that succeeded, and her courage died.

She looked round on the miserable room, with its bare walls hung with cobwebs, its unpainted and dirty floor, its scanty furniture and its degraded occupants, and she thought, with a strange, dreary pity for herself, that this was the only place she could claim as home. She realized, with a keen pain, how different her situation might have been. She remembered what she had been told of her parents, and the doting love and care that would have surrounded her, had they lived; and of her kind guardian, whose death had imposed upon her the duties that had exposed her to such changes and such trials. How relentlessly had Death pursued her! How completely had differing causes stripped her of all her friends! O, why must she be thus dealt with? Why must all the bitterness of life be gathered in the cup held to her lips? Why must she sit in the cold shadows, and see others beautiful and beloved, and bearing off carelessly all that would, if hers, have been more to her than life?

A wild and bitter feeling of rebellion seized her—an awful mistrust of the divine goodness and love. Her soul cried out, with a fierce and piercing cry, for the friends she had lost, for the hope that was fled, for the love that had passed by her to be unworthily bestowed. Alone and helpless, she felt, as she had never felt before, a craving for affection, for support, for protection; a desire to give up all struggle; a shrinking from further sacrifice; a longing for a strong arm on which to lean, for a hand to guide her; a restless, desperate wish to free herself from the present, which girded her with realities too fearful, and to be released from the future, with whose responsibilities she felt unable to cope.

Venus, who had been relieving her grief and anger by a long fit of crying, began at length to wonder at the silence of her young mistress, and, on looking up, she was startled at her attitude and expression. There was an ashy whiteness in her face, a ghastly dimness in her eyes, that seemed fixed on vacancy, a weariness and despair in the drooping figure, which was far unlike Ida's usual sprightly independence of mien. She went towards her, and, bending down, said, softly, "What de matter honey? You faint?"

"No, I'm not faint, but I'm sick, *heartsick!*" and she rested her head heavily against that faithful bosom which sheltered her infancy.

"Poor child! poor honey!" said Venus, kneeling beside Ida, so as to put her arms around her. "It do seem hard; but don't be too much 'stressed. I make sure de Lord a'n't brung you dat far t'rough all dese yer 'markable ways, to leave yer in de lurch jes' here, where yer can't help yerself. Trus' in Him, honey."

Ida sighed deeply. She was too utterly weary and disheartened to feel the consolation these words were intended to convey. Venus drew her still closer towards her, gathering her in her arms, and smoothing the dark curls that fell over her shoulder, while Ida laid her head there, as she used to do when a child.

"We'se been t'rough heap o' narrer cracks, honey," she continued, "an' sometime 'pears like de Lord didn't mind nothin' 'bout us any more; but 'pend upon it, he allers hear de poor cretures cryin' to him, and, 'fore we know'd it, he done help us. 'Pears like he be 'blidged help us mighty quick, now, an' I thinks he will, fur 'pears like you wouldn't get through dis night dis way, an' I'se allers noticed when de a'n't nothin' more we can do ourself, den de Lord, he being doin' somethin'. Don't you be scare, honey. Old Venus take care of ye till de Lord send somebody."

While she had been speaking, the mulatto girl had raised her head, as if listening to her, while her sharp, inquisitive glance rested on Ida. As she uttered the last words, the girl turned a little, to look at the overseer, who still sat before the fire, with his head resting on his hands, and a meaning smile passed between them. In a moment she rose, and, coming near him, said a few words. He raised himself a little and looked towards Ida. "By and by, may be," he replied, and the girl returned to her seat.

Ida had not heard her words, but something in her tone, and in the expression of the man's eyes, as he glanced at her, made her blood curdle, and she shivered from head to foot. A dreadful terror took possession of her—a panic that it seemed impossible for her to restrain, and it was only by a violent effort that she refrained from shrieking aloud. Venus had her back towards them, and had noticed nothing; but Ida, looking over her shoulder, saw that the girl still continued watching them, and that, occasionally, the same expressive and repulsive glances passed between them that at first had startled her. At length, however, the girl seemed sleepy again, and rested her head against the bed. Then Ida whispered to Venus, who had, for a long time, been silently supporting her.

"Don't answer—don't seem to take notice, Venus—but I think they are going to sleep, both of them, and when I give you a sign, you spring up and undo the window before they know it. We can get out there the easiest!"

"In this storm, honey! It'll kill ye!" whispered she, in reply.

"I a'n't afraid of that. I know that man means to do us harm, and I *will* get away, if I can. You'll do it?"

Venus bowed assent, and again there was a long silence. The girl was evidently asleep, and the man's head was dropped on his bosom. Ida raised herself gently, and Venus rose to her feet to approach the window; but, just then, there was a sound, as if something heavy had fallen in the room above, with a jar that shook the house; then came a rolling, rattling noise, as if fragments of some hard substance were being thrown about, and a faint sound of voices was heard above all the noise of the storm. Everyone in the room started to their feet in alarm; but, in a moment or two, all was quiet again.

"Good Lor!" said the girl, sitting down again, with a frightened look. "Dey'se at it, now, sure nuff. Dey allers wus stormy nights, like dis, but dat was uncommon powerful!"

"Throw on some fat-wood, you fool!" said Potter, "and make the room lighter. Do you s'pose we want to be in the dark, with *them* creturs 'round?"

The girl threw some pieces of pine-wood upon the embers and soon a bright flame sprang up the chimney, and threw a glow into even the dingiest nook of the room.

"There, now, that'll do 'bout right!" continued he, as he watched the flames; and then, going to the little closet, he took down a black bottle, which he raised to his lips, and drank heartily of its contents.

Ida had stood leaning her slender form against Venus, and looking at their companions in alarm and fear.

"Merciful heaven!" she cried, aloud, "how is this to end?"

"'T won't end 'fore mornin', I make sure," replied Potter, setting down his bottle; "but let 'em kick up their row, if they want to. I a'n't scared of 'em, long as I have a light room and plenty of the needful."

"Dere dey is agin—I hears 'em!" said the girl. "Didn't I tell yer dey was all 'round?" she added, turning to Venus, "In a minute dey'll come thumping' on de door!"

Hardly had she spoken, when a mingled sound of voices was heard again, and more distinctly than before, raised in a prolonged shriek, or yell, and, soon after, loud and repeated knockings were heard in various directions about the house. Wholly overcome with fear, Venus, who had hitherto kept up bravely, sank trembling to the floor, and buried her face in her aprons. She felt equal to protecting her mistress against foes of a mortal kind, but the palpable evidence of the supernatural unnerved her. For a few moments these noises continued, mingling awfully with the thunder and the rain. Ida, almost paralyzed with horror, stood listening, and watching, with a mute prayer to Heaven for help, the movements of the overseer, who was now walking about the room, with unsteady steps, evidently emboldened by the new stimulus he had taken, and casting upon her glances that grew every moment more insolent, when, suddenly, steps were heard on the piazza by the window, against which she was leaning. A violent blow struck it, shattering the few remaining panes of glass, and a voice—a *human* voice—cried, angrily, "Are you all dead, here? Wake up, and let us in!"

Venus sprang to her feet, as she heard it, and, casting one quick, delighted glance at Ida, attempted to undo the fastening of the shutter; but Potter seized her and dragged her away.

"Let me 'lone!" exclaimed she; "dey a'n't ghosts—dey's *men* dat's knockin.'"

"No you don't!" said he; "they may knock much as they like, they won't get in here this night, nor you don't get out, neither. I'm master here!"

"We'll see 'bout that!" cried Venus, releasing herself by a violent effort, and, giving him a blow that sent him reeling halfway across the room, she jumped to the window again, and had taken down one of the boards, when the mulatto girl, seizing the quilt from the bed, threw it over her head, and, thus blinded and confined, Venus was again pulled away.

Ida sprang to her aid with a piercing shriek, and, in another moment, the shutters were forced open from without, and a man leaped in through the window. Ida turned to her deliverer. It was Walter Varian, and, with a wild cry of delight, she sprang forward into his outstretched arms.

"Thank God!" he exclaimed, "I find you safe."

Three others had followed him through the entrance he had made, and, clasping close to his heart the yielding form he held, he turned his pale, anxious face towards them, bidding them close the shutters immediately, for the rain was driving in sheets in upon them as they stood, and then moving, so as to shield Ida from its effects, he said to Venus, who had been uttering various ejaculations of thankfulness,

"What was that noise I heard? Surely no one could have dared injure Miss Ida! What is the meaning of all this?" he added, with a freezing terror in his heart, glancing at the dismantled bed, the quilt that lay on the floor, the overturned chairs, that had been knocked down in the struggle, and, fixing his eyes at length with a stern, angry expression, on the man and girl, who were standing together near the fire. It was an infinite relief when Venus hastened to say,

"O, dese yer fools thinks dis ar' house is haunted, and so dey would have it you was ghosts knocking, and dey wouldn't let me open de winder, and when I tried to, de gal put de quilt over my head, and haul me away, and we hab a squabble. Dat all. Dey's fools; but dey a'n't done nothin' wus."

"You might have known it was I," said Walter, in an altered tone. "I thought you would be on the lookout for me, and have the house all lighted, to show me the way. I came near not finding it, everything was so dark, and it storms so awfully."

"*I* done 'spected you," said Venus, "*I* thought you couldn't be sich a hyppercritter as not to come, when you've allers pretended to be sich friends wid Miss Ida; but *she* wouldn't hear nothin' 'bout it."

"Surely you did not think I could leave you to bear this dreadful night alone!" said Walter, with a reproachful tenderness, bowing his face till it touched the head that lay still on his breast, and speaking in a tone intended for her ear alone.

She made no reply. Her curls fell over her face, so that it was hidden from his view, but her quietness, her silence, and the utter lifelessness with which she leaned against him, made him start with a sudden fear. Raising his hand, he put back the glossy hair. Her eyes were closed, and her face was whiter than marble.

"She has fainted," he exclaimed, gathering her light form in his arms, and laying it gently down on the quilt that was spread out on the floor.

How like a beautiful image of death she looked, as she lay there, so pale and inanimate, in the bright glow of the firelight!

Kneeling on one knee, he bent over her, chafing her cold hands, that could not feel the palpitating pressure of his own, and bathing her face with the water which had been brought, for the superstitious dread of Potter and his servant could no longer prevent the doors from being opened, and soon she breathed again. When her head was lifted and laid on Venus's bosom, she opened her eyes, and a rich color flushed her pale cheek, as she saw who it was that held her hands, and gazed at her with that strange, thrilling expression, as if his whole heart was going forth from his eyes.

Walter and Mabel had not ridden far that morning, after they had left Ida, before they fell in with a party of their young friends, who were on their way to a romantic spot, some miles distant, where they proposed having a picnic. Mabel, whose jealousy of Ida made her wish as much as possible to keep Walter away from her, yielded to their earnest invitation, and thus compelled the assent of her *preux chevalier.*[1] The morning was fine, the party was gay, and soon Walter's chagrin at disappointing Ida, who might ride out expecting to meet them, was lost in the universal good-nature and hilarity that prevailed.

Fortunately for the thoughtless party, a negro boy, who accompanied them, climbed a tree to look for squirrels' nests, and thus discovered the small cloud, which, at first, rose slowly out of the east, but which his quick eye knew boded a violent thunderstorm. They hurried to their horses and rode rapidly homeward, and it was not until Walter and Mabel had left the rest of the party that the storm broke upon them. Mabel was not afraid, for a lack of courage was not among her deficiencies; indeed, she rather enjoyed the excitement, and was gratified at Walter's evident admiration of her self-possession and skill in managing her frightened steed; and, though both were thoroughly drenched, they arrived safely at home, full of the high spirits which the young and healthy feel at overcoming difficulty and danger.

Five minutes before their arrival, Ida's horse, that, impelled by instinct, had fled homeward with frantic haste, dashed up the avenue, and turned into the stable. An old, half-blind servant, who happened to be there alone, removed his wet saddle, and

---

1 Gallant knight (French).

led him to his stall, as one of the other hostlers[1] passed through the door on his way to the yard. This man was standing near the piazza when Walter and his cousin rode up, and ran to take the horses.

"Did Miss Ida go to ride? Is she at home?" he asked hurriedly, as he ran up the steps after Mabel.

"Yes, sir; she went, but she come home now," was the reply; and, satisfied on this point, Walter went directly to his own room, where he changed his wet clothing, and made a new toilet, before he again descended to the parlor.

Meantime, Mrs. Wynn was becoming excessively alarmed at Ida's prolonged absence. The sympathy of feeling which had existed between them, of late, had aroused far warmer feelings than she had felt towards the orphan for many years, and after her anxiety for Mabel and Walter was removed by their safe arrival, she had been wandering from room to room, looking out every door and window which commanded a view of the way she should come, and almost forgetting her usual fear of these terrific storms in her greater fear lest some accident happened to Ida. Once or twice, when Mr. Wynn had come out of the library to inquire if Mabel had arrived, and to detach a servant after her, his wife had ventured to mention Ida's name, although certain that it would offend him; but he had replied, in a peremptory tone, that Ida was safe, and that she need not expect to see her again that night. Indeed, he was himself annoyed, and a little anxious at the turn affairs had taken, though he was yet too proud to manifest it.

When, in his first flush of anger, as he sat brooding over her unforeseen rebellion, it had suddenly occurred to him to send Venus after her, with that message, he did not intend finally to expel her from his house, but only to frighten and humble her. She had been a member of his family so long, that he felt a perfect right to punish her disobedience; and, just as he would have imprisoned a child in a dark closet, until it promised to be good, he determined to inflict this chastisement, which, by alarming her, and throwing her for a while on her own resources, would teach her how much she had overrated her ability to guide herself and manage her own affairs, and thus coerce her into submission to his wishes with regard to her conduct. He knew the house at the Triangle was lonely and ill-furnished, and that she would be subjected to much inconvenience and

---

1 Servants who keep horses or stables.

some discomfort; but he had no idea of the trials to which she was really exposed by his rash act. He sent Venus to her, that the proprieties of social life might be preserved, and she might not feel too entirely alone; and he carefully worded his note in such a manner that it would not compromise his dignity to have Mabel or Walter go over to inquire for her, and, at length, when she should have been sufficiently mortified, bring her to him to ask forgiveness for her conduct.

It is but justice to Mr. Wynn to give this explanation of his motives. As a lady and his guest, it would have been impossible for him to treat her so impolitely, much as her ultra ideas[1] on one subject had displeased him; but as a perverse child, he claimed the right to inflict a punishment proportioned to her offense.

It was, therefore, with concealed agitation, that he marked the fury of the storm, and it was fortunate for Dick that he was a reckless fellow, and had driven home at a perilous rate, whipping his horse all the way; for, had he made the thunder or the lightning an excuse for any delay until the rain was over, his master's irritation would have vented itself on his head. Having seen Dick, who presented himself in the library, dripping like a young Triton, and ascertained that he had left Ida and Venus together at the Triangle, Mr. Wynn felt quite like saying, "Richard's himself again,"[2] and, with his usual placid sternness, he joined his wife in the parlor just as Walter entered by another door. Mabel was already sitting by the fire, a little pale from fatigue, and attired in a blue silk *negligé*, that made her look more beautiful than ever. She turned to Walter with a smile as he entered. She was beginning to watch for his step, and to tremble and blush when she met his gaze. She was beginning to think less of absorbing him in blind devotion to her wishes, less of commanding obedience to the whim of the moment. Involuntarily, now, her feelings took their tone from his, as far as it was possible in natures so different, and the queenly Mabel was bowing her graceful neck to wear the chains of her conqueror.

"I hope you are not chilly after your involuntary shower-bath," she hastened to say, as he came near.

"O, no, thank you!" he replied carelessly, and then added

---

1 I.e., her ultra-liberal ideas on abolition.
2 This famous line from Shakespeare's *Richard III* was actually written by the actor-playwright Colley Cibber (1671–1757), whose 1699 adaptation of the play held the stage until the late nineteenth century.

more earnestly, his fine eyes lighting with admiration, "and you, *Ma belle!*[1] you were quite a heroine in your battle with the elements; do you suffer at all from it?"

"Not in the least; but I am rather fatigued," she answered, with a slight blush, as she met his ardent gaze. It had been and was still a great charm for him, in Mabel's beauty, that her face and her whole figure were so purely statuesque. She was like a living, breathing piece of sculpture, gratifying his enthusiastic love of the beautiful every time her looked at her. All her movements were graceful; each new attitude seemed more charming than the last, and either of her varying expressions seemed for the time that which most became her style of features. It was only when she spoke that the spell was broken.

Walter was about to reply, when, seeing his aunt standing near, as if wanting to speak, he turned to her inquiringly.

"O, I am so anxious about Ida!" she said, as if in reply to his question, "She has been gone since twelve o'clock, and though Mr. Wynn says she certainly don't intend coming home tonight, I know she did."

"Ida!" exclaimed Walter; "Isn't she at home?"

"No," said Mabel; "but surely, there is no need to worry. Papa never speaks positively, unless he knows."

"One of the servants told me she was at home," said Walter.

"It is a mistake," replied Mrs. Wynn; "and, what worries me more is, that I have just discovered that Venus left here, this afternoon, in the wagon with little Dick."

"It is certainly very strange!" said Walter, a good deal startled; but further conjecture was prevented by Mr. Wynn, who, standing unnoticed in the door, had heard this brief conversation, and now came forward, saying,

"I will relieve your perplexity; Ida is safe, and Venus is with her, but they will not come back here at present. She left the house this morning in direct defiance of my authority, and I have sent her such a message as will prevent her return."

"Where is she?" demanded Walter, biting his lips.

"She is at the Triangle. She went there on an errand I could not approve, and I felt compelled to treat her in such a manner as should show my displeasure. I am not to be insulted, in my own house, with impunity. She is a mere child, and a little discipline will do her good." He said these words in a slow, calm manner, as if determined to say nothing more on the subject, and, sitting

---

1 My beautiful one (French); with a pun on Mabel's name.

down by the table, took a book. It was now quite dark, and the servants had brought in the lamps. Mabel, whose eyes were fixed on Walter, rather anxiously, saw him turn suddenly, as if to leave the room.

"Where are you going?" she asked, divining his intention.

"I am going to the Triangle," he replied, in the low tone of suppressed passion. "Do you suppose I would leave any lady, in whom I felt interested, to brave the terrors she must feel tonight in that lonely house? No; she shall see that she has one friend left!"

"But the storm!—you cannot go out in this storm!" cried Mabel; "it is folly to think of it. She is *safe*, we know, and you risk your life in going." She rose as she spoke, and going to the door where he stood, with his hand on the lock she laid her hand on his arm, and looked up in his face tenderly and beseechingly. He was touched by this manifestation of interest, and, pressing her hand furtively, he said, gaily,

"O, there is no danger! I have some waterproof clothing in which I have many a time defied the elements, and my horse is well trained."

"But the trees attract the lightning; and now the clouds must be very near. You *know* it is unsafe."

They had withdrawn a little from the door, and were standing in the hall as she spoke. It was in the height of the storm, whose first fury had not been as violent here as at the spot where Ida met it; and just then a blinding sheet of lightning seemed to glide between them, filling the air with ghastly light, and the house rocked with the pealing thunder.

"Mercy! How near it is!" exclaimed Mabel, clinging to his arm.

"Still, I must go," he answered, passing his arm around her waist, for she trembled violently.

"Is Ida, then, so very dear to you that you will endanger your life for her sake?" she murmured, almost inaudibly.

Walter looked surprised, and his brow flushed. Never had he seen Mabel in such a mood—so gentle, so affectionate, so humble—and he felt vexed with himself that it moved him to no greater emotion.

"Do you really wish me to remain at home?" he said, at length.

"I do," she replied. "It is unsafe for you to go."

Never, until the present time, had Mr. Wynn been afraid that Mabel would become too much interested in her cousin; but something in her manner, as she glided from the room, aroused his fears, and at this moment he appeared beside them in the doorway.

"Are you going, sir, or are you not going?" he said, sternly.

"I am going immediately," Walter replied; and then, turning to Mabel, who, at the sound of her father's voice, had started from him, and now stood, pale but self-collected, looking earnestly in his face, he added, "Ida has been like a sister to us both, you know, and you cannot doubt but it is my duty to go take care of her. She must be glad of some protection beside what Venus can give, in that strange, lonely place. Think, if it were your situation."

"My daughter can never be placed in such circumstances," said Mr. Wynn, with frigid tones; "but if you choose to go and assure yourself of Miss May's safety, go. You can take two or three servants to aid you in finding the way, for it is very dark."

"The lightning will show me the way," replied Walter; "and I shall take only my own servant; any more would be a hindrance instead of a help."

"Perhaps so," returned Mr. Wynn; and taking his daughter's hand, he led her into the parlor, and closed the door. Mrs. Wynn had glided softly out, as they entered. She was glad Walter was going, in spite of the danger to which he might be exposed, but she shrank from saying so before her husband. Since Alfred's death, her nerves had been in a painfully shattered state, and she had hardly dared to move or speak in his presence, lest she should betray the thoughts that secretly filled her with sorrow, and meet that cold, stern look of his, which now more than ever threw her into a nervous tremor.

Meeting Walter in the hall as he came down, clad in his water-proof clothes, she gave him a long message for Ida, full of love and sympathy, and then adding numerous charges respecting his own precautions for safety, she left him to find his way to the stables, where his servant was already saddling his horse. As he stood waiting, he chanced to see that Ida's horse was standing quietly in his stall.

"How came this horse here?" he exclaimed. "What horse did Miss Ida ride?"

"She ride dis yer," said the hostler. "She come in jes' 'fore you did, massa."

"Are you sure?" he asked, turning deadly pale, as he ran his eye rapidly over the stalls, and saw that none of the animals were missing.

"Yes, massa, I's right sure. I saddle he myself, an' I in here when he came gallop in. He know nuff, dat ar! He no stop for nigger take him in out de rain. Come roun' from de front door heself."

"No he didn't," said Walter. "Miss Ida is not in the house. The horse must have thrown her, and galloped home alone."

He leaned back helplessly against the wall as he spoke. All the strength seemed to leave his frame, the blood in his veins grew chilled, and he saw, as in a vision, Ida lying alone in the dark, gloomy forest, helpless, wounded and dying. He had cheated himself with a thousand excuses, he had deceived himself with a thousand theories of platonic love and brotherly affection; but, in that moment of awful fear, the scales fell from his eyes,[1] and he realized, with a keen heart-pang, that he loved her—loved her with a deep and passionate reverence that had taken hold of his inmost being. What to him would be all else that earth might offer, if the brightness of that young life were quenched forever? Nothing. He bowed his head on his hands—that proud head, that had borne itself so loftily—and a long, bitter groan burst from his tortured bosom.

"If she be throwed, it high time somebody done go looked arter her," said the negro, whose slow brain had taken some moments to elaborate the idea conveyed in Walter's rapid words. The sound of his voice recalled the self-possession of the unhappy young man; and his servant coming at this moment, to say that all was ready for their departure, he gave hasty orders that two of the servants from the house should follow, to aid in case aid was required, and, springing upon his horse, he dashed out into the stormy night.

Sheltered somewhat by the trees that lined the avenue, they did not feel the full force of the tempest until they turned into the open road, and then they found it almost impossible to face it. The lightning was almost incessant, but its blinding glare, alternating with the intense darkness that succeeded its flashes, made it difficult to see the way; and the wind which had now risen a little, blew the sheets of rain against them so as almost to take away their breath. Nothing but such an anxious fear as possessed Walter, could have nerved anyone to persevere amid such a furious war of the elements; but, thus excited, he struggled on, encouraging his servant to follow, and shouting now and then to those who might come after them. Proceeding in this way, but

---

1 Idiom meaning to suddenly comprehend the truth, derived from the story of the conversion of Saul on the way to Damascus, Acts 9:18: "And immediately there fell from his eyes as it had been scales: and he received sight forthwith, and arose, and was baptized."

very slowly, being compelled, at short intervals, to shelter themselves among the trees to rest, and examining every object by the wayside with a sickening dread of finding what they sought, they were a long time accomplishing that part of the journey which lay between the hall and the spot where their path led off through the woods towards the Triangle. The thunder and lightning had now grown somewhat less near and frequent, but the wind was increasing, and the rain came down with a copiousness and force that was ominous of a second deluge. Pausing to rest a few moments as they turned into this road, Walter thought he heard a voice in the distance, shouting, and said to his servant,

"Let us wait here a while. I think I hear voices, and it may be the servants from the hall. Shout in reply to them, the wind will carry your voice that way."

The negro did as he was commanded, but, after listening for reply, he said,

"No, massa, dem none our folks. I reckon dey's done gone back, ef dey ever started arter us. But dem voices come up t'oder way—dey come *on* de wind. Hole yer head out, massa, an' you see de soun' come in *dis* ear," he added, slapping the side of his head against which the rain was beating.

Walter followed his advice, and found that the voice did, indeed, come from beyond the spot where they were standing.

"It is somebody calling for help," he added, debating whether he ought to go towards the spot, or continue his search for Ida. At that moment, a horse, with the wreck of a carriage hanging at his heels, came racing by; and he no longer hesitated, but, bidding his servant follow, again braced himself against the storm. In a little while they saw the remains of a carriage lying in the road; and the lightning, just then illuminating the landscape, showed, at some distance down the road, a negro waving his arms and shouting. He had seen them before they had perceived him, and, on reaching the place, they found the body of another man lying lifeless at his feet. Having ascertained, by a few questions, that these were the travelers whose runaway horse and demolished carriage they had seen, Walter ordered the two negroes to lift the white man from the ground where he lay, and carry him within the shelter of the trees; and here he found, to his great joy, that death had not been the consequence of the accident that had overtaken them. The stranger had been stunned, and bruised a little, but the act of moving him restored the circulation of the blood, and aroused his senses, so that in a little while he was able to sit up and speak. He told Walter that he had arrived at the tavern, in the little village below, just as the storm commenced, and, at first, had determined to stay there through the night; but, being very anxious to reach the end of his journey, he had become restless, and at length hired this negro to take him in a carriage to the plantation where he wished to go. The wind favoring them, they had gone quite rapidly along, until the horse, taking a sudden fright, had upset the carriage and thrown them out. Walter told him he might ride his servant's horse, if he chose to come with him, and he could conduct him to a place of shelter, which, though at some distance, was nearer than the village behind him. This offer was accepted gratefully, and the two gentlemen had in this way arrived at the Triangle, followed by the negroes on foot.

While in the shelter of the trees, they had come on with comparative ease; but when they came out into the wide, open field, they were completely bewildered, and it was their shouts to one another that had been mistaken, by the superstitious Potter, for unearthly voices. At length, just when the darkness was most intense, the lightning having nearly ceased, though the thunder still rolled in the distance, the top of the chimney blew down, and the bright flame, which the fire of light wood sent out of the orifice, revealed to them the house they were seeking. All else was perfect darkness, and, astonished to see no symptoms of life within, they had attacked various parts of the house, with little success, until the stranger, who accompanied Walter, had found the window against which Ida was leaning.

It was, therefore, with no little alarm that Walter became aware that someone from within was preventing the opening of the window, and heard Ida's cry of distress. He had been quite reassured by finding no traces of her along the way; but now an undefined, horrible dread of the treatment she might have met with in this desolate place almost maddened him, and, exerting a strength of which he had not supposed himself capable, he had burst open the shutters, and no words can tell the revulsion of feeling with which he stretched his hands towards her, and clasped her to his heart.

There had never been between them those fraternal familiarities which their early connection might have warranted—for, even in childhood, Ida had been chary of her caresses—and this act of hers had told him, more than any words could do, how much she had suffered, and how high-wrought had been her excitement of feeling.

In the first moments of awakening consciousness, Ida was sensible only of a vague and exquisite sensation of relief from some impending evil, and a certainty of safety and protection; and she looked dreamingly upon the face that bent over her, without a wish to move or speak. But Walter aroused her. In a tone the tenderness of which could not be mistaken, he said gently,

"I have been dreadfully frightened about you, Ida. How could you think I would not come to you?"

Then a quick rush of recollections came over her, and she started from her recumbent position, and withdrew her hands from his grasp. He seemed hurt that she did so, and insisted that she should remain quiet; but she had now seen the strangers who were present, and, declaring that she was as strong as ever, she persisted in rising to her feet.

"Be it so, then," said Walter, half pettishly. "You always were willful, and I always had to yield to you, Ida."

The stranger had been standing quietly before the fire during all this time. He was a tall man, with a face that had evidently been bronzed beneath tropical skies, and a keen black eye that had not lost its fire, though his hair was gray and his brow was furrowed. Yet something in his appearance indicated a degree of strength and vigor inconsistent with these tokens of age; and, as Walter looked at him standing in the warm light of the blazing pine knots, he was struck with a certain agitation in his manner, and the eagerness with which his eyes were fixed on the fair young girl, who, blushing a little to find herself so much the centre of observation, and yet languid with the ordeal she had undergone, had just seated herself in the chair he had placed for her by the chimney-corner. Leaning back against Venus, who stood behind her—with her eyelids drooping a little, showing distinctly their long dark lashes, her disheveled curls crushed back from her broad low brow, and revealing the outlines of her face clearly in the radiance of the firelight—she looked like a beautiful picture. But it was not admiration that was expressed in the earnest and restless glances that fell upon her, and then wandered to Walter, full of anxious inquiry, as if his lips trembled with a question he dared not ask.

"You are surprised, sir, no doubt, to find this young lady amid these rude surroundings, and I cannot explain the mystery at this time," said Walter to him, breaking thus the silence that was becoming awkward, and hoping to divert the regard which he saw embarrassed Ida. "I have sent the negroes upstairs," he continued, "to try to kindle a fire in the room above, and then we will retire from this room, Ida, and you must try to get some repose. You will not be afraid if you know I am within call; and you will have Venus and this other woman with you."

"O, no, I am not afraid now!" she said, turning her head a little, and raising her clear dark eyes to his face.

It was the first time the stranger had seen her face fully, and the low, musical tones of her voice seemed to strike some chord of memory, for he trembled violently, and passed his hand once or twice across his brow.

"That name! always that name!" he murmured, half audibly, and then added, with a startling abruptness, "Tell me, sir, who is this young lady?"

"It is Miss Ida May," replied he, in a reserved manner, hardly knowing what to make of his strange guest.

A convulsive trembling again seized the questioner; he turned pale, and his features worked spasmodically.

"Ida May, of Wynn Hall?" he asked, with an agitated voice.

"The same," replied Walter, with some amazement.

"The same! O, God, the very same!" repeated the stranger, and he made a quick step towards her, and held out both hands, as if to grasp her. Then, appearing to restrain himself, he turned away, and, placing his arms on the mantelpiece, leaned his head on them. They could not see his face, but his frame shook, as if he were weeping violently.

Walter, who stood near Ida, had stepped before her to shield her, for he began to think the man was insane. Now they looked at each other in great perplexity for a moment, and then laying his hand gently on the shoulder of his guest, he said, "I fear, sir, you were injured by your fall more than you thought at first."

There was no reply, but, in a little while, the excessive emotions subsided. Unwilling to seem to notice a manifestation for which no explanation was given, and thinking the man might sooner become calm if left to himself, Walter sat down by Ida, and began to tell her why it was that he had so long delayed coming to help her in her dilemma. So many were present, that he could only use the most general terms; but something in his manner made her cheeks flush and her heart beat quickly. There was more than mere friendly sympathy in that low, deep tone; there was more than brotherly affection in the depths of those brown eyes; there was a dangerous magnetism in the touch of his hands, as now and then, in the earnestness of his talking, he laid them for an instant lightly on hers. Ida saw it, and she was frightened to feel how rapturous a thrill of pleasure filled her breast. What was to become of all her just pride, of all her self-possession, if this continued long? She turned half away from him, as this thought crossed her mind, and said, in a low voice, "I am tired, Walter—very tired."

"You must be, I know," he answered, though a shadow fell over his glowing face. *He* had not a thought of fatigue. "I was very careless to sit here talking," he added. "I should have gone to hurry the preparations upstairs. I think the negroes must have gone to sleep over their fire."

"No, stay a few moments," said the stranger, now coming near and speaking very calmly. "I have something to say, which you must hear. I thought to wait until morning, lest another fainting fit should be the penalty of my rashness, but I cannot. I cannot wait! I must speak!"

He paused, and looked from one to the other. O, what an unutterable expression was that with which he regarded them! Then he spoke again, fixing his eyes on Ida's face as she gazed at him wonderingly.

"There was once a man, who had but one treasure in the world, and he lost it," he said, in a low, solemn tone. "I will not speak of his grief. Friend tell not to friend such thoughts as rent his bosom, and made his life a weariness from that hour. The Eye that searches those depths is the Eye whose comprehensive gaze takes in the agonies of a world. I will not tell of his endeavors to recover what was gone. He traveled many miles, he sought out many mysteries, he wearied Heaven with prayers— and it was all in vain. Then the Providence that guided him, led him out upon the ocean, and a storm, wilder than this which is now passing away, made a wreck of the ship in which he sailed, and he alone, of all on board, was rescued by a passing vessel from the plank to which he was lashed, and which, lifeless as he was, had upborne him for many hours. He was carried to far distant lands. He had lost everything, and he was obliged to stay there and work, to get the means of returning home; but he wrote many letters, until, at length, receiving no answer, hope died within him, and he tried to forget his native land. Years passed before he trod its shores again. Wealth had come to him; he sought it not, but it came; and yet how poor, how utterly wretched he was, to stand again in his native town and find himself lonely and unknown! In the bitterness of his heart, he prayed to die. O, foolish man! To have died then would have been, indeed, a curse! The recompense for all his woes was near him. The hours of his long desolation were over. His treasure had been found—had been tenderly guarded—was waiting to be restored to his arms. This treasure was found. O Ida, Ida May!" he cried in a burst of excited and irrepressible emotion, "does not your own heart tell you who I am?"

Many varying emotions had swept through Ida's soul, as she listened, until sudden surprise, and hope that seemed a mockery, gave place to the certainty of entire conviction, and with a wild, inarticulate cry, she sprang to her feet. There was a quick movement, a faint exclamation, and she was clasped in his arms. It seemed as if their lips would grow together in that long, long embrace, and then a gush of tears relieved the hearts that would else have burst with excess of gladness.

"My father—my dear, dear father!"

"My precious one—my child!"

They sat down together, Mr. May holding his daughter on his knee, and keeping her still closely pressed to his heart. He kissed her repeatedly, he patted her face and hands and hair, he caressed her as if she had been a child, and his lips, so long denied such words, overflowed with a thousand tender and endearing epithets of his own and of foreign languages. And Ida, her arm around his neck, and her head nestling on his breast, thanked Heaven silently for her great bliss. Her heart had so famished for such love, for such protection! and now, in the moment when her fate lowered most darkly, the boon had been granted as if by a miracle.

But it was not in her nature to think of herself alone, even in the moment of her utmost happiness. Her grateful heart longed to acknowledge its obligations to those who had been kind to her, and, raising herself a little, she held out one hand to Walter. He had been looking on with a sympathy and joy, pure as mortal can feel, and now he pressed her hand to his lips, exclaiming,

"O, Ida, this is glorious!"

She gave him a bright, beaming smile, and, drawing him still nearer, placed his hand in her father's, who clasped it cordially.

"This is Walter Varian," she said—"Walter, who is destined to be my good genius.[1] He redeemed me from slavery, and now he has redeemed me from orphanhood, by bringing you here. And this"—she added, turning to Venus, who, after the first exclamation of joy, had stood modestly aside, with tears of delight running over her face unheeded—"this is Venus, my mauma, who saved my life, when suffering and hardship had nearly killed me, and has watched over me and waited upon

---

1 As in Ancient Rome, a guiding spirit.

me ever since. My two best friends! O, father, you must love them both!"

Mr. May relinquished his hold on his daughter, that he might take the dark hand of the faithful Venus. He tried to speak, but his feelings overpowered him. The intensity of his emotion could only find utterance in prayer, and, raising the hands he held, and looking upward, with eyes that saw not for the tears that filled them, he exclaimed fervently,

"O, thou wonderful and gracious God, who hast brought us, through manifold danger and trial, to the blessedness of this hour! bless these two, I beseech thee; bless them with all the unutterable blessings that my grateful soul would crave!"

Sobs choked his voice, and his whole frame quivered and shook with agitation. His ecstasy of feeling was almost too much to bear. He had endured sorrow long and patiently, but his soul had been crushed beneath the benumbing pressure until it was like pain for it to expand to the extent of this great joy. It was really a relief when their feelings were brought down from this high and solemn intensity down to a more common level, by Venus's quaint and simple exclamations of triumph.

"Didn't I say dat, Miss Ida?" she cried. "Didn't I say de Lord, *he* know the best time? When we done drunk up all de bitter medicine, den he gives us some sugar to take away de taste. 'Pears like he been keeping dis blessing till de very minute you want it most. Bless de Lord!"

Long and absorbing in its interest was the conversation that followed, when they had all grown calmer. The hours of night wore away. Potter was stretched on the floor, under the window, in a drunken sleep, and the mulatto girl sat near him, sleeping also. Even Venus, at length, yielded to the drowsiness that weighed down her eyelids, and leaned her head on the table; but their presence was unnoticed, and the flight of time forgotten. There was so much to be told, and so many questions to be asked, there was such a perfect union of feeling and interest, that hours flew by like moments, and, resting in her father's arms, Ida felt her fatigue no longer.

All were surprised when "the cock's shrill clarion"[1] informed them of the approach of dawn. Once more Walter threw open the window. The storm had spent itself, and the clouds had rolled away. All was calm and clear as Ida's mental horizon, and the

---

1 From Thomas Gray (1716–71), "Elegy Written in a Country Churchyard" (1751).

promise for the coming day was fair as that which seemed dawning upon her life.

Without delay the servants were aroused, the horses were harnessed to a rude vehicle belonging to the farm, and the whole party departed, without any very ceremonious leave-taking, and drove toward the village, where, having seen Ida and her father comfortably established in the hotel, Walter and his servant rode homeward.

CHAPTER XV

"Mine eyes
Were not in fault; for she was beautiful:
Mine ears that heard her flattery, nor my heart
That thought her like her seemings. It had been vicious
To have mistrusted her. Yet, O, it was
A folly in me. Heaven mend all!"
CYMBELINE[1]

A gentle and affectionate nature is often roused to pride and reserve by the influence of love; a proud and cold one is often rendered more yielding and humble. Thus it had been with Mabel.
At first it had been only her vanity, her secret rivalry of Ida,
and her love of admiration, that had been gratified by Walter's
devotion, and she held the treasure lightly which she had won
so easily. But she had not been unobservant of the change that
had taken place in herself, as her own interest became aroused
and fixed. There had been no unknown, blind enchantment.
Knowing no reason why she should not marry Walter if she
chose, even in defiance of her father's wish, she had yielded to
the power that moved her, with a rare self-possession, and a
conscious enjoyment of its novelty and delight, and of the zest it
gave to days that had sometimes before been wearisome, which
would have been impossible with a more ardent and generous
disposition. Even as she sat silently before the fire that evening,
after Walter had left her, amid all the anger and jealous pain
that possessed her, the thought that recurred oftenest was not
that Walter loved another more than her, but it was that now
Ida would triumph over her, and who would restore to her the
emotion that had caused her such delightsome hours? She felt
that she had lost him—that she had condescended to him in
vain—and she racked her brain for a plan of revenge worthy of
her rage against him.

She had been sitting some time, apparently absorbed in
thought, but manifesting little of the feelings that were whirling
through her heart, when her father, who, while pretending to
read, had watched her narrowly, came suddenly near her, and
took her hands in his. She had grasped the arms of her chair, unconsciously, with such force that her fingers were stiff and cold.
He laid his hand on her brow, which was covered with a clammy

---

1 Adapted slightly from Shakespeare, *Cymbeline*, 5.5.62–68.

moisture, though her features were as haughtily impassive as ever. He looked a moment into her eyes, which shrank from his gaze, and then said, firmly, but kindly,

"You do not seem well, Mabel. Have you taken cold from your exposure?"

"No, papa. I am well!"

"Are you afraid of the storm? It is unusually severe," he asked.

Again she returned a negative answer, and, having thus assured himself of what he suspected as the real cause of her trouble, he turned quietly away, and resumed his chair and his book, apparently taking no further notice of her, until sometime later. Mrs. Wynn had been called from the room, to assist Patra in administering medicine to her sick child, and Mr. Wynn, looking up, said, abruptly,

"Consider Mabel, what it is you want in a husband. You are beautiful and accomplished; you will bury yourself in an obscure station, where, even at best, years must elapse before that can be yours which you may secure now and at once, if you will?"

Mabel turned herself half round in her chair, that she might look in her father's face, as she replied; and there was on her beautiful features a proud, hard expression, that made them strikingly like his.

"Father," she said, in a bitter tone, "I have heard it said that the happiest wives are not those who have married for rank, wealth, and display!"

Mr. Wynn uttered a contemptuous "Pooh!" and then, fixing his eyes piercingly upon her, he added, "Is it possible you think you love that young man?"

Mabel bore his gaze unshrinkingly, but the color deepened a little in her cheek, as she answered faintly, "I could have loved him."

"And now?" said Mr. Wynn.

"Now he loves me no longer," she replied. The words dropped from her lips slowly, contemptuously, as if she scorned herself for the pain she felt at this admission.

"Do you then regret this lost lover?" asked her father after a moment's pause.

"It is the lost love I regret," she answered, "not the lost lover."

She turned partly away from him again, and covered her face with her hands. She shed no tears, but her heart was almost convulsed with the mingled emotions raging there.

Mr. Wynn smiled, with a relieved expression, and, after a short silence, he said, "If you can analyze your feelings thus, you have, as yet, escaped harm from this folly; but I am not sure that I understand you. What is it you regret?"

"What is it I regret?" she answered, looking up with a compressed brow and sparkling eyes. "Papa, I think you understand me better than anyone else—cannot you think what it is? My life is growing to be a weariness. I am losing the high animal spirits that come of mere youth and health, and I tire of the monotony that surrounds me, of the sameness with which the months and the seasons succeed each other. I want something new and exciting, and this—whatever may have been the reason, it matters not now—Walter's presence, and his devotion to me, supplied. Doubtless I should have wearied of that, also, before long; but, for a little while, he has had the power to make the days pass swiftly; and, of all the sighing swains whose hearts I have broken, none other had that power. Perhaps you can tell me why it has been so. Is this love?"

Her lip curled, she spoke rapidly, and her eyes met his with a haughty and almost defiant glance. Her father's heart thrilled with admiration and fondness for her, and he came and stood by her chair, laying his hand on the silken folds of her soft hair, with a caressing movement that she could hardly remember him as bestowing upon her since childhood.

"My queenly Mabel!" he said, gently, "I don't wonder that you long for a change. I have been blind, not to have seen, before this, that the quiet which suits my habits so well, would be a dull monotony for you. You shall have change, you shall have excitement. My proudest hopes for your future are about to be fulfilled. You shall marry a man in whose veins runs the best blood of the land—a man whose ancestors were of royal race, and who has none of the low, plebeian ideas that fit so poorly with the position of a southern gentleman. Mabel, you shall marry Col. Ross! He has wealth—unlimited wealth—and a position in society, and influence in the state! He may aspire to its highest office, at any time, if he will; but, at present his intentions are to take you to England, and present you to his relations among the nobility there! You will be presented at court—you will take that station in life which you can grace so well!"

"Papa, how do you know all this?" asked Mabel, her cheek paling with excitement at this brilliant prospect, which, thus suddenly opened before her, seemed to mock her vision.

"Col. Ross was here this morning, and proposed the honor of an alliance with my daughter," replied Mr. Wynn.

"He might have asked me, first," said Mabel, pettishly.

"Mabel!—Col. Ross is a man of honor!" returned Mr. Wynn, in a tone of surprise and displeasure.

"Still, he might have been a little less guarded than he has been; and now, certainly he might condescend to consult me on the subject. How does he know but I shall refuse him?" said the willful beauty, annoyed at having her fate thus summarily fixed.

"You will not refuse him!" exclaimed her father.

"Why don't he come and see? Perhaps I shall," said she.

"He asked permission to see you alone this evening, and I granted him liberty," Mr. Wynn answered; "but the storm has prevented him from coming to solicit your consent to his wishes."

"The storm did not prevent Walter from going to Ida," said Mabel, quickly.

"Pooh! you are wayward, my child, and sport with your own desires," said Mr. Wynn, resuming his seat with his usual stern manner.

Mabel did not reply for a long time. Her eyes were fixed on the fire, and she seemed absorbed in thought. When she did speak, her words were abrupt and hurried, as with suppressed excitement.

"Papa, suppose accident had connected you with one, between whom and yourself there had ever been a secret antagonism. Suppose that person had always, purposely sometimes, and often unconsciously, thwarted your designs, opposed your influence, drawn to herself the regard and attention that would else have been given wholly to you, and established herself as your rival in hearts where you would reign alone; and, at last," she added, with heightening color and quickening breath, "at last, defeated you wholly in the one object where, most of all, you wished to triumph over her. If this were so, say, papa, what would you do?"

Her father's face grew dark, and he said, with some surprise of manner, "Is this so? Is it Ida May to whom you refer?"

"It is so," she answered. "From the first moment I saw her, a little dirty child, I disliked her. I tried to overcome the feeling, which mauma said was wrong, and to understand why the others were all so interested in her; but I could never lose that secret repugnance. She lived with us, and so I treated her well; but I never, never liked her, and now—I will no longer conceal it, I will speak out—I hate her—*hate* her, and I will be revenged!" She clenched her hand, and stamped her little foot on the soft rug as she spoke, and her eyes glowed with the rage she felt.

Her father was amazed at this excess of feeling, though he had long since divined her secret dislike of Ida; but he made no effort to check the outburst, and replied, calmly,

"I understand, then, that you do not wish her to return here."

"I do not. My food would choke me if we ate at the same table!" she exclaimed, vehemently.

"Then, rest assured, some other shelter shall be provided for her. I will have no one here whom you dislike, during the short time you will remain at home," said Mr. Wynn.

He was secretly pleased that, by this arrangement, he should probably not only remove Ida, of whose influence in his house he felt somewhat afraid, when it should become known among his servants that she was giving liberty to hers, but also separate Mabel from Walter more effectually than he would otherwise be able to do. He feared Walter's power over his daughter. Her anger and excitement made him think her heart had been more deeply moved than she chose to acknowledge.

"Are you sure you have no foolish entanglement with Walter?" he asked, as she did not reply.

"None that I cannot break thus," she answered, tearing in two pieces the delicate handkerchief that lay in her lap, and flinging it away. "Do not fear that, papa. I am no weak, heartbroken miss, to sit and wear the willow.[1] I would not marry Walter now, if he were king of the world and offered me a place on the throne beside him. No, he may have that pale-faced little girl, if he likes, but I will annoy him somewhat before I am done with her!" she added, gloomily.

"Calm yourself, Mabel," said Mr. Wynn, earnestly. "I do not like this excessive emotion. Be proud, be ambitious, be unforgiving, if you will—all noble souls have felt these passions—but never get thus excited. It is a habit that increases with indulgence, until a person has no longer control of himself at the moment when he most needs it, and so is left in the power of his enemies. And be careful what you do. I do not blame you, with these feelings toward Ida, for wishing her anywhere rather than here; but an inordinate desire for revenge often overreaches itself, and makes its possessor appear mean or ridiculous, especially when the object of dislike is a woman, and an equal in society. Be satisfied to have things as they are. Do nothing dishonorable."

"Do not fear, papa," said Mabel, haughtily. "I will be as quiet and discreet as possible. Only one thing I ask of you. Do not tell

---

1 To mourn a lost love.

anyone of my engagement to Col. Ross until I give you liberty. I prefer to keep it a secret at present."

"As you please," replied her father; "but it cannot be kept secret a long time, I fancy, for I expect Col. Ross will urge you to name an early day."

"He will find himself obliged to wait my pleasure. It seems to me, papa, you hardly consult my dignity in being thus anxious to hasten my marriage," said Mabel, proudly.

"It is your happiness I am consulting, my dear child," replied her father. "I am a quiet man myself, and my feeble health does not accord with show and noisy crowds, but all the pride of my nature is centred in you. I exult in seeing you admired. You are the crown, the glory of my life, Mabel!"

It was not possible, even for a nature so self-absorbed as Mabel's, to hear these words, the most enthusiastic and earnest he had ever spoken in his whole life, without a thrill of feeling more generous and grateful than merely the admiration they expressed would excite, and his daughter was deeply moved. She rose in her chair, and, coming to him, stooped down, with tears in her bright eyes, and kissed his lips.

"Thank you, papa," she said, in a soft and humble tone. "I will make it the study of my life to be all you wish to have me."

Just then Mrs. Wynn returned to the parlor, and calmly, as if nothing had happened, her husband took up his book, and Mabel returned to her seat. Mrs. Wynn looked a little surprised, but resumed her work without asking any questions. Mabel was the first to speak, and there was no trace of her late emotion as she asked carelessly,

"How is Patra's child? You look tired, mamma; why will you persist in fatiguing yourself so with those sick children? Their mothers ought to know enough to take care of them."

"But they don't know about giving medicine," said Mrs. Wynn, gently; "and with all my care it seems impossible to teach them, and the poor children would die, very often, if I did not attend to it myself. It is often tiresome, but I must not neglect my duties to the servants."

"Poor mamma, what a martyr you are to your sense of duty!" said Mabel, smiling.

"You will have to be a martyr also, one of these days, when you get to be mistress of a household," replied Mrs. Wynn, returning her smile.

"O, I shall never make myself so pale and tired as you are now!" said Mabel, gaily.

"It is not all my care for the child," her mother answered, "but these thunderstorms always give me the headache, you know. I am glad this one is passing away, for it has been dreadfully violent."

"Has it? I did not notice," said Mabel, dreamily, relapsing into reverie.

Mrs. Wynn looked up in surprise, and not without a feeling of envy at the strong nerves that could be unmoved through such a tumult and commotion of the elements; but her daughter seemed absorbed in thought, and she did not care to disturb her by any reply.

It was Mabel's first impulse to give voice to her indignation against Walter, and at once cast him from her as having alienated her love by his direct violation of her wishes in regard to Ida; but she wished to annoy and perplex him as much as possible, and she conceived that she had a perfect right to do so, since he had first been unfaithful to her. She was sure that while he was bound by his engagement to her, no expression would be made of his evident interest in Ida, however much they might suffer or lose by the restraint. She gave him credit for thus much of honorable feeling, even in her anger; but for Ida she had no compassion. Scrupulous as had been her conduct, Mabel believed that she had tried and would still try to win Walter from his allegiance, and if these artful designs had succeeded, and her fickle wooer was beginning to fret against the ties that bound him to her, she determined to hold them with no gentle hand, unpitying, even if she saw that they cut him to the quick. Her love for him was gone, swallowed by the torrent of angry and bitter feeling that one act had aroused. That he should have cared enough for any living being to have disregarded her expressed wishes in order to serve them, would have been cause enough for anger; but that he had done this for Ida's sake, was too much for her to bear.

Everyone knows how a feeling that has for years been kept in abeyance, making its torpid life known by a continual consciousness, and yet never manifesting itself so fully as to give evidence of its real power, kept down by social courtesy and by the predominance of other passions and interests, will in one moment spring to life, like Minerva from the brain of Jupiter,[1] with a maturity of strength ready for instant action, and armed with all

---

1 Minerva, the Roman goddess of wisdom and strategy, was born, fully adult and armed, from the head of Jupiter, highest god of the Roman pantheon.

the energies of an unceasing life. Thus it was with Mabel; and her deep-laid plan of vengeance required that for a time at least Walter should be kept from Ida's society as much as possible, lest he should discover and frustrate it; and thus another reason was added to all those which led her to dissemble and hide her real purposes and emotions with regard to her cousin. Her own contemplated violation of their secret engagement gave her not a moment's uneasiness. It was her right, she thought, since she had received so much provocation, and she would rejoice in using it.

Accordingly, the next day, when, after a long sleep, which had restored the strength lost by the exposure and watching of the previous night, he appeared in the parlor just before dinner-time, she received him with playful reproaches, and inquired so kindly after his health and Ida's welfare, and expressed such sympathy in his joy at Mr. May's return, that Walter, poor fellow, felt a bitter remorse and vexation at having so hastily condemned her as ill-natured and selfish. He was ashamed of himself, and frightened, as he became conscious of a vague disappointment at being received so pleasantly, and of an undefined hope that she might have resented his disobedience to her command. More earnestly than even in the days of his first fascination, did he, during the few moments they were alone together during the afternoon, implore her to allow him to ask her father's consent to their union. He longed to be freed, in some way, from his anomalous and embarrassing position; and, since he could not honorably leave her, he felt a desperate desire to fence himself around with such barriers as would prevent his rebel thoughts from straying away from her.

But Mabel refused his request. Gently, and with tenderness and delicacy, she begged him to wait a while longer, lest her father should utterly forbid their union, and then, with a well-feigned fearfulness of manner, she told him that Col. Ross had asked for the right to address her, and entreated him not to be angry or jealous if he saw them together, for she had promised her father that she would receive his attentions, for a few months at least, and try to love him. But she knew she could not love Col. Ross, and, if she did not, no force on earth could make her marry him. Her cousin Walter need have no fears of such a rival—O no!—and, meantime, her complaisance might win her father to consent to her union with the man she did love, if he would only be patient, and for her sake, if not for his own, refrain from rash measures that would avail nothing.

She acted well the part she had chosen to play, and Walter,

completely deceived, left her in no enviable state of mind. For a long time he walked to and fro across the piazza, in the cold, gray twilight of that winter's day, with his arms folded and his eyes fixed on the floor. The agitation he had experienced the evening previous had taught him the nature of his feelings for Ida, and how fatal it might be for his happiness if he should see her often, and yet he knew that he could not wholly avoid her society without appearing rude and unkind. Mr. Wynn had already given orders that her clothing should be sent to her, and he had also given her the deeds and papers belonging to her share of Mr. Maynard's estate, with a brief, and coldly courteous message, which was, in fact, but a civil way of saying that he expected to have nothing more to do with her or her affairs. Walter knew that, if Ida's plans were carried out, she, and her father also, would need the help he could render, and feel surprised and offended at what they must deem his unfriendly desertion of them, if that aid was withheld. He knew that there was little to choose between the dishonor of willfully breaking his engagement, and the falsehood of uttering marriage vows to one woman, while his highest esteem and strongest love were given to another; and his heart recoiled in horror at the thought of doing either. What then should he do? Could the will control the affections? Could the strong currents of the soul, which now swelled high and dashed against the barriers that opposed them, be made to flow in a different channel, curbed and quieted, and serving peacefully the occasions of daily duty?

These questions he asked himself, and, in the perplexity and confusion of his mind, he found but an uncertain answer. Other thoughts came also to trouble him; thoughts connected with his obligations to his human property, that had been for a few days imperiously urging their claims upon his conscience; and interests more important than the alternative of his own happiness or misery that loudly called for his consideration.

Wearied, at length, with the ceaseless round of thought, he determined to leave the subject, and, trusting that firm principles and right intention would in the end extricate him from the dilemma, he resolved to occupy himself with other objects, and to change his present idle life for the business and cares incident to the management of his plantation at Oaklands.

The next morning he announced to his uncle that he had given up the idea of selling his place, and, instead of going to the city to enjoy the busy idleness of a young lawyer, he should establish himself at Oaklands, and study agriculture. No objection was offered to this plan, and little surprise expressed by any except Mrs. Wynn; and, thus quietly loosening himself from his old home, Walter found himself the next evening settled at housekeeping in the time-worn family mansion at Oaklands.

Some weeks elapsed, after this, with little apparent change in the position of affairs. Walter rode over to the hall three or four times a week, and was always kindly received by Mabel. Sometimes he found Col. Ross there, and he often heard reports of his approaching marriage; but, deceived as he was in regard to his cousin's intentions, he put no faith in these rumors, and assiduously strove to recall the warmth of affection with which he had once regarded her. Ida he saw more seldom. He fancied that she had grown reserved and distant in her manner towards him, and supposed that she had divined his hidden love for her, and meant thus to discourage it. He doubted not that she blamed him, as much as he blamed himself, for his change of feeling, and his faithlessness to Mabel's love—of which in his blindness he had full confidence—and, though it gave him a heavy heart-aching continually, he accepted this loss of her esteem, as a just punishment of his offenses. Poor fellow! he would have grown nearly desperate, but for the diversion of thought and the constant occupation he found in the care of his plantation, and in improving the condition of his servants, who had been sadly neglected of late years.

Ida May and her father, one in mind and heart, delayed not a moment the work on which her wishes had been fixed so long. The happiness they enjoyed in being restored to each other, had no effect to centre their thoughts on themselves, and make them forget the welfare of those dependent on them. There were some unavoidable delays in the legal forms necessary for the manumission[1] of Ida's negroes; but, meantime, she collected them together at the old house in the Triangle, where she had passed the most miserable and the happiest hours of her life, and tried to teach them the rudiments of the free and self-dependent life on which they were to enter. At first, it was a disagreeable and somewhat thankless work. They had been so little used to unselfish kindness that they mistrusted her, and quarreled among themselves over the gifts of clothing and food;—they were all woefully ignorant; most of the good-natured ones were stupid and the bright ones were mostly vicious. It was no light talk, no "rose-water humanity," to teach such beings the decencies and arts of civi-

---

1 Release from slavery; see p. 65, n. 1.

lized life, and the moral and religious ideas, of which they were as destitute as the heathen of foreign lands. But Ida persevered patiently, day after day, with a Christian gentleness and pity for these victims of oppression, that gradually won their confidence and love; and, as time went on, her work became easier. They began to act less like savage children, helpless and incapable, and to enjoy the glimmering ideas of advancement and education that found way into their minds, so long benumbed and darkened. The most of them were of the class who are called "contented," because they sing rude songs in the intervals of labor, and are too stupid, too ignorant of a better life, too hopeless of ultimate escape from their present state, and too fearful of punishment if they rebel against it, to do aught but plod on day after day through their allotted round of labor, with the quiet obedience of brutes. These were not prepared for freedom; and it would have been better if they could have been trained carefully and judiciously for some years, before receiving that boon; but, under the circumstances in which Ida was placed, she knew this could not be done, and she wisely refrained from attempting more than she would be allowed to perform. Her father assisted her by his experience of the world, and encouraged and sustained her when she was perplexed and weary; and, thus busily engaged, the time flew by on swift wings.

They had rooms at the hotel in the village, but every morning they rode out to the Triangle, and spent most of the day. Ida taught the women to sew, and cut and make garments of various description, and Mr. May employed the men out of doors, paying them a small sum each week, that they might acquire the habit of receiving remuneration for their labor, and of spending judiciously what they received. An hour or two every afternoon was devoted to oral instruction. More than this, they did not attempt, for they knew that they should soon become objects of suspicion, and they determined to be very careful.

In the pleasant evenings they had occasionally visited some of Ida's old acquaintances in the neighborhood, but the growing coldness with which they were received caused her so much pain that gradually these were discontinued; and she tried to forget, in the exclusive devotion which her father bestowed upon her, that she was cast out from society which had once welcomed her. After receiving Mr. Wynn's message, through Walter Varian, Mr. May, justly offended at the treatment she had met with, would not allow her to make any conciliatory overtures; but they both sent many expressions of grateful thanks to Mrs. Wynn, who had learned this winter so much sympathy and love for Ida, that she was almost content, even though she began to suspect that Walter was learning the same lesson.

For the sake of principle, Ida had lost caste, and she was made to feel this in various ways as the winter wore away. Sometimes she was amused, and sometimes annoyed, by these manifestations; but she had expected them, and she clung more closely than ever to her father, and thanked Heaven for sending her such a protector at the time when she most needed his aid. She was not surprised to receive no visits and no invitations, to be met with a cold nod of recognition, or a still colder "cut direct,"[1] when she saluted her acquaintances, as she chanced to meet them in the street or in church; for, before undertaking this enterprise, she had counted the cost. She knew that no person would be received in southern families, who openly avowed a practical and earnest dislike of slavery, unqualified by any palliating "if," or "but." She was not surprised at the falling off of friends, but she was astonished, and a little alarmed sometimes, when, as spring advanced, she began to see strangers, who passed them in their daily rides to and from the Triangle, turn and look after them with frowning faces; and when the rude "clay-eaters," whom they sometimes met, stood still and gazed at them, insolently, as if they were objects of curiosity and hatred.

One day, when she came home, she found Walter waiting for her in the little parlor, with a face in which amusement and vexation were strangely blended. Her father had gone to the village shops to make some necessary purchases, and, for the first time in many weeks, she found herself alone with her old friend. Indeed, she had hardly seen him, except for a few moments together, since he had been established at Oaklands. His visits had been short, and his manner constrained.

Ida was far from suspecting the true nature of his feelings, but she thought he had begun to discover how little congeniality there could ever be between himself and Mabel; and though she shrank from acknowledging, even to herself, that Walter could ever be more to her than the elder brother he had called himself in her childish days, her pride and delicacy were alarmed lest anyone should suppose that she had to do with this change of feeling towards his cousin. Therefore she had withdrawn herself from him as much as possible. Her father wondered a little; but he had full confidence in Ida, and, believing she had some good

---

1 To not acknowledge the person at all, as though invisible.

reasons for her conduct, had asked no questions; and Walter, fancying his visits not desired, had made them quite rare.

"I don't know whether you will laugh or be offended at what I am going to say," he said, abruptly, as he seated himself at the window beside her, on this afternoon.

"Tell me, and see which it will be," she answered, smiling.

"I hope at any rate, you won't be frightened, for there is no danger, only I thought I might as well caution you," he continued.

"For pity's sake, tell me! You do frighten me now!" she said, turning pale, and looking up anxiously.

"It is nothing; only I am afraid you have been a little less cautious than is necessary, in this state of society, in expressing your views on the subject of freedom. I had a hint today, from the bar-keeper below, that something you and your father had said or done had caused considerable talk about town."

"It must then be because it has become known that I intend to free my servants," said Ida; "but surely, I have a right to do so."

"Nobody will deny that right; you know it is a fundamental principle, on which our whole social system rests, that a man has a right to do what he will with his servants," said Walter, running his fingers through his hair, and looking up with his old gleeful expression, which Ida had not seen for a long time.

"Certainly then, he may make them free men," said she.

"Certainly," repeated Walter; "but that which is lawful may not be always expedient, and I suspect that this is the 'head and front of your offending.'[1] But this is not what is alleged. It is said that your father has talked imprudently in the public parlor here."

"What can he have said?" exclaimed Ida. "I thought we had both been very careful. We expected to be watched, as soon as we became known, and therefore, have been extremely guarded in our words and actions."

"It is said," replied Walter, "that Mr. May has used the words 'master,' and 'slave,' in speaking of our domestic institution. You see I cannot treat the subject with the gravity it deserves," he added, unable to refrain from laughing heartily, as he repeated these charges; "but I assure you, the bar-keeper added several other expressions, equally seditious when used before the servants, and capped the climax by informing me that you—dangerous girl!—*you* have been seen, by two men, talking to an old woman in the woods! What do you say to that?"

---

1 From *Othello*, 1.3.80.

"Is it possible," she exclaimed, "that for such little things we are esteemed dangerous, and meet everywhere such malicious looks? I knew people here were sensitive, but I had no idea of this."

"I should have said so myself, once," replied Walter; "but I begin to think that no purity of intention, no integrity of action, can shield a person from annoyance, if he is suspected of being heretical on that one subject, which is the hinge whereon all our social and political interests turn."

"I remember my conversation with the old woman, that morning I first went to the Triangle; but it was wholly accidental, and chiefly upon religious subjects. She was a good old woman. I have met her a few times since, and given her some money, for she is miserably poor; but I think nobody has seen me since that first morning. There were two men out then, with some fierce-looking dogs, hunting a negro. I saw them look at me closely, but I feared no harm."

"They don't like to have strangers talk to their negroes, even upon indifferent subjects," said Walter; "they are always suspecting harm, and it is doubly unsafe for you, since your anti-slavery ideas happen to be well known. I would be careful, if I were you, even to a degree that seems needless, and I would caution your father, also. He lets his hatred of oppression be seen in his face, sometimes, when he says nothing; and even looks are watched, and interpreted as dangerous, in these regions."

"I will not look at anything black again, except on my own plantation," said Ida, laughing, "be it man or woman, be it brute or human, I will shut my eyes the moment I discover its color, and I will advise father to wear a mask over his too expressive face. But does it not seem ridiculous? Think of two such inoffensive beings as we are causing a commotion in town! It is too absurd."

"My dear young lady," said Walter, with affected seriousness, "it is time you should learn that nothing is absurd which offends the majesty of the sovereign people; nothing is inoffensive that, directly or indirectly, threatens harm or reproach to our beloved 'institution.'"

"Don't say 'ours,'" said Ida, impatiently. "I don't like to think of you as upholding and protecting this system, that hinders all rational liberty, in the white man as well as the negro. Don't say 'ours.' You don't belong to this order of things."

"Indeed, I wish I had not need to say 'ours,'" said Walter sorrowfully, her careless words plunging him back into the depths of perplexity from which his thoughts had for a while escaped.

"And why need you?" said Ida, earnestly. "Walter, I must ask you—though, perhaps I should not—why you thus hesitate, and struggle against your convictions of right? I know it cannot be from any paltry pecuniary motive. What is it that hinders you from following the 'more excellent way,' which your words so plainly indicate that your heart approves?"

Walter Varian rose from his chair, and paced the room hurriedly for some moments, before he could reply. Then, stopping suddenly before her, he fixed his expressive eyes upon her, and spoke one word only:

"Mabel!"

"Even your engagement to her should not interfere with this sacred duty to those helpless beings, who may, with all their posterity, be doomed to unending bondage, unless you set them free now, before other cares and other duties obscure the path which is now so plain, and render that difficult which is now so easy."

Still standing before her, with his piercing glances, that sought to read her soul, he repeated impressively, that name:

"Mabel!"

"Why should she hinder this great work?" persisted Ida, moved by a sudden impulse, that urged her on, in spite of her previous determination. "O, Walter! I know it involves a sacrifice; but should you not place your convictions of duty before your love or your happiness? And, after all, the self-denial will not be very great. You have youth, and education, and abilities, that will develop themselves more and more under this new stimulus to exertion. If Mabel loves you, she will be proud of your fame, and rejoice in your firmness of principle; and, if you love her, why not have sufficient confidence in her to believe this? You have never confided to her your trouble."

"Are you then so deceived?" exclaimed Walter, vehemently, seizing both her hands as he spoke, and holding them tightly clasped in his. "Are you so blind as not to see that it is only because I do *not* love her, that I cannot speak to her upon this subject? If I loved her—if it were a question between my happiness and my duty—I should not have refrained from all action, in this cowardly, sneaking manner. I could have given up my happiness, and thanked God for strength to do my duty. But it seemed dishonorable to me to mention this subject now, knowing, as I do, that it will surely break the ties that bind us together—now, when those ties have become like iron fetters, that gall and weary. That would, indeed, be 'stealing the livery of heaven to serve the devil in!"[1] O, Ida! I am sorely perplexed. Pity me!"

He sank down on a low bench at her feet and pressed her hands against his burning eyes. It was an infinite relief to her to escape that impassioned gaze, and she no longer sought to withdraw them from his grasp.

"I do pity you, Walter," she answered, striving to speak calmly. "I pity you, and I see that I judged you wrongly. Forgive me, that I blamed you, and do not let us talk of this any more."

"Forgive you!" he said, without looking up. "I would forgive you a thousand times more than this! Only do not despise me for my faithlessness, for my vacillation, and weakness of purpose."

"Despise you!" exclaimed Ida, in amazement. "What could have given you that idea? No, I think you are in a sad dilemma; but I can do or say nothing to relieve you. Perhaps you have mistaken Mabel—perhaps you do not do her justice. She loves you, and, therefore, she must seek to please you. Her views and feelings on this subject may change when she knows yours."

"Have I mistaken her? Have I been unjust to her?" he said, suddenly raising his head, and looking anxiously into her face. "I wish you would tell me, Ida, for you have been with her during these five years that have developed her character, and you must know better than I. Tell me, is she selfish and cold-hearted, as she seemed to be when you were at the hall, or is the gentleness she has shown since, the right index to her character?"

Ida colored violently at this question, and it was some moments before she answered. Then she said, candidly, "I do not wish to tell you what I think about it, Walter. I know that she does not like me, and I fear I do not like her well enough to estimate her character truly. I believe it must be partly my own fault, for she seems to be universally admired; but certainly, our spheres do not accord. Let us talk of something else. Time may bring you safely out from your perplexity, if you are patient."

"Do you think so—do you really think so?" he cried, joyfully. "O, if I am ever a free man again, then, Ida, then—"

He paused abruptly, and compressed his lips firmly together, as if to keep back words that struggled for utterance. The hope, which he had always rejected so sternly when whispered by his own heart, he accepted from her lips as a certain proph-

---

1 Frequently quoted line from Scottish poet Robert Pollok (1798–1827), *The Course of Time* (1827), Book viii. Also quoted in *Narrative* (1845) by Frederick Douglass (1818–95).

ecy. He gazed up into her eyes, eagerly, passionately, as if he would thus telegraph to her mind the thoughts he had forbidden his lips to speak.

Ida saw that he had understood far more than her words were intended to convey, and she became greatly confused. His glances seemed to penetrate to her very soul, and compel her to acknowledge emotions, of which she had, until now, been unconscious—feelings whose very existence she had obstinately and perseveringly ignored. He still held her hands so firmly that she could not move, and, even when she turned away her head, she felt the power, the magnetism, of his earnest eyes. Her heart palpitated wildly—her lips trembled—tears filled her eyes—she grew deadly pale, and the room seemed to whirl and darken around her.

Walter sprang up in alarm. "Are you faint? Have I hurt you? Have I offended you?" he exclaimed, bending over her with the utmost solicitude.

"O no! I am nervous and fatigued, that is all," she answered, recovering herself by a violent effort, and smiling through her tears at her own weakness.

"I have stayed too long," said Walter, after a few moments, during which he had stood silently beside her. "You are sure you are not offended with me?" he added.

"I am not offended now," she replied, hesitatingly, and a little coldly, turning her face from him as she spoke; "but you must not talk to me again about this. I was very foolish to introduce the subject. I would not, had I known—"

"I am thankful you did," exclaimed he, as she paused in sudden confusion. "I have suffered much because I could not explain to you why it was that I did not act as I felt. Now I shall feel easier, since you understand me."

"I wonder why father does not come—it is nearly tea time!" said Ida, abruptly, changing the conversation, anxious to prevent further embarrassment.

"He is coming now, and I must go. Good-bye," said Walter.

He took her hand, with a lingering pressure, and again his eyes met hers, with that expressive look which made her tremble like a reed; but she controlled herself bravely, and was giving him a message for Mrs. Wynn, when the footsteps they had heard on the stairs came nearer, and the door opened. They turned, expecting to see Mr. May; but, in his place, there appeared the pallid face, and tall, emaciated figure of Maum Abby, holding in her arms a little child.

"Maum Abby!" they both exclaimed, in surprise; and Ida, thankful for almost any interruption at this moment, sprang to her side, and clasped her hand warmly, as she led her to a seat.

A faint smile flitted over her grief-worn face, as she met this cordial greeting, and, seating on her lap the little boy who had been clinging around her neck, she said,

"You look surprised to see me, Miss Ida, and perhaps you will be still more astonished, when you know the errand that brought me. You were my best friend, my only comforter, in that dark, dark hour when my heart was broken, and I have come to you again for help."

Her voice was low and calm, and though a shudder ran over her whole frame as she referred to her son's death, she manifested few other signs of emotion.

"This little boy is Elsie's child," said Ida, inquiringly, divining at once the wishes of her companion.

"It is; and Elsie is dead."

"I heard of her death," said Ida, "and I was almost thankful; for the poor little thing was not fitted for the struggle and toil of life. It is well that her grief killed her so soon."

"Do you think it was *grief* that killed her? O, no! grief cannot kill. It blights, it sears, it tortures, but it cannot kill; else why am I here?" said Maum Abby, pressing one hand over her heart, and looking with a mournful earnestness, that brought tears to the eyes of her listeners.

"This little boy looks like her. What is his name?" said Ida, wishing to divert her attention from such sad memories.

"He has his father's name," replied Maum Abby; "but he is not a bold, bright baby, as his father was. O, how short, how short the time seems, since I held my son in my arms, as *his* son is sitting now! O, what a little time!" she added, sadly caressing the child; "and now nothing is left me—nothing but *this*!"

She bowed her face on the little head that rested against her bosom, and they all wept together. Walter walked to the window to hide his emotion, and he was the first to recover himself.

"Don't cry Mauma," he said, trying to speak cheerfully, though his voice was somewhat husky. "This baby will grow up to be a brave little fellow, and a great comfort to you."

She raised herself, and shook her head, as she answered, "God grant that the sorrows of life may have ended for me long before he grows to be a man! I love him, but I am old and feeble now, and I cannot do for him even so much as I could do for his poor father. No, Master Walter, I look for no more comfort from anything mortal. I have brought him here to give him to Miss Ida. Will you take him, my dear young lady? Will you take the orphan boy to a land where he can be educated, and made a blessing to himself and others? O, Ida, will you take my child?"

"I will do all I can for him, Mauma," said Ida, "and, with Venus's aid, I think I can take care of him. He is a dear little fellow! Will he come to me?"

She held out her hands to him, as she spoke, with the tender, winning language a woman involuntarily adopts in speaking to a young child, and he raised himself from the arm on which he had been leaning, in timid quietness; a half smile broke over his face, which was before too sad for his years; and after the glances of his large, serious eyes had wandered from her to his nurse, and back again to her face he held out his tiny hands to hers, and sprang into her arms. Her heart warmed towards him, as she felt his soft cheek touching hers with a confiding pressure.

Maum Abby smiled faintly. "He knows that your heart is large enough to give him room," she said. "He is a gentle, quiet child, and I think his mother's anxiety and sorrow have prevented him from learning to laugh and shout as most babies do, and have kept him puny and delicate. I could not bear to have him raised in that miserable, ignorant, degraded condition in which his mother's family are living, and so I took him home; but I saw that Miss Emma felt anxious, though master said nothing against it, lest something unpleasant might happen, if the child stayed there; and I am old—old in years and sorrows—and I have no life or energy to raise such a boy as his father's child must be in a few years, even if I live; and, if I die, there are evils and dangers that I shudder to think of. O, Miss Ida, if you will take him, my prayers and thanks shall follow you every day of your life, till the Lord pleases to call me to a better world!"

"I will certainly take him," replied Ida. "I am going away from here soon, but I will always provide for the little one, and see that he is well cared for, and educated as he gets older. Venus is a mighty good nurse, and she can take care of him now, and will be glad to, I know. She is fond of children."

"I hear your father has come back," said Maum Abby after a short pause, during which Ida was caressing and talking to the child, "and I bless God, every day, that you are not lonely and unprotected any more. O, this is a sad, weary world, when we feel as if we had nobody to *love best*—nobody to cling to with the strongest cord in our hearts!"

"God has, indeed, blessed me beyond what I expected or deserved, in sending back my father. It was like receiving him from the grave, for, even in my wildest dreams, I have never dared hope that he was not dead."

"You have had many sorrows and trials; I used to see them when you lived at our house sometimes, and there were others greater, that came before and afterwards; but now, I hope, they are all over, and you have nothing but happiness before you. You have tried to do right, and you have been a blessing to many poor creatures that had nobody else to help them. You have not been selfish or afraid to do your duty, and I know God will bless you," said Maum Abby, warmly. "I know you will have a peaceful and joyful life after this."

A beautiful color mantled Ida's cheek, as she heard these praises; but, as she looked up, she met Walter's gaze, and a pang of hidden sorrow shot through her heart. Alas! with all the happiness of a father's love, with all the blessings of the grateful hearts around her, was she not conscious, even now, of a heavy weight on her heart; a trial all the greater that it must be borne in secret and alone? Almost unconsciously she replied, in the words of the venerable Thomas à Kempis, and she spoke them rather to her own soul than to those who listened:

"For this whole mortal life is full of miseries, and signed on every side with crosses. But, if thou trust in the Lord, fortitude shall be given thee from heaven."[1]

"I remember that," said Maum Abby. "You read it to me once, and I have often said it to myself since. I, Miss Ida, sometimes I have felt as if no one in all the world had so heavy a cross to bear as that which is laid on me. It presses me down—it bows me to the earth. When first it came upon me, I thought it would crush me, but, through the mercy of the Lord, it is growing lighter now. In my first mad grief, I thought there was no consolation left for me; in my blindness, I dared—poor, weak worm, that I am!—to call in question the justice and loving-kindness of the Lord. I said God had forgotten me. 'So foolish was I, and ignorant, I was a beast before him!'"[2]

She had risen as she spoke, and now stood with her hands clasped, and her eyes, unnaturally large and bright, in contrast with the ghastly paleness of her emaciated face, glowing with the fervor of her emotions, as she looked upward with an earnest

---

1 Ida is loosely quoting Thomas à Kempis (c. 1380–1471), from *The Imitation of Christ*, Second Book, Ch. 12.
2 Maum Abby quotes Psalms 73:22.

gaze that seemed to pierce the heavens. Thus she stood some moments, during which not a word was spoken. Absorbed and entranced, she appeared unmindful that she was not alone, and Ida and Walter, knowing her deep sorrows, were silent with sympathy and awe. Then her lips moved at first inaudibly, and a strange, solemn expression of joy seemed to steal over her features, brightening and softening their rigid outlines.

"I will trust in the Lord," she said; "thought he slay me, yet will I trust in him! I will bear his indignation because I have sinned against him, until he plead my cause and execute judgment for me. He will bring me forth to the light, and I shall behold his righteousness. He leadeth me by a way that I knew not. Clouds and darkness are round about his throne; but the Lord is good, and from out the storm and the whirlwind I hear a voice saying, 'It is I; be not afraid!' The waves and the billows have gone over me; I sink in deep waters, where there is no standing. Bitter, bitter is the cup, but my Father hath given it to me, and shall I not drink it? Even so, Father, for so it seemed good in thy sight!"

She continued for some moments to repeat passage after passage of Scripture, with an earnestness and a readiness that showed how her troubled heart had seized upon the divine consolations they afforded. For many years she had been an untiring reader of the Bible, and since her mind began to arouse itself from the overwhelming affliction of Alfred's death, those words of healing and comfort had sustained her amid the sad memories that haunted her lonely dwelling; and often had lifted her above all trial and sorrow by the strong power of submission and faith. Dark and mysterious as the event seemed to be, she had bowed her soul to receive it unmurmuringly, as part of the discipline of her life; and, amid her bereavement and desolation, she now sometimes felt the heaven-born joy of entire self-abnegation—a joy little known, and alas! seldom desired.

Taking the child again from Ida's arms, she held him a little while, caressing and pressing him fondly to her bosom, for, at the moment of her parting, her heart feared over this last relic of her idolized son. But at length she put him away from her, and, murmuring an invocation of blessings upon him and Ida, she turned suddenly, and passed out of the room, as if she dared not trust herself to speak words of farewell.

Walter followed her, and found the wagon, which had brought her from the hall, waiting for her at the door of the hotel. He saw her safely set out upon her return, and then went back to say goodnight to Ida; but when he reached the parlor, he found it vacated. She had not supposed he would return, having been so long detained after his first leave-taking, and she had proceeded directly to her chamber, to show Venus the little boy who had been so unexpectedly committed to her care.

Venus, who was passionately fond of babies, welcomed this little veteran of two summers with enthusiasm, as a most delightful addition to the family; but he could not be induced to allow her to take him. He was tired and hungry, and he began to cry, and clung to Ida, so that she was obliged to feed and undress him, and at length the long lashes shut heavily over his mild black eyes, and he slept upon her bosom. It was quite dark before she was released from this new but pleasing employment; and then, leaving the child in Venus's care, she went to the parlor. She found her father sitting there alone. Walter had waited some time, and then, supposing she wished to avoid him, by her long absence, he had gone away, with feelings strangely divided between pain for his love and admiration for its object.

CHAPTER XVI

"O, but man, proud man!
Dressed in a little brief authority,
Most ignorant of what he's most assured,
His glassy essence, like an angry ape,
Plays such fantastic tricks before high heaven,
As make the angels weep."
MEASURE FOR MEASURE[1]

The next morning, just as Mr. May was about leaving the little parlor where he and his daughter had been sitting, waiting for their horses to be saddled for the morning ride, a knock was heard at the door, and, when it was opened, the hotel-keeper bowed himself into the room. The suppressed agitation of his face arrested Ida's attention, as she bade him good-morning, and he had hardly taken the chair she offered him before he made known the object of his visit, by saying,

"I beg your pardon for intruding, but the importance of what I have to say must be my excuse. I am sorry to have to tell you, sir and madam, that I fear you are in some danger here."

"From what source are we in danger?" said Mr. May.

"It is a matter of great regret to me, I assure you, sir, and I thought it but friendly to inform you of the charges against you. I hope you will excuse me; but it is a grave matter—a very grave matter. It is said that you are *abolitionists*."[2]

He pronounced this last word in a low, husky whisper, as if afraid to mention a term so full of infamy and danger; and when it was spoken, he sat looking from one to the other, with his face flushed, and his hands trembling from excitement. He was a kind-hearted man, and he felt truly sorry for his guests, although he was not entirely without that disgust and dread which every southerner feels, involuntarily, at the mention of that class of persons to whom he supposed they belonged.

Mr. May could hardly help smiling at his tone and manner; but, nevertheless, he knew that all sorts of difficulty and danger were connected with this charge. He glanced at Ida, who had

---

1 Isabella speaking in Shakespeare's play, 2.2.117–22.
2 During her stay in Aiken, South Carolina, Pike proudly was charged an abolitionist as well. See letter from Miss Caroline F. Putnam, Appendix E1.

grown very pale and laid her hand on his arm with a quick, nervous motion, and replied, quietly,

"Do not alarm my daughter unnecessarily, I beg. I think there will be no trouble. If, by the term 'abolitionist,' you mean a person who considers your system of domestic servitude a great wrong—an evil that affects all classes of society, and leads to untold suffering and crime—then I can only say *peccavi*.[1] But if you mean that, in the slightest possible manner, we have interfered with your servants, or those of any other man, I can affirm boldly that the charge is utterly false."

"I have no doubt of it," replied Mr. Armitage (for such was his name). "I am sure you have never meddled with my servants, and I hope you will be able to prove that you have had nothing to do with any others. I assure you, sir, I have done the utmost in my power to quiet these reports."

"Thank you," replied Mr. May; "you may be sure they are without foundation. I have my own ideas respecting my duties to the negroes left my daughter by her guardian, but I seek to control no other man's conscience, and I meddle not with any other man's affairs. Who says I do?"

"There are various persons who have been producing some agitation, by using your name and Miss May's," replied he, evasively; "and, if you will allow me to say so, I fear you may have given some occasion for the rumors, although I am sure it was through inadvertance, and ignorance of our customs. Several times, in general conversation, you have quite warmly upheld the northern side of the argument—"

"Cannot a man express his own opinions here, if they happen to be adverse to those of his neighbor?" interrupted Mr. May, with some warmth.

"In private, among his friends, certainly," replied Mr. Armitage; "but in public, it is generally unwise to do so, and when such things are said before the negroes, they are considered *seditious*. Perhaps you did not know it, but it is so. And, besides this, Miss May has been seen talking with one or two negro women in the woods, and that you know is quite contrary to custom."

"I did not know it was," replied Ida. "When I lived at Wynn Hall, we used frequently to stop to chat with the women washing in the woods, as we were riding out."

"Ah, certainly!" said Mr. Armitage; "but that was quite

---

1 I have sinned (Latin).

different. Then you were with some members of that family, doubtless, and anyone who saw you might, by inquiring learn that you were a person from whom nothing could be feared. But now, pardon me, miss, it is well known that there has been a little coolness between yourself and the Wynn family, on account of this very matter of interfering with servants; and that makes it quite a different matter, you see."

"In other words," said Ida, "because I do not live at Wynn Hall since my father came home, I am not to be allowed to bestow charity on a poor old woman, or to talk with her upon religious matters. Do you not yourself think this is making a fuss about a very little thing?"

"Well," said Mr. Armitage, apologetically, "we don't like to have strangers talk to our negroes. It makes them discontented. They can detect in a moment, the difference between one who is used to them, and persons from the north; and they are so cunning and treacherous, that they avail themselves of it at once, to tell all sorts of stories, and to give people a very wrong idea of the true state of things here. Half the stories in the northern newspapers are got in this way from the servants, and have no truth in them. The negroes will lie so, that one can't depend a moment on what they say. You get no right ideas respecting our domestic institution by talking with them. They are an ungrateful set, and will often complain of the very best of masters. Of course we don't like to be misrepresented in that way."

"Some servants seem very much attached to their masters," said Mr. May.

"Yes, O yes! No doubt the most of them are. When they have kind masters, they are always very fond of them. In fact, there is no tie so strong as that between an old servant and the family he belongs to. Many a one that has been enticed away, has come back after a little while, and begged to be taken home again. They hate the abolitionists as much as their masters do, I assure you."

"Are not most of the masters, about here, kind to their servants?" asked Mr. May.

"O yes, yes!" replied Mr. Armitage. "I know of one or two who are a little hard, but generally it has been the fault of the negroes. There are some negroes so ugly that a man can't get along without severe measures. However, that is rare; and as I said, as a general thing, they are very much attached to their masters, and would not be free if they could. Yes, it is so all around here. Most of the masters are kind. In fact there are very few bad masters. That is quite a mistake to think so."

"What harm, then, has it done for my daughter to talk to a few negro women, if they are so generally contented?" said Mr. May, quietly.

Mr. Armitage colored, for he saw that he had contradicted himself, and answered, in some excitement,

"I did not say that all were contented; and if any of the negroes find out that there is anyone about who does not exactly understand our institutions, they are apt to create trouble. In fact, sir, the negroes are all so fickle and changeable, that a man can often turn them against their best friends, if he tries; and there is such a systematic effort making now, by bad men at the north, to entice our servants away, and stir them up against their masters, that we are obliged, in self-defense, to be very strict in our precautions against all strangers who are not well known. You know, sir," he added, bending forward and speaking low, "there has once or twice been an attempt at *insurrection*, in this State."[1]

"I know it, and every humane person must turn with horror from the idea of a servile insurrection; but I don't yet understand why anything we have done can be supposed dangerous. The pillars of state must rest on an insecure foundation, if my daughter's little hand can shake them; and, as for me, I have attended to my own affairs, and I shall be much obliged to the gentlemen about town if in future they will attend to theirs."

"They consider it part of their business, just now, to watch you and Miss May," said Mr. Armitage, smiling. "I don't wonder that you are annoyed, sir, for it is a very disagreeable thing, and I regret it exceedingly. Don't you think it might be well for you both to leave town a little while, until the excitement abates?"

"I never ran from a foe yet," said Mr. May, somewhat proudly, "and I should be sorry to begin now. Besides," he added, more calmly, "I do not think it would be right for us to leave our business at the Triangle. The negroes are just getting a little in train for the life we propose they shall lead when we take them away;

---

1   He refers to Denmark Vesey's (c. 1767–1822) plot to free the slaves of Charleston, South Carolina, in 1822. South Carolina also saw the largest slave rebellion in the British colonies, the Stono Rebellion, which led to the state's restrictive Negro Act of 1740 that remained in place until emancipation. Both insurrections were put down by citizen militias.

and, as our first care was to dismiss the overseer, there is no one there to take care of them, and prevent the disorder that would be likely to follow our departure. In a few weeks more I shall receive their free papers from Charleston, and then we shall all leave, probably never to return."

"Still," said Mr. Armitage, anxiously, "I advise you to leave immediately. I cannot answer for the consequences, if you remain; and it was this I came to tell you this morning. It has been a serious matter to some men, I can assure you. I knew one man who came here from the north, and was suspected in this way, and a mob collected and nearly killed him, riding him out of town on a rail."

Ida gave a faint cry at these words, and clung to her father in great alarm.

"Let us go today," she said, "O, father, do not run such a fearful risk!"

"You shall go, poor child!" he answered, caressing her soothingly. "I will send you away with Mr. Varian; but, for me, I believe it is my duty to stay, and I shall remain. Is there no law in the land to restrain mob violence?" he added, firmly, turning to Mr. Armitage.

"If you had powerful friends to answer for you, you might take refuge in the law, in case the worst came; though the alternative the law offers is poor enough—a heavy fine and long imprisonment, for seditious language; but, unknown and unsupported as you are, I doubt if the mob could be restrained, and made to wait the slow process of the law. Again, let me urge you to go immediately. I should be very sorry to have any trouble of this kind happen in my house."

"It would be a great disadvantage to your hotel, if it became known abroad," said Mr. May, looking at him impressively, struck by the sudden thought that perhaps his fears on that point induced him to exaggerate the danger.

"Do you mean to impute my friendly warning to mean motives?" he exclaimed, angrily. "If you do, you are very unjust to me."

"I do not; excuse me that my words implied it," said Mr. May, repenting of his suspicion; "but it is no less true that it will injure the reputation of your hotel abroad, if it is known that there can be no liberty of discussion, no freedom of action, within its walls."

At this moment there were voices heard in the hall below, and heavy footsteps upon the stairs, and someone called loudly for

Mr. Armitage. He turned pale, and went out, closing the door carefully behind him.

Mr. May passed his arm fondly around Ida's waist, and, seeing how much she was distressed and agitated, he said, cheerfully, "Do not be frightened. This will probably amount to nothing more than an order from the 'vigilance committee,' requesting us to leave town and though it is certainly annoying to be thus suspected and insulted, it is nothing that perils life or limb. Go and put your affairs in readiness to leave this afternoon, my child, for I must send you out of the way before they have a chance to inflict even that slight penalty. A very secure state of society it must be that it is jeopardized by anything we have done! But these people know they walk over a quicksand that may at any moment swallow them up! Go, my dear, you have no time to lose."

"I cannot go and leave you, father," said Ida, earnestly. "Do not send me away."

"But I cannot possibly leave in less than a week, without great harm to our affairs at the Triangle; and you know Mr. Armitage spoke of danger."

"Let me remain and share it, then," said Ida. "I should die a thousand deaths in fearing one for you. O, my father! I will not leave you to brave alone the trouble you have encountered for my sake. I must remain. We have done nothing wrong, and God will protect our innocence. When I felt entirely deserted, he gave you back to me, and I cannot think we shall be given over to the malice of bad men. Let me stay with you; I am not afraid."

"But there is really more danger than you think. I could defend myself from harm, but I should be powerless to shield you from seeing and hearing what would insult and alarm you!"

"Every word you speak only makes me more urgent to stay," said Ida, growing more self-possessed as she became accustomed to the thought of danger. "If you think it necessary to remain, I should suffer far less to be here with you than to be dreading all sorts of evils, not one of which may really happen. And, in case of the worst, even if a mob should collect, I think the fact of my presence would be a safeguard instead of a hindrance to your safety. I would go with you everywhere, and they surely would not attack a woman."

Mr. May looked with admiration and love at the slight, girlish figure that was animated by so brave a spirit, and, smiling at the idea of his manly strength being so protected, was about to reply, when suddenly Mr. Armitage returned, and, without waiting for his modest knock to be answered, entered and locked the door behind him.

He was evidently much alarmed and agitated, and coming close to Mr. May he said, in a low voice,

"The danger I feared has come sooner than I expected. The sheriff is in the hall with a warrant to arrest you. There will be no time for you to escape, but I can secrete Miss May where she will be safe. There is quite a mob collected about the market. I assure you there is cause for alarm."

"Go, my child, go immediately," exclaimed Mr. May, kindly, but firmly.

Ida was very pale, and her lips trembled, but she answered with quiet determination,

"I cannot go. I shall not be any embarrassment to you, father. I can control my fears; and I do believe you will be less likely to receive injury if I am with you."

"Perhaps it will be so," exclaimed Mr. Armitage, "and, on second thoughts, I think it might be better to take her on that account."

"I cannot think of incurring any such risk," said Mr. May, hurriedly. "Take her immediately to a place of safety."

He strove to unclasp her hands from his arm as he spoke; but further argument was rendered useless by the impatience of the sheriff and his posse, who had been waiting outside the door, and now, growing suspicious that some attempt at escape was being made, struck it with their heavy canes so violently that the slight lock which held it gave way at the first shock, and they entered the room.

The sheriff was none other than our old acquaintance, Nick Kelly, who, having retired from his former active business, he settled in this neighborhood, and, investing his gains in buying a profitable plantation, had become quite an influential member of the community. Little thought he that the young lady who stood so quietly to hear him arrest her and her father for seditious language and disorderly conduct in relation to the negroes, was the same who, when a child, had barely escaped with life from the effects of his villainy.[1]

"You see there is no further question about my going with you," Ida said, looking up almost gaily into her father's face, when the warrant had been read.

"I see," echoed her father, with sigh of anxiety.

---

1 He is not recognized by Ida.

"Come on, then," said the sheriff, roughly. "We've waited long enough now."

"You must have a carriage," said Mr. Armitage, "and I will go with you. If you could send for some other friend it would be well."

"We have no friend here except Mr. Varian," replied Mr. May.

"Mr. Wynn is a man of great influence," suggested Mr. Armitage.

"I will not call upon Mr. Wynn," was the quick reply.

"Come on—here is a carriage you can have," said the sheriff, who had been looking out of the window.

They descended the stairs. The hall was full of men, who gazed at them so rudely that Ida trembled and clung to her father's arm, and it was with a heartfelt exclamation of joy that, just as she entered the carriage, she saw Walter Varian riding furiously towards them.

Reining his horse by the carriage window, he exclaimed,

"What is all this about? There is a crowd around the market-house, and I heard your names coupled with every variety of epithets."

A few words sufficed to tell him all, and, giving his horse into the care of his servant, who followed him, he got into the carriage, and drove with them up to the office where their trial was to be held. It was surrounded with men, many of them armed with clubs, and some carrying knives and pistols. As they drew near, many of them came around the sides of the carriage, catching hold by the curtains, and trying to get a glimpse of Ida's face, which was closely veiled, and shouting and bandying rude jokes with those who had followed them from the house. When they entered the courtroom, they found that also crowded, and it was not without being pressed against and pushed about in the most insulting manner, that they made their way to the place reserved for them, as criminals before the bar of justice.

Some of these men belonged to the middle classes of society, possessing moderate wealth, and calling themselves "respectable"; but the majority were of that order of the genus homo, found nowhere but the slave States, and impossible under any other combination of society. These are the poor whites, who have received distinctive soubriquets in most of the States, and are called "clay-eaters" in Carolina. Clad in the coarsest and the scantiest garments, subsisting principally upon "turpentine whiskey," and appeasing their craving for more substantial food by the filling their stomachs with a kind of aluminous earth which abounds everywhere, they are squalid and emaciated to a frightful degree; with yellowish, drab-colored complexions, eyes that are dull and cold as the eyes of a dead fish, and faces whose idiotic expression is only varied by a dull despair or a devilish malignity. Living in rude log houses, and gaining their miserable livelihood one hardly knows how, they are found scattered through the green woods and the pleasant valleys, or clustered in the outskirts of the larger towns. They are as destitute of any idea of religion or morality as the swine that feed around their doors, and are looked down upon by the negroes with a contempt which they return by a hearty hatred.

These wretched beings, crushed and degraded to the last extreme of poverty and ignorance by the operation of slavery, that cuts them off from all the labor to which their capacities are suited, are nevertheless among its warmest supporters. They have not sufficient mental vigor to originate any but the most petty schemes of vice; but, when abler heads require tools to work with, these men are ready to be led to any length of cruelty and wickedness. For two or three weeks there had been persons going round among this class, hinting that on a certain day the town folks were going to have some sport with an abolitionist who had been troubling them, and they had come from all directions, armed with their rude weapons, and gloating over the prospects of tarring and feathering, and riding on a rail, the stranger who had presumed to meddle with the niggers.

These threats, which met their ears on every side, convinced Walter and Mr. Armitage that the forms of law would probably yield to a more swift and deadly danger, and that, if the victims were to be saved, help must come soon.

An hour afterwards, Mr. Wynn, sitting quietly in his study, received the following note, written hastily in pencil:

"DEAR SIR,—Pray come to the Squire Oliver's office the moment you receive this. Mr. May and his daughter have been arrested on the most unfounded and puerile charges, and are now here in the hands of the officers; but there has a large mob collected, and great excitement prevails, and I fear we shall not be able to save them from personal violence. Come instantly, I entreat you, for your influence is greater than any other person's in this case, since I believe the fact of Miss May's expulsion from your house was the first thing that cast suspicion upon her, as very exaggerated rumors have been spread concerning the cause of her leaving you. Life or death depends upon your compliance with my request. Do not hesitate, I beg. Your Nephew,

"WALTER VARIAN"

Walter had written this note in the greatest anxiety and doubt, but Mr. Wynn did not hesitate a moment. Much as he hated anti-slavery ideas, he had too much sense not to see the danger of countenancing mob violence. He would have left the law to take its course, but his very pride and aristocracy of feeling revolted from the lawless proceedings of the *canaille*.[1] Much as he had come to dislike Ida, and her father for her sake, he would not have them treated unfairly by others on account of his quarrel with them; and, though he would never have forgiven her till the day of his death, he was too honorable not to wish to defend her from any false allegations brought against her in consequence of the withdrawal of his protection.

Therefore, in an incredibly short time, the anxious party, that scarcely hoped for his aid, saw him coming in at the door with two other gentlemen, whom Mr. Armitage had sent for, and who arrived on the spot at the same time. They were not a moment too early. The room was densely crowded with fierce, angry faces, that glared with wolfish eyes on Mr. May and Ida; missiles had been thrown and weapons brandished, a hoarse murmur of insulting epithets filled the air and coarse, hard hands had been stretched out to clutch the victims. It was only because Walter and Mr. Armitage had used threats in their turn, and finally, throwing themselves before those they protected, had declared they should be reached only over their dead bodies, that the mob had been so long kept at bay.

The presence of the newcomers, and their stern, angry denunciations of these violent proceedings, changed the aspect of affairs. It was hard to quell the appetite of the rabble, whetted for deeds of cruelty; but the movers of these fierce elements, awed by this unexpected reinforcement of the opposite party, began to soothe instead of exciting, and, after some delay and difficulty, the legal process, which had been interrupted by the mob, was again renewed.

During all this time of peril and alarm, Ida had stood leaning against her father. Her face, her very lips, were deathly pale, but she controlled with a strong will all other manifestation of fear,

---

1 Derogatory term referring to the common masses.

and remained calm and quiet amid the tumultuous noises and the brutal, wicked faces that surrounded her. Walter, who was almost desperate with fear for her safety, and who remembered how often he had seen her tremble and grow faint when there was less occasion, beheld her with amazement. He did not know how her soul had grown strong in the discipline of the last few months, and how, amid this turmoil of evil men, her faith stayed itself upon the mighty power of Him who restraineth the wrath of the wicked when it has accomplished his will.

Mr. May, when he found there was any prospect of obtaining justice, insisted upon a postponement of the trial, until he could prepare for it a little, and obtain counsel and witnesses.

The justice demurred at this, and the request renewed for a while the rage and clamor of the mob; but Mr. Wynn and his friends insisted that it should be granted, and, after some hours of contention, the obstinacy of the magistrate gave way. The crowd were appeased but five thousand dollars bond being given that the prisoners should appear the next morning, and the law should be allowed to take its course, and thus the trial was postponed.

Still there was great danger that, in leaving the room, a rush of lawless men would seize their prey in spite of all precaution; and, after waiting in vain for them to disperse, Mr. Armitage left his friends, by whom he had stood nobly until now, and, mingling with the "clay-eaters," appealed cunningly to a propensity stronger than even their hatred of abolitionists, and succeeded in drawing them across the street to a neighboring whiskey-shop, where he let it be known that he would "stand treat" to an unlimited extent, and soon the offer was accepted by nearly the whole multitude.

The way was now cleared for an escape, and, quickly as possible, Ida and her father were seated in the carriage, the others surrounding them on horseback. The first intention had been to take them to Oaklands; but some of the "respectable" heads of the mob had lingered around the door, which was hidden from view of those in and about the whiskey-shop by the market-house, that stood in the centre of the broad, sandy street, and these men, when they saw the horses' heads turned from the hotel, raised such a shout that the project was given up, lest opposition should lead to dangerous results, and they all proceeded quietly and quickly to the hotel from whence they had come.

Once more safe in their little parlor, Ida and her father could no longer refrain from expressing their warm thanks to Mr.

Wynn for the assistance he had rendered. Everything in the past was blotted from their memory, for the time, by this one act; and, as a man always feels somewhat kindly towards those to whom he has rendered a great benefit, he replied to them more graciously than Ida had dared to hope, and she was even thankful for the trial that had apparently again established friendliness between herself and the family to whom she felt bound by many an early debt of gratitude.

Mr. Wynn, and the other gentlemen, also, had been impressed with great admiration for the calmness and courage which Ida had manifested, and all now felt interested in extricating them entirely from the impending danger.

"You must get far away from here before morning," said Mr. Wynn. "It will be foolhardiness to remain, with this excited state of the community. We could control them today, but our influence will grow to be an old story by tomorrow, and these brutal creatures may destroy everything by a sudden rush."

The other gentlemen according with this view, and Mr. May saw that it was indeed, the wisest course.

"I must forfeit my bonds, then, and take 'French leave,'"[1] said Mr. May, smiling. "It does not sound very well, truly; but you will speedily find that my bondsmen will not suffer, or anyone else who has befriended me, if money can help it. It is not seemly to make a boast of wealth, but I am a stranger here, and that must be my apology."

"Wealth is generally supposed to be its own apology," said one of the gentlemen, in reply. "The only question now is about the means of getting away. You must have a carriage, and there are none in the stable here sufficiently easy for Miss May to ride comfortably all night, and she already looks very much fatigued. If you will send a servant, my place is only four miles from here, and my carriage is at your disposal."

This offer was accepted, with many thanks, and, as it was now nearly sunset, no time was lost in sending a servant. Meantime, Ida withdrew to rest a little, while Venus, who had been waiting at the door, in an agony of impatience to see her, should pack the few articles it was necessary to take with them.

Elsie's little boy was asleep on the bed, and, as Ida threw herself down beside him, she was thankful that Maum Abby had not delayed bringing him to her until this sudden change in her fortunes rendered it impossible. She lay quite still for

---

1 To leave without announcing one's departure.

some time, thinking how abrupt had been the variations in her course of life, and how deliverance had always come to her in her troubles, from the quarter whence she least expected it, and, striving to put away from there the recollections that would persist in intruding themselves, of Walter's looks and words the evening previous, and of the exertions he had made for her safety that day; and especially, of one occasion, when, believing the mob about to rush upon them, he had whispered to her, with a thrilling intensity of expression, that even then brought the color to her cheeks,

"Cling to me, Ida, cling to me! They shall kill me before harm comes to you."

In the meantime, Venus was accompanying her packing with a running commentary of words; and, rousing herself at length from her dreamy reverie to listen to what she was saying, Ida found that she was packing her own clothes, also.

"Stop, Venus," she said, "you needn't pack that."

"'T a'n't no 'count, I know, miss," said she; "but 'pears like we'd make it do, make somethin' fur de little feller. O, miss, he de mos' blessedest chile—dat ar'!"

"But you are not to go now, Venus! didn't you understand me? You are to stay and take care of the child till we make some further arrangement."

"I a'n't gwine stay take care o' no child!" exclaimed Venus. "Pretty well, too, you go off 'out no Benus take care of ye! Who say I be gwine stay?"

"There is no room for you in the carriage, mauma," said Ida, "so you see you can't go. I'm sorry, but you are safe enough here."

"*I* a'n't scare!" exclaimed she, contemptuously; "but I can't *persent* to your gwine, honey, 'thout you takes me 'long. I'se allers notice you get into strouble de minute I a'n't by to take care of ye. Dere's room fur four in de carriage, a'n't de?"

"Yes; but father and I, and Mass' Walter and the driver, will occupy it, you see."

"O, Mass' Walter gwine! am he?" she exclaimed, with a sudden exhibition of her universal giggle, winking and blinking at Ida in a manner that was infinitely amusing. "I wonders what Miss Mabel say when she know dat? Reckon she lif' up de eyelids, *so*. Mass' Walter! ki! dat good! Mass' Walter! *I'se* knowed somethin' ever sense dat ar' night de Lord sent de father back 'gin. *I* knows."

"There he is, now!" exclaimed Ida, springing from the bed, as she heard a quick step on the stairs; and, in another moment, without waiting even for the ceremony of knocking, Walter threw open the door.

"Come instantly!" he cried, seizing her hand. "The mob are upon us again, in a drunken fury! Come, don't wait for anything!"

He threw on her shawl and bonnet, and, thoughtful of her comfort even then, flung over his shoulder her cloak, that lay on the chair, lest she might need protection from the cool night air.

"Is the carriage ready?" she asked, as they ran down the stairs.

"No, it has not yet arrived, and the minute we caught sight of the mob, Mr. Warner set off on horseback, to intercept it. They will go to another street, where we will meet them."

"And my father, where is he?"

"They hurried him off into the woods, and he waits for us there," said Walter, opening a side door in an angle of the house, that sheltered them from view of the street, down which the rabble were now tramping, uniting their voices in shouting a drunken song, the chorus of which, at that moment, came to them on the wind.

> "Git out o' the way you d—d old Yankee!
> We'll burn the abolitionists."

Keeping the house between them and their pursuers, they ran down the hill and gained the shelter of a thick grove, which commenced not many rods from the house, and extended back till it was merged in an extensive pine forest. It was now nearly dark, and, once among the trees, they were concealed from view.

As he hurried her along, Ida stopped suddenly, and, looking up earnestly in his face, she said,

"You have not been deceiving me, Walter? My father tried to send me away from him once. I fear he has done so now. Has he really left the house? Why did he not wait for me?"

"He is really waiting for us somewhere here. I sent my servant with him, because it would not answer for any of the others to be absent when the mob arrive. They must be there to hold the rascals at bay, while we have a chance to escape."

"But why did he not wait for me?"

"We wouldn't let him. He was on the piazza, and we forced him to go, for his danger was more imminent than yours, if he were seen, and every instant increased it. I told him I would bring you safely. You are not afraid to trust me, Ida?" he added, reproachfully.

"O, no!" she cried, and a strange thrill of mingled pleasure and pain shot through her heart, as she realized how entirely she trusted him—how fast he was becoming dearer to her than aught beside on earth, and how, through all the peril and terror of that eventful day, there had been inwoven a consciousness of exquisite delight whenever she had felt the pressure of his hand, or met the glance of his eyes.

They passed swiftly on, too swiftly for further conversation, and soon the shouting of the mob became a low murmur, and they reached the distant spot where they found Mr. May and Walter's servant awaiting them. With inexpressible thankfulness, Ida was pressed to her father's heart. He had endured an agony of anxiety of her fate, and self-reproach at leaving her, during the short interval that had elapsed since they left the house, and was on the point of turning back to seek her, when he saw her approaching.

In a short time the carriage drove up, accompanied by Mr. Warner, on horseback; and having seen them safely placed in it, the kind gentleman shook hands with Ida and her father.

"I cannot ask you to visit me," he said, laughing, "for I suppose our rampant democracy would make that hardly a friendly invitation; but, if ever I go where you are, I shall certainly improve the opportunity to become further acquainted with this brave young lady."

Assuring him of the pleasure it would give them to see him, and with many thanks and expressions of mutual regret, they parted, and Walter's servant, gathering up the reins, drove them rapidly away from the scene of their danger.

Few words were spoken during that long-remembered night, for Walter was plunged in a chaos of troubled thought, and Mr. May was busy arranging his plans for the future. Ida was completely worn out with fatigue and excitement, and, wrapped in her warm coverings, as soon as she knew they were fairly out of danger, sank to sleep with her head resting upon her father's breast.

Thoroughly weary were they all, when, the next morning, just as day was breaking, the carriage rattled over the bridge that spans the turbid Savannah, and they entered the pretty little city of Augusta.[1]

The first thing they sought was rest, and it was not until they met at dinner, that Walter saw how pale and worn Ida looked, and how nervously she started at any sudden noise.

---

1 Augusta, Georgia, is the city closest to Aiken, South Carolina.

"You bore up bravely while the danger lasted, but, now it is past, I see you are suffering from the shock and the strain upon your nervous system. Your body is not strong enough for your soul, Ida," said Walter to her, as they sat by the window, after dinner, looking out upon the busy throng that were hurrying along Broad street.

"True," she answered, smiling. "I feel today like saying, 'my little body is aweary of this great world.'[1] It will be a long while, I think, before I shall cease having a palpitation at any unexpected sound, but I hope to be able to avoid disturbing others with my panic. It amuses me though, in spite of my annoyance, when I think that poor little insignificant I have been the cause of so much commotion."

"It was something like taking a club to crush a mosquito. The mosquito has flown away, and may sting again! Hey, Ida?"

"No, no," she replied, laughing; "impute to me no such revengeful design. I shall 'set down naught in malice,'[2] and I am quite satisfied with the mischief I was compelled indirectly to do. I suppose I did give some of those poor creatures an idea of a different order of things from that under which they live, although I tried not to. But they are quick to detect the sympathy of a tone or an expression, and I don't wonder their masters are alarmed at the presence of a person of different sentiments. If I had treated anybody as most of the negroes are treated, I should be as sensitive to slight disturbances as the Carolinians are. Really, I don't blame them for not liking to have persons with anti-slavery ideas living among them."

"I blame them, however, for stirring up a mob to get rid of such obnoxious individuals," said Walter, indignantly; "and I blush when I think that, in my native State, all laws of hospitality and of justice as well as decency, must be sacrificed to this Moloch,[3] who is so devoutly worshipped. I only hope that some day we may serve a less infernal deity. One would think that an institution which was so easily shaken might at length be overturned."

"Alas, no!" said Ida. "I fear it is like those huge stones found among the mountains, so poised that an infant's hand can rock

---

1 Shakespeare, *The Merchant of Venice*, 1.2.1–2.
2 From *Othello*, 5.2.342; Pike also cites this line in her Preface, p. 43.
3 Ancient god of the Ammonites, referred to in scriptural and literary texts as one who requires too great a sacrifice. In ancient times, Moloch worship included child sacrifice by fire.

them, but a giant's force is insufficient to hurl them from their resting-places. Humanly speaking, it seems impossible that slavery should cease, except by a convulsion disastrous and fearful as the earthquake, which alone can overthrow these vast boulders."

"Do not speak so hopelessly. There is One whose power controls the earthquake, and the designs of His providence will be worked out in spite of all human wrong-doing; yes, perhaps even by means of that which seems most adverse to all good. We see it is so, sometimes, in little things, and our faith in the ultimate triumph of right should not waver, because the weakness of our mortal vision cannot reach through the vast spaces of time, which, to the Lord, are but as a day."

It was Mr. May who said this. They did not notice his approach until he spoke, and then the solemnity of his manner prevented any reply. He felt deeply, and he spoke earnestly for, from the long discipline of his life, he had learned implicit trust in God.

He seated himself beside them, and, after a few moments of thoughtful silence, the conversation turned upon their future proceedings.

"We must go north as soon as possible, now," said Mr. May. "I was anxious to go on with our 'primary school' at the Triangle, until my agent had selected and purchased a location for our little colony, and I could arrange our affairs here without being obliged to trouble you. But, as this has not been permitted, we must leave things on the plantation to take care of themselves, until an opportunity for sale offers; and you can send all the negroes over in the cars to Hamburg.[1] You see, I take it for granted, you will still be our good genius, as you have been so long."

"Certainly," said Walter. "I am only too happy to serve you and Ida in any way. I will send them over tomorrow."

"And Venus and her little charge—you will not forget them," said Ida with a smile, and a slight blush, as she met the earnest expression of his brown eyes.

"I will see that they are made comfortable," he answered. "You will have quite a retinue to take with you to Savannah."

"Maum Venus will feel so mighty grand about it," said Ida, laughing. "It is a curious inconsistency in her nature that, notwithstanding all she has suffered from it, she yet looks upon the system of domestic servitude with a certain pride and respect. I could see that she was even a little unwilling to have me carry out my plans for the negroes at the Triangle. 'I s'pose it right, honey,'

---

1 A hamlet in Berks County, Pennsylvania.

said she, 'but it do seem mighty like comin' down to be one de poor trash 't a'n't got no niggers—an' here you'se got 'nuff to keep you comfible all de whole your life, *ef you dies in any kind o' decent season.*'"

"It is hard for any of us to free ourselves from the ideas in which we were educated," said Walter. "It is said to 'take nine tailors to make a man,'[1] and Maum Venus evidently thinks it takes twice that number of negroes to make a gentleman. But I must not linger here," he added, "for I see Tom is waiting at the door with the carriage, and I wish to get home before midnight."

"Do you go so soon?" exclaimed Ida, with a sudden heart-pang.

"I must. It will not answer for me to remain longer," he replied, with an emphasis and an intonation that expressed more than his words.

Ida cast down her eyes, and was silent. She could not urge him to remain, but her very soul seemed to grow faint as she thought of the long time that might elapse before they should meet again.

"When shall we see you again?" said Mr. May.

"I don't know—perhaps never," he replied, gloomily. His eyes were fixed on Ida's face, with that intensely earnest and sorrowful expression, wherewith a man looks on that which he most loves and longs for, at the moment when he is bidding it farewell forever. He had taken her hand to bid her adieu, but the word lingered on his lips, and the little hand, cold and tremulous, lay passively in his. Never had she seemed so dear, so infinitely precious to him as now—never had he so longed to pour out his heart to her. The events of the last two days had bound him to her with strong, entangling cords, and to leave her thus, knowing that he should not, that he *must* not see her again, seemed like tearing asunder the springs of life.

"Good-bye!" he said, at length, dropping her hand with a stifled sigh.

"Good-bye!" she answered, raising her sad eyes one instant to his.

This was all. He left the room, and Mr. May went out with him. It was no time for the manifestation of sentiment. They were in the parlor of a crowded hotel, and the groups who were passing around them must know nothing of this bitter struggle— must not hear the frown of mute despair with which these two souls were sundered—must not read on the face of the pale girl,

---

1 Proverb of unknown provenance, that a man must select his clothing from several tailors to individuate his style.

who sat in the shadow of the window-curtain, the keen sorrow, the unhappy love, she was hiding beneath that quiet exterior. One lady noticed her, and said to a companion,

"How very pretty she would be, if she had only a little color, and had not that expression of ennui."

"Yes," said the other. "I wonder who she is. That was her brother who just went out, I reckon."

"Her lover, perhaps," said the first speaker.

"No; her brother. Lovers do not part so calmly."

It is ever thus. There would be little need to write romances or tragedies, if every man carried a "window in his bosom."[1]

> "All the world's a stage,
> And all the men and women merely players;"[2]

but fortunately it is seldom the audience has a program of the play.

When Walter Varian arrived at the hotel, from which he had taken such sudden flight the preceding evening, it was past midnight, but he found Mr. Armitage waiting to receive him, and it was with no little pleasure that he heard of the safety of the guests, whom he had defended so bravely. Walter was almost equally interested in hearing how adroitly Mr. Armitage had succeeded in deceiving the leaders of the mob, making them believe their victims were secreted in his house, and appealing to them for mercy, and restraining them from violence by threats of summary justice, if any harm was done (in which he was supported by Mr. Wynn and the other two gentlemen), until, at length, believing Mr. May must be at a safe distance, they had given way, and permitted the house to be searched.

Of course, the offensive persons were not found, and the wrath of the mob was loudly expressed at their disappointment, and might have led to some injury being inflicted upon the opposing party, only that those who had excited them against Mr. May knew enough to be sure that they could not, with equal safety, proceed to violent measures against one of their fellow-citizens; and, after some trouble and ineffectual threats of vengeance, the rabble was dispersed, and the gentlemen,

---

1 Phrase from Alexander Pope (1688–1744): "The old project of a window in the bosom, to render the Soul of man visible, is what every honest friend has manifold reason to wish for ...," *Letters of Mr. Alexander Pope, and Several of His Friends* (1737).

2 Shakespeare, *As You Like It,* 2.7.139–40.

who had, until now, remained with Mr. Armitage, thought it safe to return to their own homes.

The next morning, Walter's first care was to go to the Triangle, where he found the negroes wondering at their mistress's absence, and at the strange rumors that had begun to reach them concerning its cause. Without much delay or trouble—for they had little to carry—they were put in marching order, and, having hired a responsible white person to go with them to the station, four miles distant, where they were to take the afternoon train of cars, Walter saw them start on their journey. He had previously made arrangements at the hotel to have Venus and the child, with the luggage, sent on in the same conveyance, so that he was now at liberty to attend to his own affairs.

The negroes marched silently away, with many a lingering look backward through the trees at the place they were leaving deserted. Wretched as had been their situation there, it was yet their *home*, and, notwithstanding the kindness they had of late experienced, many of them had a secret suspicion that they were to be sold, and that even a worse fate than they had known was in reserve for them. They were timid and easily depressed, and they had been the victims of so much deceit and injustice that they dreaded any change.

From the Triangle, Walter went directly to Wynn Hall, and to the library, where he knew he should find his uncle at that hour. Having recounted his adventures, and talked over the matter of the riot, and again thanked Mr. Wynn for the very efficient aid he had rendered, he inquired for Mabel and his aunt.

"Mrs. Wynn has gone out this morning to see an old friend who is visiting in the neighborhood," was the reply, "and Mabel, I think, you will find in the parlor. She was there when I looked in an hour ago. She seems dull today, and I think it may be because Col. Ross's name has been mixed up with this affair."

"Col. Ross—what had he to do with it?" said Walter, so intent upon whatever concerned Ida in the most remote degree, that he did not notice the inference his uncle intended him to make from this conjunction of names.

Mr. Wynn saw this, and though he thought it high time this game of cross-purposes should cease, he condescended to no further effort at enlightening him, but replied, carelessly,

"I don't know that he had anything to do with it. I have wondered a little who it was that put the ball in motion."

"I have thought of that myself," said Walter. "It does seem as if there must have been some private malice at the beginning, for the sensitiveness of the vigilance committee is usually satisfied with ordering all suspected persons out of town, unless they have done something worse than Mr. May or Ida were accused of doing. They do not generally go to the length of exciting a mob for the purpose."

"You should not speak sneeringly of the vigilance committee," said Mr. Wynn, somewhat sternly. "It is a very useful and proper institution, and the gentlemen who compose it should be supported in their measures. But this rising of the rabble is another matter. It is easily enough effected, but there must be an exciting cause."

"I hardly know what the cause could have been," said Walter, thoughtfully. "Ida had the misfortune to offend you, and it became public; but you, of course, had no hand in it."

Mr. Wynn replied coldly, for he was irritated by the liberty Walter had taken in this reference, "Thank you, sir; you do me the honor, then, to believe that I am not mean and revengeful."

Walter smiled, and bit his lip, in a little confusion. "Excuse me," he said; "the words escaped me unconsciously—"

"No apology is needed. You will find Mabel in the parlor," interrupted Mr. Wynn, turning back to his books. Walter saw that he was to "consider himself dismissed," and he proceeded at once to the parlor.

Mabel stood with her face half turned towards the door. She was dressed in a robe of dark silk, with wide open sleeves, that showed her exquisitely moulded arms, white as snow. Her soft, shining hair was braided with classic simplicity round her queenly head, and some sprays of the yellow jasmine were arranged with careless gracefulness among its folds. A bouquet of these flowers stood on the mantelpiece, against which she was leaning; and, as one of her delicate little hands toyed with their petals, the fragrance shaken from the honeyed cups filled the room. To the end of his life, Walter never inhaled that delicious perfume without having recalled to him this memorable interview.

She had heard him go into the library, and had been awaiting him with restless impatience. When he entered the parlor she turned quickly, and, without waiting for any of the common salutations, she said, in a sharp, mocking tone, while her blue eyes darkened with wrath,

"Well, sir, so you have carried your 'ladie love' to a place of safety, at last. I congratulate you."

He looked at her in amazement. He thought she was jealous of Ida, and replied,

"Surely, you are not angry, because I have been saving Ida from insult and danger—perhaps from death. O, Mabel!"

"And given her your heart as recompense for all she has sacrificed to the cause of freedom!" she added, mockingly.

A sudden change passed over Walter's face, as he heard this unexpected charge, and, retreating a few steps, he leaned against the corner of the mantelpiece opposite her, and shaded his eyes with his hand.

"Speak!" she exclaimed, impatiently, as he made no reply; "speak—deny it all—flatter me with smooth words, which you long to contradict as you utter them;—go on with your hypocrisy and your deceit, as you have been going on so long; play one more scene of falsehood, and make yourself believe you are an honorable man! It must be easy for you now, after so much practice!"

"Mabel, cease!" said Walter, suddenly, in a low tone, so firm and authoritative, that for a moment it stilled the tempest of her anger. He was very pale, even to his lips, which trembled a little, though all the lines of his face were hushed and calm; and his eyes, which no longer avoided hers, had an expression of patience and gentleness.

"I have wronged you," he said, "and it has cost me many bitter hours; but there should be a limit to your criminations. I was dazzled, fascinated by your wonderful beauty and grace. I thought I loved—I *did* love you, truly, fervently, with all the romance which has not yet died out of my nature, with the unquestioning faith of a worshipper at the shrine of his idol. When I told you of my hopes and you did not check them, I was in a bewilderment of enthusiastic delight—I was in a dream. Do you know what awakened me?"

"Ida's perfections, I suppose," replied she, sarcastically.

"You mistake, then. It was yourself, your own words and actions. Pardon me, Mabel, but the shock was too rude and sudden ever to be forgotten, and my blind eyes were too surely enlightened ever to be willfully deceived. I saw that we were wholly unsuited to each other—that I should make you miserable, and you could not make me happy. Since then—"

"Do you suppose I did not know all this?" she said, interrupting him; "do you suppose I was deceived by your empty professions, by your hypocrisies—"

"Hold, Mabel! I have been no hypocrite! When I adored you, I told you so in language enthusiastic as my love; but when my heart found no home in yours, the demonstrations of such love ceased. I loved you with the old brotherly affection I had felt for you from infancy, and I felt grateful to you that you had responded to a warmer feeling, but I often wondered you did not notice my change of manner. I have been no hypocrite! I earnestly strove to love you. I was pledged to you, and that pledge I would, I will redeem."

"I scorn you, and your pledges!" said she, passionately. "Do you suppose I would share a divided heart? Do you think your love so necessary to me, that I would humble myself so meanly? No! I would have spurned you from me long ago, only that I had a purpose to serve, a revenge to secure!"

"You have secured it!" said Walter, gloomily. "Believe me, there is no sorrow keener than that a man feels, when he begins to doubt the worthiness of the one he has loved best."

The color deepened in Mabel's cheek as she heard this, and she exclaimed, with exasperated tones,

"I had a revenge more sure and more lasting than that! My ultimate purpose has, indeed, been defeated, but, nevertheless, the blow struck hard; and you felt it, and *she* felt it, though you knew not the source from whence it came."

"What do you mean?" exclaimed Walter, in amazement.

Mabel did not reply for a moment; and the expression of her face changed from triumph to doubt, as if she was uncertain what to say, and again he repeated his question.

"Can you not think what?" she said, averting her eyes from his face. "Has nothing happened, of late, that you could not wholly account for—nothing that surprised and alarmed you?"

"Nothing," answered he, "except that riot in town; and you, O Mabel! surely, you could have had nothing to do with that!"

"Couldn't I!" she exclaimed, defiantly, her momentary hesitation vanishing. "I tell you it was easy to do. There is a lever here, which the weakest hand can seize, to move the deadliest forces. It needed but a few words dropped here and there, in seeming carelessness; an insinuation, now and then, that the plantations around the Triangle were hardly safe with their new neighbors; an apparently reluctant admission of what was really the fact, that our family discipline had been meddled with, and obnoxious sentiments and seditious words uttered. O, it was easy to make the girl you love an outcast from society! I gloried in it! I laughed slyly to see how the whole neighborhood were unconsciously working out my designs!"

She laughed as she spoke. Her beautiful lips were wreathed over her pearly teeth with a cold malignity, and her head was thrown back proudly.

"Mabel, you are crazy! You cannot mean what you say!" exclaimed Walter, his horror overcoming even his astonishment and his anger.

"I do mean it!" she cried. "I hate her! I hate you both! I am only sorry that my father's foolish ideas of honor led him to interfere and prevent all that might have happened."

Walter made a quick step forward, and seized both her hands with a grasp that almost crushed the delicate and jeweled fingers. She struggled to free herself, but in vain. He was unconscious of the force he exerted, and, holding her firmly, he looked straight into her eyes, exclaiming, in great excitement,

"Tell me, did you incite the movers of that mob?—did you mean to devote to insult, and pain, and death, that pure and gentle girl, who was like an angel of mercy in this house? Tell me!"

"I did!" she replied, defiantly. "I tell you I hated her! What should I care what became of her?"

"Then may God forgive you, for in your heart you have been a murderess!"

He dropped her hands as he said this, and, turning away from her, began walking across the room. He was inexpressibly shocked and surprised. Like the man in the old stories of enchantment, who beheld his peerless bride transformed into a hideous and disgusting reptile, he shrank in dismay from this blighting revelation of the worst passions of human nature in a breast which he had been striving to believe the home of its best virtues.

Mabel made no reply. The burst of passion had spent itself, and the solemnity of his look and manner, as he uttered those last words—the sudden invocation which arraigned her before that awful tribunal, where the purest must stand abashed—penetrated the whirl and the cloud of evil feelings which surrounded her soul, and, like a ray of divine light, showed her its blackness. She leaned her face upon her arm, as it rested on the mantelpiece, and stood silent and trembling.

Thus some moments passed. Then the sound of carriage wheels was heard, and Mrs. Wynn, arriving at home, sprang lightly up the piazza steps, as through the window she caught sight of Walter, and entered the parlor.

She looked pale and harassed, but her face lighted with joy as she clasped her nephew's hand, who hastily strove to hide his agitation, as he met her.

"O, I am so glad to see you!" she said. "Did you leave Ida well?"

"Very well; only somewhat shaken by what she had undergone."

"You look worn out yourself," replied Mrs. Wynn, anxiously. "Are you ill?"

"Not ill in body," said Walter, trying to smile, as he saw her fears.

"But annoyed and distressed, as we all have been! Poor little Ida! What a trying life she has had! I never loved her so well as since she came back this time; and sometimes I fear that, in former years, I made more difference than I should between her and Mabel. But where is Mabel? I thought she was here when I came in."

They looked around, but Mabel had vanished.

"Do not trouble yourself about that, my dear aunt," said Walter, more cheerfully. "Ida has a grateful heart, and she loves you. She often spoke of you to me with the strongest expressions of interest and thanks."

"I am glad of it," replied Mrs. Wynn, and then, casting a quick glance around, and drawing nearer to Walter, she said, "Sometimes of late, I have thought that, through you, she might be more nearly connected with me."

"Don't speak of that, pray don't," said he, starting as if from a sword-thrust, and averting his face.

"I will not speak of it, dear," she said, in a low voice; "but I have wished to tell you something about Mabel. I should have spoken about it weeks ago, but I was forbidden to do so by Mr. Wynn. What his reasons were I know not, but, at any rate, I shall disregard them now, for it is not right to keep you longer in ignorance."

"What can you mean to say?" exclaimed Walter, looking at her anxiously.

"Mabel is to be married in about a month to Col. Ross."

"And she dared accuse *me* of unfaithfulness!" he cried.

Mrs. Wynn looked sad, and her voice faltered. "It has been a great pain to me," she said, "that things have come to be as they are. You have always been dear to me as a son, and I hoped once that you might be really such. Now I see that perhaps you could not have been happy with Mabel. It is humiliating to a mother to speak of the faults of her own child, but I must say I have been grieved that she has been willing to deceive you, and keep you in ignorance of her change of feeling towards you. Perhaps you will forgive her for my sake."

"My dear aunt" said Walter, taking her hand kindly, "Mabel has not been wholly to blame in that regard; and, though I would never have acknowledged it to any human being but for what I have heard this morning, it is but right that I should tell you that I also have changed."

"I am glad to hear you say so. Now we shall all be happy and at peace again, as we used to be, and Ida shall be to me as a daughter. The hope that it might end thus, has been my only comfort through these stormy times we have had of late," said the gentle little lady, with a smile and a sigh.

"Did Mabel tell you of her engagement this morning?" she added, after a short pause.

"No," replied he, with a sudden change of countenance; "but she told me something else, which equally abrogated my obligations to her."

Mrs. Wynn looked up inquiringly, but just then they saw Col. Ross coming up the avenue.

"I do not wish to meet him this morning," he said, hurriedly; "And, as I wish to return to Oaklands today—"

"So soon!" exclaimed his aunt.

"I must go. Do not urge me to remain. I may not see you again for some weeks, but Mabel must tell you why."

He shook hands with her cordially, his handsome face lighting again with the affection and respect he felt for one who had been to him almost like a mother.

"My dear, dear boy," she said, "may you be happy!"

"We will try to think 'all's well, that ends well,'"[1] he said, with forced gaiety, kissing her hand, but when he turned away, his eyes were dim with not unmanly tears. Her tender and unselfish love had touched his heart.

---

1 Title of a comedy by Shakespeare.

CHAPTER XVII

"Hark, the loud-voiced bells,
Stream on the world around,
With the full wind, as it swells
Seas of sound.
It is a Voice that calls to onward years—
Turn back, and when delight has fled away,
Look thro' the evening mists of mortal tears
On this immortal Day.'"
FREDERIC TENNYSON[1]

It was one of the most balmy and delicious days of early summer, when Walter Varian found himself opening the iron gate, and ascending the stone steps of Mr. Morton's house in Harrisburg.

He had followed the Mays to Augusta, but they had already left that place for Savannah, and, knowing there was little probability of overtaking them before they sailed for New York, he had preferred returning home, and taking one of the Charleston boats for Baltimore. Thus, the very day after Ida's arrival at the house of her friend Bessie, one from whom she imagined herself severed for years, stood waiting to be received there.

The servant who answered this ring at the doorbell, ushered him into a tastefully-furnished parlor, at the further end of which a lady sat sewing by a bay window that opened into a large garden. The moment Walter saw her, he had no difficulty in recognizing her, from Ida's oft-repeated description; and as she rose, in some embarrassment to greet one whom she thought an entire stranger, he offered his hand, and said pleasantly,

"This is Mrs. Morton, I am sure; but I presume I shall have to introduce Walter Varian."

At this name, Mrs. Morton's confusion vanished, and was replaced by a cordial getting and a smile of hearty welcome that made them friends at once.

"I am very glad to see you," she said. "I feel as if I had known you for years. Allow me to introduce to you my only son. He has the honor to bear your name," she added, smiling, and pointed with a mother's pride to an infant a few months old, who lay in

---

1 From "The Bridal," first published in 1854, by Frederick Tennyson (1807–98), brother of the poet laureate Alfred, Lord Tennyson (1809–92). This contemporary popular poem foreshadows the chapter's happy ending.

state on the sofa beside her, supported by cushions. With the puzzled and undecided expression young gentlemen usually assume in such trying circumstances, Walter looked down on the small specimen of humanity, who, with his eyes opened to their widest, and his mouth puckered to its smallest capacity, was, at that moment, apparently deeply absorbed in a philosophical examination of the mystery of his own little chubby hands.

"He is a very wise-looking fellow just now, certainly," said he, uncertain exactly in what terms he was expected to express his admiration. "I was not aware that I had the honor of possessing a namesake here."

"Ida named him," said Mrs. Morton; and smiling, as she saw Walter's face flush and his eyes sparkle at this information, she added, "Ida has gone into the garden with the children. Will you stay here while I go to find her, or will you seek her there yourself?"

"I will look for her, if you please," replied he, eagerly.

"You will probably find her in the summerhouse at the foot of the garden," she said, as she opened the window to give him egress. "You can follow this broad path till you come to the pond, and then, at your right hand, you will see them if they are there."

Thanking her, he hastened down the path, which was shaded by fruit trees, and trimly bordered by a low hedge of boxwood, until he came to a high open fence of woven wire, that surrounded a circular artificial pond, in the centre of which grew different species of aquatic plants, some of which were now in blossom. He took little heed of these things, however, at this moment, for, as his eyes turned in the direction Mrs. Morton had indicated, his hurried steps were arrested by his admiration of the scene that met his view.

The summerhouse, which was simply a circular lattice work, covered with running roses, now in the full glory of their season, stood on a grass plat at one side of the pond. Three openings had been left for doors, and near one of these a beautiful little girl was playing with the mulatto boy, Elsie's child, whose black, wavy hair and clear dark skin, contrasted finely with the golden curls and delicate complexion of his playmate.

Within the soft green shadow of the arbor, Ida sat on a rustic bench, and a girl, of some five years old, stood behind her, busily employed in ornamenting her hair with the half-open buds which she pulled from the rose vines beside her. The child had removed Ida's comb, and the silken tresses, crowned with flowers, fell waving and rippling around her slight form, and, mingling with the ringlets which always shaded her fair brow, half hid her face, as she sat leaning it upon her hand, with her eyes resting on the floor, and a sad, weary expression upon her features, that was poorly in keeping with the quiet beauty and cheerfulness of her surroundings. A sudden exclamation from the little hairdresser caused her to look up, and she sprang to her feet, trembling all over, as she saw who it was that now stood in the doorway, and held out his hands towards her.

"Walter here!" she cried, in amazement.

"Yes, Walter, here," he answered, taking both her hands, and gazing into her eyes, with a glad eagerness that brought a bright color to the cheek that was before so pale. "Walter here, to tell you that he is free—honorably free—from all that could ever keep him from your side."

Then followed a few rapid words. Walter never knew exactly what he said, or how he said it, but he always retained a delightful consciousness of the moment when Ida's head sank on his shoulder, and from beneath that veil of hair some faintly breathed syllables assured him of all he wished to know.

Meantime the children had fled coyly from the unknown intruder, and now stood at the angle of the path, peeping slyly from behind the boxwood to catch a glimpse of what was going on in the arbor. Their mother's voice soon called them away.

"O mother! He *kissed* her, he *did*! That great big man, with hair all over his mouth, kissed Aunt Ida!" shouted the youngest, as she came near.

"Yes, and *she let him*!" chimed in the elder girl.

Mrs. Morton laughed heartily at the virtuous indignation expressed on the two young faces, and said, gaily,

"Why shouldn't he kiss her, if he wanted to? He is the best friend she has in the world."

"Is he?" said the eldest, thoughtfully, in a mollified tone; but the youngest exclaimed,

"O, ma! how *can* he be the *best*? He isn't her *father*!"

"You will know some time, little one," replied Mrs. Morton, laughing again; and taking little Alfred in her arms, she went with them into the house.

Unconscious of this juvenile criticism upon their conduct, forgetting even to notice that the children were gone, the lovers, sitting close together in the green, rose-scented arbor, breaking the charmed silences only by those low tones that are eloquent of the heart's purest happiness, were enjoying such moments as come but once to any mortal. Golden moments! which in fleeting leave a memory lingering and precious, like those rare perfumes contained in crystal tubes that must be shattered past remedy before the hidden essence can be exhaled.

"I cannot ask you to unite your fate with mine, now, at once," said Walter, at length; "for when I have done that which we both think I ought to do for my people at Oaklands, I shall be nearly penniless, and I cannot ask your father for his child, when I have no home to offer her. By the way," he added, suddenly, "where is your father?"

"He went directly on from New York to Ohio, where his agent has been buying some land on which our colony are to be located. Fortunately he had just concluded the purchase when father telegraphed to him; so we were driven away from the Triangle just in the right moment, you see."

"No thanks to that hateful mob, though!" said Walter, looking grave for a moment. "But I hope the purchase is sufficiently extensive to admit some of my negroes, for I shall want to dispose of a few in that way. The majority can take care of themselves, in various ways, and may as well begin at once to do so. They are bright enough, and will soon learn how to adapt themselves to new situations. There is nothing like the idea and the hope of freedom to awaken and expand a man's intellect. I shall furnish each with a little capital, and aid them in finding employment, and then I shall settle myself in some city in the free States. I can no longer live where a man is mobbed for expressing his honest opinions."

"You have not yet forgiven that tumultuous rallying of the people to protect the beloved 'institution' from the touch of our rash hands," said Ida, looking up gaily.

"And never shall forgive it!" he replied; and she silently wondered at the gloomy and thoughtful expression that gathered over his face as he spoke. She did not yet know what it was that made that recollection so peculiarly exciting and unpleasant. But he shook off his sad thoughts in a moment, and, responding to her happy mood, said cheerfully,

"Where should you like best to live? I will take an office anywhere you bid me. 'The world is all before us, where to choose,'[1] and I will compel dame Fortune to favor me with smiles."

"Presumptuous youth! Do not be too sanguine," said Ida, "for that lady's smiles are proverbially hard to be won."

---

1 From the closing lines of Milton's *Paradise Lost,* Book 12, the concluding image of Adam and Eve setting forth from Eden into the wide world.

"After the winning of today," replied he, "I may be pardoned for any amount of self-confidence; and besides, I have the secret that unlocks her treasures. She is not represented as a very industrious lady herself, but she likes to see folks work, and I will work—O, Ida! How I will work—to win a home for you, and honor and fame for your husband! You shall be proud of me yet, dearest."

"I am proud of you now," said she with charming *naïveté*, as she looked up into his face, glowing with happiness and hope. "You seem," she added a moment after, "to have full faith in that maxim which used to seem so mighty long to me, when our governess at Wynn Hall made me write in my copy-book—do you remember?—'Nothing is denied to patient and well-directed effort.'"

"I remember," said Walter; "and I remember also how she scolded you one day because you upset the ink over that same copy-book."

"And how you took my part, and insisted it was not carelessness," added Ida, laughing. "Ah, Walter, you have been my champion many times in the battle of life!"

The arm that was around her waist clasped her with a yet closer pressure, and Walter replied,

"You needed a champion badly enough when I first knew you. What a little creature you were then, Ida! Do you know, when you were sitting here this afternoon, the moment before you saw me, with your hair falling around your shoulders, and crowned with rosebuds, you reminded me, more than ever, of the little girl I saw hiding among the kalmias on that mountainside?"

"I should think so!" said Ida. "Little Bessie is never so happy as when she can disorder my hair as much as possible. You should have announced your coming, so that I might have arranged my disheveled locks in a more becoming array."

"There could be nothing more becoming—don't touch them," he added, arresting her hand as she was gathering her hair into a knot. "You have such soft, beautiful hair, that it is a pleasure to see it; and even if it were not, I should like anything that brought back so vividly the first moments I spent with you. How often, since then, have I wished I had preserved those flowers you gave me, that I might have a tangible memorial of 'little Lizzy'; and that hour I spent beside the mountain stream!"

"I am more fortunate than you—I have such a memento," said Ida; and, unclasping a small locket which she always wore attached to her watch-chain, she showed him, carefully set within, a small gold coin, pierced with a hole in the center. "Do you remember it?" she asked.

Years had passed since he thought of it, but he recognized it instantly.

"Have you kept it so long?" he exclaimed.

"Do you suppose I would ever have parted with it?" cried Ida, earnestly. "The hour when you gave me this marked an era in my changeful life. You came to me, that bright afternoon, like some puissant prince of fairy legends, breaking the spell that bound me, and giving me a revelation of the happy life which I had lost and forgotten. I could not tell you all the springs of thought that began to move confusedly through the darkness of my brain, as I watched you ride away so free and bold, so full of youth and energy. I was never afterwards the same quiet, dreamy child I was before."

"How little either of us imagined, then, of all that was to follow from that meeting!" said Walter, thoughtfully. "What a difference between then and now!"

"Yes," answered Ida, "when I look back over the past, I can almost feel the clasping of the Divine hand that has been leading me through paths which I knew not, and has at last brought me to a place of rest, so blessed that I hardly know how to believe my own happiness. My life has been strangely eventful, but now—"

"Now," interrupted Walter, pressing his lips on the eyelids that dropped over her tearful eyes, "Now your trials are all over; for, if there is power in human will and human love, your whole future life shall be free from care or sorrow."

FINIS.

Appendix A: "Who Wrote Ida May?": The Sentimental Antislavery Novel and Genre Formation

1. From the *Evening Post* (New York), November–December 1854

[The New York *Evening Post*, under its celebrated editor William Cullen Bryant (1794–1878), received an advance copy of *Ida May* from Bryant's friend, publisher, and marketing genius J.C. Derby (1818–92) and made a strong initial claim for authorship of *Ida May* by Harriet Beecher Stowe (1811–96), whose *Uncle Tom's Cabin* had appeared two years earlier. The *Post* presented—on its front page—four columns of extracts from *Ida May* and an early review. A week later, it printed a letter from the book's publisher—Phillips, Sampson and Company—stating that Stowe was not the author. The *Post* retracted, but the debut made *Ida May* newsworthy, and the hunt for its author continued.]

a. "New Novel by Mrs. Stowe," 11 November 1854

"Ida May, a new novel by Mrs. Stowe!" the reader will say, as he turns to the advertisement of the book in another part of this paper. "Why is it announced from the pen of 'Mary Langdon,' a writer unknown to fame? How do you know that Mrs. Stowe wrote it?"

We have read it; and no one who follows our example will have any doubt of it. No other living author could have written it. Besides, every circumstance connected with its publication would have justified the suspicion, if the internal evidence were less conclusive. It was natural that Mrs. Stowe should recur to a field of literary labor which she has made her own. The title indicates a purpose to meet some of the criticism which *Uncle Tom* received, and no unknown writer would have taken the precaution to publish simultaneously in London and New York, as the author of *Ida May* has done. But why, then, it may be asked, does it not bear Mrs. Stowe's name, which would insure its success, whether it had any merit or not? Anyone can readily imagine reasons for this disguise; but it is not our purpose to discuss them. They doubtless were sufficient in her eyes, and that is enough.

Suffice it to say, that *Ida May* is no unworthy successor of *Uncle Tom's Cabin*. As a novel, it is more rounded and perfect in every part, and has few or none of the remarks of hasty composition and the ordinary clap-trap commonplaces of fiction which were apparent, particularly in the concluding chapters, of its renowned forerunner—faults owing, doubtless, to the mode of publication, in weekly installments, adopted by the author in the case of the latter story. Neither is it at all inferior, as a picture of the varied phases of the social institutions at the South, where the scenes are laid—although it touches upon points which were not so fully illustrated in *Uncle Tom's Cabin*, especially that singular yet unavoidable suspicion and sensitiveness manifested by slave-owners at the least show of interference in the peculiar arrangements of their servile system.

b. "Mrs. Stowe's Anti-Slavery Novels," 11 November 1854

On the outside of today's paper will be found a synopsis, with extended selections, of *Ida May,* a novel which bears satisfactory internal evidence of being from the pen of the author of *Uncle Tom's Cabin*. Its publication on the 15th has already been advertised, but this morning we learn that the sudden increase of bookseller's orders has compelled a postponement to the 22nd, in order to supply enough copies for the first "go round." This would indicate that the public or the book trade have made up their minds as to the authorship.

It is now something like four years since the appearance in the *National Era* of *Uncle Tom's Cabin*. Little the author or her reader then supposed that before many months its circulation would only be bounded by the limits of the civilized and reading world—that it would be reprinted in every civilized language—in every possible form—and, in fact, control the action, sway the sympathies of millions, of every class and condition. Certainly this much has been done, and we need only refer to one proof of it—in the development of anti-slavery sentiment in our country. Mrs. Stowe's work appeared about the time of the Fugitive Slave law of 1850, a law the hardships of which were manifest, in its actual operation, to but few communities at the North. The practical sense of our people is always too ready to acquiesce in small interferences with the rights of humanity, provided a cessation of agitation is the result. But the vivid, almost pictorial, delineation of the poor returning fugitive's fate went to every family in the land, roused the woman-power, and diffused a discontent with not alone the Fugitive Slave law, but with the general compromise policy, which needed but the provocation of the Nebraska fraud to blaze forth and consume everything before it.[1] The political events of the present year, including the extinguishment of Messrs Douglas and Pierce in their respective states, are emphatic instances of its universal operation.

But besides the general good thus effected by Mrs. Stowe in enlarging the domain of the sympathies of a world, and the immediate effect in the political revolution of our country, she can lay claim to the credit of having inaugurated a new and characteristic species of historical fiction. Years, perhaps centuries hence, when the institution of slavery shall have like the institution of European feudalism, disappeared from the [landscape] by natural and unavoidable [changes], leaving possibly some traces of its past existence in the laws, character and habits of the people, the historian will look for a representation of the former customs and institutions, the daily life that once characterized our vast southern country, in the pages of *Uncle Tom* and *Ida May*, as we now look for a reflex of the days of chivalry in the chronicles of Froissart or the novels of Scott and Dumas.[2] And we venture to say there will be quite as much foundation for confidence in the former as in the latter.

---

1 The writer refers to the Kansas-Nebraska Bill, its architect Senator Stephen Douglas (1813–61), and its vocal supporter Franklin Pierce (1804–69), the fourteenth president of the United States. Douglas and Pierce were compromise Democrats, supporters of "popular sovereignty" (i.e., territorial autonomy in determining slavery policies) and the expansion of the United States into the West. Their efforts to compromise with pro-slavery advocates led to the "extinguishment" of Democratic Party support in their respective states, Illinois and Massachusetts.

2 *Jean Froissart's Chronicle* is a fourteenth-century prose narrative of the Hundred Years' War. Sir Walter Scott (1771–1832) of Scotland and Alexandre Dumas (1802–70) of France wrote historical novels set in their nations' chivalric past.

c. "Ida May—Not by Mrs. Stowe," 17 November 1854

To the Editors of the New York Evening Post:

The publishers are sensible of the compliment which critics have paid to *Ida May*, in attributing the authorship to Mrs. Stowe. The pen that sketched the grand outlines of *Uncle Tom* might surely a second time delight the world; but it is due to all parties to say that *Ida May* is the production of an author as yet unknown to fame.—Phillips, Sampson, & Co., Boston, November 15.

d. "Who Wrote Ida May?," 6 December 1854

We were remarking only a few months since that the most popular living novelists, in the strictest sense of that term, were women; that the fictions of American females had attained a wider circulation than those of either sex of any other nation. The author of *Ida May* strengthens that supremacy, for it is admitted by the publishers that this is her first book, and that she is a recruit to the already strong array of talented women engaged among us in writing fiction. Why her name is longer suppressed we can only conjecture. It is probably that her relations with the South are of such a nature as to indispose her to any more personal notoriety than is inevitable.

2. From the *Boston Daily Atlas*, November 1854

[The *Boston Daily Atlas* newspaper refuted the claim that Harriet Beecher Stowe wrote *Ida May*, arguing that this new novel was more realistic.]

a. 9 November 1854

We regard *Ida May* as a permanent success, both as a work of fiction, and as a picture of slavery as it really is. We regard *Ida May* as by far the most decidedly home thrust that has yet been made upon the institution of slavery, and one that will be all the more telling in its influence, because it will be found to contain no exaggerated pictures, and nothing that can be pointed to as a caricature of every day realities.

b. 16 November 1854

The publishers of *Ida May* have been so flooded with orders from the trade, from all directions, for the forthcoming work, that they have been compelled once more to postpone its issue.

By the way, the *New York Evening Post* very absurdly attributes this tale to Mrs. Stowe, the author of *Uncle Tom's Cabin*. The absurdity of this supposition should have made the writer at least less positive in his assertion of a supposition so wholly unsupported by evidence as this must have been. The very fact that it was issued anonymously, was, of itself, enough to show the improbability of the supposition, for the author of *Uncle Tom* is not given to hiding her light under a bushel, and the success of her first work, published in her own name, would furnish sufficient reason why it should not be withheld from a second. Besides, there is no resemblance in the two books, excepting that both are on the subject of slavery. *Ida May* is, to our perceptions, a far more correct representation of the institution, is much more life-like and natural in its dialogue, and will give the public a more exact idea of Southern society, slavery, and the influences it sheds around.

We never have been an admirer of *Uncle Tom*, not from any partiality for the atrocious institution against which it was aimed, but because it is a caricature rather than a true picture. Like the hospital which together collects the lame, the halt, the blind, and the diseased members of society, *Uncle Tom's Cabin* groups into one view the accumulated horrors that are scattered over a wide field and do not naturally come together. To us this has ever been a grave objection, that it is not true to the reality. Not that each picture may not be true, by itself, but that they cannot be found in such close proximity. Whatever *Ida May* may want in its power or its artistic excellence, in comparison with Mrs. Stowe's book, we think it quite makes up in its fidelity to the realities of slavery, and therefore we really believe that the advocates of the peculiar institution will have more cause to apprehend the effects upon the public of such a work, because it is so exactly true to the realities of slavery. Of course it was not written by Mrs. Stowe, but by a lady as yet unknown to fame, and who will, in all probability, whatever may be the success of her work, consent to have the veil removed.

3. From the *Portland Transcript*, 25 November 1854

[Another newspaper reviewer, this time for the *Portland Transcript*, favorably compares Pike's literary style to the wide scope utilized by Stowe for *Uncle Tom's Cabin*.]

A new anti-slavery novel, the authorship of which has been incorrectly attributed to Mrs. Stowe. To our mind it bears no marks of Mrs. Stowe's pen. It has less vivacious energy and humor than *Uncle Tom*, while the style is more calm and correct. It has more unity as a story, but not so comprehensive a grasp of the whole subject of slavery. As an exposition of the evils of that institution it is powerfully written, and must deepen the effect produced by *Uncle Tom*. It is a book that will be read far and wide, and will excite the deepest interest in all who read it.

4. From the *Boston Evening Telegraph*, November 1854

[No newspaper wrote more on *Ida May*, or more decisively in defense of its genre, than the *Boston Evening Telegraph*. Its editor, Richard Hildreth (1807–65), had written a sentimental antislavery novel on a similar theme, *Archy Moore* (1836; republished as *The White Slave* in 1852), and used his daily paper to argue for the power of fiction to effect political ends.]

a. 13 November 1854

Not having yet read *Ida May*, we express no opinion as to its authorship, nor yet any opinion of our own as to its merits; but the general verdict by the numerous critics who have read it, places it far below *Uncle Tom*. Their opinion, however, has less weight with us than that of a lady to whom, not having time to read it ourselves, we deputed the reading of the book. She expressed, after getting through a few chapters, great admiration of the artistic skill and dramatic power of the writer, but after having finished it, upon being told that some persons thought it equal to *Uncle Tom*—"*Uncle Tom*!" she exclaimed, rolling up eyes—"Why my dear sir, *Ida May* is nothing but a love story?"

b. 21 November 1854

The unsophisticated writer of the book notices in the *Courier*
thinks that the plot of *Ida May* is "unnatural, insomuch as it
principally turns upon the seizing of a white child, selling her
and keeping her in slavery. The treatment of the child by the
original kidnappers, as depicted by the author, is too revolting to
read."—"Everyone who knows with what jealousy the difference
between the races is kept up in the South, will only read with
an incredulousness which destroys all a novel's charm, the story
of *Ida May* and her adventures as a slave." Those newspaper
writers who are so continually prating about the exaggerations
and improbabilities of the anti-slavery people, are as a general
thing grossly ignorant of the slavery system. Living in a culpable
indifference to its horror, they gladly embrace the suggestion of
the slaveholders themselves, that the stories are exaggerated and
improbable. There is nothing improbable in the story of the kidnapping of Ida May. Such events not infrequently occur. As to
the jealousy with which Southern people keep up the difference
between the races—that is too broad a joke for this day. The
Courier proceeds to say that if the author wrote for money, she
will probably succeed; if for fame, she will fail, for few people will
read it more than once—(few people, we suppose, read even the
Boston *Courier's* editorials "more than once")—if to keep up a
sectional excitement, the success of the book will be for evil and
not for good. The *Courier* says:—"The negro conversation of the
book is clumsy, and is not like the talk which Southern negroes
use." This reminds us of the critic who censured the supposed
drawing of a kitten in a picture-seller's window, but was con-
siderably chop-fallen when the pictures stretched out a paw. A
number of readers who have the most thorough acquaintance
with plantation life assure us that the fidelity with which the negro dialect is imitated is really wonderful. Probably the *Courier's*
ideas of negro character have been derived from the pleasing and
natural performances of the white Ethiopians[1] wherewith our
boys are so highly delighted. The writer winds up by saying:

"However, the book will be read extensively, as the publisher's
orders indicate. It has sufficient romance about it to make it
interesting, is well conducted from beginning to end, and some
will go so far as to believe that every word of it is gospel truth, for
we know a lady in this city who seriously asked a New Orleans

---

1 I.e., minstrel show performers in blackface.

gentleman if he was 'ever acquainted with Legree,'[1] supposing that Mrs. Stowe's monster was an actual creature of flesh and blood."

The *Courier* is getting altogether too literal. It must not be so peremptory in its demands upon authors. It is doubtful whether Shakespeare could prove the existence as "an actual creature of flesh and blood" of Iago, or Falstaff, or Dogberry;[2] and though Dickens was accused by several Yorkshire schoolmasters of libeling them by his description of Squeers, yet probably no such person ever had an actual existence. Quilp is in some degree a myth, and so is Pecksniff.[3] So there are Legrees by the score and hundred, as monstrous as Mrs. Stowe's creation. Pro-slavery editors have only to study the questions they pretend to discuss, in order to cease their clamor about exaggerations.

c. "Ida May," 23 November 1854

Some newspaper writers, more careful to be consistent than to be just, have availed themselves of the recent publication of IDA MAY, to cast reflections on UNCLE TOM'S CABIN. Mary Langdon is true to life they say, but the creations of Mrs. Stowe, they would have us believe, find no counterparts in the actual workings of Southern Slavery. This is charged notwithstanding the fact that within a year or two the newspapers in the slave States have recorded several instances of barbarities practiced on slaves, equal in every respect to those of Simon Legree, and have designated their perpetrators by the very name of the monster who in Mrs. Stowe's work so offends the sensitiveness of some people. Perhaps it is not strange that writers who had decried a work which, making the tour of the globe and doing much towards forming a just public opinion, has proved a potent engine of reform, should now seek to keep alive any lurking prejudice against it. We are confident, however, that it is farthest from the desire of either the authoress or the publishers of *Ida May* that these masterpieces of fiction should be arrayed against each other. There is place for each in the literature of the country, and the anti-slavery movement. They belong to that sisterhood of pervasive influences which are every day combining the energies of free men against the slave system. They welcome other

---

1 The villainous slaveholder in *Uncle Tom's Cabin*.
2 Famously colorful characters in plays by William Shakespeare.
3 Treacherous characters in novels by Charles Dickens.

daughters of genius to join them in the beneficent work. Here there is and can be no monopoly. No historian, however great his fitness for his profession, and however complete his researches, can exclude others from traversing the same period. As long as men differ in emotions and mental habitudes, each surveys the field from his own point of view, and other explorers from other mounts of observation, may cast new light over the scene, and reveal new truth. So it is in every department of thought and enterprise. In *Ida May* may be seen the cruel wrongs which accompany the respectabilities of slavery, and are the necessary incidents of the system, however much they may be deprecated by those who inflict them. In *Uncle Tom*, side by side with lighter shades, with a dramatic power hardly inferior to Shakespeare's, are portrayed those darker inhumanities, which, in spite of all delusive theories about slavery as distinct from its abuses, are in our age and country a part of it.

d. 24 November 1854

IDA MAY.—We see that many of our contemporaries in their notices of this book speak of it as attractive *in spite* of its pro-slavery character. They consider slavery a "threadbare subject"; some even deprecate lending the graces of fiction to "controversial themes," and deplore the attempt to revive "sectional feelings." But the field of the novelist is a broad one; his mission is not merely to amuse: no topics are interdicted; and the writer who can succeed in making a story the vehicles for ideas which shall strengthen whatever is pure and noble in our natures, will deserve the thanks of mankind.

These quietists must understand that this mighty question will be discussed even though they *are* tired to death of it. There is no peace for the country upon which so monstrous a curse is fastened.

We believe that IDA MAY is but one of a series of books which will successively electrify the reading public, and quicken the impulses of all right-thinking men and women.

Therefore, although the rescued slave is among the most lovely heroines of fiction, and, although the story, as such, is one of the most absorbing interest, yet it is as a careful argument against slavery, that we most value the book. The calmness of tone which pervades it wins our entire confidence. And as we see how in its best state the system demoralizes society, hardens the hearts of masters, and crushes those of slaves, we feel our resolutions grow to an invincible strength; we determine that in our generation we will do our utmost against the evil that threatens to destroy our country.

5. From the *Boston Daily Courier*, 14 December 1854

[An insider at James S. Pike's former newspaper, the *Boston Daily Courier*, confirms the author of *Ida May*, without disclosing her real name.]

The *New York Post* is wise not to hazard any very decided opinion as to the authorship of *Ida May*, since the failure of its attempt to fasten it upon Mrs. Stowe. We happen to know the authoress, and can assure the public and the *Post* not only that her name is not Carroll, but that she does not live in Baltimore, but in a certain town in Maine. We feel bound in honor not to divulge her name, since it was given to us under a pledge of secrecy, and reasons satisfactory to us were given for concealment. We think, however, no person capable of producing such a work as *Ida May* can long succeed in keeping her secret.

Appendix B: Contemporary Reviews

1. From the *Independent* (New York), 16 November 1854

[The New York *Independent* compares *Ida May* to a contemporary release by a Southern pro-slavery apologist from Boston, Nehemiah Adams (1806–78). Both Adams and Pike rested their authority on a few months' visit to the South.]

Ida May is the story of a white child, kidnapped and sold into slavery. It professes to embody "ideas and impressions received by the writer during a residence in the South." Thus, like Dr. Nehemiah Adams's new book, it is "a South-side view of slavery"—South side, not as being in full sympathy with the great Southern institution, but as having been taken under a Southern sun. Mary Langdon, whoever she may be, has seen the South, and in this story she gives us her representation of Southern society. The picture has lights as well as shades, but none can find in it any apology for slavery. It will help even the best informed to understand that subject better. Mary Langdon has observed "things actual" with a human and a Christian eye, and with no little insight into the philosophy of human nature.

We cannot but anticipate for this book a wide circulation; and we trust we shall hear from the author again.

2. From the *National Era*, 16 November 1854

[An abolitionist weekly, *The National Era* had published the initial run of *Uncle Tom's Cabin* as a serial in 1851–52.]

This book is another terrible blow at Slavery.... It is sufficient to know that, out of such materials, the writer has produced an anti-slavery novel, second in power only to *Uncle Tom's Cabin*. It is more artificial than that—deals more with extraordinary, but still possible, events—contains more unusual surprises and coincidences; still it keeps within the ordinary limits of verisimilitude. It does not follow in the track of Mrs.

Stowe. Its characters are its own, its incidents original, it brings into view aspects and workings of the slave system not touched upon in *Uncle Tom's Cabin*; and in one respect it must acknowledge relationship with the ordinary class of novels—it does not ignore the tender passion. From beginning to end, the destinies of Ida and Walter are linked by bonds that cannot be broken.

This work will have, and ought to have, a large circulation. It may tend to open the eyes of many Southern people whose hearts are deadened by custom to the evils of Slavery, and will certainly quicken and augment the anti-slavery sentiment of the free States.

3. From "Ida May, The Kidnapped White Slave," *Liberator*, 17 November 1854

[From the *Liberator*, the premier antislavery newspaper of its day, co-founded and edited by William Lloyd Garrison (1805–79).]

... It is a work of remarkable power, without any exaggeration of tone or misrepresentation of any of the everyday actualities of slavery at the South. It will rank in popular interest next to *Uncle Tom's Cabin*. The authoress has ingeniously presented the case of a beautiful white child, 'Ida May,' subjected to all the horrors of slavery from the early period of five years of age, at which time (just after the decease of her living mother) she was kidnapped while strolling with her nurse a short distance from her home, and thrust into a close carriage by two ruffians, and driven away to a doom more horrible than that of death. In vain did her heart-broken father endeavor to discover what had been her fate—spending two years in traveling through the Southern States, and visiting every slave market, fearfully apprehending to what end she had been stolen. "One thing which he learned, in his search, impressed him with astonishment, and that was, the number of children, both colored and white, that had been in various ways stolen. From every direction, tidings of this sort came to him, sometimes from those who, with the sympathy of a kindred sorry, wished to condole with him on his loss, and sometimes from parents, too poor to prosecute the search for themselves, begging him, while looking for his own child, to inquire for theirs."[1]

---

1 Quotation appears on p. 60 of this edition.

4. From *Frederick Douglass' Paper*, November 1854 and January 1855

[Frederick Douglass's newspaper published several advertisements for the book, and three issues featured extensive extracts.]

a. 17 November 1854

The scenes of Southern Life, given in IDA MAY, are sketched by a master hand. One feels their reality. There is nothing melodramatic, nor has the authoress "set down aught in malice."[1] American slavery is shown as it really exists in the Southern States—and some of the terrible effects of this anomalous institution are depicted with startling vividness.

b. 12 January 1855

This Anti-Slavery Story is having an extraordinary run—and well it deserves the wide circulation it obtains. It has only been published six weeks, and it is, therefore, but entering on the threshold of its mission. It is a valuable addition to the Anti-Slavery Literature of the country, for it contains one of the greatest arguments against slavery that has yet been presented to view. It is bound to electrify the reading public, and to stir the spirits of all who have heads to think and hearts to feel. We, therefore, urge upon all true friends of Freedom to circulate *Ida May* in every direction, as an Anti-Slavery Missionary.

5. Negative Reviews

[Not all reviews of *Ida May* were favorable, and many negative reviews considered "improbable" the central motif of the plot: the kidnapping of a white child into slavery.]

a. From the *Daily Evening Traveller* (Boston), 22 November 1854

This is rather a story of things possible than of things actual; and in reading it we should emphasize the word "possible" as that which best characterizes its incidents. It belongs to the same class of novels as *Uncle Tom's Cabin*, and like that famous novel, aims to depict the possible evils of slavery as it exists in this coun-

---

1   See Pike's Preface, p. 43.

try, though both writers also claim to present true pictures of its actual conditions and tendencies. The plot, though extremely unnatural, is skillfully conceived and elaborated with much care. The characters are drawn with a firm touch and with a strict regard to the preservations of a self-consistent individuality. In their delineation the writer shows much power and originality.

The style too is polished and graceful; and regarded merely as a work of art it is undoubtably one of the best, if not the best, of the class of novels to which it belongs. But in reading it we could not but regret that the author should have chosen such a theme for the exercise of her rare talents. That the work will have the wide-spread popularity which powers of so high an order will always command we do not doubt; but the very extent of its popularity makes us regret that the author should not have selected some other topic less likely to excite sectional animosities. If we could separate the tendency of the work to produce such a result in the minds of readers of narrow views and strong prejudices from its more strictly artistic and literary qualities, we should feel no hesitation in bestowing the highest praise on it. As it is, we are obliged to regard it as a powerful contribution to a class of books which has become exceedingly popular as of late, but which is founded in an abuse of the legitimate functions of the novelist. The novelist should not be a controversialist; and his books should not be written to illustrate any disputed question or doctrine.

b. From the *New York Daily Tribune*, 22 November 1854

The authorship of this powerful story has been ascribed by some highly intelligent critics to Mrs. Beecher Stowe. The presumption of such an origin is, certainly, a distinguished compliment. It is almost an assertion of the superiority of *Ida May* to *Uncle Tom's Cabin*. No one would suppose that Mrs. Stowe, in the enjoyment of her high and palmy literary prosperity, would venture upon another anti-slavery novel, unless she had found materials for a still more admirable creation than her former extraordinary work.

But we differ entirely from the judgements alluded to in regard to the author of *Ida May*. It bears few traces of the pen of Mrs. Stowe. Indeed, apart from its subject, we find no feature in its composition that reminds us strongly of that vigorous and racy writer. Mrs. Stowe has more dramatic power, and greater intensity of feeling than are displayed in this story. Her plot is more consistent and natural—bears a deeper impress of real life—and is pervaded by a more vivid and indignant sense of the evils attacked, than that of *Ida May*. On the other hand, the writer in question has more repose, more dignity, more completeness of finish—her plot is more elaborately constructed—and her style is more in accordance with the best models. The great defect of the story is the improbability of its leading incidents. Even if they have a foundation in fact, it is that kind of fact which is "stranger than fiction," and finds few parallels in actual experience. The heroine is a lovely child of white parents, who is kidnapped by some southern slave-dealers, at a tender age; is transformed, apparently, into a little negress; and sold to service on a plantation. By a series of incredible turns of good fortune, her parentage is at last discovered, she recovers her freedom, makes friends in her forsaken condition, and finally becomes an heiress and owner of slaves herself. Her decision to free the slaves who had fallen to her by legacy forms one of the pivotal elements in the plot, and furnishes the motive for several situations, which are managed with great adroitness and effect. But the intrinsic improbability of the whole conception greatly mars the interest of the work as a consecutive story, and leaves the reader dependent on the energy and pathos of isolated passages. In this point of view the work is truly admirable. It exhibits less power of construction than description; but as a succession of scenes and conversation, it must take a very high rank among recent fictitious compositions ...

The evil effects of slavery are treated of rather incidentally than directly, and always without bitterness. We do not know why the book should not be read with satisfaction at the South, as a forcible representation of local customs and scenery. It assuredly has but few diatribes against the institution, the natural results of which furnish such abundant materials for forcible description. The writer was clearly less intent on "pointing a moral," than on "adorning a tale." In this respect, we find another difference between *Ida May* and *Uncle Tom*.

c. From *Putnam's Weekly*, January 1855

Whether it was the fault of the publishers, or of some Indiscreet friends, that *Ida May* was announced as from the pen of Mrs. Stowe—we cannot say; but that announcement has, no doubt, seriously damaged the public estimation of the work. All who have taken it up, expecting to find a new *Uncle Tom* in it, must have been seriously disappointed. It is not a work without talent; it is conceived with considerable vigor, and executed with ability, but it is so vastly inferior to the novel with which it was brought into relation, that we can hardly read it with patience. The truthfulness of *Uncle Tom's Cabin*—the dramatic action; the fine discriminations of character; the alternate pathos and humor, are all wanting in *Ida May*, of which the plot is quite improbable, the characters ineffective and unnatural, and the story simply romantic. There are several vigorous descriptions in *Ida*, and some scenes of remarkable power; but, as a whole, we find it on a level with the majority of stories that are published in these days. The writer would do better with a less ambitious aim, and a more quiet sphere of incident.

6. Southern Reviews

[*Ida May* did not escape the attention of the Southern press.]

a. From the *Alexandria Gazette* (Virginia), 25 November 1854

The success of *Uncle Tom's Cabin* has induced the preparation of another book, of the same school, from the pen, also it is said, of a female, called *Ida May*, in which all the bad passions of people opposed to slavery are sought to be excited by exaggerated and overstrained descriptions imputing the utmost barbarity and cruelty to the Southern people. We find numerous extracts from this new *agitator* in several of the Northern papers. The improbability of the story, and the false coloring to all the scenes, can be seen at a glance.

b. From the *Southern Quarterly Review*, 1 July 1855

Female writers are proverbial for the facility with which they get rid of embarrassing social and political questions. The dear creatures snip the Gordian knot with their neat little scissors, and smilingly request the world to admire the cleverness with which they have untied it. If there is any one of these problems which they dispose of with peculiar ease, it is that which has so long puzzled the wisest of our statesmen—the relation of master and slave.

This little book, resplendent in its cobalt blue binding, is another contribution of female genius to the solution of this vexed question. True to her sex, the author goes straight to the point, setting aside all obstacles with enviable serenity. Her story does not amount to much. It is the exceedingly improbable history of one who, when a little girl, was kidnapped, stained to imitate a mulatto, sold by slave-traders and resold to a generous and romantic young man, who afterwards manumits his slaves and marries her. A variety of still more unlikely incidents circle around this, like satellites, and those homilies on the sin of slave-holding, to which we have become so completely inured, are distributed with a liberal hand throughout the volume.

Of the details of the work we have little to say. There is an ineffectual attempt at character-painting; thus, we have a cold, decided, tyrannical planter, his good-natured, silly wife, his beautiful, selfish daughter, &c. Our author, "following in the footsteps of her illustrious predecessor," introduces us to several negro-traders, and entertains us largely with the eloquent language of that refined class, one of whom she elevates to the dignity of a South Carolina sheriff. This familiarity with slang surprises us, and makes us wonder what sort of society northern ladies can possibly select, when they visit the States south of Mason & Dixon's line.[1]

---

1   The state boundary between Maryland and Pennsylvania, named after the men who surveyed the line between 1763–67. It served as the cultural and legal boundary between the slaveholding states of the South and the free states of the North until the 1850s.

Appendix C: Advertisements for Ida May

[These advertisements were produced by the publisher of *Ida May*, Philips, Sampson and Co. They appeared in multiple newspapers, timed to announce the publication of a fresh run of copies. Included here are the earliest and latest advertisements located.]

1. 13 November 1854

IDA MAY!
A *STORY OF THINGS ACTUAL AND POSSIBLE.*

BY MARY LANGDON

"For we speak that we know, and testify of that we have seen."

THIS STORY OF SOUTHERN LIFE
is destined to produce an impression upon the nation, that is powerful, far-reaching, and permanent. As a Novel merely it equals in interest

The most brilliant fictions of modern times.

But it is chiefly in relation to the institution of

AMERICAN SLAVERY

that the book will awaken the deepest interest. The thrilling incidents to which this anomalous institution gives rise, by interweaving the destinies of master and slave in the same web of fate, are presented with wonderful vividness. It is not a re-arrangement of the old stories, but an original creation; and it will appeal to the pride of the white race

WITH NEW AND STARTLING FORCE

But a calm, inflexible adherence to TRUTH marks every page. Nothing of the 'blue fire' of melo-drama is seen; nor is the deepest tragedy marred by the *screech* and contortions of a second rate actress.

No reader, however indifferent to novels in general, can possibly leave off without finishing it. The preliminary edition has been read by a number of the most eminent literary men in the country, as well as by persons of average intellect and culture.

THE VERDICT IS UNANIMOUS,
"One touch of nature makes the whole world kin."

From the boy who devours Robinson Crusoe, up to the accomplished scholar who is familiar with the highest efforts of authorship—all bear enthusiastic testimony to the genius of the book.

IN ANTICIPATION OF AN IMMENSE SALE,
unsurpassed by that of any other book, the Publishers will be able to answer all orders as they are received.

The Work will be published
November 22d.

2. 6 January 1855

THIRTY-FIFTH THOUSAND
OF
IDA MAY

Ready on Monday, January 1st.

UPON the supposition that there are three readers for every book purchased, already
Ninety Thousand Persons
have read this
NATIONAL STORY!
There are thousands yet to be enchained as they follow the heroine through her trials and triumph.
Although this book is in the form of a novel, who that reads it does not feel and know that its principal incidents are paralleled by *well established facts*? So true is it that

Truth is Stranger than Fiction.
For sale, by all Booksellers. In one vol., large 12 mo., cloth $1.25
AGENTS WANTED to sell this book throughout the country.

3. 12 January 1855

WHAT NEXT?

AT this time, when Southern politicians are beginning to maintain the justice and morality of
CHATTEL SLAVERY,
and to consider WASHINGTON, JEFFERSON, and other early patriots as having been needlessly conscientious;—when the first principles of the
Declaration of Independence
are scoured on the floor of Congress, it becomes important to have reliable information as to the practical workings of a system that threatens to overshadow this continent,
Whoever wishes to know
Southern Life as it is,
both in the cabin and the parlor, and to trace the effects of negro slavery upon the character and manners of both classes, will not fail to read
IDA MAY,
wherein the authoress 'testifies of that she has seen.'
FREEMEN OF THE NORTH! read, and let your children read the story! Teach the coming generation not to view with indifference the extension of that system which (in the language of the author,) 'alike for master and servant, poisons the springs of life, subverts the noblest instincts of humanity, and even in the most favorable circumstances, entails an amount of moral and physical injury to which no language can do justice.'

4. *Frederick Douglass' Paper*, 27 April 1855

WHAT IS THE NOVELIST'S FIELD?

GROWN UP people are tired of reading about castles and abbeys, princesses, lords and ladies, as presented in modern romances; these themes belong to SCOTT, and no one else. And if our novel-readers are exclusively interested in representation of foreign life, where the characters and manners are necessarily unfamiliar, it is only because there are not works of fiction in which

AMERICAN LIFE AND MANNERS

Are drawn with equal vigor.

The extraordinary success that has attended

IDA MAY

Is sufficient proof of its excellence as a story and also of the deep interest of the public in its theme. And if Dickens may arraign the Court of Chancery in BLEAK HOUSE, if Kingsley may attack the social institutions of England in ALTON LOCKE, it may surely be permitted to an American author to deal in a candid spirit with

THE GREAT QUESTION

Of all others now before the public.

The Publishers commend this work to Families, as one which inculcates the purest principles, and breathes a spirit of warm and unaffected piety.

43 THOUSAND COPIES SOLD!

45 THOUSAND NOW READY.

Appendix D: Kidnapping and White Slavery

1. "The Story of Ida May," *Boston Daily Atlas*, 23 December 1854

[This defense of the probability of the plot of *Ida May* shares comparative stories of kidnapping then in the public eye. The article relates the history of Salomé Müller (b. c. 1814), who successfully sued for her freedom on the basis of race. While the abolitionist press saw Müller's story as a fissure in the racial foundation of slavery, Southerners saw the same story as a reification of the social construct of race. Recently, Carol Wilson has concluded that Salomé was in fact Sally Miller, an enslaved woman who made the best of the opportunity presented to her by her mistaken identity (see Introduction, p. 26).]

It is a criticism not infrequently made upon Ida May that the ground-work of the plot—the kidnapping of a white girl into slavery—is too probable [*sic*], too outrageously improbable, to come within the legitimate scope of fiction. Those who urge this objection are of course ignorant of the commonest facts of slavery. They are ignorant of *three things* which have been proved upon the system beyond the possibility of denial of doubt, which are, *first*, that kidnapping of free persons and selling them to the slaveholders is a crime of frequent occurrence; *second*, that whites, or persons who cannot by their appearance be distinguished from whites, are held as slaves; and, *thirdly*, that free white children have, in several instances, been kidnapped and sold as slaves.

Let us look at the facts. Judge Stroud, of Pennsylvania, in his work on the slave laws, says:

> Remote as the city of Philadelphia from those slave-holding States in which the introduction of slaves from places within the territory of the United States is freely permitted, and where also the market is tempting, *it has been ascertained that more than thirty free colored persons,*

mostly children have been kidnapped here and carried away within the last two years. Five of these, through the kind interposition of several humane gentlemen, have been restored to their friends, though not without great expense and difficulty. The others are still retained in bondage.

This is pretty strong testimony. Thirty free persons, mostly children, kidnapped from the single city of Philadelphia in the short space of two years. This was several years ago. Here is a case of later date: On the 13th of December, 1851, a young colored woman, Mary E. Parker, residing in Chester county Pennsylvania, was seized, in the evening, by two kidnappers, carried to Baltimore, and sold, and transported to New Orleans. A fortnight later, December 30th, her sister, Rachel Parker, was forcibly taken from the house of Joseph C. Miller by two men, who carried her to Baltimore and sold her. By the active exertions of their friends in Chester county, these girls were recovered, and, after legal investigation, restored to freedom and their homes in Pennsylvania.

The case of Solomon Northup is so well known, and so fresh in the public mind, that it need not be detailed.[1] He was a free colored citizen of Washington County, New York, who was kidnapped in 1841, and sold south until he reached a plantation on Red River, from which, after 12 years of bondage, he was redeemed by the exertions of an agent sent out for the purpose by Governor Hunt of New York. His kidnappers have recently been arrested, tried, and convicted of their crime.

The latest case on record is related by the Marysville (Ky.) *Gazette*, in November last. Three brothers, Henry, Lewis and Allen Young, entered a house near Georgetown, Ohio, at midnight, seized a negro girl, carried her over to Kentucky, and secreted her near Marysville, till they could find an opportunity to sell her. She managed to escape, and, getting into Marysville, gave an account of the outrage to some of the citizens, by whom the kidnappers were arrested and delivered up to the authorities of Ohio for trial.

It may be said, in reply, that these cases are all of blacks; that granting that blacks are sometimes kidnapped and sold, it does not follow that a white child could be, because her color would be a *prima facie* evidence of freedom. To set aside this objection,

---

1 See Introduction, pp. 14 and 26–27.

it is only necessary to look into those faithful and unimpeachable records of the condition of the slaves, the advertisements of fugitives which are so common in Southern journals.

In the *Richmond Whig*, Jan. 6, 1836, Anderson Bowles offered one hundred dollars reward for the apprehension of his runaway slave, Edmund Kenney, who, he says, *"has straight hair, and complexion so nearly white that it is believed a stranger would suppose there was no African blood in him."*

In the *Nashville Whig*, July 14, 1819, A.W. Johnson offered two hundred dollars reward for the apprehension of this fugitive slave Julia, whom he describes as "of common size, *nearly white*, and very likely. *She may attempt to pass for white."*

In the *Chattanooga* (Ten.) *Gazette*, Oct. 5, 1852, George O. Ragland offers five hundred dollars reward for his fugitive slave Wash, who *"might pass himself as a white man,* as he is very bright, *has sandy hair, blue eyes,* and a fine set of teeth."

In Mobile, April 22, 1837, Edwin Peck advertised "a bright mulatto man slave named Sam," who, he says, *"has light, sandy hair, blue eyes, ruddy complexion, and is so white as very easily to pass for a free white man."*

About the same time, S.G. Steward, of Green County, Alabama, advertised his slave Alfred, *"with blue eyes, light flaxen hair, and skin disposed to freckle."*

In the same State of Alabama, John Blach, of Tuscaloosa, May 29, 1845, advertised his slave Fanny, *"who is as white as most white men,* with straight light hair, and blue eyes, and can pass herself for a white woman."

These are but specimens of a large class of similar advertisements which are constantly paraded before the eyes of the Southern community in their newspapers. They show conclusively that white slaves are not uncommon, and that the fact that a girl offered for sale had the features of the white race, and even a white complexion, would not necessarily prevent her from being accepted and held as a slave.

There is, however, on record a comparatively recent and very remarkable case, which is, if possible, stronger than the fictitious one of Ida May, and which was doubtless in the mind of the author of that work when forming the plot of her novel. It is the case of the German girl Salomé Müller, decided by the Supreme Court of Louisiana, in 1815. The facts are these:

In March, 1818, three ships arrived at New Orleans, bringing several hundred German emigrants from the province of Alsace on the lower Rhine. Among them were Daniel Müller and his two daughters, Dorothea and Salomé, whose mother had died on the passage. Soon after his arrival, Müller, taking with him his two daughters, both young children, went up the river to Attakapas parish to work on the plantation of John F. Miller. A few weeks later, his relatives, who had remained at New Orleans, learned that he had died of fever of the country. They immediately sent for the two girls, but they had disappeared, and the relatives, notwithstanding repeated inquiries and researches, could find no traces of them—They were at length given up for dead.—Dorothea was never again heard of, nor was anything known of Salomé from 1818 until 1848.

In the summer of that year, Madame Karl, a German woman who had come over in the same ship with the Müllers, was passing through a street in New Orleans, and accidentally saw Salomé in a wine-shop, belonging to Louis Belmonte, by whom she was held as a slave. Madame Karl recognized her at once, and carried her to the house of another German woman, Mrs. Schubert, who was Salomé's cousin and godmother, and who no sooner set eyes on her than, without having any intimation that the discovery had been previously made, she unhesitatingly exclaimed, "My God! Here is the long-lost Salomé Müller!"

The *Law Reporter*, in its account of this case says:

> As many of the German emigrants of 1818 as could be gathered together were brought to the house of Mrs. Schubert, and every one of the number who had any recollection of the little girl upon the passage, or any acquaintance with her father and mother, immediately identified the woman before them with the long-lost Salomé Müller. By all these witnesses, who appeared at the trial, the identity was established in the strongest terms. The family resemblance in every feature was declared to be so remarkable that some of the witnesses did not hesitate to say that they should know her among ten thousand; that they were as certain that the plaintiff was Salomé Müller, the daughter of Daniel and Dorothea Müller, as of their own existence.

Among the witnesses who appeared in Court was the midwife who had assisted at the birth of Salomé. She testified to the existence of certain peculiar marks upon the body of the child, which were found, exactly as described, by the surgeons who were appointed by the Court to make an examination for the purpose.

There was no trace of African descent in any feature of the face of Salomé Müller. She had long, straight black hair, hazel eyes, thin lips, and a Roman nose. The complexion of her face and neck was as dark as that of the darkest brunette. It appears, however, that during the twenty-five years of her servitude, she had been exposed to the sun's rays in the hot climate of Louisiana, with head and neck unsheltered, as is the custom of the female slaves, labouring in the cotton or the sugar field. The parts of her person which had been shielded from the sun were comparatively white.

Belmonte, the pretended owner of the girl, had obtained possession of her by an act of sale from John F. Miller, the planter in whose service Salomé's father died. This Miller was a man of consideration and substance, owning large sugar estates, and bearing a high reputation for honor and honesty, and for indulgent treatment of his slaves. It was testified on the trial that he had said to Belmonte, a few weeks after the sale of Salomé, "that she was white, and had as much right to her freedom as anyone, and was only to be retained in slavery by care and kind treatment." The broker who negotiated the sale from Miller to Belmonte, 1838, testified in Court that he then thought, and still thought, that the girl was white!

The case was elaborately argued on both sides, but was at length decided in favour of the girl, by the Supreme Court declaring that "she was free and white, and therefore unlawfully held in bondage."

The Rev. George Bourne, of Virginia, in his *Picture of Slavery*, published in 1834, relates the case of a white boy who, at the age of seven, was stolen from his home in Ohio, tanned and stained in such a way that he could not be distinguished from a person of color, and then sold as a slave in Virginia. At the age of twenty, he made his escape, by running away, and happily succeeded in rejoining his parents. These and other examples which might be adduced are amply sufficient to defend the story of *Ida May* from the charge of improbability, which never would have been brought against it by any one conversant with the workings and developments of the "peculiar institution."

2. From William Craft, *Running a Thousand Miles for Freedom* (London: William Tweedie, 1860)

[The opening paragraphs of this memoir of the flight to freedom of William Craft (1824–1900) and his wife Ellen Craft (1826–91) highlight similarities between kidnapping and enslavement. The first chapter goes on to recount the story of Salomé Müller, as related in the previous extract.]

My wife and myself were born in different towns in the State of Georgia, which is one of the principal slave States. It is true, our condition as slaves was not by any means the worst; but the mere idea that we were held as chattels, and deprived of all legal rights—the thought that we had to give up our hard earnings to a tyrant, to enable him to live in idleness and luxury—the thought that we could not call the bones and sinews that God gave us our own: but above all, the fact that another man had the power to tear from our cradle the new-born babe and sell it in the shambles[1] like a brute, and then scourge us if we dared to lift a finger to save it from such a fate, haunted us for years.

But in December, 1848, a plan suggested itself that proved quite successful, and eight days after it was first thought of, we were free from the horrible trammels of slavery, rejoicing and praising God in the glorious sunshine of liberty.

My wife's first master was her father, and her mother his slave, and the latter is still the slave of his widow.

Notwithstanding my wife being of African extraction on her mother's side, she is almost white—in fact, she is so nearly so that the tyrannical old lady to whom she first belonged became so annoyed, at finding her frequently mistaken for a child of the family, that she gave her when eleven years of age to a daughter, as a wedding present. This separated my wife from her mother, and also from several other dear friends. But the incessant cruelty of her old mistress made the change of owners or treatment so desirable, that she did not grumble much at this cruel separation.

It may be remembered that slavery in America is not at all confined to persons of any particular complexion; there are a very large number of slaves as white as anyone; but as the evidence of a slave is not admitted in court against a free white person, it is almost impossible for a white child, after having been kidnapped and sold into or reduced to slavery, in a part of the country where it is not known (as often is the case), ever to recover its freedom.

I have myself conversed with several slaves who told me that their parents were white and free; but that they were stolen away from them and sold when quite young. As they could not tell their address, and also as the parents did not know what had

---

1 Meat market.

become of their lost and dear little ones, of course all traces of each other were gone.

The following facts are sufficient to prove, that he who has the power, and is inhuman enough to trample upon the sacred rights of the weak, cares nothing for race or colour.

3. Lydia Maria Child, "Mary French and Susan Easton," *Juvenile Miscellany* (Boston: Allen and Ticknor, 3rd Series, no. 6, May 1834)

[This short story for children by Lydia Maria Child (1802–80) introduces a plot so similar to *Ida May* that it likely served as a source text. However, there is a key difference: this story is about two little girls who are kidnapped—one white and one black. Only the white child is rescued.]

Perhaps some of my little readers may remember seeing, about a year and a half ago, advertisements in the newspapers concerning a white child, who had been stolen, and afterwards discovered to have been stained black, and sold for a SLAVE.

Mary French lived on the western shore of the Mississippi river. She was the only child of her parents. Paul Easton, a colored man, with his wife and his little daughter Susan, lived very near them.

He was an honest, industrious man, and his wife was a neat, good-humored woman. Susan was a bright, affectionate child; very merry and full of play, as colored children generally are.

The little girls had joyful times together. They loved dearly to run in the woods, to gather berries and flowers.

They had lifted a big flat stone, and placed it under a spreading oak; this served them for a table, on which they used to place acorns for cups and saucers.

A small white rabbit with two black spots on his fur, was their favorite companion. They often seated him on the flat rock, while they gathered clover for him to eat. But Bunny was a timid little creature. One day he scampered off into the woods, because he was frightened by a little shaggy dog, barking at a wild turkey.

Susan first overtook the poor rabbit; and she covered him up with her apron, and tried to comfort him; for his little heart beat violently.

While they were talking to the rabbit, they heard a voice call out, "Little girls, don't you want to buy something pretty?" They turned round, and saw a peddler, with a case full of thimbles, beads, candy, &c. They told him they could not buy anything, because they had no money. The man asked where they lived; and when they told him, he said, "I have been there; and the women have bought some things."

Mary wanted to run home, to see if her mother had bought anything for her; but the peddler gave them some candy, and persuaded them to go to his cart, under the pretense of seeing a funny little monkey. When the poor children were out of sight of their homes, he stuffed handkerchiefs into their mouths, and tied them in his cart.

In this way they traveled until night. Then the man uncovered their mouths, and gave them some bread and a piece of cold sausage: They cried very much, and said, "I want to go home to my mother." But the man told them he would whip them, if they made the least noise. He would not untie them; and, the poor little girls were obliged to get such sleep as they could, sitting upright in the cart, as it jostled over the rough road.

They were awakened by the man, who lifted them out, and carried them into a thicket, where he had kindled a fire. He spread some bags and blankets on the ground, and told them he was going to sleep there, and they might sleep too. They asked when he would carry them home; and he said they should certainly go in the morning.

Delighted with this promise, they put their arms about each other's necks, and soon fell into a sweet sleep. The wicked peddler tied their feet together, lest they should run away while he slept. But the innocent little creatures were too tired to wake early.

The first thing Mary knew, the man seized her rudely, and ordered her to jump up. He led her to the fire, where he had a kettle full of black stuff, curling tongs, and a pair of shears. He tied her arms behind her, and began to cut off her hair.

Little Susan was grieved at this; and cried out, "You shan't cut off Mary's hair! You are a kidnapper, I know; and I will tell her mother all about you." Then the peddler was in a great rage, and beat her dreadfully with his horsewhip. The poor child screamed and screamed; but there was nobody in those lonely forests to help her. The man told her he would whip her to death, if she did not stop screaming. Then she tried to be still, and only gave a sob now and then, when the pain of the lashes was too great for her to bear.

When the cruel peddler had beaten her as much as he pleased, he returned to Mary, who stood sobbing and crying on the spot where he had left her. He told her to dry up her tears very quick, unless she wanted such a whipping as he had given the other little saucebox. He cut her hair close, and curled it with the curling tongs. Then he rubbed her with soot and grease, simmered together, till she was blacker than Susan. He made her stand by the fire, till it was thoroughly dried in; and then he rubbed it on a second time. "There!" said he, with a brutal laugh, "Now you are almost as good-looking a *nigger* as 'tother one."

The unhappy children did not dare to cry, for fear of being whipped. They were again tied in the cart, and rode nearly half a day without meeting any person.

About noon, a man passed them with a large boat on wheels. Mary tried to call loud enough for him to hear; for on this lonely road the peddler had not taken the precaution to cover their mouths. The traveler stopped to ask what was the matter. "Oh," said the peddler, "it is only a couple of young slaves, that are noisy." "Give them a touch of the whip; that will make 'em quiet," replied the other. Having made this unfeeling speech, he drove on, without taking any further notice.

Before evening, the peddler came in sight of a plantation, where a good many negroes were at work, while the driver stood over them, cracking his whip and smoking his cigar. The children heard him ask this man whether the planter would buy a likely young slave. The driver said, he thought it was very probable he would.

Then the peddler untied Mary, and told her to do as she was bid, or he would make her sorry for it. The poor child trembled, and did not dare to make any answer. She only ventured to say, "Ain't Susan going with me?"

He lifted her out of the cart, without making any reply. "Oh, Susan," said she, "if you ever get home again, tell mother all about it; and take good care of my spotted rabbit." Poor Susan sobbed, as if her heart would break.

The peddler held his whip over Mary's head, and ordered her to dry up her tears instantly. Thus were these innocent little playmates separated, never to meet again.

The planter gave the peddler fifty dollars for Mary, and ordered old Dinah to take her to the negro huts. Mary told Dinah that she was a white child, whom a wicked kidnapper had stolen from her home. She looked so black, that the kind-hearted old slave did not, at first, believe her.

"Hush, hush, poor child," said she: "If the overseer hears you talking so, he will have you tied up and whipped. You needn't feel so bad; Dinah will be the same as mother. Dinah's got no children now. Massa sell 'em all."

"But I *am* a white child, and I *was* stolen," said Mary, bursting into tears.

Dinah tried to comfort her, and sung songs to her, until the little sufferer dropped asleep, to dream of her father and mother, and little Susan, and the great oak tree, and the little spotted rabbit.

When Mary was asleep, Dinah observed that there was a streak lighter than the rest of her face, where the tears had run down her cheeks; but she was afraid to go and tell her master, because the slaves were not allowed to go out in the evening.

At daylight, the loud cracking of the overseer's whip awakened them. Old Dinah spoke very kindly to her little charge, and told her she would wash her face faithfully, to see if she was a white child.

When she found that the color came off upon the towel, she promised to go and tell her master what a trick the peddler had put upon him; but she said it would do no good then, because Massa wouldn't be up.

So little Mary followed her into the fields, and picked cotton, as the driver ordered her, until noon. She got along very comfortably; only once the driver struck her across the shoulders, because she turned to look at a little bird perched on the stump of an old tree.

At noon, Dinah led her to the planter's house, and told her story. He was very angry to think he had been cheated by the peddler. He knew the laws would not allow him to keep a white child in slavery, or sell her to another. He said she might wait upon his wife, until her parents could be informed where she was.

As their residence was far distant from any post-office, he thought it would be very difficult to send them word. One of the planter's daughters begged that Joe might be sent to carry the little stranger home. But Joe was a slave; and his master was afraid he would take the opportunity to run away. When men deal unjustly with their fellow-creatures, they can no longer have confidence in them.

Mary, in a timid voice, begged that Susan might be found, and sent back at the same time with herself.

One of the boys answered, "Never mind her. *Niggers* are used to being slaves."

"But Susan Easton is not used to it," replied Mary: "Her father and mother are not slaves."

"Oh, she'll soon get used to it," said the unfeeling boy.

Mary did not say any more: but she could not understand what right they had to seize honest Paul Easton's daughter, and make her a slave, any more than they had to make a slave of *her* father's daughter.

The planter went off in search of the peddler, to recover his money; and he promised to bring back Susan, if he could find her. He returned in the evening, saying he could not discover what course the peddler had taken, and must make up his mind to lose his fifty dollars. I wish this had taught him never to buy another human being. He wrote a letter to Mary's father, and promised to send her home, if he did not receive an answer before long.

In the meantime, the parents of these poor children were in an agony of doubt and fear. The woods were searched in every direction. The acorn cups still stood on the flat stone, as if arranged for a mimic tea-party; and an apron at a little distance showed that the children had wandered towards the road.

Paul Easton's first thought was of kidnappers; for he knew very well that it was a common thing for colored children to be stolen from their homes, and sold for slaves. He said he did not believe that peddler came into the neighborhood for any good purpose. But Mr. French did not believe this; because he thought kidnappers could have no motive for stealing a white child, whom the laws allow no man to sell or buy.

They all watched anxiously for the appearance of travelers, of whom they could make inquiries.

The first one that came along, was the very man to whom Mary had called for help. He said he had seen an advertisement for lost children in the newspapers; and when he read it, he thought about the children that screamed from the peddler's cart; but he could not tell them anything more. If his heart had not been hardened by the wicked system of slavery, he would have stopped and spoken to the children, and they might both have been saved.

Paul Easton was afraid to go in search of *his* child: because a free colored man traveling is liable to be kidnapped and sold, or shot through the head for a runaway slave. But Mr. French took his pack on his back, and went in search of his lost treasure. After many inquiries, he found the planter who had bought Mary.

The poor child saw her father before he reached the door. She ran out to meet him, and sprang into his arms, sobbing and laughing at the same moment.

When Mr. French had taken some rest and refreshment, they

set out for home. Sometimes Mary walked, sometimes her father carried her, and once they found a chance to ride in a baggage wagon. There was no end to the child's questions about her dear mother, and the spotted rabbit; but when she thought of poor Susan, she wept aloud.

They returned to a house of joy; but poor Mr. Easton and his wife were almost broken-hearted. They never heard any tidings of *their* child. She is, no doubt, a slave—compelled to labor hard without wages, and whipped whenever she dares to say she has a right to be free. Yet the only difference between Mary French and Susan Easton is that the black color could be rubbed off from Mary's skin, while from Susan's it could not.

4. From Francis Colburn Adams, *Our World, The Slaveholder's Daughter* (New York and Auburn: Miller, Orten, and Mulligan, 1855), 213–16

[This scene of white children at auction appeared in a novel by Francis Colburn Adams, *Our World, The Slaveholder's Daughter* (1855), also set in South Carolina. The title character, Annette, is the daughter of Clotilda, an enslaved woman, and her master Marston, whose creditors have come for his property. This scene takes place at Graspum's slave pen. Annette is accompanied by Nicholas, her younger half-brother. *Our World* was the next new novel with an antislavery theme to appear, six months after *Ida May*, and it featured a nearly all-white cast of enslaved characters, including Annette, Clotilda, and Nicholas.]

Annette speaks feebly, looks pale and sickly. Her flaxen curls still dangle prettily upon her shoulders. She expected her mother; that mother has not come. The picture seems strange; she looks childishly and vacantly round—at the dealers, at Graspum, at the sheriff, at the familiar faces of the old plantation people. She recognizes Harry, and would fain leap into his arms. Nicholas, less moved by what is going on around him, hangs reluctantly behind, holding by the skirt of Annette's frock. He has lost that vivacity and pertness so characteristic on the plantation. Happy picture of freedom's love! Happy picture of immortalised injustice! Happy picture of everything that is unhappy! How modest is the boast that we live to be free; and that in our virtuous freedom a child's mother has been sold for losing her mind: a faithful divine, strong with love for his fellow divines, is to be sold for his faith; the child—the daughter of the democrat—they say, will be sold from her democratic father. The death-stinging enemy Washington and Jefferson sought to slaughter—to lay ever dead at their feet, has risen to life again. Annette's mother has fled to escape its poison. We must pause! We must not discourse thus in our day, when the sordid web of trade is being drawn over the land by King Cotton.

The children, like all such doubtful stock, are considered very fancy, very choice of their kind. It must be dressed in style to suit nice eyes at the shambles.

"Well! Ye'r right interesting looking," says the sheriff—Messrs. Graspum and Co. look upon them with great concern, now and then interrupting with some observations upon their pedigree—taking them by the arms, and again rumpling their hair by rubbing his hands over their heads. "Fix it up, trim; we must put them up along with the rest today. It'll make Marston—I pity the poor fellow—show his hand on the question of their freedom." Mr. Sheriff, being sufficiently secured against harm, is quite indifferent about the latent phases of the suit. He remarks, with great legal logic—we mean legal slave logic—that Marston must object to the sale when the children are on the stand. "It is very pretty kind a' property, very like Marston—will be as handsome as pictures when they grow up," he says, ordering it put back to be got ready.

"Why didn't my mother come?" the child whimpers, dewy tears decorating her eyes. "Why won't she come back and take me to the plantation again? I want her to come back; I've waited so long." As she turns to follow the gaoler—Nicholas still holds her by the skirt of her frock, her flaxen curls again wave to and fro upon her shoulders, adding beauty to her childlike simplicity. "You'll grow to be something, one of these days, won't ye, little dear?" says the gaoler, taking her by the hand. She replies in those silent and touching arguments of the soul; she raises her soft blue eyes, and heaven fills them with tears, which she lifts her tiny hands to wipe away.

Nicholas tremblingly—he cannot understand the strange movement—follows them through the vault; he looks up submissively, and with instinctive sympathy commences a loud blubbering. "You're going to be sold, little uns! but, don't roar about it; there's no use in that," says the gaoler, inclining to sympathy.

Nicholas doesn't comprehend it; he looks up to Annette, plaintively, and, forgetting his own tears, says, in a whisper, "Don't cry, Annette; they'll let us go and see mother, and mother will be so kind to us—."

"It does seem a pity to sell ye, young 'uns; ye'r such nice 'uns—have so much interestin' in yer little skins!" interrupts the gaoler, suddenly. The man of keys could unfold a strange history of misery, suffering, and death, if fear of popular opinion, illustrated in popular liberty, did not seal his lips. He admits the present to be rather an uncommon case, says it makes a body feel kind a' unhinged about the heart, which heart, however rocky at times, will have its own way when little children are sorrowing. "And then, to know their parents! That's what tells deeper on a body's feeling—it makes a body look into the hereafter." The man of keys and shackles would be a father, if the law did but let him. There is a monster power over him, a power he dreads—it is the power of unbending democracy, moved alone by fretful painstakers of their own freedom.

"Poor little things! ye 'r most white, yes!—suddenly changing—just as white as white need be. Property's property, though, all over the world. What's sanctioned by the constitution, and protected by the spirit and wisdom of Congress, must be right, and maintained," the gaoler concludes. His heart is at war with his head; but the head has the power, and he must protect the rights of an unrighteous system.

An old negress, one of the plantation nurses, is called into service. She commences the process of preparing them for market. They are nicely washed, dressed in clean clothes; they shine out as bright and white as anybody's children. Their heads look so sleek, their hair is so nicely combed, so nicely parted, so nicely curled. The old slave loves them—she loved their father. Her skill has been lavished upon them—they look as choice and interesting as the human property of any democratic gentleman can be expected to do.

5. Charles Sumner, "Another Ida May," *Boston Telegraph*, 27 February 1855

[In this letter to Dr. James Stone, Massachusetts Republican Senator Charles Sumner (1811–74) introduced Mary Mildred Botts, a young enslaved child whom he had helped redeem from slavery in January 1855. Stone forwarded Sumner's letter to Richard Hildreth, the editor of the *Boston Telegraph*, to drum up publicity for the speech Stone and Sumner had planned for April. Her resemblance to the fictional Ida May caused a media sensation in the months that followed.]

Washington, Feb. 19, 1855.

Dear Doctor—I send you by the mail the daguerreotype of a child about 7 years old, who only a few months ago was a slave in Virginia, but who is now free by means sent on from Boston, which I had the happiness of being trusted with for this purpose. She is bright and intelligent—another *Ida May*. I think her presence among us (in Boston) will be a great deal more effective than any speech I could make.

Meanwhile I send this picture, thinking that you will be glad to exhibit among the members of the Legislature, as an illustration of Slavery. Let a hard-hearted Hunker[1] look at it and be softened.

I send another copy in a different attitude to John A. Andrew. Her name is Mary.

Ever yours,
CHARLES SUMNER.

P.S. Such is Slavery! There it is! Should such things be allowed to continue in the City of Washington, under the shadow of the Capitol?

---

1 Obdurate conservative who sought to minimize the slavery question.

Appendix E: Mary Hayden Green Pike's Racial Politics

1. Caroline F. Putnam, *Liberator*, 21 October 1859

[In this letter submitted to her regular column for *The Liberator*, Caroline F. Putnam (1826–1917) recounts a story Mary Hayden Green Pike told her, of being accused of abolitionism during a visit to South Carolina.]

Calais, 30th. The authoress of *Ida May*, Mrs. Pike, has just left us, after giving us an hour's entertaining and animated conversation. She resides in this place, and her husband, a member of the State Senate, gathered a fine audience for Miss Holley last evening. Mrs. Cooper, with whom we have a delightful home, and Mrs. P[ike], with another Maine lady, spent a winter in South Carolina, as invalids, a few years since, when Mrs. P learned much which suggested to her the narratives of *Ida May* and *Caste*. She has given us this afternoon many reminiscences of that Southern winter—some shocking atrocities which she could not shut her eyes to. How do so many Northern ladies visiting South? Once the Mayor of Aiken, S.C. waited on these ladies with a warrant! They were addressed, "Ladies, you are suspected of being Abolitionists!" Their landlord soothed the alarm of the town by favorable reports of their demeanor, and they were suffered to remain.

2. From Mary Hayden Green Pike, *Caste: A Story of Republican Equality* (1856), 375

[Pike's second novel shares *Ida May*'s antislavery theme but more directly confronts Northern racial prejudice. In this scene, Henry Lane, a free black child attending a predominantly white school in New York City, "takes the stump" to confront a group of boys about name-calling in the schoolyard.]

"Since I have been in the school, some of you boys have somehow got an idea that I'm a nigger—picked up out of a sand bank—and you have taken particular pains to inform me of the fact. Now, I just want to tell you that I remember where I was born as well as you do, for I was there first, and upon serious reflection, I have come to the conclusion that I *am* a nigger, and probably always shall be."

"No, you'll be a colored gentleman, by-and-by," interrupted one of his hearers.

"Interruptions not allowed. I claim the stump. Mr. Chairman, please preserve order," said Henry, turning to Ned, who proceeded to shout "Order," and was echoed with such zeal by a dozen other voices, that order was some time in being restored. When they were still he went on.

"If any of you think I'm ashamed of not being white, you are much mistaken. I don't think my color is any disgrace at all, and I am sure it is very becoming to my style of beauty! So you see the more you kick me, the higher I'll rise; for I can't help it if I am smarter than the rest of you, and I hope you'll try not to feel bad about it. If you kick me too hard, I may go up so high that I shall never come down again—like the football that lodged in the belfry. Gentlemen and ladies, I'm done finished, and I thank you for the stump."

He jumped down as he uttered the last words, and Ned, throwing up his cap, called loudly for three cheers for "Hen, the boy that wasn't ashamed of himself."

3. From Frederick A. Pike, "Tax, Fight, Emancipate" (Congressional address, 5 February 1862), *Congressional Globe*, 7 February 1862: 658 (Library of Congress)

[In the conclusion to his speech to Congress on the Legal-Tender Bill, Pike's husband Frederick made the first call in Congress for emancipation as an expeditious necessity of war.]

The next sixty days are to be the opportunity for the nation to reassert itself. In them, past blunders can be remedied and the memory of inefficiency be lost in the brilliancy of triumph. I have all faith in the war, when it shall move to the tones of our new Secretary. It has already done much to enlighten our people as to the destiny of the Republic. Civilians in high station and officers of leading rank have been converted by it to sound doctrines of political action. It is the measure of our civilization and Christianity. In its grand march in the future, it shall carry with it, like a torrent, the sophisms and theories of vicious political organizations; and presently clearing itself of all entanglements, it will make plain to the world that this is a contest of ideas. It will try aspirants for the leadership; and when one fails another shall supply his place; until in God's own time, the appointed Joshua shall be found who shall lead us into the promised land of peace and liberty.

Our duty today is to tax and fight—twin brothers of great power; to them, in good time, shall be added a third; whether he shall be of executive parentage or generated in Congress, or spring, like Minerva, full-grown from the head of our army, I care not. Come he will, and his name shall be Emancipation. And these three—tax, fight, emancipate—shall be the trinity of our salvation. In this sign we shall conquer.[1]

4. Mary Hayden Green Pike, "John Brown in Prison" (c. 1859)

[Pike published this rough but enthusiastic poem in response to John Brown's 1859 raid on Harper's Ferry and his subsequent execution. Rachel Reed Griffin found this poem as a newspaper clipping, with no date or source recorded, in the *Washington County Scrap Book*, New England Historic Genealogical Society, and reprinted it in her thesis "The Life and Writings of Mary Hayden Green Pike."]

"I thought him monomaniac because he talked in a mysterious way of having been appointed by Heaven, a Moses, to lead the slaves out of bondage." —A Writer to the N. Y. *Tribune*

Defeat or victory! What is it?
    For my soul is dark,
And it heareth through the midnight,
    Only slavery's ban-dogs bark.
Hears alone the Southern pouring
    Curses o'er my children's grave
And the false and frantic protest,
    Of the cowering, trembling slave.

Can I tremble? Can I falter?
    Such a man as I—

---

1 The motto *In hoc signo vinces* (Latin) refers to the sign of the cross.

Who for years have seen the watch sign
    Flaming in the Southern sky?
Who have heard the spirit whisper
    Through the solemn night to me,
"Go—the Red Sea shall be opened—
    Thou shalt set thy brethren free."

Was it then a lying vision?
    Did I do a wrong,
When I sought to aid the helpless—
    Arm the weak against the strong.
Saith the word that never faileth,
    "Aiding these, thou'rt aiding me."
Oh my Lord! whose death was victory!
    Humbly thus I follow Thee.

When the Jewish host beleaguered,
    Jericho's old town,
Sword in hand, 'twas by their shouting,
    That the walls fell down.
Emblem of the mighty power
    Given to the spoken word,
That the souls enclosed in error,
    May be reached without the sword.

Living, I had been a unit,
    Dying, men shall see
What a strong and countless army
    Wait to set the bondmen free.
Never could my voice th'oppressor,
    From his fatal slumber wake—
O'er my grave the shout of thousands,
    Shall the guilty silence break.

Lo! I see the vision brightens—
    Clearer grows the sign—
And the "Red Sea" is a river,
    Red with blood that once was mine.
They, who perished, I who follow,
    'Neath that Jordan's swelling wave,
Through defeat accept our victory—
    Gain our triumph through the grave.

Works Cited and Suggested Reading

Works by Mary Hayden Green Pike

Langdon, Mary [Mary Hayden Green Pike]. *Ida May: Story of Things Actual and Possible*. Boston: Phillips, Sampson & Co.; New York: J.C. Derby, 1854.

——. *Ida May: Story of Things Actual and Possible*. Edited by an English Clergyman. London: Simpkin, Marshall & Co.; Ipswitch: I.M. Burton & Co., 1854.

——. *Ida May: Story of Things Actual and Possible*. Author's Edition. Leipzig: Bernhard Tauchnitz, 1855.

——. *Ida May, ou Encore un triste face de l'enclavage aux Etats-Unis*. Paris: Librairie de Ch. Meyrueis et Co., 1855.

Pike, Mary Hayden Green, *Agnes*. Boston: Phillips, Sampson & Co., 1858.

Story, Sydney A. [Mary Hayden Green Pike]. *Caste: A Story of Republican Equality*. Boston: Phillips, Sampson & Co.; New York: J.C. Derby, 1856.

Secondary Material

Barnes, William Horatio. "Frederick A. Pike." The Fortieth Congress of the United States: Historical and Biographical, Vol 1. New York: G.E. Perine, 1869. 273–78.

Bassett, Charles. "Pike, Mary Hayden Green." *American National Biography Online*. Feb. 2000.

Baym, Nina. *Women's Fiction: A Guide to Novels by and about Women in America, 1820–1870*. Ithaca, NY: Cornell UP, 1978. 268–69.

Clymer, Jeffory. *Family Money: Property, Race, and Literature in the Nineteenth Century*. New York: Oxford UP, 2013. 59–61.

Durden, Robert Franklin. *James Shepherd Pike: Republicanism and the American Negro, 1850–1882*. Durham, NC: Duke UP, 1957.

Foner, Eric. *Gateway to Freedom: The Hidden History of the Underground Railroad*. New York: Norton, 2015.

Griffin, Rachel Reed. "The Life and Writings of Mary Hayden Green Pike." MA thesis. University of Maine Orono, 1947.

Johnson, Walter. "The Slave Trader, the White Slave, and the Politics of Racial Determination in the 1850s." *The Journal of American History* 87.1 (June 2000): 13–38.

Liedel, Donald E. "The Puffing of *Ida May*: Publishers Exploit the Antislavery Novel." *Journal of Popular Culture* 3.2 (1969): 287–306.

Mitchell, Mary Niall. "The Real Ida May: A Fugitive Tale in the Archives." *Massachusetts Historical Review* 15 (2013): 54–88.

Mitchell, Sally. "Pike, Mary (Hayden) Green." *American Women Writers: A Critical Reference Guide*. Ed. Taryn Benbow-Pfalzgraf. Detroit: St. James Press, 2000. 3.279.

Morgan-Owens, Jessie. "'Another Ida May': Photography and the American Abolition Campaign." *Imagining Transatlantic Slavery*. Ed. Cora Kaplan and John Oldfield. London and New York: Palgrave Macmillan, 2010. 47–60.

Newlyn, Andrea K. "Undergoing Racial 'Reassignment': The Politics of Transracial Crossing in Sinclair Lewis's *Kingsblood Royal*." *Modern Fiction Studies* 48.4 (2002): 1041–67.

Sánchez-Eppler, Karen. *Touching Liberty: Abolition, Feminism, and the Politics of the Body*. Berkeley: U of California P, 1993.

Sinha, Manisha. *The Slave's Cause: A History of Abolition*. New Haven, CT: Yale UP, 2016.

von Frank, Albert J. *The Trials of Anthony Burns*. Cambridge, MA: Harvard UP, 1998.

Weinstein, Cindy. *Family, Kinship, and Sympathy in Nineteenth-Century American Literature*. New York: Cambridge UP, 2004. 95–129.

Wilson, Carol. *The Two Lives of Sally Miller: A Case of Mistaken Racial Identity in Antebellum New Orleans*. New Brunswick, NJ: Rutgers UP, 2007.

Winslow, Elizabeth. "Pike, Mary Hayden Green." *Notable American Women: A Biographical Dictionary (1607–1950)*. Ed. Edward T. James, Janet Wilson James, and Paul S. Boyer. Cambridge, MA: Belknap Press, 1971. 3.68–69.

From the Publisher

A name never says it all, but the word "Broadview" expresses a good deal of the philosophy behind our company. We are open to a broad range of academic approaches and political viewpoints. We pay attention to the broad impact book publishing and book printing has in the wider world; we began using recycled stock more than a decade ago, and for some years now we have used 100% recycled paper for most titles. Our publishing program is internationally oriented and broad-ranging. Our individual titles often appeal to a broad readership too; many are of interest as much to general readers as to academics and students.

Founded in 1985, Broadview remains a fully independent company owned by its shareholders—not an imprint or subsidiary of a larger multinational.

For the most accurate information on our books (including information on pricing, editions, and formats) please visit our website at www.broadviewpress.com. Our print books and ebooks are also available for sale on our site.

On the Broadview website we also offer several goods that are not books—among them the Broadview coffee mug, the Broadview beer stein (inscribed with a line from Geoffrey Chaucer's *Canterbury Tales*), the Broadview fridge magnets (your choice of philosophical or literary), and a range of T-shirts (made from combinations of hemp, bamboo, and/or high-quality pima cotton, with no child labor, sweatshop labor, or environmental degradation involved in their manufacture).

All these goods are available through the "merchandise" section of the Broadview website. When you buy Broadview goods you can support other goods too.

broadview press
www.broadviewpress.com

The interior of this book is printed on 100% recycled paper.

PERMANENT

100%

Ancient
Forest
Friendly™